The Degas Trove

Stephen Timbers

DORRANCE
PUBLISHING CO
EST. 1920
PITTSBURGH, PENNSYLVANIA 15238

The contents of this work, including, but not limited to, the accuracy of events, people, and places depicted; opinions expressed; permission to use previously published materials included; and any advice given or actions advocated are solely the responsibility of the author, who assumes all liability for said work and indemnifies the publisher against any claims stemming from publication of the work.

This is a work of fiction. Names, characters, places and incidents are the product of the author's imagination or are used fictitiously. Any resemblance to actual persons, living or dead, businesses, companies, events, or locations are entirely coincidental.

Cover: Dancers Practicing at the Barre, 1877. Edgar Degas, Mixed Media on Canvas. 29 ¾ x 32in., The Metropolitan Museum of Art, H.O. Havemeyer Collection.

All Rights Reserved
Copyright © 2023 by Stephen Timbers

No part of this book may be reproduced or transmitted, downloaded, distributed, reverse engineered, or stored in or introduced into any information storage and retrieval system, in any form or by any means, including photocopying and recording, whether electronic or mechanical, now known or hereinafter invented without permission in writing from the publisher.

Dorrance Publishing Co
585 Alpha Drive
Suite 103
Pittsburgh, PA 15238
Visit our website at *www.dorrancebookstore.com*

ISBN: 979-8-88812-499-4
eISBN: 979-8-88812-518-2

To our Boys
Alexander, Christopher and Brendan

PART ONE
LOST

Chapter One

"They're gone!"

Those were the words that had stunned Charlie Bailey twenty minutes ago. His mother, Claire Bailey, had called sounding uncommonly angry. Immediately Charlie sensed that she meant the paintings that she had donated to the Yale University Art Gallery just yesterday.

"What's gone, Mother?" Charlie asked to be sure.

"Two of my pictures. That awful man called. I was out in the garden cutting flowers when James brought me my cell phone. He said that Mr. Vance was on the phone. Hugh Vance—that pompous Yale official with the fake British accent. I can't stand him."

"I know, Mother." Charlie added. "You made that clear on the company plane back to O'Hare from New Haven early this morning. What did he say?"

"That man said that two of my pictures were gone. Can you imagine? We were there yesterday. What an incompetent nincompoop.'

"I knew this was a mistake. I should have never let them talk me into it. They were safe here before we shipped them to Yale last month. Now who knows where they are? I'll never see them again. And the gift was supposed to honor your father. I feel Yale has disgraced his memory. Shame on them!"

"Mother, you're distraught. You have every right to be, but I worry about you getting too stressed out. It's not healthy. Try to calm down. Did Vance tell you how it happened? What does he know?"

"That idiot said that after the reception yesterday afternoon, they put all three pictures in a storeroom in the basement of the gallery and locked the door. With that curator woman—what's her name?"

"Susan Parker."

"Yes, Susan. He said that she came in at noon today to arrange for them to be moved to the art warehouse. She discovered that two of the three pictures were gone. Vanished."

"Incredible. Who had the key? Was the room broken into?"

"Frankly I was too shocked and angry to ask. I got off the phone before I said something a lady should not. What am I going to do?"

"First, try to calm down. I'll call Hugh and get more details. As soon as I know more, I'll be back. Should Kate and I drive up to Lake Forest tonight?"

"No, that isn't necessary. James will get me dinner and then I'll try to go to bed early. We'll see how I feel tomorrow. Thank you for calling Mr. Vance. You are so clever. I know you can handle this mess. I don't want to talk to him again. He so upsets me."

"Good night, Mom. We love you."

Charlie was sitting in the library of his Lake Shore Drive co-op apartment. He was shocked by what he had heard. Only yesterday his mother, his wife, Kate, and he had been in New Haven at a reception and dinner honoring his family for donating three important works of art to Yale. That occasion had left him exhilarated. He had forged an important bond between his family and *alma mater*. Now he felt crushed. What had happened? Were they misplaced, stolen, destroyed?

Charlie thought back to a meeting at his mother's house with the Yale Art Gallery representatives two months before. They had sat outside on the large stone patio off the drawing room. While they talked, he could see how impressed Hugh Vance was viewing the ten acres of landscaped gardens and lawns, which adorned the Lake Forest estate. The other two visitors, Susan Parker and Cynthia Newgate, sat quietly while Hugh did the talking.

Charlie saw in Hugh a short, delicate man with white hair, who was dressed classically in a blue blazer, gray trousers, white shirt, and a bow tie. Despite saying that he was born in Boston and attended Harvard before working at the Metropolitan Museum of Art in New York, he spoke with the clipped precision of someone who might have grown up in England and attended Oxford or Cambridge.

While he dominated the conversation, he gave way to Susan whenever the topic was specifically one of the paintings. Susan was the curator of American paintings. She was most expert in the historical significance and authenticity of the works of art. Charlie noted that when she arrived, she contrasted with Hugh in that she was taller, thinner, younger, and less sophisticated looking. She wore a cream-colored cotton dress, silver earrings, and flat shoes.

The most junior of the three visitors was the most anticipated by Charlie and his mother. Cynthia Newgate was a name that immediately registered with Claire Bailey when Hugh's secretary had called a week before to give her the names of the people coming to Lake Forest.

Claire had asked Charlie, "I wonder if Cynthia is my sister's grandchild? Helen, my sister, your aunt, has three daughters, one of whom is Eleanor."

"Yes, I remember cousin Ellie. She married Harold Newgate. They're in Ohio. Right?"

"I think so. I lost track of Ellie after Helen died. Cancer. Only fifty. Their Christmas cards come from Cleveland. Occasionally they include a photograph. I remember that they have a daughter. I can try to find their cards to see if the daughter's name is Cynthia."

"She would be about the right age to be a graduate student," Charlie guessed. "If she is related and is studying art history, Yale would usually want her here on this visit. After all, they are hoping to convince you to make a gift from your collection. The Yale Development Office rarely misses a trick."

Hugh Vance did not bring up the issue of a gift at first. Rather he tried to ingratiate himself by complimenting Claire.

"Mrs. Bailey, your house is exquisite—a French Château-style limestone house from the twenties, I presume? Who was the architect?"

"David Adler," Claire answered. "A friend of my father-in-law."

"Your father-in-law had talented friends—famous as well. Walking through the house, I was impressed by the formidable paintings and sculptures in the foyers and drawing room. You are an impeccable collector."

"You flatter me. You needn't. But before we talk further, I wonder if I could take Cynthia aside to ask her a few questions. Personal matter. Charlie will join us. I'll ask Kate, my daughter-in-law, to come out and answer any questions about the house or Lake Forest."

"Of course," Hugh said.

Charlie followed his mother and Cynthia into the library where they sat facing each other.

"I am curious about you," Claire began. "My niece is named Ellie Newgate. I haven't seen her in years. I remember that she had curly blond hair and was tall like you. I wonder if we are related?"

"We are. Mom. I apologize for not calling before, but I did not want to impose and felt awkward arriving at your front door with Mr. Vance asking for one of your paintings. I'm naturally shy. I'm sorry."

"Don't worry, sweetheart," Claire said with feeling. "I'm so happy to meet you."

"When I told my mother a year ago that I had been accepted to Yale for my graduate studies in art history, she mentioned that her aunt and uncle were connected to Yale. She said that I should keep an eye out for the Baileys from Chicago. So when Susan, who is my supervisor at the gallery, mentioned that the Baileys were considering an important gift, I remember my mom's conversation. She'll be happy that I met you."

"Marvelous. You bear a resemblance to your grandmother," Claire remarked. "Helen was shy also."

"I'm delighted to meet you as well," Charlie added. "Having you here is a treat. It's wonderful that we all share a love of art."

After Cynthia brought Claire and Charlie up-to-date with news about the Newgate family, Claire suggested that they shouldn't keep Mr. Vance waiting and led them back to the patio.

The conversation then turned to Hugh assuring Claire that Yale would be a wonderful place to showcase her works of art.

"Students, scholars, and the general public would admire and learn from them for generations. In addition, a gift would honor your family's generosity to Yale over the years."

"I suppose so," Claire said softly. "Robbie loved Yale."

By the lack of enthusiasm in his mother's voice Charlie sensed that she had misgivings about giving up any of her artworks. Still Claire did offer to take the Yale visitors on a tour of the house. Charlie followed and heard her single out the significant paintings and sculptures found in several of the rooms.

Hugh praised all of the artworks but expressed greatest interest in the American Impressionist paintings. He said, "Your American impressionists are unquestionably superb. If I may add, a couple of them would fill gaps in our gallery's collection—particularly the Mary Cassatt in the guest bedroom and the Childe Hassam in the library. If we had them at the gallery they would stand out immediately."

During the tour of the house and the ongoing discussion, Charlie noticed that Claire kept looking over at Cynthia. She seemed fascinated by this young woman with straight brown hair, full figure—some might say plump, and plain features. Charlie thought that her nose and green eyes resembled features he remembered from photographs of Claire's family. Overall he judged her appearance as unremarkable to most people. She dressed simply, befitting a thrifty graduate student.

His mother had a sharper assessment of Cynthia. After the guests left she declared that the girl was pleasant and intelligent but "mousy". Her words only confirmed to Charlie that his mother was hard to please.

After two hours of prodding and flattery by Hugh and intense negotiation, Claire agreed finally to donate the paintings by Mary Cassatt and Childe Hassam and an unusual charcoal sketch of the very ill Edgar Degas—presumably by Cassatt also. They were all favorites of Charlie, but he was not about to challenge his mother's choices. She was near her wit's end to see anything that had been part of her house leave permanently.

Once Claire had determined the components of the gift, Hugh became giddy with excitement—unctuously praising Claire, Charlie, Kate, and anyone named Bailey since the beginning of time. If he were not so practiced and obvious in his sentiments, Charlie would have found him funny. Instead, he could barely tolerate the man. Still good manners prevailed, and the Yale trio departed exuding a glow of success.

Now, two months later, Charlie wondered if they had made a mistake trusting Hugh Vance and his staff. He had not liked Hugh, and his mother had been reluctant to make the gift. Charlie could have stopped the process at any point, but he had not.

As much as he needed to call Hugh immediately, Charlie wanted to ask Kate's advice. He feared he would burn bridges with Yale if he were too inflamed. He found her in the kitchen starting to prepare Sunday dinner. Charlie admired her tall, lean, athletic figure from behind and felt a brief sexual stirring for this young, attractive brunette only ten feet from him. She wore khaki shorts, flats, and a long-sleeved, rolled-up white men's dress shirt two sizes too big with the tails hanging out. He was so comfortable with her and delighted that they had bonded so well in the mere seven months since they had married. He loved every thing about her.

Kate turned around when he spoke.

"Bad news, I'm afraid."

"Is your mother ill?

"She's not feeling well to be sure."

Charlie told her what had happened and how angry he was.

"I feel guilty. I encouraged mother to donate the paintings. Without me I doubt she would have done anything."

"It's not your fault," Kate countered. "Yale lost the paintings. Don't beat yourself up. And don't beat up Yale -yet. Unload on them after they get the paintings back, if that is possible. You need them at this moment. Unfortunately."

"You're right."

"I can imagine how upset your mother must be. Should we drive up there tonight?"

"Mother said no. Let me call Yale now. Then we'll know what to do."

Charlie walked back to the library and sat down in his favorite, brown-leather chair and telephoned Hugh Vance. Since it was late Sunday afternoon, he was not sure if he could reach him. Nevertheless, Hugh answered on the second ring.

"Hugh, I'm glad you're still there. This is Charlie Bailey. My mother told me about your call."

"Oh, oh, yes," Hugh stammered. "We're so sorry. I've been here since one—trying to make sense of what happened. But they're gone. Gallery security doesn't know what happened. Susan doesn't either."

"Know this: my mother is beside herself. She thinks she made a huge mistake in giving you the paintings and, frankly, she's right. Now tell me all you know about the disappearance."

"What I know is that Susan came in late this morning to supervise the crew who were to move the paintings to our warehouse. The storeroom door was locked, as is our protocol. She used the key she kept in her desk. Two pictures were missing. She had the guards search every room in the gallery. Nothing. Then she called me at home.'

"I drove in immediately and called the Yale Police. They came over and started a search of the campus. As of now, they haven't found anything."

"So two of the paintings are gone? The other one is there?"

"Yes. Strange, isn't it. The Hassam oil and the charcoal sketch are missing. It makes no sense. Why not all three? The Cassatt beach scene is worth far more than the sketch and, probably, the Hassam. Either the thief is naïve, or there is some unknown explanation. I'm baffled."

"So you think they were stolen—not misplaced."

"It must be. What else could it be? Susan said that she and Cynthia locked them in the storeroom after the reception."

"Besides Susan who else had a key to the room?"

"There are a couple, I guess. The police are looking into that."

Charlie did not say anything for about fifteen seconds. He wanted to yell at this man for being incompetent, but that would accomplish nothing. Hugh had to know that he was upset. Instead, Charlie tried to sound calm.

"What are you going to do next?"

"I'll wait for the police report. While we have never had a loss of this magnitude before, we have some experience in these matters. You may remember the instance of the dealer who stole several valuable, historic maps from our Beinecke Library. We recovered all of them over time. The police did a fine job—with Yale's assistance, of course."

"I remember that incident," Charlie said.

"In your case, I'll make sure to notify the insurance company first thing tomorrow and file a claim. Since you have already made the gift, your tax deduction is safe."

"Stop," Charlie demanded through clenched teeth. "I'll say this only once. My mother did not give these paintings to Yale for a tax write-off. She doesn't care a whit about deductions. She gave these works of art—which she loved—to honor Dad's memory. In fact, the Hassam *Flags* painting was his favorite painting. So, to be clear, this gift has emotional currency far exceeding the painting's monetary worth. Do you understand me?"

"Of course, I meant no harm," Hugh said, chastened. "Our first priority is to find the paintings. Rest assured. I just thought you should know that we have insurance covering loss or theft. But that fact will not stop us from recovering these works of art."

Charlie hung up abruptly but was anything but assured. At his core, Hugh was a patronizing bureaucrat. For him, if the paintings were stolen, that's fine. Yale will get the insurance money. The Baileys had given the paintings to Yale and now were not involved legally anymore. Vance was clueless to the emotions attached to the long, previous ownership of the art and the meaning of the gift. So be it. Screw Hugh Vance. Charlie had a mission: make sure the paintings are recovered. He knew where to start.

mother-in-law invariably looked elegant whether she wore a gardening smock or a ball gown. Even her silver hair, as always so well coifed, was such that the color did not make her look old — instead, rather grand.

"Relax, Mother," Charlie said sensing her undisguised qualms about making the gift. "We've been through this a hundred times. Dad would have loved to see his pictures go to Yale, his *alma mater*, after all. You are doing the right thing. You'll see."

Kate remembered that she had tried to help by walking behind her seated mother-in-law and gently put her hands on her shoulders.

"Let's remember why we're here," Kate added. "Yale has arranged a reception to recognize your gift. What a happy event! I'm excited. Let's enjoy the day."

Kate felt tense herself. The magnitude of this gift was beyond her experience. These extraordinary paintings were prime examples of the best of American Impressionists, Mary Cassatt and Childe Hassam—worth millions at auction. Kate recognized that once this gift was made public, reactions would be swift and dramatic. Museum directors around the country would be envious of Yale and art dealers would chafe that these works of art had not been sold through them. She guessed that an important gift like this would be talked about for years.

Of the three of them, Kate knew that Charlie was the most enthusiastic. It was a momentous day for him. Like his father, he had graduated from Yale. This gift would establish a significant, permanent bond between the great university and the Bailey family. He obviously relished that link.

Fifteen minutes before the scheduled beginning of the reception an anxious Kate said, "Time to go. Let's have fun."

The trio had walked silently up Church Street until they saw their destination—the Louis Kahn Gallery. All glass and steel, it resembled to Kate a jewel box floating in air. Charlie tried sounding enthusiastic, "Look, Mother, your paintings will find a home in that architectural masterpiece. Up until now, only a few lucky scholars—and insurance appraisers—have seen them in the house in Lake Forest. That all changes today."

"I know, but I shall miss them. With us they already had a home."

"We'll have to come to Yale often," Charlie offered in commiseration. "They will always be here when we visit."

Chapter Two

While Charlie was making his phone call, Kate stopped chopping cucumbers and radishes for the dinner salad. She could hear the angry tone in his voice from two rooms away. She could not concentrate—critical when wielding a knife. Her mind kept asking what went wrong? How could a famous university art gallery not have sufficient security to protect its works of art? How could Claire's paintings have been there yesterday and gone today? Her mother-in-law must feel violated. How could a happy event turn so sour?

The trip to Yale was so vivid in her memory. She had accompanied Charlie and Claire on Charlie's company plane. They had checked into the New Haven Omni Hotel and changed into their clothes for the reception and dinner. Kate remembered clearly what bothered her then—trivial now. She had not been sure if her black knee-length cocktail dress and Ferragamo pumps were dressy enough for the evening. To provide some color and style, she had added a gold and ruby pin to the dress and put on smart gold and diamond earrings. Nevertheless, she had felt insecure in how she looked because she had never been to a reception honoring a donor of important works of art. Her mood improved, however, when she and Charlie went to Claire's suite to meet before leaving for the reception. She was relieved to see that Claire had dressed in a light-blue classic Chanel suit—an outfit Kate had seen her wear several times to church and lady's tea. Claire had also forgone wearing her very expensive jewelry in favor of beautiful, but unpretentious, pearls and earrings and a gold watch. Of course, Kate thought her

"I hope so. One thing though: you are going to have to help me with those nice people at the Art Institute back home. They have been after me for years to donate some things."

"They can wait, Mother. Their collection is already one of the best in the country."

"I feel I have let Chicago down."

"You have not. There will be time for the Art Institute."

"Yes, when I die. Let's hope they will have to wait a long, long time."

"Hear, hear," Kate had chimed in. "You're going to outlive all those curators. But, Charlie, stop for a second. We're almost there. Which door do we go in?"

"The reception is on the first floor up those stairs."

She remembered how handsome and commanding he looked at that moment: tall, athletic, impeccable in his blue, pinstripe suit, white shirt, and Yale tie.

As they climbed the steps she had recalled what Charlie had told her of its history and importance. Louis Kahn had won the commission for it on the recommendation of Eero Saarinen. Much to the dismay of some hidebound alumni, Kahn designed the first modernist building on this neo-gothic and colonial brick campus. Conversely the design blew away the faculty, the press, architects, and boards of museums across the country, when it opened in the early 1950s. Originally, it housed both the art and architecture students and the art gallery. Now it was entirely an art gallery. Its genius was in its flexibility and its revolutionary use of reinforced concrete, unique glass walls, and open ceilings. Aspects of the building had been copied for over fifty years. Yet, as new and revolutionary as it was, Charlie had argued that it blended in with the older, neo-gothic Yale Art Gallery on the right to which it was connected. Now having seen it in person Kate had to agree.

A crowd of about sixty people had already assembled in the reception area holding drinks and chatting. Drawing Kate's eye, she recalled, were three easels, each bearing a painting covered by light-gray cloths and illuminated by lights attached to the distinctive tetrahedral ceiling structure.

"The reason we're all here," she had thought.

Almost immediately Hugh Vance had bolted through the crowd and greeted them in his unctuous manner. Kate had recalled that weeks ago Claire had remarked, "I wonder if that man oils his mouth after brushing his teeth." Vance was wearing a similar blazer and bow tie ensemble to that which she remembered from Lake Forest.

Kate had turned him off after he punctuated his greetings with mention of "sons of Eli", "bleeding blue", "bulldogs", and "Boola, Boola".

Fortunately, at that moment a tall, thin man in his fifties, dressed in a light tan suit, blue and white striped shirt, and a Yale blue tie, walked up and interrupted Vance.

"Hello, Charlie. I'm Chauncey Adams. We had dinner in Chicago three years ago. I'm happy that you, Kate and your mother can join Rebecca and me for dinner tonight."

"Thank you, Chauncey. We shall be honored to join you and Rebecca. Let me introduce my mother Claire Bailey and my wife Kate.

"Ladies, Chauncey is the President of Yale, who I have talked so highly of."

Claire and Kate shook his hand and sounded respectful. President Adams then had led them to their seats in the front of the room. Remarkably without a word from anyone, the crowd had stopped talking and took their seats. Hugh Vance welcomed the audience, introduced the Baileys and President Adams.

"Now let's talk about why we are here," Vance began. "Mrs. Robert Bailey is gifting to the university in the name of her deceased husband three extraordinary works of art. They are not only valuable, they are important from a scholarly point of view and meaningful to Yale's collection of American Impressionist paintings."

A woman came forward and removed the cloths from the paintings. The audience murmured in approval.

"The first, which Susan Parker is unveiling now, is entitled *Mother and Child on the Beach*, an oil painted by Mary Cassatt in 1894. This beautiful painting is important to the Yale Gallery, because not only instantly is it recognizable in theme and style as Cassatt, but also it is the first Mary Cassatt oil in our collection.'

"The second painting is *Flags on Fifth Avenue, November 11*, by Childe Hassam in 1918. Another oil on canvas. Classic Hassam, celebrating Armistice Day. As you know, Yale owns several Hassams—but alas, until now, no *Flags* painting. This work of art will be extremely popular in this gallery.'

"The third piece—in some ways the rarest and most extraordinary—is a charcoal sketch. The sick man in the bed in the sketch is the dying Edgar Degas, drawn by his friend of many years, Mary Cassatt. A private moment. Pathos.'

"These works of art have been in the private collection of the Baileys in Lake Forest, Illinois, two for almost one hundred years. Few scholars have seen them until now, as the family desired privacy and had understandable security issues. Now they will be available for the whole world of art lovers to study and enjoy. We are extraordinarily grateful."

The audience had applauded and then stood at their chairs to acknowledge the magnitude of the gift. As was her temperament Mrs. Bailey appeared flustered by the display and urged Charlie to quiet the group. Kate had smiled because she thought that despite her momentary embarrassment, Claire would remember positively the way she was celebrated. After a few minutes the applause subsided, and the audience again took their seats. During that demonstration, three faculty members had walked forward to the easels to view the paintings and sketch up close. Meanwhile Hugh Vance had begged the assembly for decorum.

"George, Hal, and Ryerson, please sit down. There will be time to examine the paintings later. Obviously, we are all thankful and moved by the Baileys' generosity. As a delightful surprise now, our benefactor, Claire Bailey has agreed to reveal a few personal facts about the provenance of each work. Mrs. Bailey, you grace us with your presence."

Once again the crowd had burst into applause. Charlie had steadied her for a second. Then, by her side, he walked her to the podium. Finally, there was quiet. Kate had felt that Claire looked beautiful in her tailored suit and pearls. She adjusted the microphone to her height to speak.

"Excuse me. I'm not used to public speaking, but I'll try. As most of you are aware, we Americans purchased a great deal of French Impressionist art from about 1890 to the time of the Great Crash in the late 1920's. Until the Impressionists came along, most people of that era thought paintings should depict classical themes-that is, noble or mythical people drawn realistically, positioned in romanticized settings. Much as they are revered today, the Impressionists were rebels in their own time. As you can appreciate, since many wealthy Americans of that period earned their money during their lives instead of inheriting it, they had little time for a cultural education. These wealthy types admitted readily that they did not know good art from bad. They relied on the opinions of friends and the advice of art dealers to help them buy art. Acquiring art made them feel cultured—even if they weren't. Fortunately a handful of the dealers of the time did appreciate the French Impressionists—and some of the local American Impressionists as well—and directed many rich Americans their way.'

"In our case, my grandmother, Sophia Meade, lived in New York and was a close friend of Louisine Elder, who married Harry Havemeyer. You all know the Havemeyer collection at the Met in New York City. Louisine was an enthusiastic traveler and met Mary Cassatt on her first trip to Paris as a teenager. During that trip and subsequent ones, Mary introduced Louisine to the work of her artist friends from Paris: Degas, Manet, Monet, Morisot, Pissaro, and Cézanne—the lot. Louisine trusted Mary's taste, bought some paintings, and mentioned these painters to my grandmother.'

"Over time, my grandmother, who came from a good family and had been widowed, bought four works by Cassatt, including the two here, two by Degas, a Monet, a couple of Renoirs, and three Cézannes. She bought two or three directly from the artists, a few through Mary Cassatt, two from a Paris dealer, and some at dealer shows in New York. These works of art were passed down to my parents and then their children. Fortunately for me none of my sisters cared for art.

"So that's how I have these two Cassatts. The Childe Hassam was purchased by my father-in-law in a more conventional way. Mr. Bailey—Terrence was his name—needed some artwork for his home in Lake Forest. He had heard of an art dealer in New York named Durand-Ruel. So in the 1920's he traveled east once on business and paid George Durand-Ruel a visit. Georges showed him several French and American paintings, and my father-in-law bought two of them and several others later on. Since my husband's father was very patriotic to his death, he particularly liked this Hassam *Flags* painting. He liked both its theme and the colors.'

"So that's my story. My family has always been lucky in its friends and advisors. I should add now that it gives me great pleasure to honor my late husband, Robbie, with these gifts to Yale in his name. Thank you. I hope you like them."

Once again the applause had been strong, and it continued until she sat down. Kate had squeezed her hand and told her she had done well. Hugh returned to the front and introduced Susan Parker. Susan wore a mid-length blue crepe dress adorned with a large yellow brooch, which looked like a sunflower. Her straight hair was cut to her jaw line and held in place by a black hairband. She was tall and gaunt, looking almost ascetical and appeared to be in her late-thirties.

Susan's presentation had been more detailed and academic than Hugh's introduction. Kate had assumed that she was talking to scholars in the audience. Kate tried following her talk, but she lacked the knowledge of art history necessary to understand the references and technical comparisons. She did retain, however, some fascinating information from Susan's talk.

"The Mary Cassatt painting was done in her prime using her familiar mother and child themes," Susan had pointed out. "But in a setting, the beach, that she rarely used. Cassatt was a master in capturing the tenderness of a mother with her daughter.'

"You may be aware that a major argument among scholars was whether Cassatt was an American or French Impressionist. She was American by birth who lived and painted for most of her life in Paris. Her closest artist friends were Manet, Morisot, Renoir and, in particular, Degas. My considered opinion is that Cassatt should be recognized as an American painter first. Accordingly, Claire's gift will be exhibited in Yale's American collection."

No such question existed with paintings by Childe Hassam. Susan had stressed, "He was an American painter of urban settings and seaside landscapes in the Northeast. He contrasts with Mary Cassatt in that she painted figures principally—usually inside a structure, and he captured the outdoors in its colors and play of light. Mrs. Bailey's gift depicting a parade up New York's Fifth Avenue with brightly colored flags displayed outside buildings was one of a handful of such paintings."

Kate did not need to be convinced that the patriotic theme and the energy of the flags waving in the wind would be popular.

The third gift, the charcoal sketch, was entirely different from the other two. Kate had remembered that it had hung in a guest bedroom in the Lake Forest house. It looked dark and the theme was dark: a dying Degas.

Susan said, "Mary Cassatt visited Degas frequently at his Parisian apartment studio. Degas had been her mentor but was a difficult friend. Now in his early eighties, nearly blind and deaf, he was dying. Cassatt, herself suffering from diabetes and rheumatism, was also losing her sight. The moment is poignant, even though the sketch itself is not her best work. In fact, the sketch might be special only to art historians—a scene between two remarkable artists. The sketch is Cassatt's last remembrance of the man whom she considered the greatest artist of his time."

Kate had been touched by this description of a relationship long ago. Her respect for this stark and depressing drawing increased as Susan had explained the meaning. With that context the sketch was significant and moving.

When Susan had finished, she took a few questions. Kate remembered that she had said that the three pictures would be on public display in early October, after classes resumed. Susan expected that the interest in viewing them would be immense. These works of art were attractive, very valuable, and important in the history of art.

With the audience's questions exhausted, Hugh had called an end to the reception. Several people came up to thank the Baileys and others gathered around the paintings and sketch for a closer look.

Meanwhile, Kate had recognized Cynthia, standing at the far end of the reception area with two other individuals. She went over to talk to her.

"Cynthia, remember me? We met briefly in Lake Forest. Are you joining us for dinner?"

"Yes, Mrs. Bailey, I'm lucky. Usually such dinners are for the bigwigs. I'm going even though I'm just a lowly graduate student. Let me introduce my colleagues. This is Marie DiGracoine and Christopher Von Buch. They love the paintings and wanted to meet you and Aunt Claire."

Kate had shaken their hands and thanked them for coming. She knew she could not linger, so she turned to Cynthia and asked her to join them in the car.

"I'm sure we could add you, if we ask."

"Thank you, but I have to stay and store the paintings now. I'll catch up later."

"That's fine. Will talk then. You should know that all of us want to talk to you some more. Later. You must have excellent security here. I noticed the cameras up near the ceiling. Standing here, looking around, I see three already. Are these everywhere?"

"In the exhibition galleries, yes. We also have motion detectors and guards twenty-four-seven."

"Air tight?"

"Almost."

Then Charlie had waved to Kate to come over. President Adams had joined Charlie and Claire. When Kate had arrived, he led them to the door. His car was waiting to drive them to his house on Hillhouse Avenue. As they left the gallery, Kate noticed that Claire had stopped and given a wistful look back at three old friends resting on easels by themselves. Kate had thought that, unlike Degas with Mary Cassatt, at least these old friends would be there when Claire came back someday.

Now Kate reflected on how foolish that sentiment was in light of the theft. Charlie came into the kitchen, suggested that she join him at the table, and reported on his unsatisfactory conversation with Hugh Vance.

"Charlie, sweetheart, I have been thinking about this tragedy for Claire. I just don't comprehend how a thief could walk off with those pictures, considering how many cameras and guards I saw there. It's something out of the movies."

Charlie frowned at her and said softly, "Inside job."

Chapter Three

Claire could not sleep. The news from New Haven dominated and tortured her thoughts. If only..., she pondered. The Hassam was Robbie's favorite painting. If she had to make a gift, why had she not chosen some paintings with less family history or which had less appeal to her? Yes, the Pissaro or the J. Adler Weir landscape qualified; neither was among her favorites.

She lay in her bed remembering the good and the bad from her trip to Yale the day before. She had dreaded making that speech at the reception for over a month. She was not accustomed to speaking in front of a large group. Yet the speech had gone over well. In fact, everyone there had been gracious and appreciative to her. They had made her feel as if she had done the right thing in making the gift. Even that awful man, Hugh Vance, sounded genuine in his praise.

In contrast, Claire liked President Adams. He had invited Kate, Charlie and herself to join him in his car for the trip from the art gallery to his home. Instead of a stretch limousine fit for a corporate CEO, the president of Yale had a Toyota four-door sedan with room for a driver and passenger in the front seat and three average-sized adults tightly fit in the backseat. Claire was impressed that a rich university such as Yale would economize on an unessential luxury like a limousine even for their top official. Its money must be going to teaching, facilities, and scholarships.

Ever courteous, President Adams sat in the front seat next to the driver and turned to talk to them. Claire sat squeezed between Kate and Charlie, but she did not mind the minor inconvenience.

"Mrs. Bailey, have you visited Yale often over the years?"

"Yes, I suppose you could say that. But not at all during the past twenty years since Charlie graduated. In the 1950s when I was a proper young lady at Vassar, when there were only women there, I attended a few football games and some formal dances here in New Haven. My, how things have changed—new buildings, chain store retailers, scruffy-looking students. But I suppose the school is only a reflection of how our society has changed. Still, my mother would have had a heart attack if she had seen us dressed the way young girls dress now."

"Did you meet Mr. Bailey here?" Adams inquired.

"Claire replied, "At the time, I was being escorted around by one of his roommates, and we were introduced only after we both graduated. He said, 'out of respect for his roommate', even though that relationship was sporadic and platonic. I also recall visiting here once during that period at the invitation of my cousin Alexander. He was a student at Yale one year and then transferred to Purdue to do engineering."

"A shame," the president admitted. "We're much better at engineering now. But you and your husband must have visited here when Charlie was an undergraduate?"

"Yes, of course. Parents' weekends and commencement. It was fun to go to a football game and meet Charlie's friends and some of his teachers. I always found the school very welcoming."

"Reunions, also?"

"Oh, yes. Three or four over the years. Robbie had lots of friends and kept up with the Yale ones after a fashion. Yes, reunions were fun. Of course after Robbie died, I would not come here alone."

Chauncey Adams broke the momentary silence. "Well, we are here now. This is Hillhouse Avenue, and that big rather forbidding house on the right is my official residence. Come join me and Rebecca inside."

Looking out the window of the car, Claire remembered that Robbie had brought her here after they were married. He had said that Charles Dickens had described Hillhouse Avenue as "the most beautiful street in America". And she recalled that all the elm trees gave New Haven its sobriquet. The Elm City. Quite lovely.

The car stopped in front of the large Greek revival mansion. As Chauncey Adams was helping Claire out of the car, he said,

"I hope you know, Mrs. Bailey, I don't actually live here. We have a nice, comfortable house in Madison near the ocean. This formal residence with the priceless artworks and antiques and the lovely gardens in the rear of the property is used almost exclusively for occasions like this."

Once inside, the Baileys checked their coats and were greeted by Rebecca Adams and a row of waiters with glasses of champagne. Charlie guided Claire and Kate into the large drawing room decorated with eighteenth and nineteenth century American furniture, porcelain, and paintings. Claire thought she recognized paintings by Gilbert Stuart and Winslow Homer on the long walls. Chauncey Adams rejoined them immediately.

"I shall not attempt to introduce you to everyone at this party. Rest assured, none of them will refrain from introducing themselves. They are not shy. Suffer it to say, present tonight are the luminaries from our Art History Department, the provost, head of Development Office, and the heads of a few of our residential colleges. In addition, of course, you have met Hugh Vance and Susan Parker. Oh, and your great-niece, Cynthia, may be able to join us. Please feel comfortable to wander. We'll serve early—at seven. I have been told that you have a morning flight back to Chicago; so we'll get you out at a decent hour."

"That's very considerate of you."

At that point, Claire recognized Adrian Greene, an old friend of Charlie's, coming up and grabbing his shoulder from behind.

"Charlie, you have come back like the Magi bearing gifts."

Claire knew the history of this relationship. Adrian Greene was Charlie's teacher from his first survey course in art history when Charlie was a sophomore. Adrian was a young teaching assistant leading a weekly, seminar breakout from the massive main lecture course. They hit it off from the start. Now Adrian was the head of Pierson College, coincidently Charlie's residential college as an undergraduate.

Charlie laughed and shook his old friend's hand. "My mother's the one bearing gifts. Kate and I are along for the ride."

"How is your investment firm doing? And how is that partner of yours?"

"All is well, thank you, and Ollie is his same quirky self."

Claire understood this reference, of course. Her Charlie had been an investment manager for sixteen years. After college, serving in the marines, and earning his MBA, his father had given him startup funds with the stipulation that Ollie Richardson, an old friend of Robbie's, come on as a partner to offer his many years of experience and credibility.

"Where's your better half?" Charlie asked Adrian.

"Taking care of the baby. Amy said to say hello to you."

"You know my mother, of course, from your visits to Chicago."

"Of course. The guest of honor. Our benefactor. It's wonderful to see you again."

"My pleasure. Now, Charlie, introduce Kate. Be polite."

"I'm getting there. This lovely woman is my bride of last year. I am an extremely lucky man. We had hoped that you and Amy could have come to the wedding."

"My apologies again. We hated to miss it. I had this commitment to lecture on a Yale-sponsored cruise. I hope I told you then. We plan to make it up to you both some time in Chicago. Kate, it is a great pleasure to meet you now. You know you married quite an athlete. He used to beat me regularly in squash back when he was an undergraduate. Of course, now he is no match."

"Ha," Charlie interrupted. "Don't believe him, Kate. I've still got his number. He's an old man."

"Okay. Tomorrow at nine-thirty at the Payne Whitney courts. If I'm forty-seven, you must be forty at least.

"Next time, codger. We have a plane to catch."

For the next half hour Claire met a whirlwind of people. All thanked her for her gift and complimented her family. She was becoming tired and overwhelmed when thankfully dinner was announced.

As the group moved towards the dining room, a breathless Cynthia came up to Claire.

"I am sorry I'm late. Everything at the gallery took so long. I wish I could stay, but I have a paper due on Monday. I should have finished it, but I need to go to the library. I promise to visit properly when the exhibition opens in the fall. Please give my apologies to Kate and Charlie."

"Certainly, dear."

In a flash Cynthia was gone. Claire had shaken her head in bewilderment. Youth, she concluded.

She was the last to enter the back dining room, which overlooked the gardens. Since it was June, the flowers and colorful landscaping were still splendid. The guests circled an elegantly set mahogany table searching for their name card. One-by-one they stopped at the appropriate place.

Claire was positioned between the president and Hugh Vance. She saw that Kate was seated directly across the long Georgian table from herself and between Adrian Greene and Edward Ravenel, head of the Art History Department. Charlie was seated a bit farther down the table next to the head of development and wife of the provost. All sat at Chauncey Adams's bidding, and the Yale Chaplain Howard Biddle said grace—with a special tribute to the Baileys.

Claire noticed that one spot was empty. She assumed that it had been for Cynthia.

"It's too bad that Cynthia could not stay," Claire mentioned to Hugh.

"Yes. Susan said that Cynthia was feeling sick."

"Sad. I had hoped to get to know her better."

As the first course was being served, Hugh detailed to Claire his plans for the paintings.

"During the summer we'll display the three in a separate room in the gallery. Only authorized scholars, accredited journalists, and specially invited individuals will be allowed to view them. Our normal protocol. Then in autumn, we'll mount a public exhibition of new acquisitions. Your works of art will be the central pieces. Afterwards we'll add the Cassatt and Hassam paintings to our permanent exhibit of American art and send the sketch to our Hamden facility.

"What is the Hamden facility?" Claire inquired.

"It is our huge, state-of-the-art storage facility in Hamden, Connecticut. We also have one in West Haven. Understand, we have viewing space in the gallery for only about six percent of the works of art we own. A select few we display at all times, and we rotate other works in and out depending on interest and special exhibitions. For instance, now we are displaying more antique silver pieces than we normally would. Of course the whole collection is available to scholars upon request. Yale is very fortunate to have the Hamden facility. It was designed specifically for preservation and conservation of works of art."

"Why would the sketch of Degas on his deathbed be kept in Hamden?"

Claire had not liked where this conversation was going. She had not donated the sketch to gather dust in a warehouse. She would have rather it be back in the bedroom in Lake Forest. As she listened, her facial expressions tightened and her voice cracked when she spoke. She had tried to control her emotions but the pitch of her voice crept higher, "I don't understand."

"It is our view that this charcoal will have special meaning only to scholars," Hugh explained. "Cassatt was well past her productive period and probably meant it to be a personal memento. How this sketch came to be in the art market for your grandmother to purchase, I have no idea. We are all lucky it was available. While its value as a work of art is significant in itself, its overwhelming importance is in how it reveals the close, caring relationship between Cassatt and Degas."

"So its importance is principally in the eyes of art historians and not the public?" Claire remarked quizzically.

"We think so. In no way am I minimizing the piece, but most museum goers have no idea that Cassatt and Degas even knew each other. Cynthia insisted we should have it—for researchers. We agreed with her."

"So be it. Maybe I should have kept it at home. I have always been touched by the story behind it."

"Oh, I hope I haven't offended you in any way! I was merely making a distinction as we art historians are prone to do."

This contretemps had spoiled the dinner for Claire. Her emotions were so full that she barely heard what anyone else said after that. Hugh and Susan had been so enthusiastic about all parts of the gifts before. Now one of the artworks would be exhibited only temporarily before being shipped to Hamden. She felt as if she had been conned.

After dinner, the president had the driver take the Baileys back to their hotel. The dinner had broken up early enough so that they could have some good sleep before being picked up the next morning to get to their plane at Tweed Airport.

A glum Claire had invited Charlie and Kate up to her suite when they arrived at the hotel. She had not spoken to them since they left the party. When they sat down in Claire's room, Kate began with an assessment of the dinner. She had excitement in her voice.

"I met some knowledgeable and personable people tonight. When I went to school, I thought all art historians were as dull as dishwater. My opinion is changing. Charlie's friend Adrian, for instance, has a good sense of humor, and Professor Ravenel is a true Southern gentleman. I had a good time. And the meal was wonderful."

"How about you, Mother?" Charlie asked. "Was everyone on good behavior?"

"I suppose so. I must admit I heard enough tonight about paintings and artists for a lifetime. But I imagine it is to be expected with this group. Maybe we are shallow, but my crowd at home prefers to talk about social events, current political affairs and family and children. These people are aloof. And I particularly did not like Mr. Vance. He is a bit of a dandy and full of himself. I thought him a martinet. I don't think he much likes our little sketch of Degas. At any rate, I can't take it back. We'll have to come back next year to see what they have done with our paintings. I'm not optimistic."

So in bed at home the next day, Claire attributed her restlessness to the combination of a foul-mood brought on by Hugh Vance's pronouncements at the dinner party and her heartbreak from the news of the theft. Her stomach was churning.

Chapter Four

"May I speak with Officer O'Connell?" Charlie asked the operator at the Yale police office. He hoped that he was not calling too early this Monday morning. He was eager to talk to Marty O'Connell ever since he had heard of the theft the day before. In fact, he had tried calling then but he had been told that Officer O'Connell was not expected until Monday. That night Charlie had had a hard time sleeping and had given up, climbing out of bed at five thirty. He was careful not to disturb Kate, but his ever-vigilant bulldog Dickens woke and joined him in the kitchen. He fed Dickens and grabbed a yoghurt himself.

Since the time was so early Charlie decided to dress and call from his office when it would be nine o'clock eastern. Marty picked up immediately.

"Marty, my favorite cop. This is Charlie Bailey. How are you? You must be getting close to retirement."

"Well, Charlie, some people around the station think I retired several years ago. But I am still hanging around for a couple more years, racking up pension credits. By the way, thank you again for inviting Margaret Mary and me to your wedding last year. We hated to miss it. We would love to meet Kate someday."

"You will, of course."

"I thought you might call. I know the art theft yesterday involves paintings your family gave to the university. It must have been quite a shock."

"It was—and I am calling to find out if this is an instance where the artwork is likely to be recovered. My mother is shattered."

"I guessed as much. I am not leading the investigation. At a school this size we see lots of burglaries and larcenies, but they are usually small books, personal computers, clothes—that sort of thing. But this one is of such high profile and so embarrassing to the university, the chief is personally involved—as well as Lieutenant Burke and myself in a supporting role. As we always do in major cases, we have asked the New Haven Police to join us. They have excellent resources, and we have a great working relationship with them. Several of our officers came from there. I can't tell you anything that isn't public information, but I don't suppose you get the *New Haven Register* in Chicago?"

"No, and I didn't see anything in today's *New York Times*."

"A theft of this magnitude will make the *Times* eventually. First, the art theft. If we don't find the paintings quickly, we'll call in the FBI. Someone in the department might have already. The FBI has a special art-theft program. They also have ties into Interpol if it looks like the artworks might leave the country. The bottom line is that we are still gathering evidence.

"Now the second part," Marty continued. "An art-history graduate student was found dead early this morning in the stacks of Sterling Memorial Library. It may be on the local news programs already. The deceased is Cynthia Newgate.

"Stop!" Charlie shouted. "Not Cynthia! She is a distant cousin. No!"

"We didn't know that. Another connection. I'm sorry for you. Ordinarily an art theft and what may be a homicide would be two isolated incidents, but there is a link here too close to be a coincidence. Ms. Newgate was writing her dissertation on Degas. More telling, she had been helping out the curator at the art gallery with your family's paintings."

"Do you mean Susan Parker?" Charlie asked, trying to be calm.

His mind was racing. His mother will be devastated. He knew that she had had a mysterious falling out with her sister—which explained why she had not been close to Ellie and that part of the family. But this tragedy was too egregious and personal not to cut deep into Claire's sentiments. And poor Ellie!

"Yes, that's the curator. So the deceased probably had special access to the works of art in question."

"What makes you think she was killed?"

"The crime scene guys from the NHPD are still over at the library, and the state medical examiner may not have arrived yet. But this woman died in a lot of pain. Anyone could see that. From my experience she looks like she was poisoned."

"Why do you say that? She wasn't assaulted, stabbed, shot, or strangled?"

"No, so far no signs of a struggle or trauma. It looks like she had been writhing in pain on the floor and vomiting."

"God. We talked to her on Saturday. This is terrible. Do you have any leads or suspects?"

"Nothing yet. The last person who saw her was the guard checking passes to enter the stacks. It was late Saturday night. He said he often saw Miss Newgate and spoke to her regularly. He said she looked pale, tired, and agitated; so he asked her if she was okay, and she said she might be coming down with the flu. She had a stomach ache and had thrown up, but she had some work to do, as she had a presentation due the next week. Like many graduate students, she had a stall in the library stacks—on level Six *M*. You know, a desk, chair, bookcases, and lots of books, which had been ordered to be brought to her stall. The guard sees lots of strung-out students, so he didn't think anything was unusual. At any rate, Miss Newgate probably took the elevator to her floor, may have used the ladies room, and gone to her stall. Of course, the medical examiner will do an autopsy, including a clinical analysis to test for poison. We'll have to wait for his report."

"You think it will show poison?"

"Yes. The evidence points that way. Poisoning introduces lots of investigative complexities. Was it a suicide of a stressed-out student or a homicide? If a homicide, there is not a conventional weapon as evidence. Even if you identify a suspect, with poisonings he generally has good trial defenses."

"Between you and me, what do you think happened?"

"I can't say. This is an ongoing investigation."

"Between friends," Charlie pleaded. "She was my cousin."

"Okay. I didn't say this, but I think Cynthia Newgate got in over her head, assisted someone in stealing your pictures, and was rewarded by the thief with a slow, painful death. Her accomplice probably used some sort of heavy metal poison like arsenic, which takes less than an hour to cause vomiting. It leads to severe diarrhea, dehydration, and heart failure within twelve to twenty-four hours. Now he is probably long gone with the painting."

Charlie shook his head in disbelief. Cynthia seemed like a nice, young woman—obviously intelligent and apparently respected by the people with whom she worked. Even hard to please Mother had taken a fancy to her, a distant grandniece. Murdered? It made no sense. Marty had to be wrong. Cynthia could not have been involved in the theft. She had to have been a victim only. Somehow she had been a threat to the thief. Now she was dead and two pictures were gone. This situation gets worse and worse. How am I going to tell Mother?

"Marty. I'm sorry. I didn't answer because I had to compose myself. What you say is a lot of terrible news at once. Is there anything I can do?"

"Just hold tight. The events of the past two days were well planned out. This case is going to be a bitch to solve. We're doing our best. Call me in a few days, and I may have more news. Again, I'm sorry for you and your family."

Charlie sat back in his chair in his office in Chicago's Loop, the financial district. He knew that he had to tell his mother. It would be awful if she heard about Cynthia from another source. He dreaded that conversation; his mother was already devastated. He would have to talk to her in person. He and Kate would drive up as soon as they could get out of work.

Another murder. A year before, a client of his had been murdered, and circumstances had drawn him into the investigation. The Bradshaw Affair. As a consequence of his involvement, his then fiancée Kate had almost been killed. He too had been targeted and only saved by his remarkable Kate. While New Haven's events seemed very remote and different, he could not help but think of what had happened last summer and how upset with himself he had been for playing amateur detective. True, he had been treated by the police and the press as a suspect, and he had felt highly motivated to clear his name. In that regard, everything worked out and in the end, the murderer had been killed. Justice was done. Yet the recollection of those events remained strong in his mind and especially in Kate's. Not only had she narrowly escaped death in a drive-by shooting, she had shot a man in self-defense. That circumstance haunted her still. Her life had been transformed. Charlie had had to comfort her and soothe her whenever something shook that memory loose. She was a strong woman, but nothing in her past had prepared her for shooting a person. Considering the trauma that these events had caused Kate, Charlie was thankful that she had gone ahead and married him last fall as planned. Now Charlie hoped that the current events would not raise a connection with what had happened the year before.

Still, needing to talk to someone, Charlie tried Kate's office. But he had forgotten that she had told him that she would be at client meetings all day, so he was unsuccessful. He left a message instead asking her to join him on a visit to his mother.

He thought about his conversation with Marty. Marty was a long-standing friend who confirmed their relationship by being so candid with him. He doubted anyone else in the Yale police department would have told him all Marty did. Their connection went back to Charlie's freshman year. After a Saturday football game Charlie and his two roommates had hosted a party in their two-bedroom suite entertaining their friends and dates. Unfortunately, one particularly spirited classmate threw a large, full plastic container of beer out of a third-floor window to the courtyard. The beer doused a student who called the campus police.

A short time later two officers arrived at the suite and demanded to see the hosts. Charlie and his roommates met the officers in the hallway. Marty O'Connell, the senior officer, took down names and details of the incident, including the presence of alcoholic beverages in a room housing underage undergraduates. He warned the boys that this incident could lead to various punishments including probation, suspension, and even expulsion from school.

The impact on Charlie was immediate and profound. He was scared. What a way to begin his stay at Yale. Shaken and contrite, he feared the worst for about three weeks, until he was told he had received only a warning against a further violation, which went into their school files, but which fortunately was not sent to his parents.

Much relieved, Charlie eventually attributed his light sentence to three factors: the officers dealt with such events all the time; Marty O'Connell was a nice guy; and most convincingly, his last name was Bailey and those of his roommates were Doyle and O'Brian—probably warming the heart of an Irish-American Officer O'Connell.

Over his next few years as an undergraduate, Charlie would run into Marty on the street or in a local restaurant and greet him enthusiastically but respectfully and bring him up-to-date on his scholarly pursuits and, always, his good conduct.

After graduation, the two saw each other only occasionally—when Charlie came back to New Haven for a football game or a reunion. Still, each Christmas without fail Charlie sent Marty and his wife a Christmas card. Over time and with age, Charlie felt that they had become friends who had shared many common, enjoyable experiences over many years. Marty's openness this morning simply affirmed his trust and regard.

Charlie's remembrances were interrupted suddenly when his secretary reminded him that the weekly staff meeting was about to start. A money management firm like Bailey, Richardson and O'Neill scheduled staff meetings each Monday morning. They would review the news from over the weekend that might affect the financial markets. They also discussed current portfolio strategy to determine if it should be changed. Then at the end of each meeting, Charlie, as head of the firm, always asked if any of the clients had made any special requests.

Julian Anderson, the chief operating officer, also used this meeting to pass along administrative updates. Because of its importance, Charlie required that all senior officers attend these meetings. He also knew that once the week began and the markets opened, everyone became extremely busy and would be hard to bring together.

Charlie hurried down the corridor of offices to the conference room, vowing to hide the turmoil he was experiencing. So to cover up his feelings, he asked more questions of his portfolio managers and analysts than usual and sipped his hot tea slowly and calmly throughout the hour the meeting lasted.

As soon as it ended, Charlie headed back to his corner office. He looked moodily out of the floor-to-ceiling glass windows at Lake Michigan. Just then Adrian Greene called.

Adrian began, struggling for the right words, "I am so sorry. I don't know what to say. I assume you have heard about Cynthia and the stolen paintings? My condolences."

"Yes. Sadly. The world has lost its bearings."

"I had learned only two weeks ago that Cynthia was related to your family. I am sickened by what has happened to her."

"Thank you. I had hoped to get to know her much better."

"She and then the paintings. We lost them. Inexcusable. I never thought I would see Hugh Vance shamefaced, but he is now. As a member of this institution and part of the art history department, I am equally mortified. I can't apologize enough, dear friend. We have to find these works of art immediately and find out what happened to Cynthia."

"I don't blame you. Not at all. And I am heartened that you see the importance of finding the pictures. When I talked to your colleague Hugh, he seemed more interested in the insurance money than the artwork. He emphasized to me and my mother—rather cavalierly I might add—that Yale owned the paintings, after all."

"I am sorry he said that. Believe me, the people I talked to at the university do not think that way. We are determined to recover the paintings. On the other hand, we can't bring back Cynthia."

"Thanks. I appreciate that. I like to think best of the school. Do you know anything about Cynthia's death?"

"Her death is on the news now—local radio and TV. The school is all abuzz. I knew her reasonably well, although she never took any of my classes. Most of the people in art history here meet each other over time—parties, dinners, departmental meetings. I met her that way. Anyways, Cynthia was found dead in Sterling Memorial Library today. The media is saying she was murdered, although the police have not confirmed that yet. I can add that no one I talked to is linking her with the theft of your paintings. She was a Barbizon and Impressionist specialist and, like many others, had access to the art gallery. Maybe she saw something she shouldn't have seen. Her death—possibly murder—would appear to be related to the theft somehow."

"God, I hope not. What can you say about her personally? I'm sorry to say I barely knew her. I regret I did not spend more time with her."

"She was bright, articulate, worked hard. I think she was doing well in her academic work. I don't think she was a teaching assistant, but she did help out at the art gallery. She would have worked with Susan Parker. I think you met her. As far as her thesis, her faculty advisor is, was, John Hamilton. He was at the president's dinner on Saturday. He is an expert on nineteenth century French painters."

"Did she have a boyfriend?"

"I never saw her with any particular man."

After a moment, Adrian continued, "I think someone told me that she did her undergraduate work at Columbia."

"New York. Lots of museums and galleries. A good place for an art-history student," Charlie commented. "Who would kill that lovely girl? I guess that the police will piece it all together. What do you think is next?"

"I imagine the police and the FBI will be asking questions. I'll keep you informed if I hear anything."

After Charlie hung up, he tried to picture Cynthia Newgate. Adrian made her sound like any one of a number of young, industrious students. After graduation from college, they put their life on hold while they focused entirely on learning enough to complete their doctorates. That was the certification they needed to land a teaching position at a university or a decent curatorial job at a museum. Once situated, they could have a fuller personal life and pursue a career as a scholar.

Of course, while someone was still a student, there would be almost no money. Cynthia Newgate would have had to rely on generous parents, loans, fellowships, and, if lucky enough, the odd stipend for helping at the university. The prospect of cashing in on a stolen work of art could be tempting. The risk, however, would be huge. Charlie knew almost nothing about Cynthia. From what his mother had said about Cynthia's mother, she came from a good family—upper middle class Midwestern. She had studied at top schools. Plus, she was a relative. She did not seem the type of person to con her own family—however distant.

Waiting for Kate to return his call, Charlie found himself temporarily free from meetings and distractions and sat down in front of his computer. He wanted to read the *New Haven Register*'s online accounts of the theft and the murder

Finding the site was easy, and, since the Newgate murder was the lead story, he did not need to subscribe online to read the articles. There was not much new in them. The paper reported that Cynthia's parents confirmed that she had grown up in Cleveland and developed an interest in art from visiting Cleveland's excellent museums. The article went on to say that her parents were shocked at her death and knew nothing about an art theft.

Looking at the newspaper coverage, it was clear to Charlie that the theft was secondary to the newspaper's interest in the murder. The details of a murder case were far juicier to the public than the disappearance of two works of art attributed to painters dead for more than eighty years. If the police found no hard evidence to link Cynthia to the theft, the public interest in the missing pictures would fade. In that case, he would have to look for a monthly update on the theft on the ninth page.

Kate called around noon and Charlie immediately informed her of Cynthia's death and Marty's speculation around it.

"No way, José," Kate said dismissing the notion that Cynthia was involved in the theft. "It's terrible that she is dead. Absolutely tragic. Such a pleasant girl to talk to. It's cruel that Marty thinks she was part of the theft. You need to set him straight."

"I'll try. He will have to consider all possibilities. I prefer to think she was an unfortunate victim. We have to tell Mother as soon as possible. In person would be best. I'll call and say that we are coming to Lake Forest after work. Hopefully, you can leave early."

"Of course. And you and she must call the Newgates."

On the trip north Charlie attempted to divert the conversation to mundane matters such as what Kate accomplished at her job that day and how the stock market performed. She went along with Charlie's lead, but Charlie imagined she would rather have discussed the murder.

Claire met them at the door and announced that she hoped they would stay for dinner.

"Thank you, Mother. We have important things to discuss. Let's sit down in the dining room and talk. We can eat whenever the food is served."

"Okay," Claire agreed. But she was visibly perturbed. Charlie knew she liked to run the show and do events like dinner in her usual format.

"Excuse me. I'll have to talk to Cook. Otherwise she'll be upset."

Five minutes later Claire returned. She bade them to sit and demanded, "Let's at least await serious conversation until after soup."

Charlie bit his tongue. He was resigned to wait awhile—however weird in this situation.

Dinner at Claire Bailey's house was a throwback to another era. They were in a formal dining room decorated with Georgian furniture and a table setting of Limoges plates, silver flatware, and Baccarat crystal wine glasses. James, the houseman since Charlie was a boy, served the courses of soup, salad, entrée, and dessert. When Charlie was dating Kate early on, she was intimidated by this show, but time and familiarity had lessened that response. Of course, Charlie was used to this formality, but he was happy that Kate had never copied it at home.

After James had served the soup and left the room, Claire assured her son and daughter-in-law that she was doing better today after a dreadful Sunday. The theft was an awful shock, but the police would likely recover the pictures. At least she hoped they would.

Charlie agreed with her regarding the art, but then added, "I am afraid that there is even worse news. We learned today that Cynthia was found murdered early this morning."

Claire gasped and turned pale.

Charlie continued, "She may have been poisoned. The police don't know much yet, but her death and the theft must be linked somehow."

"Gracious," Claire said. "Poor girl and poor Ellie. I have to call her. I had high hopes that Cynthia would be the reason to bring us closer to the Newgates. I wanted to get to know Cynthia well and help her get ahead. When we saw her at the Yale reception she looked so good—lost a few pounds and perky. This is horrible, shocking. Who cares about a couple of paintings when this happens? I hate to think—."

"What?" Kate asked.

"I hate to think that my gift has caused all this pain. No gift, and Cynthia would still be alive and the paintings in their old places on the wall. How could I have done this? I feel guilty."

"Don't think that," Kate counseled. "Your gift came with wonderful intentions. What happened has nothing to do with you. You have been so generous."

"I should have been kinder to Eleanor and her family. Some silly spat with my sister kept me away. And then Helen died and I just acknowledged them with Christmas cards. I have been so wretched."

Claire grimaced and then looked up. "I am not feeling so well. Please excuse me. Please finish your dinner. I have lost my appetite." She stood up and left.

Charlie looked over at Kate and said, "How are you?"

"I've been better. Death does not agree with me. I have a request, though. Do you mind if I stay over tonight? Your mom needs someone. She likes me and could use a woman to confide in."

"How about your work?"

"I have a light day tomorrow. What I have, I'll reschedule. The advertising world will survive my missing one day."

Charlie was impressed with Kate's concern. He married her for lots of reasons and her heart was one of them. This kind of emergency was precisely why they kept a change of clothes in their upstairs bedroom.

"Very good idea. I'll call tomorrow morning to see how Mother feels."

Chapter Five

Although the sun was shining through her bedroom window when Claire woke up, it did not cheer her one bit. She felt depressed and deflated. She was also embarrassed that she had left Kate and Charlie in the middle of dinner last night. She knew that they would understand, but such rudeness was beneath her usual standard of conduct.

Surprisingly, she had slept deeply. The bad news piled on the previous bad news had exhausted her so thoroughly that sleep came quickly. It had not refreshed her however. She decided that she would stay home until this depression passed. Why burden others with her problems? Contrary to her current state, she prided herself on being a positive, energetic person. She felt that people expected her to be lively and upbeat.

She had to call Ellie. Claire assumed that the police would have informed Cynthia's family. She hoped that Cynthia's death had nothing to do with the missing pictures, but, whatever the connection, Ellie should know that Claire was thinking of her and praying for Cynthia. Claire would offer any help that Ellie and her family would need.

When Claire went downstairs, James informed her that Kate had stayed over and wanted to join Mrs. Bailey for breakfast. Claire welcomed the idea of talking to her daughter-in-law, although the fact that Kate had not driven home with Charlie increased her embarrassment.

Claire always ate breakfast in the dining room, even though the kitchen was large and comfortable. Her family always had help in the house and she enjoyed the tradition of eating in a formal room, being served by a butler.

She liked to skim the headlines in the papers folded neatly next to her place at the table and order the same breakfast: orange juice, hot tea, half a grapefruit, one soft-boiled egg, and unbuttered wheat toast. She remembered that her father had often said that if you are in a foul mood always maintain the usual order of things. Structure can be reassuring. Kate joined her at the dining room table after a minute or two. She ordered something simple and smiled at Claire. "How are you feeling this morning?"

"I'm upset. What happened is so dreadful. I think I'll stay close to home until I am my usual self. When I'm off, my big mouth can get me into trouble. At any rate, it was nice of you to stay over—although it wasn't necessary."

"It's the least I could do." Kate replied, paused, and then added, "Let me volunteer to listen. A thousand things must be going through your mind. Sometimes it makes you feel better to air them."

Claire had grown to like her daughter-in-law. Kate was smart and logical. She provided a good balance to Charlie, who could be impetuous and stubborn. In the months since their marriage, Claire had frequently confided in Kate, mostly on small matters, and never regretted their conversations. Similarly, Kate had shared with Claire some of her hopes, fears, and ambitions. This familiarity made Kate's offer unsurprising and welcome.

"All right. Where do I begin? Clearly Cynthia's death is the worst thing. Maybe if we had not made the gift, she would still be alive."

"The gift was a wonderful and selfless act," Kate countered. "You are in no way responsible for her death. And who knows if what happened to Cynthia had anything to do with your gift."

"I hope God sees it that way. The missing paintings bother me a lot, also. I know I didn't lose them, but the impact is the same. I am concerned that I let down Robbie and my family. In a way, I was the trustee for their legacy, and I failed."

"They are missing through no fault of your own. Besides, Charlie assures me that Yale will recover them."

"You're a dear, Kate. I hope so. Of course nothing will bring back Cynthia."

"True, but Charlie says he would feel better if the police determine what happened to her and catch the murderer. He called Marty O'Connell of the Yale Police yesterday and learned that thorough and vigorous investigation of the murder and theft has already begun. You know Charlie. He'll be on the police constantly until they succeed."

"Yes. That's Charlie."

Seeing that Kate had finished her breakfast, Claire suggested that they go out to the garden to cut some flowers. Some activity might relax her. Claire was already dressed in a white cotton dress and added a broad-rimmed, cotton hat and a pair of Wellies from the mudroom off the kitchen. Kate tagged along in the clothes she had left at the house—her just-in-case casual outfit. She wore a short-sleeved, pink blouse and white Capri pants, which Claire thought would be fine in the garden.

"Maybe I'm just curious," Claire began as she wielded her shears on some white peonies. "But why did the thief only take the Childe Hassam and that sketch? The Mary Cassatt oil is certainly worth more than each and would have been in the same storage room?"

"I wondered the same thing." Kate said as she cut three peonies and put them in her basket. "Does the Childe Hassam have some special meaning?"

"Only to me. Robbie's father, Terrence Bailey, bought it. He purchased the painting in New York some time before the 1929 Crash and the subsequent Depression and had it shipped to his home in Lake Forest. There it hung in his wood-paneled library for years—except for a time when he moved it to his house in Palm Beach. When Mr. Bailey died, he bequeathed it to Robbie, who told me that he had always been enthusiastic about the colors and the patriotic theme. When we bought this house, we considered several places to display it effectively. Finally we decided that the entrance hall was the place. As we had expected, our guests entering the house loved it. The picture was so upbeat it put them in a festive mood.'

"Over the years I think that painting—more than any other—came to be identified by our friends with the Bailey house. It was so memorable and striking. It may sound silly, but I felt as if I had lost a family member when I sent it to New Haven. Even in that short time I felt as if the personality of this house had changed. I have tried hanging other paintings in its spot, but nothing seems right. I wished I had said no to that one. But Charlie had said that it was the one painting that Dad would have wanted at his *alma mater*.'

"It's gone now. Robbie would have been sick to hear that. Almost any other painting would have been better. I miss Robbie more than ever"

"We'll just have to get it back," Kate promised.

"Do you really think that is possible?"

"As Charlie likes to say, 'Failure is not in our vocabulary'."

Chapter Six

By nine o'clock on Tuesday morning, Charlie had called Kate's cell number twice—once from home and once from his office. He guessed that she must have turned her phone off while she spent time with his mother. He understood that she did not appreciate interruptions at times like that, but he found her practice irritating. He loved his wife, but she did try his patience at times. He considered calling his mother's house phone but rejected that idea because she might pick up, and he waited to talk to Kate first to see how his mother was coping. He decided to wait until he saw Kate tonight at their apartment.

Charlie was full of nervous energy. He knew the day would be busy. Crucially, he wanted to get an update from Marty O'Connell as soon as he thought his friend would be on duty. He looked at the meeting schedule that his secretary, Kathy, prepared for him. Between meetings with a client and with his bond trader, who was considering a job offer from a competitor, he saw an opening at ten-thirty. He would just have to wait until then.

Managing an investment management firm was a constant challenge. Securities markets were volatile by nature. Clients wanted positive results constantly. Employees were highly paid and high-strung. Most individuals would find such an environment too unsettling, but Charlie loved it. His personality thrived on risk—the greater the risk, the greater the reward. He acknowledged that some perceived him to be impatient and arrogant, but he accepted that he could not please everyone. Neither his mother nor his wife could change him. But as long as they put up with him he was fine. He glanced at his watch for the third time in five minutes and frowned. His client was late and might throw off his schedule.

His mood improved when the meeting ended on time despite the late start and the client seemed to have left with a clear understanding of Charlie's strategy for his investment portfolio. Faced with a half hour of free time, Charlie closed his office door and called Marty O'Connell.

"Hi Charlie. I've been expecting you to call. Things are really hectic here. Lots of excitement but no culprits yet. One thing is pretty sure. The immediate cause of Cynthia Newgate's death was cardiac arrest brought on by arsenic poisoning. Arsenic trioxide, to be exact."

"That sounds awful," Charlie said, imaging Cynthia's suffering.

"The ME's report will not be out for days, but he confirmed our suspicions by an analysis of her hair and by two other chemical tests. She had all the classic signs: dehydration, clammy skin, vomiting, diarrhea, and garlic odor. She probably ingested the powder in a flavored drink—maybe hot tea or wine. Once the poison is absorbed by the stomach, it enters the bloodstream and attacks the vital organs. The process usually takes a day, but eventually her muscles spasm, she goes into shock, and her circulatory system and heart fail. It's a tough way to die."

"Is arsenic always fatal? I mean, would the murderer have been certain she would die?"

"If the dose was large enough and she didn't immediately go to a hospital, she was definitely going to die. Since we found her in the stacks, I think she had no clue what was going on. She probably thought she had a bad stomach flu, and unfortunately, when she felt really sick, she had no one to help her. Remember it was a weekend, and other scholars normally using the stacks were not there. She might have called a security guard, but she didn't. Library security found her Sunday already dead."

"So when did she die? When was she poisoned?"

"The ME has not said yet. I would guess she was poisoned late Saturday night and died about twelve or so hours later."

"Since the paintings were taken presumably late Saturday night, could she have witnessed the theft and then had been poisoned?

"Witnessed? I don't think that's the right word. Poison is a bit slow. Besides how did the murderer get her to take it? No, Charlie, I'm sorry since the deceased was related to you, but she had to have been a participant in the theft. Her partner or partners planned her death and killed her."

"I'm not convinced," Charlie countered.

"You will be. Of course we don't have all the evidence yet. Our forensic guy says that her prints were on the door of the room where the paintings were kept before they were stolen."

"Only hers?"

"No, there were other prints—the curator, guards, and the gallery director. Several people had reason to go in that room. The only unsecured set of keys to all the storage rooms in the basement were kept in the curator's desk drawer—unlocked. Susan Parker. There was easy access. Look, if she hadn't have been killed, she would have only been one of the suspects. With poison, someone planned her death—the method and the timing."

"Did Susan Parker always leave her desk drawer unlocked?"

"She said that only her close associates knew her keys were there. She usually locked the drawer when she left but must have forgotten to do it in her haste to attend President Adams' dinner. But she confirmed that Cynthia Newgate was one who had a key to the drawer for those instances when she called in for Cynthia to get something out of the storage room and bring it to her—for instance for a lecture Susan was giving."

"So Susan or other of her associates had access to the keys to the storage rooms—not just Cynthia?"

"True and we are investigating all of them. But none of them are dead."

"Still...," Charlie argued.

"Charlie, you have a point. Everyone in that area is under suspicion. But if the theory is that Miss Newgate was poisoned because of something she saw someone else do, why would she have sat down with the murderer for a drink and why would the murderer suddenly have arsenic available? That scenario seems farfetched."

"Did one of the guards see Cynthia with the paintings?"

"No. The guards monitor the exhibition space with cameras—not the basement. Anyone knowing the basement connections can come and go without being seen. Security could be a lot better. Nobody saw her. She may have come by way of Street Hall."

"If it was she."

"Believe what you want. I'm just a cop who has been doing this for over thirty years. I'm telling you this because you are a friend, and what I have told you will be in the papers tomorrow. Anything else I know, I can't say."

"Of course, ongoing investigation."

"There is something funny. The keys from the curator's desk were there. After the thief used them, he or she took the trouble to return them. Only an amateur would do that."

"I guess I'm not in a laughing mood," Charlie declared. "What do you do next?"

"I have the art theft. Billy Schwarz is assigned to the murder. At some point we'll bring everything together. The New Haven PD is working with us on both. As you can imagine, most of the interest is in the murder. We also contacted the FBI—about the art theft, not the murder yet. They are the pros in art thefts. I'll be working with them. Expect a call from them. I may need you later to ID the paintings when we find them."

"That's the most encouraging thing you've said—that you'll locate them."

Charlie found focusing on his business difficult after this conversation. He visualized the poisoned Cynthia, retching and sinking away. Hideous. He tried to come up with an explanation why she was murdered other than that she was a part of the robbery scheme. Nothing was convincing. *Am I in denial because she seemed so ingenuous, and she was related? I see her as a victim—not a thief.*

All afternoon Charlie pretended he was listening to his staff on their concerns and to stockbrokers who called to pitch him on investment ideas. He put on a good face, but his mind was elsewhere.

Kate never called back. However, she was at the apartment when Charlie arrived.

"Your mom is the best. She has good reason to be depressed, but she took the time to confide in me some of her feelings. She made me feel like a daughter."

"Well, you are. She's better now?"

"I spent most of the day there. I think she is reconciling things. I'm sorry I didn't return your call. I knew I would see you tonight. Did you have a good day?"

Charlie told her about the call with Marty. He avoided the details of arsenic poisoning because he feared Kate would react poorly. Instead he highlighted Marty's theory of Cynthia's involvement. He admitted that it made sense, although Charlie could not agree with it emotionally.

"That poor girl," Kate remarked with emphasis. "She went through hell. I hope Marty is wrong. Your mother does not need another shock. It's easy to see a connection though. Cynthia was close to the art and knew the gallery intimately. The 'why' I cannot understand. Steal art from Yale? Partner with a thief? It makes no sense."

"We need to get to the bottom of this mystery. Find the answers. If we can retrieve the paintings in good condition quickly, then Mother might calm down a bit. And Dad's memorial would be restored. We would probably also learn if Cynthia was mixed up with the theft. Of course, Yale would also benefit—the art and its reputation."

"Hold your horses, Cowboy. How are you going to 'retrieve the paintings'? Come down to earth. Finding the lost artworks would have positive results all around, granted. But also clear is that we cannot do anything about a recovery. The police will do that job."

"We can hope so. In the meantime, I'll think about how we can help them."

Charlie saw Kate's face and body language turn quizzical; so he dropped the subject.

Chapter Seven

"A woman from the FBI is in our lobby and asked to talk to you," Kathy announced from the door to Charlie's office. "Also, Mr. Donato called to confirm your squash match at five."

Charlie turned around from typing an email and told her to bring in the FBI agent. Out of habit he straightened the piles of papers on his desk and checked that there were no dirty coffee mugs from a previous meeting.

"Hello, Mr. Bailey. My name is Jackie Farrell."

Charlie shook his visitor's hand and pointed to the couch as a way to direct her to sit down.

"Coffee? Tea? Water?" Charlie asked politely.

"No, thanks. I've already been to Starbucks. You have attractive offices and a great view of the lake from here."

"Thank you. What can I do for you?"

Charlie took note of the striking figure sitting across from him-tall, thin, athletic build in a navy suit. She wore little makeup and looked pretty in a wholesome way. Her medium length, blond hair framed her face and her wire-rimmed glasses gave her a serious appearance. Charlie guessed she was in her mid-thirties. More than anything, he was surprised that the FBI had female agents and disappointed in himself to think that way.

Jackie Farrell spoke very professionally, with a strong New York accent.

"I am a special agent for the FBI's Art Crime Team—out of New York. Here's my card. I'm here to talk about the art theft that took place in New

Haven last weekend. I am hoping that you could answer a few questions that might help us locate the paintings and return them to Yale."

"I'm happy to help."

Charlie was amused at the woman's body language. She was uncomfortable in her suit, stockings, and pumps. He speculated that FBI agents did not wear such formal clothes to work every day.

"Here are descriptions of the two works of art that were taken. Could you verify that these descriptions are correct?"

Charlie studied the paper handed to him. "This appears to be accurate—the Childe Hassam and the Cassatt sketch."

"Do you have any idea why the Cassatt oil was left behind? Is there something unique about it or is its authentication in doubt?"

Charlie bristled at this suggestion but he controlled his temper. "No. The Cassatt painting was purchased from Mary Cassatt's principal dealer and has been in our family for almost a hundred years. No one has ever questioned its authenticity."

"You must admit that it is strange that it was left behind."

"Yes, but I have no idea why. It's very valuable."

"If our research is correct, Childe Hassam painted many variations of the theme of that stolen picture."

"That is true. People like "flag" paintings."

"The sketch, on the other hand, seems to be one of a kind. Do you know of another like it?"

"I am not aware of another deathbed sketch of Degas by Mary Cassatt."

"Do you feel that it is as valuable as the other two paintings?"

"No. Although I am not an expert, neither its artistic nor its monetary value places it on a par with the two paintings."

"Then it's curious that the thief took the sketch instead of the Cassatt oil."

Charlie was enjoying the conversation now. The agent seemed to value Charlie's opinion and also exhibited a knowledge of art. Moreover, instead of a phone call, she had taken the time to fly to Chicago from New York. Such effort was impressive. Maybe the FBI knew what it was doing, he thought.

"Maybe the thief lacked expertise," he suggested.

Jackie disagreed. "Anything is possible, but what he took is very valuable. Is anything else noteworthy about the sketch?"

"Like what?"

"A provenance. A connection to another painting. Did Degas ask for it? Did he help in the drawing? Anything?"

"Nothing I can think of. I believe that our family has been the only owner of the sketch. No art expert ever suggested a special history to it. It's just Mary sketching her very ill friend."

"Did anything suspicious happen in the weeks leading up to the theft? Did anyone contact you about the works of art beforehand, to ask you which paintings you were donating, or to ask you anything about the artwork irrespective of their being part of a gift?"

"Nothing unusual. For over a year my mother and I had discussions with Yale personnel about the gift and which artworks were to be selected. Still nothing seemed unusual or unexpected. The Yale people were delighted with our choices. They did seem to like these in particular. However, if we had chosen some others from my mother's collection, I feel they would have been just as delighted. I must say we were surprised that they wanted the sketch. I guess the curator liked it because it is unique. I suppose it is a nice footnote to the history of art."

"I see," said Jackie, taking notes as Charlie spoke. "No one ever expressed any particular interest over the years in any of the artworks?"

"Nothing strikes me at this moment. All three were admired by viewers over the years—including art historians and dealers. But no one ever seriously offered to buy them from us."

Charlie started to grow impatient. While he liked Jackie, he did not want to answer questions only. He had questions of his own.

"Now let me ask you a question," said Charlie. "What does the FBI do with regard to art crimes and are any other entities involved in finding stolen works of art?"

"We are the Art Crime Team out of the Department of Justice. We currently have twelve special agents and three prosecutors. Art theft has become a big business in this country—about $6 billion worth each year worldwide. It's number four behind drugs, money laundering, and arms trafficking. Because these crimes require a specialized knowledge, local police call us in if they think the theft isn't routine. If possible, we gather evidence and testimony at the crime scene working closely with the police and then follow the trail wherever it leads. We maintain the National Stolen Art File—a database of all missing artworks. Some items have been on it for decades. If we think the artworks might have left the country, we contact Interpol, which has its own Stolen Works of Art database. Practically all countries of any size have membership in Interpol. If we have to go abroad, we often use our Legal Attaché Office to open doors. We are very serious about recovering stolen art and bringing the thieves to justice."

"I'm impressed," Charlie offered sincerely. "I had no idea. I am feeling more confident that our pictures will be found. Wait. Should I feel better? Do you recover most stolen works?"

"We recover many, but not as many as we would like, and sometimes it takes years. Often an artwork appears suddenly, and we check it against the file. Then we focus on the case until we find the thief or group of thieves."

"So what is your recovery rate—say fifty percent?"

"Nowhere near that high. But our methods, resources, and experience are improving. Sometimes we use an undercover agent. Our biggest problem is the cult of secrecy in the art world. Museums and dealers are reluctant to report thefts, for fear that donors, artists, and consignees will think them unreliable. On many occasions they try to hide the theft, talk quietly to their insurance company, attempt to recover the work of art through their own sources, or simply pay a ransom to the thieves. After the trail is cold, often we are notified. Some see us as the last hope. Then they expect miracles."

"But in this case you were notified quickly. Should I be encouraged?"

"Yale and its insurance company worked with the local police and wanted us on the scene immediately. Nevertheless, this case may take some time. Because the theft was high profile—Yale, famous artists, and because the death of the young lady who may be related to the theft—there has been lots of publicity. In such circumstances, if insurance money is the goal, the thief usually remains silent until the noise settles down."

"Are most art thefts done for insurance money?"

"Yes, most thefts are for money, not beauty. However, sometimes the thieves have a buyer in mind. Maybe a Dr. No type."

"Who is a 'Dr. No' type?"

"Didn't you ever see the James Bond movie? Dr. No was a secretive, obsessed art collector who paid for and hid artworks he desired. There are many wealthy Dr. No types around the world."

"Do you have a list of them?"

"We have lots of suspected illegal collectors under surveillance—but certainly not all of them."

"You make them sound glamorous."

"I'm sorry. They are glamorous only in the movies. Most thieves are scumbags—drug dealers, conmen, organized crime groups."

"Not so glamorous," Charlie admitted. "Yet there must be big money involved to attract those kinds of low-lifes."

"There is. The value of art can be so high that even though the black-market value may be only ten percent of open market, there is ample incentive to steal."

Charlie learned a lot about the stolen art market in only a few short minutes, but he did not like what he heard. He feared that prospects of recovery were dim.

"Can I ask if you have any clues?"

"We always have clues, but it is still early in our investigation."

"Of course, we'll do anything to help you find the paintings. You see, we aren't interested in an insurance company writing a check to Yale for the loss. My mother gave two paintings and the sketch in memory of my father to allow the public to view and enjoy these are works of art. She is very upset they are lost."

"I understand," Jackie said sounding sincere. "First, you and your family should tell us anything that might lead us to the thieves. Next, if Yale or the insurance company does not offer a reward for the return of the works of art, perhaps you could. Rewards can be effective."

Charlie thought that was an interesting idea. Maybe part of the reason Jackie came to visit was to plant that seed. It would be reprehensive to pay a thief to purchase our own gift, he thought, but the main objective is to get the pictures back. We certainly have enough money.

"Good idea. I'll ask Yale what they intend to do. Alternatively, I would be happy to offer a sizeable reward. You just tell me how much is appropriate."

"If it comes to that, I'll let you know. Now I would like to visit your mother today or tomorrow. Do you know if she is at home?"

"She is, but she is quite depressed by this whole affair—not only the theft but—the murder of her grandniece. Let me call her to prepare her. Give me an hour, then call her. I assume I'll be hearing of any developments from you, and I'll call you if I think of anything."

Jackie stood up, shook Charlie's hand, and left quickly—as if she were late for another appointment. Charlie sat back at his desk and reflected on the visit. He thought that Jackie was knowledgeable, matter-of-fact but not brusque, and committed to recovering the artworks. He was encouraged.

When he called, Charlie's mother surprised him by saying she was eager to meet Agent Farrell. She seemed to want to be involved.

"I've had my down days. I'm still angry, but your father would want me to be a Bailey—look forward, not back. Let's find the paintings. The FBI can help.'

'Oh. One thing. I called Ellie about Cynthia. She was so upset. I'll keep in touch with her during this awful time."

* * *

At five o'clock Charlie was sitting in an oversized leather chair in the center of the spacious, open-form men's locker room of the Racquet Club. He was waiting for his squash playing partner, Dan Donato—"Dashing Dan" as he called him—to show up. He had not cancelled the match because he wanted to take his mind off the events surrounding the art theft. He had already decided to use the next morning to visit his old friend, Seth Price, a professor in the Northwestern University Department of Art History. After Jackie Farrell's lesson in the realities of art theft, he thought that Seth's insights—from an academic's prospective—might add depth to his understanding. Charlie was determined not to sit back and wait for developments. He was going to be proactive.

"Hey, Bails. Ready to lose?" Dan asked entering the room from behind Charlie.

"Dashing Dan," Charlie replied to his stocky, middle-aged friend. "You're ever hopeful, seldom gratified. You're the Chicago Cubs of the squash world."

"Watch yourself. Just because you are taller than me doesn't give you an edge. Besides this is the year for both the Cubs and me. Ye of little faith."

"Faith, it is. Fact, it's not. So how's the investment banking world at J.P. Morgan?"

"Super. Good markets make for lots of deals. I'm really busy."

"I wish I could be as sanguine as you. The Fed is tightening."

"You worry too much."

Dan sat down on the bench of an empty cubicle and started to change into his white squash clothes. Charlie was always in a good mood around Dan. They had been friends and regular squash partners for fifteen years since college. Banter and trash talk between them were normal. They knew each other too well to offend the other.

"Nice deal you have," Dan said. "Five blocks from here to your apartment. Are you doing take-out tonight or is Kate joining you after your defeat?"

"Take-out. It keeps the wife happy."

"I heard by way of a lawyer-friend of mine in New Haven that your mother's art donation was stolen. I am sorry about that."

"Yes, most unfortunate. Word seems to get around," Charlie said, annoyed that Dan had heard already. "We're really furious with Yale. The police are on the case, but it's early yet. I'd appreciate it if you wouldn't talk to others about this episode. I'd rather not have lots of folks asking me about it. We're feeling sensitive and trying to handle everything discreetly."

"I understand. Let's play squash. You know though that if I win I'm going to blab about my victory to our friends, classmates, and anyone within hearing distance."

"I'm shaking in my boots."

Chapter Eight

"Welcome to academic clutter," Seth Price remarked without apologies. "My office is not very glamorous, but believe it or not, I know where everything I need is in this mess."

Charlie had called his friend early in the morning and begged to see him as soon as possible. Seth was a tenured professor of art history and had published several books and monographs in his field, Italian Renaissance paintings and sculptures. Charlie had read two of Seth's impressive offerings a few years ago. They had not seen each other in a month or two and Seth said that he welcomed Charlie's call and the opportunity to catch up. Luckily, he had no lectures or departmental meetings in the morning. They settled on ten o'clock, which gave Charlie more than enough time to drive up to Evanston. In fact, he was happy to be able to drive the slower but more picturesque route up: Lake Shore Drive through the park to Sheridan Road.

Seth's office was on the second floor of a stand-alone Victorian house on a residential street on the edge of the Northwestern University campus. The door of the house was open and Charlie found Seth at his desk wearing a tweed sports coat, button-down shirt, khaki pants, and tortoise-shell glasses. Very preppy as usual, Charlie thought.

The room was cluttered with books and papers on the desk, a side table, and bookshelves. Seth sat in one of the two chairs in the room to the right of a computer screen.

"A lot of people work better amidst clutter," Charlie said sitting down. "My office is only marginally cleaner. And I have to talk to clients in it. At least you have a window where you can see trees and people walking on the sidewalk. All I can see is other office buildings. Anyways, it's nice to finally see where you hang out during the day."

"I'll swap you for your view of the lake but I suppose that is a non-starter since I usually see you at some benefit in black tie. Your world really differs from mine."

Charlie proceeded to catch Seth up on the theft, Cynthia's murder, and the efforts of the police and the FBI. "Based on your experience with stolen artworks, what should we expect to happen?"

"Can I offer you some coffee or tea? It's not Starbucks, but it keeps me awake."

"No, thanks. I know you're busy, so let me get right to the point of my visit."

Seth defected Charlie's urgent plea, "You can understand that I'm more comfortable working here in khakis. You on the other hand look rather distinguished in your tailored suit."

Then Seth got to the topic, "You know, I did hear about the theft two days ago. Bad news travels fast. Usually universities try to hush a story like this, out of embarrassment, but apparently it received widespread press coverage in the East. What I did not know is that it involved artworks that had belonged to your family and the death of a relative. I would have called you to offer my help, whatever I can do."

"Thanks, Seth. The two stolen works of art have been at my mother's house for decades. You might remember them from a visit. The donation obviously triggered the theft. The campus police believe that it was an inside job. The FBI was not encouraging that we'll see the paintings again. What do you think?"

Seth sat back and stroked his close-cut beard. He shook his head and said, "What a story! Theft of extremely valuable works of art and a murder! My short answer to your question is recovery is not very likely. These pictures by celebrated artists are undoubtedly too high profile to appear for sale at a dealer or an auction house. More likely they will end up with a secret collector or be offered back to the Yale gallery. The art world is very secretive. The biggest art theft I know of was from the Isabella Stewart Gardner Museum in Boston in 1990. The theft received a huge amount of publicity.

Five hundred million dollars of masterpieces—Rembrandt, Vermeers, other paintings—were there. I am not aware that everything was recovered. Rumor has it that organized crime pulled it off with insider information. In any case, sadly, even when stolen paintings are found, often they are damaged—sometimes beyond repair. I hope none of this occurs here, but the facts remain. Has a reward been offered?"

"Not that I know of. But I am ready to offer one if Yale or the insurance company do not."

"That's generous of you. One of the most unfortunate aspects of art theft is that the public thinks that it is a harmless fleecing of the rich. It's hard to get people sympathetic over rich people losing something. That movie *The Thomas Crown Affair* did enormous harm. People think art theft is glamorous with no real victims. Art thieves are more brutish than suave, and the victims—rich or not—feel violated. If I may sound like a professor for a second, art theft is a harm to society. Art viewers, art historians, scholars—they are all victims."

"I agree completely. Besides a reward, I would like to help in the recovery process, but I am out of my element. Is there anything I can do?"

"Not much," Seth said. "The FBI has specialized investigators. I assume they have called on you for information. This is their kind of case. I would like to see more of a collaboration between art scholars and law-enforcement officers. We academics could help in collating documents, interpreting data, providing perspective, and perhaps even taking part in interviews. I know several cases where I could have been an immense help, but the FBI didn't accept my offer to assist them. Still the FBI does one thing well; they maintain a database of stolen art, which they share with international law enforcement officials, Interpol, Scotland Yard, the Spanish Policia, the Italian Carabinieri, and so forth. There is also a private company in London, the Art Registry, which you should know about. It maintains a database on the Internet, to which the company sells access. Their clients are principally auction houses, dealers, and insurance companies. I am told that they also act as go-between in sales back to the owners."

"Hold on one minute, Seth," Charlie interrupted and reached in his coat pocket for a pad and pen. "Let me write down the name of that company."

Charlie thought that this company might be a good source of information—especially because the FBI's database was probably off-limits to him. In addition, if it functioned as a go-between, maybe the thief would contact it.

"Are you sure about the Art Loss Registry acting as a conduit?"

"I have no direct knowledge, but several people I know have suggested a role like that. Again, the art world is secretive. Many, many owners are willing to pay ransom. A discreet go-between can be very useful. If it plays that role, I am sure the London company receives a commission for its work. Now that I think about it, someone told me that the Art Loss Registry lists about 175,000 stolen works of art in its database. That would include paintings, sculpture, antique furniture, antique silver, antiquities, jewelry, and probably other valuables. I would not be surprised if they had offices in New York or Hong Kong. You should ask the FBI if they use this database to supplement their own."

"I need to make sure that our pictures are on both lists. I'll talk to Yale about it. But bottom line, how low is the probability of seeing our gift back at Yale?"

Seth paused, searching for the right words. "Charlie, as I said, don't get your hopes up. Your best chance is if there is a breakthrough quickly. As time goes on, the trail will get cold. But please use me as a resource. I may be able to help explain something that comes up. I hope the FBI succeeds. These thefts hurt the art world immensely, and I would like to see a happy outcome for you and your family personally."

"Thanks. I am sorry to have bothered you with our problems, Seth. You have been enormously helpful. Next time, we'll chat about less serious things."

As Charlie walked to his car, he felt he had learned a lot from Seth, but he was also discouraged. Despite the databases and the global investigatory groups, Seth had made it sound as if the only ways to recover an art theft were through a ransom negotiation or because of a blunder by the thieves. One would almost have to be lucky to regain stolen artworks.

Charlie reflected that they had a lot in common. They were classmates at St. Mary's Elementary School in Lake Forest and at Yale College. They played Little League baseball together and rowed in the same boat on the

Yale Freshman Crew before Charlie switched to football. Charlie and Seth had lost touch for several years after college but met again at a wedding in Winnetka. They rediscovered that they both shared a keen interest in art: Seth as a professional art historian and Charlie as a collector—of twentieth century American art. Following up on this interest during the past few years, they arranged several times to have dinner together before going to a gallery opening or a museum show.

Charlie drove slowly up Sheridan Road through the wealthy towns known as Chicago's North Shore. He had decided to skip work and visit his mother instead.

He called ahead on his cell phone. The large homes with manicured landscaping lining the road were familiar to him, but his mood was too gloomy to admire them. He disliked the helplessness he felt. He was accustomed to achieving successful outcomes in his life and business through intelligence and effort. Almost everything was possible through hard work and application. The current situation felt foreign. Money, which solves many issues, might not even be relevant in this case. The thieves might have a buyer in mind who would not even consider returning or reselling the pictures. In that case, he could do nothing. Unless the police and FBI were successful, he might have to resign himself, however reluctantly, to a permanent loss.

The overcast weather matched his mood. Not even an upbeat song on the radio improved his outlook. Soon he was driving through Lake Forest, the peaceful, beautiful town where he grew up. The leafy streets meandered like country lanes past stately houses set back behind gates and walls or thick branching trees and shrubs. He drove past the Potawatomi Club, where he often played golf. He passed the park where his father had taught him how to catch a baseball and ride a bike. He passed a handful of estates where he had played with friends and classmates. Then he was home before the open gate and long driveway to the house where his mother lived. He drove in and parked in his favorite spot in the large, front courtyard under an old oak tree where shade would keep his car less steamy when he returned after lunch.

James must have heard his car on the driveway and opened the front door when Charlie stepped up to it.

"Charlie, your mother is out on the terrace reading a book. She said you called; so she had us set up a table for lunch on the side veranda. That way you can enjoy the fresh air without enduring the direct sun. We don't expect any bees at this time of year."

"Fine, James. You know me; I'd be happy at the kitchen table. It's Mother who is so formal."

Charlie made his way through the hall and large drawing room and through the French doors to the terrace where his mother sat.

"Hello, Mother. What a glorious day it has become suddenly. It was so gloomy only a half hour ago." Charlie kissed his mother's cheek and made a concerted effort to be cheerful.

Claire turned and looked up. "Hello darling." She pointed to the left. "Please sit over there where I can see you. The sun is in my eyes."

"You look well."

"I am. Did you play golf today? The weatherman says rain tomorrow. Today would have been a better day."

"Yes, I've heard about the rain. No, this morning I dropped in to see Seth Price at Northwestern."

"I remember the Prices. They moved away, I think. Seth was that polite little boy. Art history, right? Too bad. My recent exposure to art historians has been poor, hasn't it? Well, Seth had nothing to do with what happened."

James approached to announce lunch. When they sat down at the table, soup and iced tea were already in place. Charlie was happy his mother was in better spirits.

"I hope you like the centerpiece. I picked the flowers myself this morning. Of course, James arranged them. He always does such a nice job. I ordered a toasted ham and cheese sandwich for you with a pickle. Your favorite."

"Thank you, Mother. Now tell me about your visit from the FBI."

"Nice lady. Not at all what I expected. You know you watch those awful television shows about the FBI and you expect some overweight, bald, tired=-looking fellow in a rumpled suit with an awful accent. This young woman was well groomed and solicitous—although she did have that accent. She asked a lot of questions and seemed to want to help. I hope she can."

"What did she ask about?"

"She asked about the history of the paintings. When did we buy the paintings? From whom? Where did we keep them? Who had seen them here? Did we ever lend them for exhibitions? That sort of thing. She also wanted to know why after all these years we decided to give them to Yale."

"Was she surprised or especially interested in any of your answers?"

"Interested but not surprised. She took notes the whole time. She seemed most curious about who might have been familiar with the paintings before Yale had them. She may have been disappointed that I could think of no one in particular. I know that over the years that people we have had by to see our paintings and antiques have said nice things about them, but no one stands out. Of course, I have been very wary of the museum people, who always seem to be hoping for a donation."

"It sounds as if Agent Farrell was thorough. I am happy she did not upset you."

"Not at all. You know, the loss has left me out of sorts. At times I feel crushed. But the idea that this young woman might work hard to find them is comforting."

"Did she ask anything else?"

"Oh, yes. She wanted photographs of the paintings. I know where we have some. I want you to send them to her."

"Photographs?"

"Years ago, your father had photographs taken for insurance purposes. Standard procedure. We kept them in a folder in a safe in my bedroom. You know, in my closet. We have photographs of all the artwork and furniture in the house—in case of a theft or damage."

"Very smart. I'll go up after lunch and take the photographs with me. I'll have Kathy copy them, package them up, and send them to the FBI. Do you know the combination?"

"Of course I know the combination. I'm not senile yet. I keep my everyday jewelry in the safe. The 'heavy artillery', as your dad called it, is kept in the safe deposit box at the bank. I can't remember the last time I wore any of those pieces."

"We'll have to make a special event for you so you can."

"Maybe a celebration when you have your first baby," she said with a twinkle in her eye. "I want to be a grandmother. Who's holding back, you or Kate?"

"She's not ready yet. She has her job, which she adores. It's difficult to raise a child and be nine-to-five."

"Don't make excuses for her. I hope you know, I love Katie. You made a good choice. I enjoy our little chats—like last Monday morning up here. Perhaps, though, you both need to get your priorities straight. She married into wealth. In my circles there are options for young women besides having a career. My friends' daughters and daughters-in-laws don't work for money. They do charitable work—volunteer, plan benefits, oversee foundations. They have time for babies and their husbands."

Charlie sat up in his chair. He was uncomfortable with this kind of talk. It was out-of-date, out-of-touch. Today was not the first time she had expressed her opinion on Kate's duties.

"Mother, be serious. Our culture has changed. Women today are admired for their success in business. They have careers. The standard is not your friends' daughters—half of them can't write a sentence, work on a computer, or implement a strategic plan. Kate would do her job for free if they would let her."

"Then we have lost something in the social order. Everyone has a place—and duties. I still believe that. Someone has to create and support our culture and charitable institutions—which do so much good for society. I hope you and Kate will think about that soon."

"Of course."

"When we are finished, I need to call Ellie Newgate again. Cynthia's death bothers me so. The FBI is sure to visit her and Hal. They will be asking all those personal questions like Agent Farrell did with me. Recalling the past happy times could be a terrible experience for them. I should warn her what to expect. Being prepared might make the ordeal easier."

"I agree. We need to keep in mind how awful these events must be for them."

Chapter Nine

From the kitchen, Kate heard the door of the apartment open and knew that Charlie was home finally. Dickens knew the sound as well, as he waddled off to greet his master.

"Where have you been all day?" Kate shouted in Charlie's general direction. "I called you twice this afternoon at the office. I even left a message on your cell."

Charlie entered the kitchen carrying a large manila envelope, which he placed on the island countertop. He went over to his wife who was facing the sink and wrapped his arms around her waist and kissed her neck. Kate felt her irritation start to dissolve. "I'm sorry. I changed my plans after I visited Seth. I went up to see Mom and then spent the afternoon there working in contact with my office—talking to portfolio managers and telephoning clients. I know you called, but I was very busy and your message didn't sound urgent. Then the traffic was terrible driving back into the city. Please forgive me."

"Okay, you're forgiven this one time," she teased him. "I do worry when I can't reach you."

"I have something I want you to see. Mother gave me these photographs of the paintings she donated," Charlie said as he opened the envelope he had brought. "She said that Agent Farrell had asked for them. I'll have copies made and FedEx them tomorrow."

Kate sat down at the kitchen table and examined each photograph closely—front and back of each painting. Meanwhile she caught a glimpse of Charlie peeking in the oven, checking on dinner.

He turned and added, "I thought that Jackie Farrell would have had photographs from Yale, but I guess she was being thorough. As you can see, Dad had three or four shots taken from different angles and even included one of the back of each painting. They make a good record."

"I see, Charlie, that there are both black and white and color pictures. Some of the black and white ones may be quite old, since your parents had the paintings for so many years. There are no dates. The color ones may be updates. The picture is the same. Did you notice that the photograph of the back of the sketch shows some writing? The missing sketch has a label identifying the picture, the artist, and the date, but the sketch also has some French words written on the backside. They are hard to make out, faded. I wonder what it means?"

"I missed that. I was planning to send only the frontal views. I did not pay any attention to the shots of the back."

"Come over here and look."

Charlie walked over behind Kate and looked down at the photograph. She pointed to the left side. Starting at the top there seemed to be a list in two sections. The first section consisted of one item, and the second part listed eight. The writing was hard to make out because the photograph was old and in black and white. Moreover, the writing may have faded on its own by the time the photograph was taken.

JF
Petite Danseuse de Quatorze Ans - sculpture (cire)

ZC
Danseuse à la Barre - pastel
Les Blanchisseuses (Le Repassage) - pastel
La Toilette (Le Bain) - pastel
Portrait à l'Artiste - fusain
La Chanteuse - pastel
Le Petit Déjeuner Après le Bain - pastel
Au Louvre - pastel
Nature Morte aux Fruits - peinture à l'huile (Cézanne)

"You are better at French than I am," Charlie conceded. "But I think I can make out a few words: *Blanchisseuses*—I can't make out the ending, *Bain, Petit Déjeuner, Fruits*, and *Quatorze*. *Laundry, bath, breakfast, fruits,* and *fourteen*. It sounds like a list of chores or activities and perhaps a shopping list –or something else."

"Your eyes are better than mine," Kate said. "Maybe after Mary Cassatt finished her sketch, she made a list of things to do. Who knows? I wonder what these letters before each section means: It looks like *JF* and *ZC*. Could they be stores or people? But wait. See the words *sculpture*, (cire), and *pastel*. So this must be a list of works of art. *Sculpture* is obvious; *cire* is wax; and *pastel* is just that. I don't know if the handwriting is Mary Cassatt's, but if it is, she wrote down a list of paintings and a sculpture on the back. Maybe they are paintings by Degas—or maybe just a list of her own or of paintings by others. I see 'Cézanne' next to one of them."

"Oh, of course," Kate said in recognition. "The first one, everyone knows that one: the famous sculpture of the young ballet dancer. Foot turned out. I took a year or two of ballet lessons when I was a little girl. The dancer is in one of the basic positions. I wish I had stayed with ballet but soccer and basketball became more interesting."

"I learn something new about you every day. But you're right about this page. It looks like a project for someone—decipher the list. It may be nothing more than a reminder of a collection of paintings, or maybe it has some other significance. At any rate, I'll try to get a clearer image tomorrow and blow it up. Then I'll send all the photos to Jackie Farrell."

"Maybe Dickens can solve the riddle." Kate laughed as their dog made his way into the kitchen toward his bowl.

"If he doesn't drool on the pictures," Charlie countered good-naturedly.

"While I put the food on, tell me about your day. Is your mother feeling better? Did Seth say anything?"

"Mother is almost back to her old feisty self at times. Still I could see this affair depresses her. She needs time. My visit to Seth was useful, but the bottom line is that the prospects of a near term recovery of the paintings are poor. We'll need luck and patience."

"Bad news. Here's dinner—almost as good as take-out."

"You do yourself an injustice. You're a great cook. Which reminds me—Mother repeated that she was very appreciative of your visit last Monday. You helped her get her bearings."

"That's nice to hear. Anything else?"

Kate immediately regretted such an open-ended question where the topic was Charlie's mother. In many ways she liked her mother-in-law—a smart, generous, helpful woman. At times though, Claire had strong opinions, some of which annoyed Kate to the core. For the sake of a tranquil dinner, she hoped that Charlie would ignore the question.

"I'm afraid she did lecture me on two sore points: children and your job."

"Not again."

"Yes, again. It's natural for a woman of her age to want grandchildren. She wants to enjoy them before she is too old. Selfish, perhaps, but normal. She probably thinks that at forty-one I am getting too old to start a family. Funny, I don't hear a biological clock ticking in me. The other thing—your job—is a cultural phenomenon. The generation of her social class doesn't believe women should work if they can afford not to. She won't listen to the other side of the argument. Her belief is ingrained."

Kate had heard these sentiments many times. Kate's mother had warned her before she married Charlie that very wealthy people were different. Their class had rules, not-to-be-questioned standards of conduct. The older women of Claire's social group strongly pressed these standards on the younger women. According to the code, ladies should work only in public service—volunteers to charitable, cultural, not-for-profit, educational, and civic organizations–and participants in philanthropic endeavors. They should not run for an elective post or accept money for their efforts. While Kate acknowledged that such work promoted the good result of a better society, so did the work of enlightened employees, dedicated jurists, doctors, religious leaders, and sensitive politicians. Claire's attitude seemed medieval to her, and she was angry she had to justify herself.

"*Noblesse oblige*," Kate said. "Your mother should get with the times. I'm not quitting my job."

"I didn't ask you to. If you ever want to, though, that would be all right with me. I am fully supportive of you."

Fine, Kate thought, but Charlie never puts up much of an argument on this issue with his mother. I love him, she thought, but he tries to avoid conflict in family discussions. He defers to her. She admitted that she was not assertive either, but she was the new member in the family. Besides, Claire intimidated her. She wanted Charlie to win this argument for her—or at least try harder.

"As for her other complaint, someday we'll have a big family," Kate declared. "Wait and see, Charlie. In the meantime we have our very own Dickens. Don't we?"

Chapter Ten

On his way to work the next morning, Charlie decided to call Marty O'Connell again once he got in. He had brought up the *New Haven Register* website on his computer each day to see if anything new appeared on the theft or murder. The story seemed to be shifting farther back into the paper—possibly because the police were not releasing any new substantive facts. A talkative Marty seemed to Charlie like the best source for an update.

"Marty, anything new on the theft?"

"Yes, I would say so. No surprise, but we have evidence that Miss Newgate stole the pictures."

"Do you know where they are?"

"We still don't have them. Dead people don't talk."

"What evidence?"

"Things we found in her studio apartment on Park Street."

Charlie leaned forward in his chair and grabbed a clean sheet of paper to take notes. He had been incredulous that she was culpable—despite the high probability that Cynthia's death connected her with the theft. Now, however, he would have to accept what he feared.

"Okay. Specifically what things?"

"When you were at the reception last Saturday, did you notice anything different about the three pictures compared to when they hung in your mother's house?"

Charlie paused and thought back a few seconds.

"One thing. The two paintings looked the same, but the sketch had a new frame—modern looking. My father would have been appalled. I never said anything because the art gallery could do what they wanted."

"Very observant. The paintings were kept in their original frames, but the sketch was reframed. In her apartment we found pieces of the new metal frame and also new staples and fragments of old velum that were attached to the wood part of the frame. The sketch must have been torn away from the frame without taking care to remove the staples. I suspect whoever killed the girl rolled up the sketch and concealed it in a cylinder or his coat pocket. On the other hand, with regard to the Hassam painting, we have found no traces of the original frame. I assume the painting was still in it when the murderer took it from the apartment."

"You're assuming that the Hassam painting had been there."

"Correct. That's a good assumption. But what's important is that the stolen sketch was definitely there."

"Is there any chance that Cynthia might have been coerced?"

"Not in my mind. We also found two dirty wine glasses near the efficiency kitchen sink. One was wiped clean of fingerprints and the other had several from the deceased. In her glass we tested positive for red wine and arsenic. We'll test both of them for DNA. The thieves probably toasted their success in stealing the pictures. The poisoner left with them, and Ms. Newgate went to the library—probably to give the impression that she was just maintaining her normal routine. While there, the arsenic progressed through her system and eventually killed her. She probably did not suspect anything other than a stomach ache until it was too late to do anything."

Marty's story sounded plausible enough to Charlie. Of course, he had no idea why Cynthia would have committed the theft. She must have had a good reason. She also must have trusted someone to work with her without understanding the danger.

"Why didn't Cynthia's murderer wash both glasses?"

"He washed his but Cynthia may have not finished hers before he left. Fortunately she didn't wash her glass before she left for the library."

"Was there anything in the apartment that gives a clue to the other person or persons?"

"No. Whoever killed her knew what he was doing. He was thorough."

"Is anyone helping you on the investigation?"

"A woman from the art-theft unit of the FBI was here this week. She went through the apartment and yesterday interviewed every member of the staff at the art gallery—administration, curators, researchers, and guards. Careful and professional. I can work with her."

"Was that Agent Farrell?"

"Yes, she said she had been to see you and your mother. I guess she did."

"Was there anything in Cynthia's personal life that would lead you to suspect someone?"

"Miss Newgate was a reserved type. She had few close friends. She had dated a graduate student for a year or so, but they broke up last winter. His name is Larry Kendall. Most of her friends worked at the art gallery. Last summer she interned in New York City at a dealer's gallery. That would have broadened her circle of acquaintances, but we have found no red flags so far. Since she was a cousin of yours, maybe you know of someone who might have been close to her?"

"I never even knew she existed until a few months ago. I'm no help. Have the New Haven Police been of much assistance?"

"That's a sore point. The powers that be still are treating this situation as if there are two separate cases. I am working on the theft, and one of our lieutenants and the New Haven PD are working on the murder. The separation is ridiculous. Find the thief, and you will find the killer. I know some things they are doing—but not all. I keep telling the chief we need to combine the investigations. No luck so far."

"They'll have to combine efforts at some point."

Charlie hung up shaking his head in disbelief. Typical bureaucracy and turf battles. If they can't get their act together, they'll never be successful. That bothers me. Maybe I can be helpful in bringing those efforts together. I'll need to delegate my duties around here. Then I could devote more time to this mess. The police might benefit from fresh thinking. Besides it's obvious that the Bailey family is right in the middle of both the theft and the murder.

The more he thought about his direct participation in the investigations, the more enthusiastic he became.

* * *

"You want to do what?" Kate snapped frowning. "Amateur detective in a murder case! Over my dead body—no pun intended. Last year, that Bradshaw murder nearly killed us both. You promised me then that you would never get involved in another police investigation. Moreover, remember how upset the police were with you. They were clear: murderers kill people—especially nosey people."

"That was different. The police initially treated me as a suspect. I had to clear my name and ensure that the reputation of our firm wasn't undermined by innuendo. Remember, my efforts to exonerate myself somehow became a threat to the killer, and then we were targeted. If I had been able to work more effectively with the police, there would have been no danger to either of us and the case would have been resolved much sooner. In retrospect I learned a lot from that experience. It could be useful now."

"No, no, no, no!"

"The paintings and the thief are probably long gone," Charlie kept arguing. "This time there would be no danger. I would like to think in the end that we tried to do everything we could in this case. After all, Cynthia is dead and despite a brave front Mother is heartbroken. Spunky one minute but depressed the next. You know that maybe we can clear Cynthia's name. Anyway, I wouldn't do anything foolish without talking to you first."

Kate stared at him angrily walked toward the kitchen, and turned back saying, "Charlie, some times you are bone-headed and reckless. Get your own dinner."

Charlie knew he had not won her over and that she would talk to his mother. Then there would be two strong and opinionated women against him. Nevertheless, he was convinced that he could add value. In the end, he rationalized, the capture of poor Cynthia's murderer and the recovery of the art would justify everything he did. The girls would come around.

* * *

"Mother, I am going to fly out to see Ellie and Hal Newgate tomorrow morning. Would you like to join me?"

Charlie made this call not only to offer his mother the opportunity to travel with him to Cleveland to meet with and console her niece, but to learn if Kate had already called his mother to organize a campaign against his involvement. From her response Charlie believed that his mom was still ignorant of his new plan.

"Such a good idea that you're going. I don't think I'll join you. After talking to Ellie briefly when we heard about Cynthia I wrote her a long letter expressing my sorrow. Then I called again to offer any help. If I were in her shoes, I wouldn't want to be entertaining some relatives at this time—especially a relative who had had a falling out with her mother. Then I also feel awkward because of the stolen paintings. If just you go, we'll be expressing our sympathy, but not burdening her. There will be another time later on to visit."

At this point, he held off telling her of the evidence of Cynthia's involvement in the theft. Let her think only positive thoughts of Cynthia at least until she was laid to rest.

The flight to Cleveland's Burke Lakefront Airport took less than an hour. Although Charlie was licensed to fly, he employed two pilots to be available on short notice. He kept his plane at Palwaukee in Wheeling, about twenty miles from downtown Chicago. That location was more convenient than the bigger and busier O'Hare and Midway airports. Although he occasionally flew commercially, a short trip to Cleveland on his own timetable made sense to him. He arranged for a limousine to meet him and bring him to the Newgates' house in Shaker Heights.

Charlie had telephoned Ellie Newgate the day before to ask if he could see her. She recognized his name immediately and agreed to meet her cousin without hesitation. She regretted her husband would not be there because he was in New Haven making arrangements to bring Cynthia's body back home.

Charlie had never been to Shaker Heights, but he had heard of it favorably from time to time. This long-established suburb eight miles east of downtown Cleveland, founded by bankers, shipping executives, and steel men, boasted excellent schools, safe and quiet neighborhoods, and a professional, cultured citizenry. Charlie confirmed this reputation as his limo drove by the charming, big Tudor-inspired homes set back from the tree-lined streets and sidewalks. The town reminded him of Winnetka and Glencoe on Chicago's North Shore.

The Newgates' house was more modest than its neighbors, but its concrete driveway and traditional landscaping blended in appropriately in the area. He arrived at the time he had promised. What was surprising to Charlie were two white vans parked across the street with local TV station markings. Five people gathered around the vehicles talking and drinking coffee. The media people are the lowest form of humanity he thought. Can't they leave the grieving parents alone?

Charlie walked up the flagstone path and rang the doorbell. Ellie Newgate appeared in a subdued navy dress almost immediately, as if she had seen Charlie walking up to the house, and invited him in. She extended her hand to shake Charlie's but he embraced her instead and said how sorry he and Kate and his mother were for her loss.

"I saw Cynthia only twice but she impressed me with her intelligence and good manners. She had a wonderful future ahead of her. I wish we could bring her back."

Ellie began to cry quietly still hugging Charlie. After a few moments, she broke away and led him into the large living room. He sat on a comfortable couch facing a coffee table and two upholstered chairs. A black Steinway piano was positioned in a corner in front of windows looking out at a well-landscaped backyard. On the piano were several photographs in wooden frames, one of Cynthia presumably at her college graduation, one of Cynthia with her parents in front of a huge, columned stone museum, and one of many people in a family reunion pose. Charlie wondered if his aunt appeared in that photograph.

"Excuse my tears. It's a difficult time. Can I get you anything?"

"No, thank you. I'm quite all right. Take your time. I'll wait until you feel okay."

"Excuse my emotions. Cynthia was everything to us." She stopped trying to compose herself. "This situation has been very frustrating. The New Haven police won't release Cynthia's body. They are doing tests. But we need to plan her funeral. We can't make a date for visitation or the service. The funeral home has called twice already. I feel guilty that I didn't fly out there, but Hal said it would only take a day and he would take care of it. My friends want to know when they could come. I know I'm silly to worry about this schedule. But I need to focus on something. I feel lost and don't know which way to turn. Now Hal is gone and I'm alone and confused. Thanks for coming."

Charlie stood up and walked over to where Ellie was sitting. He knelt and held her hand while she sobbed. He handed her his handkerchief. He waited until she was ready to continue.

"The delay is terrible," Charlie said. "It's been a week. The medical examiner should have finished by now. I wish I knew how to expedite things. Surely Hal's presence will move things along. But don't worry about the timing of the service. Your friends and the people who matter will understand. They will pay their respects when you say so."

"I suppose so," she said sniffling. "Do you mind if I change the subject? I'm such a bad host. How's your mother? She has been nice to call—twice now. And she wrote a wonderful letter. I appreciate her sympathy."

Charlie answered her questions about his family and he asked about her side of the family in return. Eventually the conversation came back to Cynthia.

"She told us about the magnificent gift your mother was making to Yale. She said the paintings were very valuable and important in the history of art. She was very enthusiastic. She was also excited to meet you and your mother. What a coincidence."

"Was she happy at Yale?"

"Oh, yes. She was happiest when she was immersed in her studies. Yale has fantastic teachers and resources at hand. She was committed to earning a doctorate eventually. She wanted to teach or work for a museum or auction house—like Sotheby's or Christie's. I remember taking her to the museum over at University Circle, not far from here. I think that is where she first started developing an interest in art and art history."

"I have not spent much time in Cleveland, Ellie. But I remember a concert with the Cleveland Orchestra at Severance Hall. It was marvelous. Isn't that part of University Circle?"

"Yes, of course. Also the hospitals, Case Western Reserve, the botanical gardens, and the various museums. Clevelanders are very proud of the area."

"As well you should be. Did Cynthia have time to enjoy herself outside her studies? Did she have a boyfriend or suitor?"

"Not recently. She said her last boyfriend was too moody and had a temper. Cynthia never dated much before—she was so devoted to her studies. In college, at Columbia, she did see quite a bit of New York City, mainly with her group of girlfriends."

Charlie wondered how this studious, socially cautious girl could have become mixed up with major theft. She did not have a risk-taking profile. Her mother's description only confirmed what he had heard from Adrian Greene and Marty O'Connell. He wondered if she had changed her personally recently.

"Someone told me that Cynthia spent last summer in New York with a dealer. Was that useful in helping her decide what she wanted to do eventually?"

Since Ellie seemed to be more in control of her emotional state, Charlie let go her hand and returned to the couch across from her.

"She told us that she learned a lot. She was an intern at the Ludyard Gallery. The firm is a prestigious dealer in Impressionist works of art—mainly French and American. That was her specialty. She did research and cataloguing and sat in on some purchases and sales. Hal didn't think she liked the people. She seemed withdrawn and noncommittal about parts of the experience. I thought there was something she didn't want to tell us. She didn't always confide in us on personal matters. Maybe her mood had something to do with her relationship with Larry Kendall and nothing to do with the gallery in New York"

Charlie listened closely to this recent history. He thought immediately that he needed to visit the New York gallery and talk to Larry Kendall in New Haven. Something or somebody had to have convinced this quiet, scholarly, young woman to participate in an illegal and immoral act. From what he had been learning, so out of character. This transformation must have been recent.

Looking at Ellie, Charlie saw an aging, spent woman. She slumped in the chair and her eyes had prominent bags under them. He wanted to ask many questions but understood he needed to go carefully lest she go over an emotional edge. He stated in a gently voice, "You said that recently she was excited with our gift to Yale. She seemed to be working close with the director and Susan Parker to put together their initial exhibition."

"They gave her a lot of freedom to set things up. She said she knew your paintings intimately and helped to produce a brochure describing the gift."

"It pains my mother that our donation could have had anything to do with what happened to Cynthia. Nevertheless, the sequence of events seems to be more than coincidental."

Charlie saw Ellie's body stiffen from his suggestion. He wondered if she had thought about the connection and felt that Cynthia would still be alive if the gift had not been made.

"I try not to think that my little girl was murdered. It might be less painful if she died of natural causes. But she didn't. She was killed. She must have known who stole Aunt Claire's paintings. Of course, it's not your fault. But somehow these particular paintings attracted a thief. I'm sorry I didn't ask, but is your mother very upset with the theft?"

"Certainly. They were a part of her life for decades. She donated them in honor of my father. Nevertheless, our loss pales in comparison with yours."

Ellie began to cry again. She still had Charlie's handkerchief and used it to dab her eyes.

"I'm sorry. Hal said she was poisoned. Who could do such a thing? I can't stand to think of her pain."

"The police need to catch the murderer. Since he probably is also the thief, the path to him should be through the paintings. The FBI contacted us to say they are on the case and have specialists on art thefts. They may contact you as part of their investigation."

"Someone talked to Hal in New Haven. She said she would visit here as well. Do you know that according to Hal there are newspaper writers who think Cynthia was part of the team who stole the paintings? That idea really saddens me. My only child is dead, murdered, and some ignorant bastard is saying that she was a thief. If she was, why was she killed? That makes no sense. I am so angry. What's more, those leeches outside are shouting questions at Hal and me, hounding our neighbors, and staying there day and night. The police won't move them. I'm drained of energy and good manners."

Charlie was sympathetic to Ellie's suffering. He was not about to tell her there was hard evidence linking Cynthia to the crime. Let the police deal with that issue. However, her comments allowed him a chance to ask her a few more questions. "I wish I could help with the media, but I have thought about what I could do to help the police and FBI identify the murderer. Cynthia may have known him—in a different context. Do you know someone who had a grudge against her?"

"No," Ellie murmured. "She was a sweet girl who never said a nasty thing about anyone. Of course, Larry may have been upset about the break-up. But you don't love someone one day and kill her a day later. Do you?"

"Sadly, it happens. What about New York? Where did she live?"

"She was lucky. She found someone she knew from college who had a spare bedroom. Apparently her friend's roommate had moved away a month before and left Sandy—Sandy Rasmussen—with the lease and extra space. Cynthia was a godsend for the summer."

Charlie reached within his sport coat's inner pocket and brought out a pad and pen. He asked if she would mind if he wrote down these names and the Ludyard Gallery.

"Go ahead if you think it is useful."

"Ludyard Gallery. Where's that and who owns it?"

"Ludyard is just off Madison in the seventies—near the Frick. Jacob Stern hired Cynthia. She said he was a kind man who went overboard to treat her like a professional. I don't remember any other names. Hal and I were going to visit her in New York last summer, but we had to cancel our trip. Thinking about it now, we should have gone no matter what."

Charlie paused as Ellie sobbed. When she stopped, he said, "That's a shame. What about the pictures that were stolen? Did Cynthia say anything specifically about them?"

"Yes, I remember one thing. She said that Yale was getting a marvelous Mary Cassatt. A mother and child painting. She said Yale was light on Cassatt. She also knew of my fondness for Mary Cassatt paintings and prints. She was probably hoping that her father and I would visit to see her and the paintings. It's too bad it was stolen."

"Surprisingly, that one was not. The thieves took a small Cassatt sketch and a Childe Hassam painting. The Cassatt oil was left behind. It is probably more valuable than the two that were taken. If the thieves were knowledgeable, it is puzzling that the Cassatt was not stolen as well.'"

Charlie thought he detected a slight smile on Ellie's face. Something he said had registered with her. She put her hand to her face—as if in thought, and then said,

"What you said is very interesting. It proves that Cynthia had nothing to do with the thieves. Yes, she would have known which painting was worth the most. No one steals the least valuable painting if they are knowledgeable. The notion that Cynthia could have been involved in a theft is absurd. The idea that she would steal artwork is incomprehensible. She lived for works of art. I'm glad you told me about the Cassatt painting."

"I hope you don't take this wrong, but how did Cynthia support herself at school? Did she rely on you and your husband? Her internship could not have paid much. Did she have a part-time job?"

"No, we are fortunate enough to be able to support our daughter until she could find a permanent job. She did win a fellowship this year, which paid a modest stipend. But, in general, she lived very modestly. Why do you ask?"

"It's probably nothing. If she was in debt to someone, he might have a reason to be unhappy with her."

Ellie straightened up a bit. She appeared to be considering something that Charlie had said.

"Charlie, you are serious about working with the police, aren't you? In your situation you probably have contacts and power in the art world to help find the missing pictures. It's nice of you to want to help. You are right—Cynthia's murderer is where the pictures are. Please find him. It won't bring Cynthia back, but it would help us find a type of closure."

On his plane ride back to Chicago that afternoon, Charlie evaluated his conversation with Ellie Newgate. The Newgates were a prosperous, professional family with seemingly traditional, conservative values. They were justifiably proud of their daughter and devastated by her loss. They were also sensitive to the implication that their daughter could have participated in the theft. On the other hand, they seemed to know very little about Cynthia's life after she left home. She had told them little and they did not visit her frequently enough to learn much on their own.

In deciding what to do next, Charlie did learn a few names of people Cynthia knew well—Larry Kendall, Sandy Rasmussen, and the gallery owner, Jacob Stern. All three would be worth a visit. Also, there must have been other friends and colleagues with insights on Cynthia whom she had neglected to mention to her parents.

As Charlie thought more about Cynthia, he was sad that Marty had found evidence that established her participation in the theft. From the start poisoning was the problem. Poisoning takes time, expertise, and knowledge of the victim's eating and drinking habits. If someone stumbles on a theft, the thieves would presumably eliminate any witness immediately and violently. In that situation poison is out of the question. The evidence in the apartment only confirmed what should have been obvious to Charlie. Cynthia was part of the scheme. Of course, Charlie would have been insensitive and tactless to make these points to Ellie. She was in enough anguish.

Chapter Eleven

Charlie sat in a particularly comfortable chair in his suite at the Carlyle Hotel in New York City reflecting on where he had been the past two days. He had flown to Cleveland on Saturday morning. After his conversation with Ellie, he returned home, slept in his own bed, and at noon took his plane to Teterboro Airport just over the river from New York in New Jersey. Now he was staying in his favorite room in his favorite hotel in the city.

Situated at the corner of East 76th Street and Madison Avenue, the Carlyle is surrounded by expensive apartment buildings, art and antique galleries, upscale bookstores, and boutiques. The staff rarely changes, and they recognized Charlie by name after his many visits over two decades. Of note to the business community was its dining room located on the ground floor—the site of breakfast for many of the financial power brokers and corporate titans of the rich and famous.

Charlie regularly booked a two-room suite on a high floor facing south and west, overlooking the roofs of apartment houses and Central Park. The high price of the rooms was an indulgence that Charlie granted himself for having to leave Chicago and come to a city that constantly declared self-importance. The comfort and excellent service of the hotel made the trip bearable.

He had not planned to travel east this soon. He knew that if he were to progress in an investigation of what had happened to the paintings, he had to get to Yale. However, he had thought he could clean up work at the office first and take the time to convince Kate that what he was doing was necessary. What had transpired the night before at home had changed that timetable.

From the moment he walked into the apartment, Kate confronted him. She blocked his way to the library and looked vexed.

"This adventure of yours has to stop. You're just being foolish. Do you think you are some kind of hero riding in on a white horse solving crimes for the dithering FBI and police. You are Charlie Bailey, investment manager to the wealthy in Chicago, art collector, civic contributor, and forty-something husband. You are not Superman, John Wayne or even Dick Tracy. Let the FBI do its job. They are the pros. You can be my hero—but not as a detective."

He had hoped that after her speech she would come over and give him a forgiving hug. She stared at him instead.

"Okay," He said. "I understand that you are serious. I don't mean to upset you. My trip to Cleveland was intended to console Ellie for her loss. We are family—however distant—and connected to Cynthia's death, however unintended. If you had been there, you would have seen how distressed she was. She clearly appreciated my visit."

Kate's body seemed to soften a bit. She moved out of the way and followed him into the library. They sat across from each other. She glared at him for a moment and the tone of her next question spoke continued annoyance. "That was it? You didn't question her about Cynthia's activities?"

"She talked about Cynthia. I think it made her feel better. I did not tell her about the evidence the police believe incriminates Cynthia. That would have only depressed her more. In fact, she is angry that the media is reporting that her daughter wasn't an innocent victim."

"She'll find out sooner or later."

"That's just it. The sooner everything is clear, the better it will be for everyone."

Kate shook her head and tramped into the kitchen. Charlie grasped that she was still disgusted with him. He knew that he had failed to convince her of the need for the mission he was committed to. She was focusing on his lack of qualifications or experience to be involved in solving a murder and a theft. She probably also felt there was unnecessary danger in his pursuit. He did not deny that she had a strong argument, but he felt more confident in his abilities and was driven by the desire to ease his mother's and Ellie's pain.

Matters turned worse over dinner. Kate told Charlie that his mother had called him earlier to warn them that the social editor from the *Chicago Tribune* had telephoned her to question her about the theft. She said that she was surprised that the newspaper knew or cared about it. She emphasized to Kate that she had been evasive to the writer. As a result, Charlie should expect a call.

"Damn it," Charlie said in frustration. "I was hoping this news would stay out of the Chicago papers. It's embarrassing to be the focus of a theft and a murder. Mother doesn't want to talk about it—nor do we. Notice that it is the social editor, Peaches Kenney, who called. To him it is not the crime itself that is important; it is that something sensational happened to a family in the social spotlight. We don't need the notoriety or exposure. I'll call him to try to head him off. He is a client of ours."

"Don't you see your inconsistency?" Kate said, sharpening her tone. "You want to avoid publicity on the one hand but get more deeply involved in the case on the other hand. Your efforts could make it a bigger story. 'Socialite turns Amateur Detective'."

"Granted there's a risk, but I think I can handle it. Let's eat."

After dinner Charlie went alone into his library to think this situation through. Kate could not be convinced—at least not today. Increasingly, Charlie felt an urgency to do what he wanted. The longer it took to recover the paintings, the longer the pain and uncertainty would linger. And the longer the Baileys would be vulnerable to public scrutiny of their wealth and misfortune. Rather than reconsidering his resolve to continue, this sense of urgency made him want to move forward faster. Sitting there quietly, Charlie admitted that he was not constitutionally equipped to sit and wait.

The next morning he announced his intentions to fly east to visit the FBI and Yale. By that time Kate seemed angry but also resigned that Charlie would do what he wanted.

"Do what you will. I can't stop you. You're foolish but you obviously don't care. So when are you coming back, Sherlock?"

"Tuesday night. I hope you understand."

"Nope."

Charlie took her last word as a dismissal and walked over to his desk in the library to gather his notes for the trip to New York. Being in New York on Sunday meant to him that he could get an early start on Monday when it was usually easy to reach people at work. His absence also created a cooling-off period for Kate and himself. He didn't minimize that his wife was unsupportive of his activities. She was usually approving and sympathetic. This dispute bothered him. Perhaps this time apart would calm her down.

Charlie made a to-do list for the next morning: call Kathy at the office and reschedule appointments until Wednesday; set up meetings downtown in New York with Jackie Farrell and with Jacob Stern after lunch at his gallery; call Marty O'Connell to arrange to meet him on Tuesday morning; and see if Adrian could put him together with Cynthia's faculty advisor, John Hamilton, and Susan Parker. With good fortune Charlie could talk to a handful of people who might spark an idea or theory to pursue. Then having learned a lot, he would track down Larry Kendall.

Charlie had Jackie Farrell's telephone number and address from the business card she had left at his office. He called at eight o'clock from his hotel room and arranged to see her at ten. They met in a small conference room on the second floor in a building not far from City Hall and the district courthouse. The room had no windows and standard issue Steelcase chairs and a metal table. There was an old model telephone but no amenities.

Jackie looked more comfortable this time in a white blouse and tan, cotton trousers.

"I didn't expect to see you again so soon, Mr. Bailey. Especially not here in New York. What's the occasion?"

"I'm on my way to New Haven, but I have a couple questions for you and an offer."

"Shoot."

"First, did you receive the photographs you asked for? My office should have sent them."

"Yes. FedEx brought them this morning. I only had a chance to glance at them, but they appear to match what Yale supplied us. Your mother's photos have a few more angles and back and front. Thank you. We'll put them out on the wire to the authorities here and abroad. At least everyone will know what the artworks look like."

"That's why you wanted them," Charlie observed. "It's true that hanging on our walls all these years there wouldn't be pictures of them available in books or catalogues. The second thing—has a reward been offered yet?"

"That's in the works. Yale, in consultation with their insurance company, will offer one this week."

"For how much?"

"I don't know. I expect that it will be high enough to interest the thief but well below auction value. Rewards, ransom, I call it—can be very useful. That's two. What's your offer?"

"I want to offer to help in an active way. I may be able to find out things that people may be reluctant to talk to the FBI about. I may see connections that may not occur to someone else. I am not constrained by protocol or bureaucratic obstacles."

"Thank you for your offer, but I can't think how you can be helpful now. It's early in our investigation. Police work isn't like what they show on TV. We don't solve every case in sixty minutes. We work carefully, always hoping to have a breakthrough that will speed everything along. I told you that this case might take a long time. Also, the case is complicated by the murder."

"Are you working on both aspects at once?"

"I work on the missing art. If the FBI takes on the murder, the Violent Crimes section will handle that."

"Having two separate units working this case sounds counterproductive to me."

"Different specialists. What you don't know is that the Art Crime Team reports to the Violent Crimes. Anyways, that's our issue—not yours."

She was dismissing his offer. Charlie felt frustration invading his whole body. He wanted to try again. "I know I can help. I know the missing art. I know Yale. Cynthia was a cousin of mine."

"All true, and if I need your expertise or familiarity I'll call you. However, direct involvement is out of the question. You have no idea how dangerous it is for civilians to be involved. These thieves can be extremely nasty. While museum thefts usually require an insider in the gang, the other members often number drug dealers, money launderers, underworld criminals. The fact that

Miss Newgate was killed confirms the type of people we are dealing with. I can't permit you to be involved."

"Everything will just take longer."

"Are you unhappy with the pace of our investigation so far?"

"I can anticipate a slow process—based on the bifurcation of the investigation and your rejection of my offer."

Jackie frowned and leaned forward at him. She spoke sternly, "Bear with me. You may be pleasantly surprised. We know what we are doing."

Charlie was not convinced but could go no further with her. By nature he was proactive. He was always making decisions without perfect information. At work he relied on his analysts but always made final decisions himself and accepted responsibility. He hated people who were so bound by procedure and bureaucratic rules that they missed the one clue or piece of information that solved the mystery—in his case, of an investment. Then they would usually blame someone else for their failures.

Charlie stood up abruptly and offered to shake her hand. He controlled his anger but barely touched her hand. The conversation had not ended well. As he walked out of the room he turned back briefly and snapped, "Better have your hot shot analysts check these photographs completely. Who knows what you'll find?"

Jackie said nothing in response.

As Charlie descended on the elevator he steeled himself. He was convinced that his approach would be just as successful in solving a theft or a murder as it was with investing. Jackie Farrell was undoubtedly well meaning, but Charlie was determined to go ahead anyway. She would want his help eventually. Perhaps his natural competitiveness or his lack of confidence in her approach explained why he was eager to continue his trip to New Haven.

Chapter Twelve

As Jackie saw the elevator door close on Charlie, she thought 'What the hell was that all about?' Here was this rich guy calling up out of the blue this morning, demanding an appointment, implying we are disorganized, and swearing he can help find stolen art. Bullshit!

She didn't remember him being so pushy last week. It must be the "woman" thing and the "Ivy League" thing. Prejudices, she lived with all the time. She recalled how proud her dad was when a cop's daughter from the Bronx was accepted into the FBI. Of course she couldn't forget that once she got to training she was told two or three times a week that the only reason she was there was to please the EEOC. Since only four girls were in our training class, she understood that they had "token" status. That hurt. Not much changed after graduation. Rotation through different squads, never given the lead.

Jackie got a coffee from the office machine and returned to her desk. She tried to concentrate on a case but her emotions were still stewing. She disliked whining—even if it were to herself. But sometimes acting aggrieved made her feel better.

She remembered her first big break. In 2005 the agency set up the Art Crime Team first in Philadelphia, then in New York and other towns. Her boss, Penn Olson, recruited the first team of eight. He said in his avuncular tone, "Jackie, we want you on this team. You're smart and the pay is better. I like the way you work with the prosecutors from DOJ. What do you say?"

"I'm flattered, but my classes in criminal justice at City College never mentioned art. Am I qualified?"

"Never mind. We'll send you to classes."

Those classes were tough at first, but eventually they became fun. Field trips to the Met and MOMA. Nice duty. Now because of turnover she was top dog.

Her major regret was that Art Crimes reported to the Violent Crime Division. That's where the detective superstars roamed. They considered art sissy. Sam Petrino once said, "A girl in charge of art theft, that makes sense." Of course Sam was full of himself but his attitude was common in Violent Crimes.

Despite assholes like Sam, Jackie liked her job. She had eight people in the department and they were working on twenty-three cases right now. The work was intellectually challenging.

She thought back to Charlie Bailey. He seemed to have a bias against women in authority. With him it may also be that he thinks you have to go to Yale or Harvard to know art. At least that kind of elitist prejudice doesn't exist in the FBI. Everyone here went to Fordham, Baruch, St. John's, or Fairfield and are just as smart as any Yalies.

As Jackie was assessing her situation, she was calming down. Her inherited Irish temperament meant she was easy to rile but also quick to moderate her moods. Soon she realized that she was absent-mindedly fingering through photographs of the Bailey artworks. The two paintings were both gorgeous and heroic and touching, individually. The sketch was another matter—somber and dark. That one was certainly not worth killing for.

"What are you looking at?" Penn Olson interrupted, looking over her shoulder.

Jackie turned around to look at her boss, now one of the group leaders in the Violent Crimes section. He was an imposing figure—tall and stocky, with a round head looking larger because his blond hair was balding. If he weren't married with two small boys, Jackie admitted that she would have been tempted to do something about the physical attraction she felt.

"The Yale pictures," she answered. "They're in black and white because they were taken by the donor years ago."

"Beautiful. They must be worth a pretty penny. Am I right, the thieves only took two of them?"

"Yes, they left this one behind," Jackie said pointing to the Cassatt painting. "Why?"

"Don't know yet. Maybe the bad guys were fulfilling an order—a specific request for the two from a collector. Then there would be no sell-back to Yale."

"How does the dead girl fit in?"

"Since these were in a private collection, the thieves probably never knew of them. She must have mentioned the paintings to them. I don't know why she would have agreed to the theft. But she was their access to the pictures—the insider. The timing was good, because they were on display at a reception and then held in the basement before being sent to permanent storage or display."

"Good point. Then I guess once the girl let them in she was unnecessary."

"And potentially dangerous, since she knew the thieves."

"Where do you go from here?"

By this time Jackie had stood up. Even standing, Jackie was dwarfed by Penn. Intimidated by his hulk and always nervous when asked by her boss about her next activities, she said, "I'll keep interviewing and following up leads from the local police. Nothing promising yet. I posted the three pictures on our website and contacted the Art Loss Registry as well as Interpol, the French, Italians, and Brits. I know you don't like to hear it, but I could use some help on research. I may be able to profile suspects from knowing the art and the artists better."

"Jackie, you know what I'm up against. We are on budgetary lock-down on hiring—even consultants. Violent Crimes always has first call on resources over property thefts—especially art. Museums and rich people don't tug the heart strings of our supervisors in Washington. Do your best."

"I've heard that song before. Throw in, 'Women are second-class citizens', and I can say I have heard it all."

"Now, there's nothing personal. If I had the help, you'd get it. By the way, I saw you in the conference room. What's that?"

"That was Charlie Bailey—from Chicago. His mother was the Yale donor. I think he has too much money and not enough to do. He offered to help us find the pictures—and probably the murderer as well. When I said 'no thank you', he insulted the FBI in general and me in particular for being slow and screwed up. I was pissed but bit my tongue."

"I'm proud of you. You never know who these rich guys know—maybe a congressman or the President."

Penn left, and Jackie sat down. Even though she had been with the FBI more than five years, she instinctively guarded herself in her answers to Penn's questions. She rated her responses just now average and regretted not saying anything insightful or original. At least she avoided saying that like most art thefts the case would lead to a dead end unless the thieves tried to sell the art back to the owner. Penn always hated that prospect because months or even years could pass before any resolution. He liked action—after all, he was a Violent Crimes guy now.

Jackie admitted that the inconvenient truth was that most art thefts were never solved. The insiders who facilitated the theft were often identified, but by then the art was long gone with the real thieves. She liked to compare herself to a major-league baseball player who was doing fine if he batted .300.

The one approach she had never tried but which intrigued her was to go undercover. That meant that she would pose as a fence or go-between, spreading the word among known art-world predators that she was looking for a specific stolen work of art. If lucky, she would get a promising lead. Undercover work was extremely dangerous, and only a few FBI had ever tried it. Still Jackie was curious, but Penn had shot down the suggestion a couple of times. He may have been showing his bias but not admitting it.

The longer she was part of the Art Crime Team, the more she loved the art aspect of the job. She had not been brought up in an art conscious family. Her parent's idea of culture was Archie Bunker on TV. As a result, her first time in a museum didn't occur until a trip by her sixth-grade class to the Metropolitan. Her only lasting memory was of the nude Greek statues of boys. At her age she confessed that she was more interested in anatomy than art.

Now she visited museums and dealer showrooms around the country. She knew the difference between Manet and Monet. She could differentiate between art nouveau and art deco. She was conversant about strengths and weaknesses of Greek versus Roman ancient sculptures. She had even developed a philosophy about art in a society. She believed that there was always a rich variety of art works reflecting and interpreting the cultures and societies in which they were produced. The ambitions, visions, and philosophies of the people of a specific time and place appeared aesthetically in their works of art. When a change occurred in the culture or society, it was signaled immediately by the radical fringe of artists. Later that change would be picked up by the mainstream. Tell her that society was becoming more liberal, and she would forecast the demise of conservative principles in art forms. She felt that the little Irish girl from the Bronx had come a long way.

Despite the poor odds in art thefts, Jackie had had some successes. She found a Delacroix canvas wrapped in brown paper under the couch in the apartment of a janitor. Two Tiffany table lamps were left in plain sight in the garage of a museum lighting specialist. Sadly some of her FBI colleagues were not impressed by these triumphs. These people she considered philistines and morons. More highly educated and successful people than they appreciated what she had accomplished and mentioned it.

"They should make a movie about you," one happy art collector gushed when he was reunited with his oil painting. "The movies glamorize the thieves. The real heroes are you and your colleagues."

In more than one instance she and Penn appeared in the newspapers with a mayor and a museum director shaking their hands. Because of these occasions, she was more visible publically than her Violent Crimes colleagues. That fact probably didn't endear her to that crowd.

The recovery of a work of art was a reward in itself, but she particularly liked the process of problem solving and the fact that her job was unique. Very few people did what she did. The specialized expertise that she had gleaned over time made Charlie Bailey's offer so naïve. If only he knew.

She opened the file to read the material on the Yale theft a tenth time. There was no question that authentic, valuable, identifiable art had been stolen. The timeline describing the theft and death was relatively accurate. The site of the theft was clearly evident. The involvement of Ms. Newgate was certain. No fraud or con was likely. No eyewitnesses had come forward. Forensic evidence at the scene of the theft and death was inconclusive. The interviews of gallery personnel, Newgate colleagues and friends, and the Baileys had produced no significant leads but were helpful in putting the artwork and theft in perspective and in learning about the personality, background, and activities of Ms. Newgate. As Jackie read through the evidence, she had to conclude that while this case profile was informative, there was no hot lead.

The photographs from Yale differed from the Baileys in that they were all in color and shot recently. Jackie preferred to look at them. On the other hand, the Baileys photographs showed the front and the back of each picture.

The backs of the paintings were shot in black and white, and each revealed a paper plaque citing the title and the artist and date the picture was painted. In the case of the sketch there was no such citation. Instead there was a fuzzy, handwritten list of French words. Jackie could translate some of the words, but it was unclear what the writing meant. What was the context? Who wrote the list? What did the initials mean? Jackie wondered where she could grab a French-speaking analyst—just for a few minutes or so. Was this list what Charlie Bailey had alluded to?

Rather than moving on to another case, Jackie picked up the file again and remembered that she had intended to call Cynthia Newgate's parents. She reread their police interviews. The one point that stood out was that they were certain that their daughter had not willingly participated in any theft and that she was murdered—perhaps because she knew the thief's identity.

Jackie reached Mrs. Newgate in Shaker Heights on the third ring.

"Mrs. Newgate, I am Jackie Farrell of the FBI. I am familiar with your daughter's case. I am sorry for your loss. The police are working hard to find out what happened. I am a member of the Art Crime Team of the FBI. We try to recover stolen art. Although I know this is a difficult time for you, I do have a couple of questions.

"You are trying to find Cynthia's murderer?"

"Not directly. The police are working hard on that. I am trying to find out who stole the painting and where they are."

"Whoever stole the paintings killed my daughter."

"Possibly."

"I know you are concentrating on the paintings. But my husband and I want the police or the FBI to find our daughter's killer and bring him to justice. I talked to someone yesterday who can help. I mean my cousin, Charlie Bailey. I suppose you two have talked. He came to visit me—to express his sympathies and to suggest that, if he could find out who stole his family's paintings, he would also likely be identifying Cynthia's killer. From our talk, I am sure that if you do not solve the crime soon, he will try to solve it himself. I urge you to open up to him and work with him. I told him that my daughter needs to rest in peace with the knowledge that whoever did this to her has been caught and punished."

"Of course, but you should understand that we are doing our best right now, and we don't need any extra help from Mr. Bailey. Murder investigations can be very dangerous and should be left to the proper authorities. People become frustrated when their case is not solved quickly, but unauthorized involvement can slow things down. I'm going to talk to Mr. Bailey and dissuade him from doing anything on his own."

"I am surprised by your attitude, Ms. Farrell. I would have thought you would welcome any help—especially from someone as smart and familiar with what was stolen as Mr. Bailey. Do reconsider. You may be missing something."

"Thank you for your ideas. As I said, I'll talk to Mr. Bailey."

Jackie was irritated by Ms. Newgate's ignoring her advice and pushing Charlie Bailey on her. She grounded her pencil into notepad until the tip broke. Nevertheless she continued the conversation in a calm voice.

"If I may, I have a few questions. In your conversations with your daughter recently did she mention anyone who might have wanted her to do something she didn't want to do?"

"Like what?"

"Like help him steal these paintings."

"What?" She shouted indignantly. "She didn't do that. She wouldn't do that."

"Not ordinarily. But sometimes a person can be pressured to do something against their better judgment."

"No. You are missing the point," Ellie insisted sounding annoyed. "Cynthia was murdered. She must have seen the thieves in the act or overheard their plans. Go down that path."

"I am, but I must tell you that there is evidence to place the stolen art at Cynthia's apartment. She must have participated."

"Impossible. Listen young lady. I lost my daughter. Incredibly, the police won't send her body back to her family. Now you have the gall to say she was a thief."

Ellie started to cry loudly and uncontrollably. Jackie waited in silence. She knew she had pushed the idea of Cynthia's involvement indelicately. Her irritation over Bailey had made her lose her cool.

When Jackie heard Ellie's cries soften, she apologized for upsetting her and offered to call back later.

"No, no. I don't want to talk to you again," Ellie sobbed. "Get this over. If you found a painting in Cynthia's apartment, then she was forced to have it. She didn't participate! She was murdered."

Jackie was getting nowhere, and Ellie was disconsolate. She made one last attempt.

"I know. But please try to remember anything that even hinted at somebody forcing her to remove the paintings. Was there anything unusual about these pictures that Cynthia mentioned? Anything?"

"No," Ellie wept.

Jackie then thanked her and hung up gently. She sat back, then slammed her fist on her desk. Damn it, she thought, Charlie Bailey was trouble. Who else had he talked to? Under no circumstances did she need Bailey's involvement. She would have to stop him immediately.

Chapter Thirteen

After meeting with Jackie, Charlie took a taxi up to the Ludyard Gallery, housed on the ground floor of a brownstone on East Seventh Street between Fifth Avenue and Madison Avenue. To be safe he had made a two-thirty appointment with Jacob Stern but he was early; so he looked around the neighborhood. He recognized the Frick Museum where he had not been in for at least five years. He remembered its magnificent collection of European art and decided to pay a visit. Considering the great number of art collectors and enthusiasts drawn to the Frick, Charlie could appreciate why the Ludyard Gallery was located where it was.

An hour or so in the Frick and a leisurely lunch in a Madison Avenue coffee shop brought him up to his appointment time. He walked down three steps from the sidewalk to the black wrought-iron gated door and buzzed for entry. A chic, attractive young woman greeted him, said her name was Christina Hidalgo, and asked if he had an appointment. Charlie presented her with his card and said he had called ahead to meet with Jacob Stern.

"Please stay here, and I'll see if he is free."

Left alone, Charlie browsed around the front of the gallery, looking at some colorful Impressionist paintings by Pissarro and Bonnard. His first thought was that this was a very high-end art gallery and a likely place to employ a budding scholar like Cynthia Newgate for a summer's internship. Soon a bearded older man dressed in a tweed sport coat and dark-brown trousers came out from a door in the back of the building with Christina a step behind.

"Mr. Bailey, I am pleased to meet you. Please join me in my office in the back. Christina, if Marshal Cohen comes by, please ask him to wait until we finish."

Charlie followed the gallery owner through two smallish galleries, up a staircase to a large exhibition room, and through to a single door. In the back were three offices and a kitchen. Stern's office consisted of a partner's desk with two Chippendale-style visitors chairs facing the desk, and a large, comfortable leather chair for the owner behind the desk. The walls were covered with either bookcases or multiple paintings hung above and below and to the side of each other. On his desk were several large art books, catalogues, and a computer. The room gave definition to the word *clutter*. Most likely only the owner had an idea where any specific thing could be found. Stern made room for Charlie to sit by moving a mound of auction-house catalogues to a bookcase shelf.

"Excuse the mess, Mr. Bailey. Someday I'll clean it all up, but I'm too busy now, thank God. What can I do for you?" He paused and sat down. He pushed aside a book and took a sip of some coffee from a colorful mug. Charlie waited for him to get settled.

"When I heard that you had called, your name rang a bell. I went into the art news service I have on my computer, and I realized that you were the one who had his donation to Yale stolen. What a shame! And from Yale yet! It's hard to believe. And then there is the related tragedy, which is close to me. Young Cynthia is gone. You know, she was here working for us last summer. A smart, beautiful girl. She helped us tremendously. What a tragedy! Did you meet her?"

"Yes, she helped with the gift and in talking with her and my mother we learned that we were distantly related."

"Then my condolences. Everyone here in New York—at least in the art community—is talking about what happened. Both the theft and the death. People will be reviewing their security systems. As long as I can remember there have been attempted thefts in this business. Unfortunately, some are successful. You can imagine what my insurance premiums are like. No, you don't want to know."

Stern laughed at his own comment and sipped more coffee.

"Mr. Stern, I had been told that Cynthia interned here last year. I know she was studying the period that you specialize in. I am very interested in recovering the artwork for Yale—as well as seeing Cynthia's murderer brought to justice. Tell me about her time here. Did anything about her work seem odd or abnormal?"

Charlie thought he saw Stern change his body position as if Charlie's question made him guarded. He took out a pack of cigarettes from his desk but did not light up. Rather he played with it in his hand.

"No," Stern answered. "She did research for us. Checked provenances. Talked to the academic community. She helped out when a potential buyer asked a technical question. She knew her stuff or knew where to go to find it. We have had an intern each year for the past eight or nine years. She was one of the best. Yale, after all."

Stern stood up and walked over to the window to open it. Charlie noticed the security bars around the window frame. The room lacked air-conditioning. The temperature was pleasant outside and a slight breeze made the air fresh in the tight quarters. Charlie waited patiently until Stern sat down again.

"Did she seem particularly close to anyone—collector, other dealers, scholar, boyfriend?"

"No one I know. She was shy and all business. She kept to herself—rarely went to lunch with the others from the gallery. She worked closest with my nephew, Ron Gelb." Stern sat back in his chair and folded his arms across his chest. "If I may ask, and I don't want to be rude, why are you asking these questions? I imagine the police and FBI are doing their jobs."

"You are quite right to ask. Yes, the police and FBI are conducting their investigation but are not making much progress from what I can tell. I am trying to help the FBI to find these paintings sooner rather than later."

Stern leaned forward and asked, "Do you have any experience in this type of thing?"

"Not really. But I do know artwork and Yale. I might be able to piece something together for the authorities."

"Generous of you, though I would be very careful. My experience tells me that art thieves are dangerous people. Sadly, it sounds like they killed Cynthia."

"I am aware of the risks," Charlie asserted with conviction. "If I may continue, did Cynthia ever indicate that she had financial problems or needed money?"

"It never came up. We don't pay interns. They are here for the experience and learning. At first she didn't dress to our standards. I couldn't have her interface with clients. I talked to her and she improved her wardrobe. I assumed she had support from her family. She never asked about money."

Charlie sensed that Stern was becoming more nervous. His voice was wavering slightly.

"Your question seems to imply that Cynthia may have had something to gain from the robbery—that she was a participant."

"I may have given you the wrong impression," said Charlie, backtracking. "All I know for sure is that she was murdered."

"Murdered? Are you sure? That's the second time you said that."

Stern fidgeted in his chair and frowned—but said nothing.

Charlie realized that his inexperience in questioning was showing. To cover up, he changed the subject. He said that he wanted to make sure that Stern knew what was stolen so he could notify Charlie if it was offered to him. Charlie described the Hassam painting and the deathbed sketch.

"Degas," Stern said with confidence. "Mary Cassatt's irascible friend and mentor. The sketch sounds like one of a kind. I could have easily found buyers for both pictures. They sound so recognizable; I doubt we'll see them on the market unless the thief is an idiot. His goal is ransom or he has a very private collector. He won't show them to a dealer—at least not to an honest dealer. That's what will happen. I'm sorry I never saw the pictures. If I hear of anything about them, I'll call you—and the police. For my curiosity, do you own others from those artists or from the period?"

"Yes, but my family has not bought or sold anything for decades. Considering what happened, I doubt my mother will entertain any thought of gifting or selling anything else for quite a while. But if that changes, I will keep you in mind."

"Thank you. Ordinarily I would spend more time with you, Mr. Bailey, but today I have a client due now. Will you leave your number on the way out?"

"Of course."

Jacob Stern stood up, and the interview was over. Charlie thought it had ended abruptly—as if Stern had lost interest in the conversation the moment Charlie had said that nothing in the Bailey art collection was for sale. Still, he was pleased to have seen where Cynthia Newgate had worked and had had confirmed what she had done for Ludyard.

Stern was a puzzle to him. He seemed defensive when the conversation turned to Cynthia. He also appeared to want the interview to end. Why? Was he hiding something?

On the way out Charlie noted several other first-rate Impressionist paintings for sale and speculated that Ludyard was an important gallery for this type of work. While only the younger woman, Christina, was in the up front space of the gallery, Charlie had seen fleetingly three or four people in the back rooms and guessed that there was where Cynthia had worked.

"Christina, by chance, is Ron Gelb here? I'd like to talk to him."

"No, he's not back from lunch. I could have him call you."

"Thanks. Never mind. I'll call later."

On the sidewalk, Charlie checked his emails on his cell phone and called Kathy to check on messages and questions from clients and his staff. Kathy responded that it was a slow day but that Jackie Farrell from the FBI had called and left a message in Charlie's voicemail.

"Okay. Patch it through now."

"Mr. Bailey. This is Jackie Farrell. It has come to my attention that you have been talking to certain people of potential interest in your case. In particular you visited Mrs. Newgate in Ohio. I know she is a relative, but she said you were going to investigate the case yourself. Don't do that. You are only interfering in our ongoing investigation. As I told you before, when the FBI has some findings in the case, we'll let you know. In the meantime, be patient and stop interfering. I repeat, <u>stop</u>."

Charlie was disappointed but not surprised by Jackie Farrell's message. He recognized from the time he decided to visit the FBI that the idea that Farrell would welcome his help was a long shot. Still he had had to try. Now he was on his own—at least until the FBI appreciated what he could bring to them. Of course, he would not be frightened by her warning. Charlie did not scare off easily.

Chapter Fourteen

Charlie spent the late afternoon on keeping his business humming along without the boss in the office. He also hired a limo and driver for the next day. This arrangement allowed him more flexibility than in renting a car that he would have to pick up and return to some obscure garage on the East Side. Also, he would not need to find parking places on the crowded streets around Yale.

After another dinner from room service, Charlie rehearsed in his mind a call to Kate. He assumed that she would still be angry. In a way it was a silly disagreement. She was worried about his safety. Wonderful. He should be hugging and kissing her for her concern. Instead he was sulking and arguing. Clearly, Kate had the high ground in this dispute. On the other hand, in the short run recovering the works of art and finding Cynthia's murderer were more important to him than domestic tranquility. Kate would forgive him eventually, he was certain. Nevertheless he should call now and try to mollify her feelings.

"Hi, Katie. I miss you. I'll be back tomorrow night."

"I can't wait. I'm sorry I was cross the other night, but I don't want to see you hurt."

Charlie was relieved that Kate seemed to be feeling better about him or, at least, reconciled to his *"adventure"*. Nevertheless he wasn't so confident that he would push his luck; so he told her about his visits to the FBI and the gallery in careful terms—avoiding Jackie Farrell's demand. Not knowing if he was safe talking too much about his investigations, Charlie changed the subject to ask what she had done that day. In the end Charlie figured that a volcano of emotions was at most between eruptions and he was free to pursue his curiosity for another day.

Charlie checked out of the Carlyle early the next morning. After a two-hour drive northeast out of the city through the leafy suburbs along the Connecticut shore, the driver turned off the interstate into the heart of New Haven. Along the way Charlie read the *Wall Street Journal* and called Adrian Greene's office to see if Adam had succeeded in arranging lunch with John Hamilton. Adrian told him that Professor Hamilton could not stay for lunch but would meet Charlie at eleven-thirty at the Elizabethan Club. That news delighted him. He admitted that he was never literary enough to aspire to membership there while he was at Yale. So he would enjoy seeing the inside of a club he had walked by hundreds of times as an undergraduate.

"Remind me, Adrian, who is John and what is he like?"

"He was the faculty member overseeing Cynthia's studies and thesis preparation. He may strike you as stiff, but he is congenial enough once you get to know him. He is well thought of and has published a couple of books—one on Manet, another on Manet's sister-in-law, Berthe Morisot. He also serves on an advisory board at MOMA. Otherwise he keeps to himself. Although he is here now, as you might expect he visits France most summers. He is on a fast track at the University. He's only forty."

"I assume he knew Cynthia well. Was there ever any talk of them being an item?"

"Not at all. I think he is happily married to Sue. They have a couple of young Hamiltons. He doesn't seem the type to fool around."

"Is he paid well?"

"No one in academia is paid well—except those lucky ones at the law school and the business school. That type of consulting pays well. The Hamiltons have expensive tastes, but I have never heard they were in trouble. I do recall that one of their sons, Prescott I think, has a medical issue. A genetic disorder. He has been in and out of hospitals all his life. But John has never complained about the cost. Why do you ask?"

"I'm just reaching. Money has to be a factor in this sad story. It seems the most likely motivation."

"Well, I wouldn't know about that. Maybe John can provide some illumination on relationships and background information for you."

Charlie's first stop in New Haven was the Yale University Police Department building located behind the Payne Whitney Gymnasium. Marty O'Connell met Charlie in the reception area before leading him to a nondescript conference room. These old friends were happy to see each other face-to-face after talking on the phone.

"Marty, you look great. It must be all that Guinness you drink. You need it to keep up with the students."

"They get younger each year, don't they? The wee folk do say that Guinness is medicinal. I wouldn't know. I never touch the stuff—except on weekdays and Saturdays. The missus says that Sunday belongs to the Lord, and if the missus says so, it must be so."

Same old Marty thought Charlie—a touch of the blarney. He probably hasn't drunk an ounce of alcohol in forty years, he takes his job so seriously. It's fun to joke with such a man.

"I suppose you are wondering why I'm here," Charlie said with a grin. "I hear the great university mislaid a couple of paintings."

"Right you are. At first I was just embarrassed for the gallery like everyone. But then we found the young girl and the mood changed. We don't expect homicides here."

"Forgive me. I know that there is nothing funny in what happened. Do you have any recent news?"

"Only one thing. The New Haven Police and we have brought in the FBI. Today, as we thought should happen, the murder and the theft are now joined as one case."

"That makes sense. Any new evidence or suspects?"

Marty stood up and poured himself a coffee into a paper cup.

"Want a cup?"

"No thanks."

Charlie assumed that Marty was stalling while he considered how much he should say. Friendship only goes so far.

"I can't talk about that. Anyway, what are you doing here?"

"I need to talk to a few people about the paintings."

"Like who?"

"John Hamilton, Susan Parker, and Larry Kendall."

"Kendall? He's not in the art department. Why him?"

"Come on, you know. The boyfriend may help me understand Cynthia's state of mind."

"Don't get your hopes up. They broke up a couple of months ago."

"He's a suspect, though?"

"I can't say."

Charlie was learning that Marty was becoming a dead end. His involvement in the murder case now apparently precluded his sharing knowledge. So be it. Marty was doing his job.

Charlie looked at his watch and used the time as his excuse for moving on. In leaving, Charlie promised to call if he came upon something that might be useful to Marty.

"Watch yourself. This case is serious business," Marty warned.

It was about a ten-minute walk across campus to the white, two-story, New England style building housing the Elizabethan Club. Charlie had told the limo driver earlier to park somewhere near campus until he called him on his cell phone.

Charlie enjoyed the walk past the weathered stone structures comprising the center of Yale's undergraduate campus. Each building brought back memories of his own days as a college student—friends, teachers, and events. No doubt the place would not appeal to him as much as now if he lived in it every day. But his visits were infrequent enough to evoke a pleasant emotional tie each time.

All too soon he reached his destination and tentatively opened the door of the Elizabethan Club. Inside he introduced himself to an employee who led him into a comfortable reading room toward the back. As he entered, a tweedy-looking man Charlie assumed was John Hamilton immediately got out of his chair to greet him.

"Mr. Bailey, come in. Let me suggest these couple of comfortable chairs where we can talk privately."

Hamilton sat down where he had been sitting and Charlie took the other chair. Charlie looked at a trim, athletic six-footer with sandy hair and wire-rimmed glasses. His red bow tie, buttoned-down blue cotton shirt, and loafers put him comfortably in this academic setting. He was by Charlie's standards exceptionally handsome.

Hamilton offered coffee but Charlie declined. Hamilton began, "Adrian called me and asked me to see you about the art theft and the tragic death of Cynthia. I think she would have been a recognized scholar in her field eventually. My wife and I do miss her."

"I understand that you were her faculty advisor," Charlie stated. "Was there anything about her or these paintings that might have provoked someone to murder her?"

"That's a rather direct question," Hamilton answered sounding offended. "But the answer is no. She was a serious student who kept to herself. Not a party girl or someone anyone would hate. It was a shock to me that she was murdered."

"Did she have boyfriends who might have been angry with her?

"I don't think she dated much. The only man I remember her with was a graduate student, Larry Kendall. She introduced him to me last fall, and I saw them together a couple of times. I don't recall having seen him for several months. I never asked her if anything happened with Larry. It was none of my business."

"I understand. But did you form an opinion about Larry?"

"Kind of an odd ball. I thought Cynthia could do better than a chemistry student mixing compounds. If you knew her well, she had a brilliant mind. I was quite fond of her."

"How about the paintings?"

"What can I say? They are marvelous. They would fill out our collection. They are worth an extraordinary amount. On a par with others we exhibit. It's no wonder the thieves targeted them."

"They are from your area of study. Correct?"

"Absolutely. Manet and Mary Cassatt were acquaintances. Berthe Morisot was also a good friend of Cassatt. Everyone knew Degas. They were the original Impressionists. Childe Hassam was influenced by their technique and use of color. We were all excited about your pictures coming here."

"When did Cynthia learn about the gift?"

"There was talk in the department about a year ago about a potential gift, but I don't think we knew exactly which paintings were coming until recently. Cynthia would have heard definitively from Hugh Vance or Susan Parker."

"How had her work been lately? Did it fall off, or did she seem stressed?"

"Actually she was doing quite well. She was looking forward to finishing classes and starting her dissertation. Lately she was exceptionally excited by your family's gift. She had never been so close to works of art new to the gallery nor participated in the planning that went into their exhibition and installation as she was with yours. Also she admired Mary Cassatt—a sort of iconic role model for women in the field of art."

Hamilton paused and sipped a cup of coffee that sat on a side table next to his chair. He seemed to be thinking about something and considering whether to mention it. Charlie leaned forward to study the man. His one tic was that he crossed and recrossed his legs at one-minute intervals. He never looked Charlie in the eyes. Charlie assumed he was nervous—although he had no idea why.

"But since you asked, I do remember now that she was depressed about something the day or two before your reception at the gallery. I thought nothing about it at the time. Maybe she was overworked or had a personal problem. She wasn't a moody person normally."

"Did she say anything unusual during those last few days before her death?"

"No. As I said, she seemed depressed, so I let her be. I had said to her a couple of times that she could confide in me—and she had one or two times in the past. But this time, no. I thought she would snap out of it."

"I saw her at the reception. My wife talked to her. Did you know she was a cousin of mine?"

"I heard that from Susan. Her death must be especially difficult for you."

"We were only beginning to know her. Do you know anything about the circumstances of her death?"

"Only what I read in the papers and rumors in the department. She was murdered, and her death was linked somehow to the robbery. Very upsetting. She was a wonderful person."

The manner in which Hamilton spoke of the murder lacked emotion. He said all the right things, but Charlie could not gauge how sincere he was.

Hamilton's relationship with Cynthia was not fathomable yet. He had described a bond closer than purely professional. A father figure? A confessor? A lover? Maybe his tone was meant to cover up his closeness.

"Did she ever talk about her internship in New York?"

"I had a hand in arranging her position. She did not know much about dealers or individual collectors before that job. The experience helped round her out."

"Did she have any problems there?"

"No. She said old Jacob Stern treated her well. She learned a lot and made some contacts.

"Anyone worth mentioning?"

"Not that I remember. As I recall, Stern and his nephew handle the clients. By contacts, she may have met other dealers and institutional acquirers like the museums. In my world there aren't many good university positions available. It behooves a young person to branch out for job opportunities."

"Did Cynthia have any competitors in her age group here at Yale?"

"There are four other graduate students whom I advise currently. They each have a different niche. Because our current staff is relatively young, it is likely that none of them—and I include Cynthia—would find a teaching position here, let alone, tenure. Practically speaking, I don't think they see each other as competitors. Once someone like Cynthia was to be awarded her doctorate, she would apply for a curatorial position or a teaching job at another college or university. If she published well, she might have a chance to move up. It's a tough world out there. I'd say that she was making progress."

At that point John Hamilton looked at his watch, said he had to leave for a luncheon engagement, stood up, shook Charlie's hand, and left quickly. Charlie sensed he was annoyed. While Hamilton's departure was abrupt, it was understandable, as Charlie had asked to meet him at short notice. Charlie recognized that he should also leave, as he was not a member of the club. As it was around noon, Charlie walked up to a sandwich shop on the corner of Elm and York Streets where he could eat and plan his next meeting.

He knew very little about Larry Kendall except that he was a graduate student in the Chemistry Department. So after he finished his sandwich, Charlie went up to the counter and asked if a New Haven phone directory was available. The cashier called over the manager who found one in back. There was only one listing for a Lawrence Kendall—on Whitney Avenue, a few blocks away. That address was next to campus in an area full of high-rise apartment houses, presumably renting to students who lacked university housing. Since the address was only a ten-minute walk away and the main chemistry building was fifteen minutes up Science Hill, he decided to try the apartment house first to find Kendall.

The building was one of a pair of towers higher than most buildings in New Haven—twelve of fifteen floors up. The front door did not require a key, but there was a buzzer system in the lobby. The lobby was dirty with two baby strollers left against the far wall, newspapers and fliers on the floor, an empty Coke can on a windowsill, and cigarette butts littering the space. None of the buzzers had a name associated with it—only the number of the apartment. Nevertheless Charlie guessed that finding Kendall's apartment would be no trouble, as it appeared that the building was experiencing frequent traffic by its many residents. In fact, within two minutes, a pair of women and a man walked into the lobby and produced keys to open the second lobby door leading to the elevators.

Seizing the chance, Charlie asked the women if they knew Larry Kendall. They looked at him carefully and decided he was no threat to security. They both shook their heads and said they had never met a Larry Kendall. They added that the building was large and there was a large turnover of residents. Then the single man said that he had overheard the conversation and mentioned that he knew Kendall.

"I know Larry. We live on the same floor. Friends. I doubt he is there now. I haven't seen him in a week. He might be at his lab unless he went out of town for some reason."

"Sterling Chemistry building or Kline?" Charlie asked.

"I don't know. I'm an English Department post doc."

Thanks. Say, did you know Cynthia Newgate?"

"Do you mean the girl who was murdered?"

"Yes."

"I saw her here with Larry quite a bit until a few months ago. Larry said they broke up. He seemed upset about it. Didn't tell me why. The murder must have really done him in. As I said I haven't seen him in a week."

"Did you socialize with Cynthia and Larry?"

"Occasionally. But you know graduate students. They socialize mainly with other wonks in their field. Why do you ask?"

"I knew Cynthia. I can't figure out why she was killed."

Charlie detected a shift in the man's attitude. He seemed to look at Charlie suspiciously and glanced toward the elevators.

After the man exited, Charlie left the building and called his driver while he walked up Science Hill. He told him to wait outside 225 Prospect, the Sterling Chemistry Lab. Of the two huge chemistry labs adjoining each other, Sterling is the bigger and older. Charlie decided to start there. He walked in the front door and asked the seated guard at the information desk where he could find Larry Kendall. The guard said he would call Kendall's lab and have him come to the front if he was there.

"Name?"

"Charlie Bailey. Tell him that I am a cousin of Cynthia Newgate."

The guard reacted visibly at that name. With raised eyebrows he slowly made the call. He was successful which Charlie surmised when the guard stuck his thumb upwards while still on the phone. Ten minutes later a short, unshaven, twenty-something, visibly tired Larry Kendall appeared. He was wearing a Yale hoodie, blue jeans, and sneakers. He came over to Charlie and shook his hand.

"Is there somewhere we can go to talk?" Charlie asked.

"Of course. There's a buttery in the building. Follow me."

They walked down the stairs to the basement level and reached an open area with vending machines, a grill/sandwich bar, and tables and chairs. Only a few people were sitting there, nursing coffees or soft drinks and studying papers and books. They sat down at an empty table in a far corner.

"Mr. Bailey. I remember your name. Cynthia mentioned it last fall when she talked about your potential donation. Considering what has happened, I'm sorry you went through with it."

"I agree with you. Our intent was to make a gift honoring my father. What happened ten days ago is tragic. We did not know Cynthia well, but her death has affected us deeply."

As he talked, Charlie was studying Kendall, who was looking down at the table and his moving hands. Charlie read him as nervous and morose.

"From your comment, Larry, I take it that you still had feelings for Cynthia even after you two broke up."

"I loved her. We were together for a year. I thought we would marry after getting our degrees. I didn't want to break up, but we had to. I hoped that things would work out. Now she's dead. Gone. Christ, it's tough."

Kendall kept fiddling with his hands. As he talked, he never glanced up at Charlie. Observing his face, Charlie thought he might begin to cry.

"Larry, nothing can bring her back, but I am determined to find her killer. That's the least we can do."

"Yeah. I talked to the police—the campus and New Haven guys. It wasn't very helpful. I hadn't seen Cynthia for a week. We work so far apart. Since we broke up, it's unlikely I'd see her. The last time was when I went to pick up a pizza to take home. She was alone waiting for take-out and I nodded to her. She smiled back but did not invite me to join her. So I left and went home."

"That was when?"

"A couple of days before the reception. I tried to call her the night of the reception. Even though we weren't really talking, I thought I would congratulate her on receiving your paintings. After all, it was a big event for her. I called her cell, but she didn't answer."

"When was that?"

"Around eleven. The police asked me about the call. I wish she had answered. I could have talked to her one more time."

"I understand. She may have been still working."

"Yes," Kendall whispered.

He sat silently for a moment. Kendall kept gazing at his hands. He appeared sad and tense. Then he looked up and asked,

"Do you know how she died? The police wouldn't tell me and the newspapers only mentioned that she was found in the library stacks."

"Maybe it's best you don't know. Remember how she was alive."

"Damn it. I want to know," he cried pounding the table. "I wanted to marry her."

"She was poisoned."

Charlie immediately regretted telling him that. Although Kendall seemed genuinely grieved, he might be a suspect. He might have been angry over the break-up. He knew Cynthia's schedule. He was a chemistry expert. If he was the murderer, he probably would be interested in what the police knew.

Kendall reacted explosively to the mention of poison.

"What! Which poison? That can be a slow, terrible death. How could she have taken it?"

"I don't know," Charlie lied.

"Who told you?"

"The police let it slip."

"No wonder they seemed so interested in me. The lab has access to all kinds of poisonous compounds. Now I am pissed."

"After seeing how upset you are over her death, I can't believe anyone could think you were involved."

"What? Nobody thinks that."

Charlie wanted to calm him down by sympathizing with him. But there was a comment Kendall had made earlier that Charlie wanted to pursue.

"I know the break-up tore you apart, but you said that you had to break up. Why was that?"

"None of your business."

"Come on. I have been upfront with you. What ended your relationship may have relevance to finding out what happened ten days ago."

"Drugs. She got hooked on drugs. Cynthia was the last person on earth I thought that would happen to. I couldn't get her to stop. I thought if we broke up, maybe she would come to her senses. I don't know if she tried to stop. I'll never know. She's gone."

"Drugs. That can be really hard on a relationship. I can see why you broke up. When did she start taking drugs?"

"Last summer. I was working here in the lab, and she had a job in New York City—an art dealer. Before that, when we started dating she was sweet, innocent, disciplined, and devoted to her work. Then when I visited her in New York, I noticed a difference. She was hyper—intense and nervous. Outside of work she became sloppy about her dress and time management. Also she had lost some weight and complained that she couldn't sleep at night. I guessed she might be taking some anxiety drugs, because her job might have been more stressful than school. I was concerned but not panicked."

"Did you confront her about these changes?"

"Yes. This conversation took some weeks, since I didn't see her every day. She got angry and withdrew from me. Denied everything and suggested that we stop seeing each other until we were back at Yale. Foolishly I agreed."

"Were things different when she returned here in the fall?"

"Not really. If anything she was worse. One day I found some pills on a piece of aluminum foil on her dresser top. Amphetamines, like I thought. When I pointed them out, she said they were diet pills. Since I had known her, she was a little chubby and said she needed to lose weight. I reminded her that there were other ways to thin down."

"What happened after that?" Charlie asked thinking that he finally understood what may have been driving Cynthia's actions ten days before. Drug usage is powerful. They push us to do things we ordinarily wouldn't do. What he had heard about Cynthia from her mother and colleagues didn't jibe with a user of heavy drugs.

"I tried," Kendall said with emotion. "I really tried. For months. She was in denial and tried to hide the pills. I still found them. Finally, I blew up and called it off. Deep down I thought that if I left, Cynthia would come to her senses, drop the drugs, and want me back. Stupid. I was more miserable without her than with her."

"Where did she get the drugs? On campus?"

"I don't know. It started in New York. Maybe she met someone at the gallery or her roommate or someone at a party. Does it matter now? Drugs are available if you want them."

"When the police questioned you, did you tell them about the drug problem?"

"Of course not. I didn't want to put Cynthia in a bad light. Also I didn't want them to hassle me. They would have asked a million questions. Besides, what is the connection? The guy who killed her was an art thief—not a drug dealer."

"I don't know who killed her. Taking drugs is expensive. I wonder where she got the money. I don't suppose that graduate students in art history make any money. Did she borrow from you? From friends?"

"She borrowed a little from me but I don't have any money either. She said it was for personal items. I never got it back. Yale pays me a stipend for some lab research and my parents fund the rest. I knew that Cynthia's parents sent her an allowance. I doubt that amounted to more than subsistence. Art History would have paid peanuts. Anyway I don't know how she paid for the drugs."

Kendall seemed to become even more uncomfortable with the last few questions. Charlie sensed that he did not want to talk about Cynthia's drug problems and regretted that he had brought it up. Charlie was afraid that Kendall would stop talking if he went much further, so he changed the topic slightly.

"When you and Cynthia had dinner—at her place or at a restaurant, did she enjoy a glass of wine?"

Kendall looked up quizzically. "Yes. She liked red over white."

"So do I. She was a social drinker, right?"

"Yes. That reminds me. Sometimes, she would pop a pill and wash it down with wine. Said it was a vitamin. Not likely. That obvious lying got to me after a while."

Kendall straightened up suddenly as if he had just thought of something. He stopped playing with his hand. Charlie sensed his tenseness dissipating. He seemed to mellow. A very visible mood shift. He said, "I'm talking too much. I know you are a relative of Cynthia's but I don't know you. I'm giving the wrong impression. Cynthia was a wonderful, loving person."

"I know. Remember, talking can be therapy for a horrible event. You have been through a lot emotionally. It takes time to heal, but our conversation has helped me and I hope it helps you. Thank you."

Kendall appeared to accept Charlie's analysis and got up to lead Charlie back to the entrance on the ground floor.

"Do you think the police will call me again?"

"Expect it. Tell them what you told me and you'll be okay."

They shook hands and went in opposite directions.

Charlie hailed his driver and sat in the back thinking. He was considering whether he wanted to make his last stop on his itinerary before heading south to his plane. He had arranged to meet Susan Parker—late afternoon, he had said. Susan had worked closely with Cynthia at the gallery for many months. If Cynthia had brought her drug problem to work, Susan would have been in an excellent position to recognize it. Nevertheless, Susan might be wary to speak of Cynthia's difficulties. Charlie would have to be skillful to get Susan to discuss the issue. He might be better off waiting until he had formulated his line of questioning.

Deciding to postpone until next week, Charlie called Susan at her office to reschedule. She agreed and then commented that she would be on vacation in England for the next three weeks. Dreading that delay, Charlie reversed course and offered to meet her now as originally planned.

Having an hour to kill, Charlie sat in the parked limo reviewing his conversations of the past two days. Jacob Stern struck him as a wily businessman—confident on the outside but guarded and measured in what he said. If Cynthia had begun taking amphetamines while working at the gallery, he should have noticed the changes in her. He was silent on this fact. Charlie was suspicious of him already since the murder was tied to artworks of the same specialty as his gallery. Could Stern or someone else at the gallery have corrupted Cynthia? Charlie needed to dig deeper and start with Ron Gelb, Stern's nephew.

John Hamilton is a participant in the same niche of the art world and knew Cynthia intimately. Maybe too intimately. He was demeaning of Larry Kendall which attitude seemed to Charlie impolite by a professor towards a student. Adrian had suggested that Hamilton might have financial pressures because of his son. He also was uncomfortable in answering questions. And he left abruptly. Charlie felt Hamilton knew more that he had said.

Finally, Kendall the ex. Granted he acted depressed and had revealed a great deal of new information about Cynthia to Charlie, but he had reason to be angry at her and knew her habits well. He professed strongly against drug usage, but what if he was lying? What if he supplied the drugs? He also would know poisons. On the other hand, if he were the murderer, he was a magnificent actor. His performance as the bereaved ex-lover just now was believable.

Three possible suspects but no clear culprit. Maybe the meeting with Susan Parker would shed new light on those puzzling relationships.

Susan Parker met him in her second floor office in Street Hall. As Charlie sat down across from her desk, he could not help but recall that this desk was where Cynthia must have taken the key to the storage room where the paintings had been. Unlike Jacob Stern's office, Susan's was tidy and orderly. The two art professionals might have the same books in their shelves, but their personalities were apparently opposites.

Susan began the conversation by updating Charlie on the status of the stolen artworks. Yale had heard nothing from the thieves despite the millions offered in reward. She spoke confidently that eventually there would be contact and a successful negotiation. She apologized for having been so lax in the security of the storage room and admitted that her lapse made her doubly committed to regaining the paintings. She also acknowledged a failure in judgment in trusting Cynthia.

"My disappointment over Cynthia's involvement does not mean I am not dismayed by her death. What she did does not justify her murder. Heavens, no. She deceived us, but she must have been in way over her head."

"Undoubtedly," Charlie agreed noticing that this prim, intelligent woman—perhaps in her late thirties—was looking straight into his eyes. She impressed him as sincere and determined.

"I am heartbroken, Mr. Bailey. We are doing all we can to assist the police on both matters. I believe that whoever stole the works of art also killed Cynthia, but the possibility exists that we could recover the art and not identify the thieves."

"How's that?"

"The thieves might well go through an intermediary who would not reveal the seller. In fact, if there is contact from the thieves, most likely it will be in the form of a ransom demand or a response to our reward—both through an intermediary. The FBI can be a great help in this event in trying to identify the thieves, but there is no guarantee they will be successful."

"Our biggest surprise in this sad tale so far is Cynthia's involvement," Charlie said. "Did you notice any signs of discontent or unusual behavior on her part leading up to the theft?"

"I have thought about that question every day since the robbery. She worked for me the past nine months. She did research and cataloguing and assisted on planning exhibitions. She was quiet and very organized—extremely dependable. Never complained about the work or the late hours."

Susan shifted in her chair and leaned forward to emphasize her next point:

"Cynthia was very excited about your three pictures. They were new to her, and being related to your family, made them even more special. In particular, she was touched by the Degas sketch. She said it was a rare historical artifact. It appealed to the scholar in her."

Charlie nodded agreement. He liked her. She was direct and informative. He liked matter-of-fact people.

"What you say makes it even more remarkable that she would have been involved in stealing them."

"I was dumbfounded at first. Of course, she had access and knowledge, but she was straightforward and honest. If she made a mistake, she came to me immediately and admitted her error."

"What about her personal life? Did you know much about it? Did she have money or boyfriend problems?"

She reacted to his change of topic by shifting her eyes from his face to a framed picture on the right wall. She paused a moment then answered frankly as before, "I think that her work was her life. Except for a single boyfriend with whom she broke up a few months ago, she never mentioned men—or even girlfriends. If she came to a departmental function, she came alone and might have a single glass of wine, which she nursed for the entire time. I think that her social life was limited by design. Money? She never talked about it. I had the impression that her family had some money. She got by, like all graduate students. We paid her a little bit, but I always felt she would have worked here for free."

"Academic pressure?"

"All graduate students feel pressure about their classes and their thesis. Ask John Hamilton. I think she was doing fine."

"You feel that she was acting normally up to the robbery. What about drugs? They seem to be common on university campuses."

"Okay. You had asked about the one issue where I am uncertain. She missed a few days of work—nothing excessive. Once in a while she would have mood swings. I have chalked that up to her woman's calendar. She didn't seem the type to experiment with drugs—too fixed on self-control. Still, something made her act against her personality. Sometimes she was hyper—almost confused. I chalked that up to her passion for her work. She also lost some weight. That was good. If she did take drugs, she concealed it well."

"Did you know her before she interviewed in New York?"

"Of course. We interviewed her in the spring, before she started at the gallery. All her references were glowing."

"Did she seem different after New York?"

"I can't say that she did. I thought her internship was a wonderful experience. She saw firsthand how the commercial side of the art world functions. I still think she was more comfortable with the academic side, but the gallery broadened her thinking. If anything, she was more sophisticated after her summer work. She saw that different people put different values on works of art-that there is a marketplace importantly influenced by factors other than aesthetics."

"If she was taking drugs, she must have hidden that fact well, Charlie concluded. "On the day of the reception, do you know what Cynthia did after the presentation?"

"I talked to her briefly before the dinner at President Adams's house."

"What did you talk about?"

"I asked her to see that the paintings were carefully placed in the storage room downstairs by the movers and that the room was locked. I gave her my key. Then before she left, I wanted her to check the reception area to make sure no one had left anything behind."

"What did she do with the key?"

"She returned it here to my desk. I assume it was she. After the pictures were reported missing, I checked and the key was here. I trusted her."

"Could someone have taken the key and then returned it unnoticed on Saturday night?"

"I suppose so. We do have two guards here at night. One is in front and the other does a tour each half hour. If they saw Cynthia, they would not be alarmed. Anyone not working here would have been another story."

"Did they see her?"

"Once right after the reception, but she could have avoided them. She knew their routines."

"Did the key itself reveal anything?"

"The police took the key to analyze it—to look for fingerprints, I imagine. But so many people have used that key over the past few months. I can't believe that the police would have found it useful, but they are smarter than me. The sad fact is that, if someone else had used the key, Cynthia would still be alive. I hate to admit it, but her murder convinces me she was involved."

Chapter Fifteen

Claire Bailey was in her yard checking her birdhouses for eggs or fledglings when James walked up to her with a FedEx envelope that had just arrived. Claire could not recall anything that required a FedEx delivery, but she was intrigued enough to stop her inspections.

The envelope contained an unaddressed smaller envelope. She opened that and found a typed terse letter printed on a plain white sheet of computer paper. The message was direct and ominous:

> *Stop your son.*
> *The paintings are gone.*
> *If you continue,*
> *there will be consequences.*

Claire felt a sharp pain in her chest. If the sender's intent was to frighten and intimidate her, he succeeded. She thought of her doctor's visit earlier in the week. She had gone to him because she felt so stressed by the events at Yale. She had put up a controlled front for her family and friends, but a constant, latent anxiety engulfed her.

While she was in the doctor's office, he had reviewed the recent cardiologists' report in her file that detailed the two cardiac episodes she had experienced during the past five years and her history of medical treatment, including the heart drugs she was taking. He recommended that she continue with her prescriptions and avoid all stressful situations.

So much for that advice, she thought. I hope that pain in my chest meant nothing. "James, I'm glad you are still here. Would you help me back to the house? Suddenly I'm not feeling well."

Claire held his arm and walked slowly up the incline to the house. She worried that she might be having a heart attack and needed to sit down and slow her breathing. If the pain passed quickly, she might be able to avoid telling Charlie and Kate about this. She didn't want to worry them.

Despite her qualms, Claire recognized that she had to tell Charlie about the letter. He would know what to do. *Consequences* might refer to him as well. They had not talked about the theft since he returned from New York two days ago. What had he done to prompt such a threat from the thief? He had told her only that he was visiting the FBI to offer to help them and to go to Yale to see if there was anything new on the case. That itinerary sounded innocent enough. He must have done something else.

When she felt calm enough, she called Charlie at his office. She read him the letter and heard him pound on his desktop.

"What? Mother, I'll drive up to your house as soon as I can get out of here. Don't tell anybody else about the note."

Claire felt better knowing Charlie was coming. Her chest pain had abated, but she thought she should call her cardiologist anyway and lie down on her bed for an hour.

The day passed at a snail's pace for Claire. Try as she could, she could not shake the grasp of the letter's message. The thief and probable murderer was threatening her. She thought of herself as a strong woman, but this threat—so serious—could test her to the limit.

At last, Charlie arrived with Kate. Claire led them into the library, which was located far away from the household staff. Claire handed the letter to Charlie, and Kate looked over his shoulder. He had put on white, painter's gloves to hold it.

"Short but powerful," Charlie said, holding it up for Kate.

"Charlie," Kate said. "What are you to stop? Your meetings with people who knew Cynthia? Do you think one of them could have sent this?"

"Maybe—or someone who learned of my meetings. The conversations I had out east had an edge to them. People were nervous in talking about

Cynthia. At times I felt they were holding back information about their relationships with her. They seemed happy when the conversation was over. In fact, two of them simply left abruptly. Still, I didn't think I shook a bee's nest. But this letter suggests otherwise.

"It sure does," Kate said.

Claire sat across the room looking glum, fretting. She remembered Charlie's involvement in the Bradford murder a year ago. He had pushed his investigation—outside the police—too close to the murderer so that he and Kate had nearly been killed. She hoped he wasn't doing the same. But now she needed their advice.

"Kids, I am glad you came. I'm scared. What do we do? One side of me wants to kill this guy—excuse the use of the word. The other side of me says, 'Call the police!'"

"Let's call right now," Kate suggested.

"Let's wait a minute," Charlie argued. "What do we know and what are our options? First, this letter was produced on a computer. If the writer was Cynthia's murderer, I doubt the FBI will find any prints on it. Based on what Marty didn't find at Cynthia's apartment, this murderer is careful."

"Second, he wants us to panic and give up—call the FBI and do nothing. As an aside, that is what Jackie Farrell wants us to do as well—leave everything to her."

"I agree with Jackie," Kate interrupted. "She's a professional."

"People say things to me that they won't to the FBI or police," Charlie countered. "They are afraid of the FBI. Also, I don't bow to bullies."

"You're just like your father," Claire said. "Head-strong, impervious to risk, stubborn. Maybe foolish. Remember the Bradford murder."

Charlie stood up and appeared to ignore the criticism from his wife and mother. He walked across the room, then turned back to the women.

"One thing is obvious. We are hiring security personnel for you, Mother. Also for you, Kate. We have to take this threat seriously."

"Son, I know you mean well, but I don't want some army-types hanging around the house. Is there a better way?"

"No, and no negotiation. The men we hire will blend in. No goons or military-types. Fearing the worst, I have already talked to Dave, our head of security at the office. He's a former cop. He recommended two former Chicago policemen who started their own firm."

Charlie fished a piece of paper out of his sportcoat pocket. "One man is named Milosz Zielinski, called Rocky. The other is Stanlislaw Bartkowski, Stan. I'll meet them and, if they pass muster, I'll insist they start immediately."

"I pray they are better than Roman Spartek from the Bradford murder last year," Kate snarled.

"Yes, he was working for the devil," Claire agreed.

"I made a huge mistake taking Jamie Bradshaw's recommendation for a bodyguard. I learned my lesson. But you both must have protection."

Kate frowned but shrugged her shoulders in resignation.

"Next, regarding the letter. I'll call Marty O'Connell and see what he thinks. If he says, call the FBI, I will. By the way, Mother do you have the FedEx package? Let's look at the sender."

"I did already. The sender was a *Mr. Mailbox* in Stamford. So I threw it in the trash."

"Stamford. Half way between New York and New Haven. Let's retrieve it. The package may be useful at some point."

Charlie was silent for a minute staring in Claire's direction. Then he said, "Excuse me for taking time to notice, but, Mother, you look pale. I can understand that this note upset you. How's your heart and chest?"

"I had a pain," she admitted. "Now I'm just exhausted. I'll call my cardiologist this afternoon."

"Please do," Charlie said.

* * *

That letter should do the trick. Of course, the local police and the FBI would be all over the theft. I think I thought out how they would proceed and I covered my tracks. Cynthia did what I asked her to do and no one saw me. I couldn't rely on her to keep quiet after the theft. Drugees are undependable. She had to go. The arsenic worked well. The plan has come off perfectly so far. No one will find the artworks until I am ready to move.

He finished off his glass of wine, stood up, and walked over to the window. He looked out at the fading light and the emerging moon in the eastern sky. He liked the dark. Soon he would disappear and pursue the second part of the plan.

Now Bailey may force me to the next steps. I might not have thought about him if he hadn't asked questions. If he backs off, then I'll proceed on schedule. If not, I'll take care of him. He knows the pictures better than the FBI. He may be more motivated than the FBI because Cynthia was related to him. I can't take the risk. Worst case, I may have to dispose of the painting sooner than I wanted.

Chapter Sixteen

The threatening note changed the situation for Charlie. Now there was potential danger afoot. Before, he felt removed from the theft and murder. His involvement was voluntary. He could help the formal investigation from a distance with impunity. If he came up with something useful to the FBI, he would be pleased and the FBI would be surprised.

Now the stakes had been raised. If he stopped pursuing clues, the note implied that the threat would dissipate. Once out of the case he could sit back and wait for the FBI investigation to run its course. Realistically, their effort might take months with no guarantee that the pictures would be found or Cynthia's murderer identified. Charlie recognized that if they failed to solve the case, he would regret his inaction and blame himself for the failure.

On the other hand, if he continued his own investigation he would be putting his family and himself at risk. He had to consider that he may have already caused his mother's health to worsen. Such a decision was difficult, but today weighing the risk against inaction, he chose to be proactive. He did not take lightly a physical threat to his mother or Kate, but he thought that the danger could be minimized with the employment of security personnel. He also expected that his efforts would be successful and completed quickly. In spite of this confidence, he acknowledged that perhaps he was being too sanguine. But he was not backing down. The simple fact was that the note made him even more motivated and energized than before.

Charlie was crystallizing these thoughts on Friday morning as he sat in his office waiting for his appointment with George "Peaches" Kenney. Charlie had known George as Peaches since they were small boys. The name aptly described George's complexion and rotund shape. The senior Kenneys, Peaches' parents, had been major clients of Charlie's for over a decade. In his own name, Peaches had a modest portfolio with Charlie. Beyond that, since Peaches was an only child, Charlie understood that the plump Mr. Kenney Junior had great expectations financially.

Despite the obligation to talk to any client who requested a meeting, Charlie had delayed this session as long as he could. He anticipated that the topic of conversation would be the art theft. Charlie and his mother had agreed that no good could come from publicity in Chicago. Public notice would expose the Baileys to ongoing expressions of pity, ridicule, and a few "I told you so's". Charlie preferred that the events at Yale be a private or, at most, an East Coast topic of conversation. Unfortunately, in asking for this meeting, Peaches had mentioned that he had learned of the events at Yale. As society editor of the *Tribune*, he would be expected to write a sensationalized column highlighting the misfortune of the socially prominent Bailey clan. As a consequence, Charlie knew he would have to persuade Peaches to bury or better yet, ax the story.

Peaches came into the office with a rush, put out his hand to shake Charlie's, and posed briefly with his left arm akimbo.

"How are you, Charlie B.—my favorite money manager? If truth be told, my only money manager. I hope I am making gobs of money. Momsie says I am. Can't have too much, can we?"

Charlie acknowledged this flamboyant entrance with a smile and a handshake and then nodded toward the sofa to indicate that Peaches should sit there. Charlie stared at this short, chubby, balding man wearing a pink and white seersucker suit, blue bow tie, no socks, and tasseled loafers positioned across from him.

"I always love your offices," Peaches said as he sat down. "They are so comforting and masculine. We need that when the stock market is so jumpy. How is that stunning young wife of yours—last year's bride of the year?"

"Kate is fine. She's climbing the ladder as an advertising whiz at Hunter, Freeman."

"Marvelous. I love women who work when they don't have to. It's so modern. I'd like to write a column about the phenomenon, but who has the time what with weddings, benefits, and art thefts I have to cover."

"That's a strange litany of events," Charlie responded lifting an eyebrow.

"Don't be coy, Charlie. Although I am interested in my investments, the reason I am here is to get the scoop on those exquisite paintings that were removed from Yale recently. That must have been a blow to you—and Mrs. Claire Curtis Bailey. You make a gift, and the thank yous are still coming in when the pictures are stolen. Rather untoward."

"I'd rather not comment. Would you like to review your portfolio?"

"You're trying to change the subject, dear boy. I'm just a poor scribe with a job on the line. It's not every day that art is stolen from an illustrious Chicago family like the Baileys. I may have even seen those pictures on your mother's walls. She must feel violated."

"Watch your language, but she's doing fine. She made the gift in good faith, and it was received as such. What happens afterwards is out of our control. I'm sure the pictures will be recovered in time. There's no story."

Peaches shifted his weight slightly to allow himself easy access to a notepad in his suit-coat pocket. He took it out, adding a pen, and set it on his leg. Meanwhile Charlie pondered how to get control of this conversation.

"There is a story," Peaches retorted. "Not only the art theft, but there was a girl murdered. The *New Haven Register* said she was related to the donor. Our readers would be very interested."

Charlie was becoming increasingly angry and considered briefly how he could intimidate this stubborn, obnoxious, casual acquaintance of his. If he could have bullied Peaches, he might have, but Charlie's manners got in the way.

"Do me a favor on this," Charlie asked finally. "The loss is painful enough. Publicity would make matters worse—and not bring the pictures back to Yale. I know you don't want to hurt my mother. This wound is still sore."

"Sorry. But my editor already knows about this and expects a story. Like it or not, the Baileys are a story in Chicago—especially a society story."

"Okay. I have an idea. What if you bury or kill the story now in exchange for an exclusive when the case is resolved? The news has been out there for a while now—on the East Coast. No need to rehash. If you have an exclusive later, you will look good, and time will heal all wounds."

Charlie knew he had no power to stop Peaches, but his offer might buy him time. Who knew what might occur? In a sense his offer was a bluff.

Peaches said nothing for a long minute. He was obviously considering Charlie's offer.

"All right. I'll talk to my editor. I can't guarantee anything. If we hadn't known each other for so long, I wouldn't trust you. Charlie Bailey's been a man of his word. You better have something special if I wait."

Charlie felt that he had dodged a bullet. If all went well, thee would be no article on the theft, no mention of Cynthia, and no interference with his pursuit of evidence at least for a while.

The conversation then switched to investment information and the state of their respective squash games. After what seemed like an eternity to Charlie, Peaches announced he had to leave to meet the newspaper's photographer to cover a luncheon to honor the chairwoman of a future charitable benefit. He put his pad away and asked Charlie to give his regards to Charlie's "redoubtable" mother.

Peaches had just left when Charlie asked Kathy to reach Rocky Zielinski. Considering the lack of enthusiasm his mother and Kate had shown for a bodyguard, he had to be sure that Rocky and Stan were reliable.

Kathy put Rocky Zielinski through in two minutes.

"Rocky, I think Dave Doyle talked to you about my situation. I need bodyguards for my mother and my wife."

"Yes, sir. Dave said you might need two men for a protective assignment that could be dangerous."

"Exactly. We need to meet first."

"I can come over this afternoon at two with my partner, Stan Bartkowski."

"I'll see you then."

A few hours later, Charlie was impressed by the physical appearance of the two security men he met. Both appeared to be strong, fit men in their forties. Rocky—"like the boxer", Milocz Zielenski added—stood over six feet tall with short, blond hair and a scar over his left eye. Stan was a few inches shorter but stockier—built like an offensive lineman in football. He had dark, curly hair. Both wore navy blue suits, white shirts, and conservative ties. Except for their muscular builds, they blended in as businessmen in an urban setting. Charlie judged that in most situations they would be inconspicuous until needed. Perfect.

He asked about their credentials, experience, and availability and then he outlined the assignment. After an hour, Charlie was confident that they could do the job.

"You might be on duty all day and night, in Illinois and elsewhere, and maybe for months. Okay?"

"Okay."

Charlie didn't haggle over the cost. He could not put a price on protecting his family.

"You start tonight, assuming the ladies are comfortable with you. We had an unfortunate experience with bodyguards last year. So they are sensitive. Assuming all goes well, Stan, you will be with my mother in Lake Forest, and Rocky, you will look after my wife in Chicago. Kathy will give you addresses, phone numbers, and the like."

Charlie felt better as they left. That task was likely done. He recognized that the women would complain that he had not added protection for himself. But he was confident that he could take care of anything he faced. He laughed to himself—confidence, my character fault.

Charlie remembered then that he had promised the women that he would consult Marty about the note, but he decided to delay that call. He was sure that if he told Marty or the FBI about the threat, they would reinforce their insistence that he stand down. What else would they say? Besides, they already knew the thief was capable of murder. Of course, he would strike out at anyone coming close to himself. Considering the situation, Charlie concluded that nothing useful would be served by alerting the police or FBI about the note at this time.

Satisfied that the ladies would be as safe as possible, Charlie told Kathy to hold all calls and shut his office door. He sat behind his desk and started listing the suspects so far. He began with the assumption that most art thefts were done by insiders or with the aid of insiders and that most murders were committed by persons who knew the victim. Cynthia was both an insider and the victim. She was the key. Who knew Cynthia? It most likely was one of the persons who had learned of his questions recently.

The motives seemed clear. Money in the case of the theft and the removal of the person who could identify the thief in the case of the murder. So again who was close to Cynthia?

Larry Kendall was certainly close to Cynthia for a long while. He could use the money that came from selling or ransoming the pictures. He was not an art expert, but he could have conspired with Cynthia, who was knowledgeable about the artworks and knew when and where they would be. Maybe she had actually broken up with him and he may have been angry enough to kill her. Or they may have plotted the theft. Then they broke up. Maybe he then learned that she was going ahead anyway and he took advantage of the situation.

Did this scenario make sense? Charlie judged it a stretch. First this explanation assumed that Cynthia was the prime mover. He was convinced that she was forced somehow to participate in the theft. Dedicated art scholars and relatives of the donor do not steal paintings. At least, so it seemed so to Charlie. She was not the type. Maybe the influence of drugs changed her.

Second, Kendall seemed upset about his former girlfriend's death. In addition, what did Kendall know about the disposition of the artwork? Cynthia would have had to arrange that. If she had, then this story might make sense. True or not, Charlie was sure that the FBI would see Kendall as a suspect and keep him on the list.

Who else was close to Cynthia: colleagues at the art gallery and in her field of study? What about Susan Parker? She knew the importance and value of the paintings. She had access to the storage room and could tell Cynthia to remove the pictures and put them elsewhere. She could have visited Cynthia at her apartment and poisoned her to direct attention at Cynthia and her role in the theft. Afterwards, Susan could have pointed to Cynthia's use of her key and suggested that Cynthia was acting a bit strange recently—both distractions for the authorities.

This scenario struck Charlie as a clever ruse. However, Charlie had difficulties in seeing Susan as the killer. She seemed open with him and was convincing in pointing out Cynthia's involvement. While Susan was closest to Cynthia at the art gallery, Charlie could see that variations of this story could apply to any one of several persons working there. Still, he should not eliminate Susan Parker as a suspect.

John Hamilton was close to Cynthia. With his knowledge and contacts in the art world he could have masterminded the affair. Money might have been a motive for him.

Stern had to be on the list as well. During Cynthia's time there she developed a drug problem. He might have used drugs to manipulate her.

There may be others. The notion that some unknown acquaintance of Cynthia could have plotted and carried off the crimes forced Charlie to admit that he did not know enough yet. He realized that he could not thoroughly answer his question: who else was close to Cynthia? For instance, maybe she met someone during her internship in New York City who impacted her and carried out the theft and murder. Maybe someone else? He had a long way to go. His list was only beginning.

The positive was the appearance of the threatening note should help to narrow the list. His own efforts had come to the attention of the murderer. Charlie had not talked to many people in many locations. Maybe he learned of Charlie's involvement from a conversation with Stern, Parker or Kendall. The culprit's action tended to focus Charlie's search. Stamford, Connecticut?

What was clear was that the answer did not lie in Chicago. Charlie had to return to New Haven and New York. If his search hadn't been urgent enough, the note had made time more critical. He would start again on Monday in New York where he still had not talked to Cynthia's summer roommate and her Ludyard Gallery boss.

Chapter Seventeen

Kate had completed her project for the day and sat back to consider her frustration with her husband's activities. She sighed that it wasn't easy being married to Charlie Bailey. He was a talented but stubborn man. Still Kate thought that she was the luckiest woman in the world to be his wife. She loved him dearly and couldn't imagine not being with him. But why did he have to get involved in matters that were dangerous and beyond his experience, she wondered? Because of him his mother had been stressed out. And because of his compulsive need to right the wrong done by the thief and murderer, Kate worried about him constantly. He was almost insanely confident always. After they were married, she thought she could calm him down, bring balance to his fixation on tasks outside his job and family, and convince him that the world did not expect him to be a superhero. For a while she felt she had succeeded. But now she recognized that he had just not had a challenge—a dragon to slay-recently.

Her biggest concern was that Charlie's activities were putting himself and his family at risk. Kate had tried to persuade him to step away but he ignored her advice and went off to New York and New Haven anyway. She recognized that her arguments so far had failed.

At least Charlie had followed through and hired a bodyguard. Rocky Zielinski seemed capable enough in their meeting. So she agreed to have him watching her. He was waiting on the sidewalk when she had left work. He didn't say a word to her, but he was always a half block behind her as she walked up Lake Shore Drive to the apartment. She found the situation humorous until it occurred to her that if he was following her, he wasn't watching Charlie. Charlie didn't think he needed anyone, she thought. His disregard of his own safety was another reason why being married to Charlie Bailey wasn't easy.

After she had spent a few minutes alone in their apartment, Kate decided that she should talk with Rocky. She wanted to make sure that they mutually understood the general rules of this vigilance. So she called down to the front doorman to send Rocky up to the apartment.

"He's the athletic-looking man in the blue suit and short haircut. He should be on the sidewalk away from the main door trying to look inconspicuous."

"I see him, Mrs. Bailey. You can't miss him for being so inconspicuous," Sean, the doorman, laughed. "I'll send him up."

Kate was waiting at her front door when the elevator arrived at the landing. She smiled and shook Rocky's hand, escorting him inside.

"It's nice to see you again. I am feeling more secure because of you."

"Thank you. My job is to see that nothing bad happens to you."

"I'm all for that, but we need to be on the same page. I have to be able to do my work and do ordinary things without feeling your overwhelming presence."

Kate remembered that the last time she had a bodyguard she had been always aware of his being nearby and sometimes even felt that good manners dictated that she watch out for him. Did he have lunch? Were Charlie and she out too late or up too early? The situation had been new and awkward for her.

"Try to forget I am around," he suggested. "You just do whatever you normally do. The only time you will see me is when you need me."

"I hope I don't need you—ever. No offense. I'll just have to get used to having you around. Now beyond me, what about my mother-in-law and Charlie? Is there another person like you?"

"Stan is in Lake Forest. Mr. Bailey said nothing about himself. He's an ex-marine."

"Almost twenty years ago. He thinks he's tougher than he is. He's not twenty anymore. I'll have to talk with him."

"Are you and Mr. Bailey going out tonight?"

"Not that I know. Give me your cell number. If we are staying in, we'll call you and you can go home."

Charlie arrived home an hour later—just in time for dinner. He kissed Kate with some passion, then stepped back and seemingly waited for a reaction. Kate sensed that he was trying to gauge whether she was still upset with him for not dropping his efforts. Kate responded in a noncombative manner.

"I see that Rocky is on the job. I like him. He takes his job seriously."

"Yes, Rocky is the best. I'm sorry we need him, but we can't do better."

"How is he going to look after both you and me?"

"His job is to protect you. At this point I don't need anyone."

"I would think you are most at risk. You're the one travelling places and asking questions."

"If I need someone, Rocky will know someone. We'll see. What's for dinner?"

Kate let him change the subject, acknowledging that Charlie would not be persuaded to hire a bodyguard for himself at this point.

After dinner they sat in their bedroom watching television and flipping through magazines. Dickens slept at the foot of the bed. Kate waited patiently for him to bring up the subject of his investigation. During a commercial Charlie said, "I'm sorry but on Sunday I need to return to New York. I need to talk to Cynthia's boss from last summer and her roommate there."

"Won't the FBI do that?" Kate asked.

"I have no confidence that they will. I need to find what, if anything, happened in New York. Someone put her up to helping steal the pictures. It must have had something to do with the drug habit I told you about. If we eliminate New York, then we can focus solely on New Haven."

"If you say so," Kate sighed. "I don't know much about crime solving. You are not going to let this go, are you?"

"No, I take this personally. The more time that goes by the colder the case becomes."

"Okay. I give up. But I'm not going to sit here and listen to what you do. If you go to New York, I go to New York. I love you too much. I have to be there—in case you are in danger. We can bring Rocky, too. He can protect both of us."

"I appreciate your support, but it is not necessary that you come. While it might be fun, you have your job."

"So do you. I can postpone things at work for a few days. My decision is not negotiable. I have to be there—insuring my investment—you."

Kate smiled, thinking that she had at least won part of the argument. He was probably doing something foolish, but she would feel better if she were there. Maybe he would take more care if she were accompanying him. Perhaps also, she might understand this obsessive need of his to be involved.

Trying to start contributing, Kate revealed, "While you were in New Haven last week, I took another look at the blow-up your office did of the writing on the back of the sketch. Remember?"

"Yes, the list in French."

"It's definitely a list of paintings. I looked in the book of paintings by Degas that you have in the library. He did lots of paintings depicting ballet dancers and scenes from ordinary life. Of course, I have no idea why the list is on the back of the sketch. Maybe the list means something. Why don't you show it to Seth Price? He might have a theory."

"That's a great idea. I should have thought of that. I'll do that. See, I need your help. In many ways."

Kate watched Charlie get up and switch off the remote. He joined her on the bed and kissed her. Since their disagreement they had not made love. While not entirely reconciled to Charlie's attitude, she had mellowed and missed their intimacy. She did not stop him while he undressed her and himself. She was excited about the love-making but also about the prospect of working with him on the investigation. She reached up to him as he embraced her. Suddenly he stopped and said in fake concern,

"What about Dickens?"

"That's okay. The boy needs to learn sometime."

Chapter Eighteen

On Sunday afternoon after an uneventful trip in Charlie's plane to Teterboro Airport and a limousine transfer to New York City, the Baileys checked into the Carlyle Hotel. The man behind the front desk welcomed them by name as they entered the lobby and announced that their suite was ready immediately. Charlie was relieved that there would be no wait. They could unpack and then relax or work before dinner.

On the flight Charlie let his pilot fly while he was in the back of the luxurious eight-seater busy researching on the Internet. He wanted to learn whatever he could about Ron Gelb before he met him. He had begun googling Ludyard Galleries. Fortunately, the gallery supported a robust website illustrating its inventory for sale and posting a list of principals with their photographs and direct phone lines. Ron Gelb was featured in the main Impressionist section. He appeared to be in his mid-thirties, wore his curly brown hair closely cropped, and looked scholarly in his wire-rimmed glasses. His features were nearly symmetrical, framing deep brown eyes, and a large, boney nose. His eyebrows were a bit bushy, and his ears and lips proportional to his head size. Although Charlie could not tell from the picture how tall Ron was, his thin face and posture suggested that he was above average height. On balance, Gelb struck Charlie as handsome, well groomed, intense, and intelligent. The narrative on the page claimed that the gallery enjoyed a stellar reputation as a dealer in European and American Impressionists and that Ron Gelb would be happy to assist the needs of buyers and sellers.

Satisfied that he could pick out Gelb in a crowd, Charlie then brought up all *Ron Gelb, art dealer* entries provided by Google. There were over seventy items. While many of the entries were repeats, Charlie learned that Ron Gelb had contributed articles to art magazines and journals, had responded to reporters' inquiries with pithy and colorful quotes, and had spoken at a few academic symposia. His expertise went beyond Impressionism to all styles of nineteenth and twentieth century European and American paintings and sculpture. Charlie concluded that Gelb's professional interests were consistent with supervising the work of a graduate student like Cynthia Newgate.

Gelb's academic credentials consisted of a bachelor's degree from Brown and a master's degree from Columbia. In several citations Charlie noticed that Gelb was listed with a middle initial of *T*. That fact proved quite helpful as Charlie learned when he checked the telephone directory in the room of the Carlyle. He was surprised to find that there were scores of Ron Gelbs in New York City. However, only one listing contained the correct middle initial. That Gelb lived at 1010 Park Avenue in Manhattan. Based on his familiarity with the East Side, Charlie recognized that that address was in the same swank neighborhood of his hotel and was most likely a prewar cooperative-apartment building. Gelb would have to be doing well to afford such an apartment.

On the flight to New York Kate had offered to interview Cynthia's summer roommate, "I'd like to talk to Sandy Rasmussen. She might be more comfortable chatting with another woman. You can be intimidating. I'll try to get her relaxed and to open up."

Charlie was pleasantly surprised that Kate had volunteered. Considering her prior opposition to his investigation he had not anticipated her direct participation. Clearly she was warming to his efforts.

"Great idea. Cynthia's mother gave me the address."

"I'll try tomorrow after work," Kate said seemingly enthusiastic. "I won't call ahead. I think catching her off guard may produce franker comments."

"You sound like you have done this kind of thing before, sweetheart. I picked a good partner."

Kate smiled and said, "I'm happy to help."

Rocky had sat in the back, separate from Charlie and Kate. He had said nothing unless they asked him a question. All during the flight he had a book in his hands, although Charlie never saw him turn a page. Charlie had no idea what was going on in his head. All Charlie knew was that he could never do Rocky's job. He lacked the patience to watch from a distance and do nothing until the client was in danger. As much as Charlie was proud of his service as a marine, he hated the "hurry up and wait" aspect of military duty. As his mother always said to him, he was in perpetual motion.

The Baileys ordered room service Sunday night. Charlie wanted to make sure Kate was current on everything he knew about Cynthia. He had no idea what to expect from Sandy Rasmussen. But the more Kate knew about Cynthia, the more likely Kate would elicit useful information from Sandy.

"Here's my plan tomorrow," Charlie said when they sat down over their meal. "I'll walk down to the Ludyard Gallery, ask to meet Ron Gelb, and invite him to lunch. Over a glass of wine I'll try to have him describe Cynthia's work and his relationship with her. I'll test his knowledge of the art theft and inquire about the chances that the paintings will be recovered.'

"After he returns to work, I'll visit Gelb's apartment building and try to get anyone on the staff to talk about Gelb. Meanwhile you meet Sandy and we'll compare our findings tomorrow night."

"Let's hope that everyone is talkative," Kate added sounding amused.

With their missions defined, Charlie slept well and woke eager to learn more about Cynthia's summer in New York. After he and Kate shared a sumptuous breakfast buffet at the ground-floor restaurant, they kissed goodbye and went in different directions after Charlie helped find Rocky and Kate a taxi to take her to midtown to take advantage of Charlie's membership at the Yale Club. The club had a marvelous library—quiet and comfortable for paperwork or for reading a book. She planned to stay at the club until after lunch when she would do some shopping and then cab it over to the West Side to wait for Sandy to return from work.

Charlie found Rocky outside the hotel on the sidewalk and briefed him on Kate's schedule and told him to follow her. He was to wait outside the Yale Club and then trail Kate over to Sandy Rasmussen's apartment.

"What about you, sir?"

"I'll be in the neighborhood. No danger here."

Charlie had booked a single room in the Carlyle for Rocky. Rocky told him after he had his instructions that he had never stayed in such a luxurious room. He added in all sincerity, "The sheets were soft like a baby's ass."

Charlie laughed and told Rocky that he preferred not to think of an infant's bottom. "Reminds me of diapers and all that mess."

Charlie returned to his room to read the *Wall Street Journal* and call his office for messages. He assumed that the gallery would not open until ten. At a quarter to ten he left the hotel to walk the nine blocks down Madison Avenue to the gallery. The day was beautiful—sunny and cloudless, temperature in the low seventies. Charlie took his time looking in the windows of a bookstore, a men's shop, and a fine porcelain store.

When he arrived at the gallery he rang the bell and was buzzed in. He began to look at the paintings to the left when the same well-dressed young lady he had met the week before came up to him.

"Christina. I'm back. Obviously I like your paintings."

"Yes, I remember. I apologize that I don't remember your name. I recall you talked to Mr. Stern."

"I am Charlie Bailey from Chicago. Last week I asked to meet Ron Gelb, but he wasn't in. Is he available now?"

"No, he is expected a little later this morning. Perhaps I can help you."

Charlie did not expect that Gelb would not be there. He wondered if Gelb took his job seriously. He tried not to look frustrated.

"It would be kind of you if you could ask Mr. Gelb when he arrives if he could join me for lunch—say at the Carlyle at twelve-thirty."

"Of course. Should he call to confirm?"

Charlie gave her his cell number. Then, since the gallery was deserted of clients, he decided to ask her about Cynthia. "Besides your great art, I am here to talk to people who worked with my cousin Cynthia Newgate last summer. Do you remember her?"

"Of course. Mr. Stern said she died recently—up at Yale. He didn't say what happened to her. She was an intern for two or three months. So sad. I liked her."

"That's nice of you to say," Charlie said sincerely. "Our family is trying to find closure. We intend to write a memorial. Last summer here was important for her professional growth. I want to learn more about the experience."

"Ron would definitely be the man to talk to. He directly supervised her. Ron is Mr. Stern's nephew—the son of his youngest sister. He is an expert in his own right. Cynthia worked in the back doing research. I work in the front with customers."

"Still you must have talked about things. Did you go out to lunch or social events with her? You are about the same age—in your twenties."

"You flatter me, Mr. Bailey. I'm thirty-two. Yes, we went to lunch a couple of times. One or two of the other girls in the back joined us. We talked about the usual—the works of art, exhibitions, other staff members, other dealers, clients. She talked some about Yale. I think this was her first time working for a dealer."

"It sounds as if she learned a lot. What a terrific experience. Did she have time for a social life? New York must offer a lot to young people."

Charlie noticed that Christina frowned at his comment. He wondered if she was reacting to her own situation or did not associate Cynthia with a successful social life.

"Cynthia was pretty quiet. She didn't talk about dates or even men in general. Her work came first. I doubt if I'm telling you something you don't know."

"I always knew her as serious and personally reserved. But we wondered if she opened up when she was away from family and school. I always hoped she was having a lot of fun on her own."

"Maybe but I never saw her like that."

"That's too bad. During her year at school after her internship here she seemed different. Jittery. Lost weight. I worried about her. Did something happen here?"

Christina looked surprised at Charlie's question. She stopped looking straight at him. Charlie wondered if she was hiding something.

"Talk to Ron. I don't know anything. If you excuse me, I have a painting for shipping. I'll tell Ron to call you about lunch. I'm sorry about Cynthia. Did she have a disease?"

"No she was murdered."

"Oh, my God. Mr. Stern just said that she had died. I assumed she was sick. That's terrible. My condolences."

Christina was obviously shaken. She turned and walked to the back of the gallery. Charlie was puzzled by her reaction. He would have thought that Cynthia's death and the art theft would be well-known and discussed in the art world. In particular, he thought it would be a prime topic in a gallery where she recently worked. Maybe Jacob Stern had a reason to suppress this news within the workplace, or Christina was simply naïve. Perhaps Ron Gelb would shed some light on this puzzling situation.

Charlie left the gallery and walked over to Central Park. The day was so beautiful and the park was in full bloom. It was so inviting that he felt the best place to wait for Gelb's call was on a park bench. As he entered the park he remembered that the model sailboat pond was nearby. He would find a bench near the Hans Christian Andersen statue and watch the miniature sailboats being maneuvered around the buoys by remote control.

Around eleven o'clock his cell phone rang, and Charlie heard a baritone voice asking for him. It was Ron Gelb who apologized for missing Charlie earlier at the gallery and agreed to meet for lunch at the Carlyle. He said that his uncle had told him about Charlie's visit the week before and added he was heartsick to have learned about Cynthia's death.

Charlie perceived a sincerity in Gelb's sentiments. He must have been fond of his summer intern. Charlie wondered if the FBI had interviewed Gelb. Certainly his relationship with Cynthia was relevant. He was an expert in her field and her boss.

Whether the FBI had talked to Gelb or not, Charlie was aware that people were often reluctant to talk to the authorities out of fear of being dragged into a situation that might be, at best, inconvenient and, at worst, personally threatening. On the other hand, if they felt comfortable, most people liked to talk about serious matters like murder and robbery. It made them feel important and knowledgeable. As he had discussed this point with Kate, their roles as investigators were to function as foils, making Sandy Rasmussen and Ron Gelb feel relaxed enough to open up about their true feelings and specific memories.

After the call Charlie remained sitting on the bench enjoying the picturesque setting and contrasting the brisk tempo of New Yorkers with the more leisurely pace of Midwesterners. Ten minutes before his meeting time with Gelb Charlie started to walk the couple of blocks to the Carlyle. There were a few items that he wanted to prod Gelb into talking about—drug usage was number one. Had he observed Cynthia using drugs? When did she start? Larry Kendall was convinced she was introduced to drug usage last summer in New York. The second item was her social or love life. Had she become close to anyone who might have influenced her behavior enough to have her commit an out-of-character act—such as assisting the stealing of the paintings? Finally, had she talked to Gelb or others this year about the Bailey gift—what it consisted of and when the pictures would be at Yale?

The Gelb connection appealed to Charlie. Gelb knew Cynthia well and would have been familiar with the stolen artwork. This was a powerful combination. As a professional investor, Charlie was trained to look for relevant connections—relationships and cause and effect. Most things happened for a reason. His experience gave him confidence that his current pursuit of information was worthwhile—despite the disbelief of the FBI.

Charlie recognized Gelb from his internet picture as Charlie entered the hotel lobby. Gelb was seated, leafing through a magazine. Charlie went straight to him and offered his hand.

"I hope you haven't been waiting long?"

"No, I've just arrived. How did you recognize me?"

Charlie explained about the gallery's webpage as they walked into the dining room.

Although the Carlyle was situated in a predominantly residential neighborhood, Madison Avenue was home to a variety of high-end clothing boutiques and art galleries. The hotel was a favorite at breakfast for "power" business meetings and at lunch as a shopping respite for ladies with means. In fact, Charlie and his guest were the only men in the restaurant that day.

Gelb dressed the part of the art dealer—or a university professor. He wore a tweed sport coat, light blue shirt, and blue and red patterned bowtie. He looked fit, was easily over six feet tall, and had distinctive curly brown hair. His glasses added to his scholarly look.

When Charlie had shaken his hand, he had glanced down on Gelb's left hand and noticed no wedding band.

"Thank you for joining me," Charlie said. "I'm sure you are a busy man. My family and I are quite upset at losing Cynthia and the works of art. The happy event of a major gift to Yale went so utterly wrong."

"You have my condolences. All of us at the gallery were fond of Cynthia and impressed by her knowledge and work ethic. She would have made a wonderful art historian in time. It was my good fortune to work with her."

"You're kind." Charlie picked up his menu and asked, "Shall we order? Let's get the food out of the way."

They both chose salads and iced tea. Charlie sat back on the banquette and decided to get Gelb talking about the art world before returning to Cynthia.

"The loss of the works of art we donated to Yale has profoundly distressed my mother. She is a wonderful, generous woman, but is becoming a bit fragile. She made the gift in the name of her deceased husband, my father. I am trying to comfort her. The best thing would be for Yale to recover the stolen paintings. We talked to the police and the FBI, but they don't have much to tell us. I thought that perhaps you, as an expert and dealer in Impressionist paintings, might know what our chances are of seeing them again."

"You flatter me, Mr. Bailey. True, this is my field, but I know very little about stolen art. Our gallery is very respectable, and we would never deal in stolen goods. We check provenances assiduously and, knock on wood, have never had a problem with anything we have bought or sold. I wish I could say the same about the auction houses, but then, our staff does better work. Tell me, what paintings were stolen? I'm afraid, I didn't pay much attention to the news reports."

"Two pictures. An oil, *Flags on Fifth Avenue, November 11*, by Childe Hassam. And a charcoal sketch, *Untitled, of a dying man, Edgar Degas*, by Mary Cassatt. Both had been in our family for decades.

"Extraordinary. A Hassam flags painting and a Cassatt sketch of her friend, Degas. First rate, I'm sure. A fine gift. Clearly, though, in terms of recovery, these would both be too recognizable to be offered by a thief through a gallery or auction house. I suspect either an unscrupulous and secretive collector had heard of them and taken them for his own purposes or the thieves stole them to offer back to the insurance company or Yale as a ransom ploy. In the first case, Mr. Bailey, you will never see the pictures again. In the second instance, unless the thieves are too greedy, you will see them at Yale someday, but probably not soon. I have no idea which is the more likely case. So I guess I can't be very encouraging to you."

"I was afraid of that."

Charlie eyed Gelb closely as he explained the two outcomes, which Charlie had heard before from others. He had asked not to learn something new but to see how Gelb responded. Gelb spoke matter-of-factly. He showed no empathy. His attitude seemed to be: too bad, you will be lucky if you ever see them again. This side of Gelb contrasted with his comments about Cynthia

"If Yale is approached about buying them back, why did you say 'not soon'?"

"Because the thieves will probably wait until the spotlight on the theft dims and goes black. Then it would be safer to approach the former owner—in this case, Yale. But remember, I am not an expert on these recoveries. I would advise you to talk to the FBI."

"I will. Still there is one thing that puzzles me about the theft. Please help me understand. There were three pictures in the gift—all stored at the same place at Yale. Yet the most valuable one was left behind by the thieves. Doesn't that imply that either the thieves were not aware of the relative values to steal only the two? That might be your first case—the secret collector."

"Maybe. What was the third painting?"

"A Mary Cassatt. *Mother and Child on the Beach*. Thematically in the mainstream for a Cassatt."

"Yes, of course. You know we could sell such a painting in an instant for a big number. I can't believe that the thieves left it behind."

"It must be worth much more than the sketch."

"Most likely. Sight unseen, it sounds to me as if the thieves didn't know what they had. They blew it. Although a 'flags' painting has lots of appeal. I would say that Yale was very lucky the thieves did not grab the Cassatt."

At this point the salads arrived and the men began to eat. This time Gelb brought up Cynthia.

"I am completely confused about Cynthia. We heard that she had died. The impression we had from the initial press report was that she committed suicide. We assumed that her death was a coincidence unrelated to the theft. We were surprised that she would commit suicide although she was intense and held her feelings inside. Then my uncle said you said she was murdered. That suggests her death was related to the theft. What happened?"

"The police seem to think she was implicated in the theft and was murdered afterwards."

"No! Not possible! Cynthia was a sweet, innocent young woman. She could not have been involved in an art theft. How horrible that the police would have come up with such a bizarre story. Let the girl rest in peace."

Gelb was the most animated he had been since Charlie met him. He seemed to be defending an old friend against terrible accusations.

"I have no idea if she had a role in this. The police seem to think she had access to the paintings in storage and understood the value of these works of art."

"The whole idea of her involvement is ridiculous. I worked with her for over two months. She was an academic. She was practically afraid of her own shadow. It's inconceivable that she could have participated in a sophisticated plot to steal and fence expensive works of art. Preposterous!"

"I agree. I'd like to convince the police they are wrong. More likely Cynthia was in the wrong place at the wrong time. It might help if I knew more about her summer here last year. What was it like? Was it all work and no play? Did she mention anyone you might have concerns about?"

"No. She was a workaholic. I don't think she knew many people in New York."

"Did she date or have a boyfriend?"

"Not that I am aware of. On second thought, oh, yes, she did mention a boyfriend at Yale. Another graduate student. I can't remember his name."

"So she did not go out with anyone here in New York last summer?"

"I don't think so."

"Could her behavior have changed subsequently—due to taking drugs, for example?"

Gelb straightened up a bit and laughed. He appeared incredulous. "Drugs? Not Cynthia. She was the definition of virtue. Straight as they come. Did the police say she was taking drugs?"

"Not to me. I'm just exploring different possibilities."

"I see. Don't bother to explore. You are wasting your time. Cynthia could not have anything to do with the theft. If I were you, I would be patient and wait for the thieves to contact Yale. From my experience, that's your best chance of recovering those pictures. Let the police find out who killed Cynthia."

"You are undoubtedly right. What about last winter and this spring? Did she stop by the gallery? Did you talk to her? Did she seem the same, or was she different?"

"I don't know. I have not talked to her since last summer. No one told me that she visited the gallery."

"That's strange. If she was so well liked, no one tried to keep up? Did you plan to bring her back this summer?"

"We have a new intern from Columbia. We always bring in a new person each year."

"We know Cynthia was very excited about our donation. I would have thought she would have told someone here about it. She said it was quite a coup."

"From what you described, it was. The fact is, she never talked to me about it. I would have congratulated her."

Gelb had finished his salad and glanced at his watch.

"Are you staying at the hotel?"

"Yes, my wife and I are in New York briefly. We fly back to Chicago tomorrow."

"Too bad. There are so many things to do in the city at nights."

"I know. I'll see how she feels, but we may take in a show tonight."

"Well, I notice that Barbara Cook is at the Café Carlyle this month. She's great."

"Good suggestion. We'll see."

Gelb looked at his watch again and stood up to go.

"I have to get back to the gallery. I'll keep an ear open for anything relating to the Hassam painting or the Cassatt sketch. People talk to each other in this industry. If someone says something, I'll call you right away. I am sure Yale is red-faced over this incident. Do you have a card?"

Charlie produced one from his wallet. Gelb glanced at it and said, "Good luck and thank you for lunch."

Charlie sat alone at the table for a few minutes. He had not learned much from Gelb. Maybe there was not much to learn. Maybe Cynthia just worked hard all summer, made no friends, took no drugs, and was poisoned by the thieves for no good reason—since most people swore that she couldn't have been involved.

But I know that version isn't correct. Marty convinced me. What about Gelb? Either he was particularly unobservant, or he was not telling everything he knew. Maybe both.

Although Charlie had no reason to distrust Gelb, he also was not about to cross him off his list of possible suspects. He knew Cynthia, and he knew art—or should have.

As planned, Charlie headed to Gelb's apartment house to talk to the staff or a neighbor. Charlie needed less than ten minutes to walk over to Park Avenue and then up to his co-op building. He knew that this neighborhood was one of the most upscale in the city. People walking by and entering the buildings were all fashionably dressed. Most of the men wore tailored suits, and the ladies looked as if they had just come from a *Vogue* shoot. Even the children wore classic-style coats and ties over gabardines or jumpers and white-collared blouses—private school uniforms. Limousines parked outside a couple of buildings waiting for their riders. The streets were clean. Planters with seasonal flowers adorned the median of the avenue. Trees lined the sidewalks. An abundance of security personnel guaranteed a peaceful atmosphere. Charlie knew none of this came cheap.

Gelb's building was a large, twelve-story, prewar brick structure with a masonry façade. The entrance featured a canopy extending to the street, double glass doors, a large, marble lobby, and a uniformed, Hispanic-looking doorman. Charlie walked confidently through the doors and asked the doorman to ring Mr. Gelb.

"I'll do that, sir. But I am almost certain that Mr. Gelb is out."

The doorman turned to the brass plate built into the wall and pressed one of a multitude of buttons to produce an intermittent buzz. The doorman listened attentively and pressed the button again with no response.

"That's a nice system you have there," Charlie said. "We need to upgrade ours at home. But I do need to see Ron, and I don't have his cell number. Do you know where his office is?"

"No, but it must be near here. He takes off each morning walking down Park."

"Am I right? He's not married. I haven't seen him in months, so I am not up-to-date. But I do recall he was dating some younger woman last summer. I thought he might have married her."

"He's not married. Unlike some people in the building he doesn't have many visitors or throw parties."

"Too bad. I liked that girl. I'll have to kid him about her. So he never has a woman visitor?"

"I shouldn't say anything, sir. But I remember one lady. Young. She was nice. Remembered my name. Always said, 'Francisco, nice to see you. Is Mr. Gelb in?' I liked her."

"Polite. Was this last summer?"

"Yes. And then about a month ago. I remember. I said, 'Long time, no see.' She said, "I never forget you, Francisco.'"

"Do you remember if her name was Cynthia Newgate?"

"'Newgate'? I think I called up a Miss Newgate before. But I don't know if she was there for Mr. Gelb."

Charlie thanked Francisco and walked south on Park Avenue. Of course, he understood that the woman visitor could be anyone. It would be telling, though, if the woman who came last month was Cynthia. After all, Gelb had said he hadn't talked to Cynthia since last summer. He might be lying. Maybe he had a relationship with her beyond work—sex, drugs, a plan to steal paintings. And maybe not. Charlie's imagination was running wild. He was way ahead of the facts. Still, Francisco's timetable was consistent with Charlie's concocted story. Walking back to the hotel, Charlie felt lucky he had learned as much as he had. Even so, he hoped that the doormen at his own building were not as chatty with strangers. His mother would be mortified if she learned that a staff member talked about his employer.

Standards aren't what they used to be, Charlie thought and chuckled. He assumed that Francisco would mention his visit, but he had not given him his name. Still Charlie did not mind if Gelb was confused and unsettled by the events of this afternoon. A nervous man makes mistakes.

Chapter Nineteen

From a fifth-floor window of the Yale Club the figure of Rocky looked small to Kate. To a bystander he must have appeared to be a middle aged businessman waiting for a companion outside a side entrance into Grand Central Station. Kate smiled at the sight and thought she would make a poor member of a European royal family or a Hollywood celebrity. They were used to constant security protection. They probably did not even notice bodyguards as they went about their daily lives. On the other hand, Kate knew she would always feel uncomfortable with Rocky watching her. She amused herself, "I would flunk royalty." Still she recognized that Rocky made her safer and that this arrangement was only temporary.

What did make her feel comfortable was the library of the Yale Club. She had been in this series of rooms spread over the entire fifth floor of the club once before. The library consisted of several alcoves of full bookshelves and nooks housing big, comfortable leather chairs. The larger rooms also had long tables with lamps and wooden chairs much like the reading rooms of large university libraries. The nooks presented inviting places to read and sleep while the long tables were favored by lawyers, authors, and businessmen writing papers longhand or on computers. Kate had come there before, specifically to work on an art project for a consumer-goods client of hers. She knew the room would be quiet and full of energy generated by all of the serious workers around her. She might be helping Charlie but she still had her job to do.

At lunchtime she called Rocky on her cell, "Go eat something. I'll be here until two. Then I'll walk up to Saks to do some shopping."

Rocky said nothing, but when she peaked out the window five minutes later he was gone. Good boy, she thought and chuckled to herself. Directing a bodyguard amused her.

At two Kate packed up her work and left the club as she had promised. She noticed that Rocky was back looking inconspicuous and did not nod to him. She guessed that she had three or four hours to kill until a young working woman like Sandy Rasmussen would be arriving at her apartment. She spent the time in Saks and Bergdorf's viewing the latest fashions and thinking about the upcoming meeting with Sandy.

It seemed simple enough to meet Sandy and ask her about her roommate of last summer. She chatted with women each day about their experiences and relationships. Nevertheless, this meeting would be different. She had a mission to learn if Cynthia had taken drugs or befriended someone who might have conspired with her to steal Claire's paintings. She would have to be subtle but dogged. She might have only one chance to garner information to further Charlie's investigation. Unquestionably she wanted to help Charlie and Claire in an important way. Having volunteered to meet with Sandy alone, she pressured herself to deliver.

At four-thirty Kate hailed a cab to go to the West Side. Charlie had obtained Sandy Rasmussen's address from Cynthia's mother. The apartment was in a walk-up brownstone on West End Avenue in the eighties. Before ringing the bell, she decided to get a feel for the neighborhood. It was clearly a residential area with many large, doorman-serviced apartment buildings, delicatessens, ATM's, small grocery stores, commercial garages, schools, churches, and boutiques. Walking around, she saw a cross-section of elderly couples and young mothers with their children. Blacks, whites, Latinos, and Asians blended together on the sidewalks. Cars filled every parking place on the avenues and cross streets. The area was a busy, middle-class, residential urban neighborhood.

Eventually Kate returned to the address she had written down and mounted the stone steps to the front door and small vestibule. On the right wall were small mailboxes and twelve buzzers with nameplates next to them. S. Rasmussen lived in 3B.

Kate pressed the buzzer, but no one responded. Meanwhile, two residents had entered the vestibule, retrieved their mail, and used keys to unlock the door. Kate could have followed them into the building, but why enter if Sandy was out? Kate left and walked down the street half a block to wait. From her vantage point she saw four women enter the building over the next thirty minutes but had no idea if any of them was Sandy Rasmussen.

Thinking that it was possible that Sandy had returned, Kate climbed the stairs again and buzzed the apartment. This time a voice rewarded Kate's patience.

"Yes?"

"Hello, is this Sandy?"

"Yes, who is it?"

"My name is Kate Bailey. I am familiar with Cynthia Newgate and her family. I wonder if I might talk to you about her. I'll only be a minute or so."

After a moment of silence, the buzzer unlocked the door to Kate's left. She entered before Sandy could change her mind and climbed the stairs to the third floor, where 3B was in the back of the landing. The landing was empty except for two apartment doors with doorbells. Kate pushed the bell, and the door to 3B opened a crack.

A tall, light-skinned African-American woman in her twenties peeked out at Kate for a minute and then let her in the door.

"Come on in. The apartment is a mess. Sit on the couch over there. Can I get you coffee or water?"

"No, thank you. I'm quite all right," Kate said, recognizing a slight Caribbean accent.

She glanced around the small living room of what appeared to be a two-bedroom apartment. The kitchen had a pass-through to the room where she sat. The apartment was simply furnished with a dhuri rug and furniture one might find in a college dorm room or in the back of a Crate and Barrel store. Posters were on the walls of past art exhibitions in New York and Boston. One featured a Rastafarian musician who was probably Bob Marley. A TV, DVD player, and a stereo balanced on a Lucite table in the corner by the window suggested that this room was used a lot.

Sandy followed Kate and sat across from her on an upholstered chair. She was a strikingly beautiful woman—thin; marvelous clear skin; high cheekbones; large brown eyes; and long, lustrous black hair. Her clothes were simple with a brown belt, designer high-heeled shoes. Kate guessed she was a model or worked in the fashion business.

"Sandy, my husband, Charlie, was Cynthia's cousin. I hope you heard about her recent tragic death. We are here to learn more about her last year to try to make sense for her parents and her family of what happened to her. Frankly, we are confused. I hope you can help us."

"A friend of mine from Connecticut called last week and told me Cynthia had been murdered. She remembered that Cynthia had lived here last summer. I was shocked. Totally. So sorry."

"How did you come together as roommates?"

"Columbia. She was in my art classes for two years. We hit it off. Hung out together once in a while. After graduation I didn't see her until a friend of mine luckily told Cynthia that I needed a roommate. She was looking to come here to work in that East Side art gallery. So Cynthia called me and reminded me that we knew each other in college."

Kate was intrigued to hear Sandy speak—sounding educated with a slight island lilt and British clip. Definitely international, maybe Jamaican. She looked exotic and Kate wondered if she had seen her on the cover of a fashion magazine. She did look familiar. Of course, her name was incongruent. Sandy Rasmussen? Black? White? Swedish-American father?

"She moved in and was nice to have around—quiet, clean, paid the rent on time. We talked some but we had different lives. I had to travel a lot for shoots, so I'd say we didn't get to know each other well. The summer flew by really fast. I liked her but didn't know her, if you know what I mean?"

"Of course," Kate said.

"You could say she was a godsend. I haven't been able to find anyone since she went back to Yale. Frankly, the rent is killing me. Oh, that's a bad choice of words. I really feel sorry for Cynthia and your family."

"Thanks. Tell me more about last summer. We knew her mainly as an academic—completely into her work."

"That was Cynthia. She was very smart and knew art. She had what sounded like a great summer internship. She said the work was fascinating, and she was learning a lot. She certainly worked long hours over there."

'Cynthia wasn't a party person. Academics were her thing. She didn't hang out at bars or do the club scene. I love to. It helps me get jobs.'

"So she had no boyfriends?"

"Actually she did have at least two boyfriends, which I found surprising. Most of my friends would consider her boring and too focused on her career. Graduate students are like that, you know. Also fashion versus art history. Duh. Different."

"Oh, yes. Does that mean that her boyfriends were also in the art world?"

"One was. The other was from Yale. A chemist. He was also in grad school. I met him only once. Here."

"I think I know who you mean. But what about the one who was in the art world?"

"I never met him. Cynthia said she met someone from work. She said he was smart and handsome—an expert in her field. She fell for him but said very little about him. It could have been that some of her late nights were with him rather than at work at the gallery. She kept personal things to herself. And I guess I didn't ask her much."

"Do the names Ron Gelb or Larry Kendall mean anything to you?"

"No."

"Did Cynthia talk about her work at the gallery?"

"A little bit, but I was only half-listening. Sorry."

"Did you ever visit the Ludyard Gallery? Maybe she invited you to a reception or something?"

"I've gone by the gallery. Never been inside. I had a shoot at the Frick last fall. It was nearby. Art is not my thing anymore."

"Was there anyone else from the art world she talked about knowing or working with?"

"I don't remember anybody. I mean her idea of who she wanted to know were Monet, Degas, Cézanne. You know—dead, white guys." She laughed and played with her hair.

Kate sensed that she was somewhat nervous.

"Mary Cassatt?"

"Probably, too."

"Was she determined to own a painting by one of them?"

"What? Of course. Possible? No way. She had no coin. Look at this apartment. Not great. I work regularly and can barely pay the rent. New York is expensive. That gallery and Yale doesn't pay. Fuggetit."

Sandy had been animated and gesticulated with her hand to make her point. She had started out a bit bored with the conversation, but Kate sensed that she might now speak openly about more sensitive topics. First she had to get her to relax.

"I'm fascinated, hearing you speak," Kate said. "May I ask, are you Jamaican?"

"Part. My dad's American. Mom's Jamaican."

"You're a remarkable combination. Where in Jamaica?"

"Montego Bay—Mo'Bay for short."

"I've always wanted to visit there. Can you speak the patois?"

Sandy brightened up, smiling and pointing a finger up, "Yo, mon. No problem." Then "Come, Mr. Tally man tally me banana."

"Harry Belafonte," Kate responded laughing.

Sandy giggled. "When I started modeling, I had to drop the Jamaican talk and I even changed by working name. I'm Sandra."

"Upscale," Kate said. "Simple name model. Good. Well, Sandra. Let me change the subject to a delicate one—but important. Drugs. Some people have said that Cynthia's behavior changed over the last year. Did you see anything?"

"Drugs? Pills? I guess so. I remember one day seeing some pills on her dresser. I don't know what they were. As I said, I do the club scene a couple of times a week. Hope to get my picture taken. I see a lot of people taking pills. Bad stuff. I don't do it. Seen models with runny noses and passed out on assignment. Not me. Not worth it."

"Were you surprised that Cynthia had these pills? Maybe they were prescriptions?"

"I didn't see any prescription bottles. And she didn't act slick. Sometimes she was really tired and sometimes tense—kinda hyper like. But I didn't ask her about it. I figured she was going to be here only a few more weeks. It was her business."

"I take it that you saw these pills late in her time here?" asked Kate.

"Yes. Listen. A lot of people our age take drugs. I don't pass judgment—unless it messes with me or my work. Cynthia was okay."

"Did you have any idea where she could have bought those pills or have been given them?"

"Maybe on the street a few blocks from here. Maybe someone at work gave them to her. Who knows?"

"How did you end things with Cynthia? Did you part friends? Did she owe you anything?"

"We hugged and wished each other good luck. I have never talked to her after last August."

"By the way, have the police or FBI contacted you about Cynthia's death?"

Sandy sat up at this last question. Kate realized that Sandy had not connected the murder with the possibility that Cynthia's relationships and experiences in New York may have contributed to it. The FBI had not contacted her yet and she clearly did not welcome a visit. Kate guessed that Sandy was weighing the possibility that she might be in trouble in some way. At any rate, their conversation changed in character. Sandy was only willing to answer yes or no to Kate's questions. Kate realized that it was time to go. She thanked Sandy for her help today and for being a good roommate to Cynthia.

Kate walked down the brownstone's stairs and recognized Rocky across the street. She proceeded around the corner and stopped to evaluate the meeting. Cynthia and Sandy were opposite personalities but had put up with each other for a few months. The two substantive items Sandy had revealed were that Cynthia had been fond of an unknown man from work and that she used some non-prescription drugs. Kate sensed that these revelations would be important somehow to piecing together the mystery. Eager to tell Charlie what she had learned, she hailed a cab for the Carlyle. As she got in, she waved to the ever-present Rocky across the street and pointed toward the East Side.

* * *

Charlie welcomed Kate with a long kiss when she arrived at the room. He told her that he had an eventful day.

"So did I," Kate said excitedly. "You are going to be proud of me."

Charlie smiled and they both sat down on the couch. He said that she should go first. She described the exotic Sandy Rasmussen and then gushed out the news that Cynthia had a New York boyfriend, and as Charlie had reported from his visit from Yale, she was taking some kind of drugs—probably starting late in the summer.

"Do you think those two facts are related?" Charlie asked.

"Sandy didn't say, but the timing is suspect to me."

"Yes, indeed. You're pretty good at this questioning thing. We make a good pair."

Kate admitted to herself that the experience had been exhilarating. She was still opposed to Charlie being involved in a murder investigation, but she had enjoyed her part. She had been helpful. It had been fun.

Charlie then recounted his day. He mentioned Christina Hidalgo at the gallery, his lunch with Ron Gelb, and the chat he had with Francisco, the doorman. While there were no stunning revelations in his conversations, he surmised that with what Kate reported, Gelb had been either oblivious or was intentionally withholding the truth about Cynthia.

"I don't trust Gelb," Charlie concluded.

"Do you think he was the boyfriend?"

"Cynthia doesn't strike me as his type. He is more sophisticated and worldly than she was. Still, he may have had baser motives than a mutually romantic relationship."

"Like pure sex?"

"Or setting her up to conspire in a theft."

"Wow! That would be something."

"Stop me, Kate, if I throw these theories out there. There is no evidence that he was the boyfriend or that he encouraged her to experiment with drugs. I have a tendency to get ahead of myself."

"Okay, you are officially reprimanded: don't get ahead of the facts."

They laughed and agreed it was time to shower and get dressed for their dinner downstairs at the Café Carlyle. Charlie remembered that Rocky was still on duty and called his room to tell him that they did not need him any more that night.

A half hour later Charlie felt primed for a fun evening and escorted Kate down the elevator and around the corner to the nightclub restaurant.

* * *

"I think these tables and chairs were made for midgets," Charlie groused as he sat down. "Imagine if I were a football player."

"Now, now, Charlie. They are made for dainty women and their lean lovers. At least all the other tables are the same size. If you like, we could switch to the banquettes along the wall."

"No. I like where we are. I can wink at Barbara Cook. Not everybody can do that. Here's the waiter. I'll order two Kir Royales to begin."

Soon they had settled in, and the room began to fill. They had almost an hour before the show. The waiter brought their drinks and wedged the glasses between the small lamp and the salt and pepper shakers.

"I guess nothing has changed since I came here years ago as a student from New Haven to hear Bobby Short. He was the best cabaret singer ever. The famous murals are still on the wall–in the bar, the spotlights, the small stage—all for seventy to eighty diners like us jammed together."

"You really like this place. Nostalgia."

"Brings back memories of a misspent youth."

"Ha, I doubt you were so wild. Though tonight I must admit I share your concern as to where the waiter will place our plates when dinner arrives. Maybe we'll eat on our laps."

Miraculously, when dinner arrived the waiter expertly found room for the plates—including the butter plates. All went well, so Kate and Charlie could focus on the talent and songs of Barbara Cook.

"Great entertainer, remarkable voice," Kate declared. "I love Broadway and café tunes. We have to come back next time."

"A perfect ending to a good day. I tell you what. Once I pay, let's take a walk outside. It's a beautiful night. We can look at the stars and apartment lights in the tall buildings."

"Sounds magical," Kate purred.

They left the hotel through the Madison Avenue door. This entrance had no doorman but was closest to the Café. Charlie put his arm around Kate's shoulders, and she held his wrist. They both looked up to the sky and walked slowly on the sidewalk. Taxis buzzed by heading north on the Avenue taking people home from the theaters and restaurants. Suddenly without warning Charlie and Kate were hit in the back by a powerful body block, which sent them both off their feet and stumbling into the street and traffic. Charlie's body pushed Kate forward in front of him and down into the pavement and over the curb. Charlie also fell and rolled onto Kate. A speeding cab braked before them and swerved out towards the middle of the street. It never stopped but straightened out and drove up the avenue. Kate and Charlie scrambled back towards the sidewalk, desperately trying to avoid the cars.

Kate was scared but felt no pain initially. Pedestrians arrived, asking if they were all right. Charlie bent over Kate and attempted to help her up. After a couple of minutes they both were able to stand. Their clothes were stained and torn. Kate began to feel pain from the cuts on her hands, knees and face. Blood drained down her hands and legs.

"Are you okay, Kate?" Charlie asked. "That was close. Some asshole hit me from behind. I'm sorry I bumped you out into the street."

"I'll be fine in awhile," Kate said bravely. "I'm more frightened than injured. Did you see who it was?"

"No, he was gone by the time I stood up. He may have turned the corner. Let me take you to the emergency room. There is a hospital nearby,"

"I'd rather not. Maybe the hotel has some antiseptic and bandages. Also a pain killer."

By that time a doorman and the hotel security man had arrived. The Baileys followed them back inside for treatment. Kate limped along and became increasingly angry. That was no accident, she thought. Someone wanted to hurt us.

Chapter Twenty

"Katie, I'm so sorry," Charlie apologized for the third time since they had gotten up in the morning at the hotel. "I'm so stupid and bullheaded. It never occurred to me that you could be hurt. Why did we go outside? Why did I excuse Rocky?"

Charlie was sitting directly opposite from Kate on their plane. He held her bandaged hand on the little folding table between them. Kate's head, cheek, and knees were also bandaged. Most of the injuries were scrapes, but Charlie had called ahead to her internist to make an appointment for her after they landed. They wanted to be certain there was no concussion and the wounds had been treated properly by the hotel doctor.

Kate was obviously in pain, which explained her subdued mood. Nevertheless, she did not blame Charlie.

"We went outside because we were both feeling good after our conversations during the day and Barbara Cook. If I thought for one second that we were going to be in danger, I would have said no. Still, I hurt all over. I would love to get a hold of the guy who pushed us. That's who I blame."

"We'll get him," Charlie said, trying to console her. He was furious at himself for not reacting quicker during the incident to see who had hit him. All he was certain of was that the assailant must have been a strong man to hit him with such force. If only Rocky had been there, Charlie was convinced that the man would not have escaped.

Unfortunately, "if only's" do not count.

Despite his assurances to Kate, he knew that locating the attacker was a remote possibility. He had described the incident to the police officer the hotel had called in. Nevertheless, unless an eyewitness appeared, the police had little to pursue. The man was gone. The attack had to be related to their investigating. Kate had said so as well. Someone was extremely serious about scaring them off. Therefore, they must be doing something right. They had either talked directly to someone involved in the theft and murder or by their actions had alerted the guilty one that they were getting close to him. If that person thought he could intimidate Charlie, he was mistaken. Charlie was only more resolute. Kate might be a different story. She had reluctantly agreed to participate in his investigation. Now she was injured. Charlie knew she was one tough lady when pushed. She could be resilient and firm. But now he was not sure how she would react. However, he would wait until she wanted to talk about her view of the situation. First he had to ensure that she was going to be all right. Then he had to see where she stood.

When they arrived in Chicago, they were met by a limo driver who took them directly to her doctor. After he examined Kate and treated her abrasions, he told her to stay home for a few days to confirm his opinion that her head injuries were only superficial. He said she could talk to her office but be sure to take the prescribed pain medications. He also dressed Charlie's scrapes and told him to take it easy. Of course Charlie had no intention of staying out of the office. His injuries would have to be much worse before he would stay home. Right or wrong, that was the way it was. First though, he accompanied Kate home.

With Kate sitting on the couch next to a phone in their apartment, Charlie asked her if she minded if he went to his office

"Go make some money. I'll be fine. I have my pills. Remember to bring home some dinner. I'm not cooking tonight. Take Rocky with you and be careful."

In the taxi downtown, Charlie fumed at himself. He had messed up and was not sure if Kate blamed him for what happened to her. If she did, she was justified. He owed her a lot. She was so positive and excited the night before at dinner. Now time would tell. The sooner he finished his investigation the better. He needed to work harder and faster.

As he walked into his office, his good intentions became waylaid by events.

"Charlie, I'm glad you are here," said Ben Watenabe, one of his senior portfolio managers. "The Middle East is blowing up. Israel went into Gaza and shot missiles at Iran. The stock market is down a thousand points."

"Damn it. Staff meeting in the big conference room in ten minutes. Portfolio managers, analysts, and head traders. Ben, notify everyone."

Major events resulting in huge valuation changes in the financial markets happen rarely, but when they do, investment management firms like Charlie's have to drop all the daily, mundane chores they must perform to regroup and evaluate the significance and impact of the new development. Charlie understood immediately that such an event was taking place. War in the Middle East brought into play alliances among major powers, religious passions, critical economic factors such as energy production, and potential large-scale loss of life. Above all, wars brought uncertainly, and financial markets hate uncertainty. Investors have to recalibrate risk leading to exploding volatility. High volatility means that portfolio values jump up and down significantly.

Charlie's immediate concern was for the firm's clients. They would be nervous and upset. They would want to know how these new events would affect their investments and future well-being. They would look to the investment managers they are paying to make sense of confusion and, in spite of all that is happening, to have a plan to meet their objectives and needs—and then to communicate that plan calmly and articulately.

Charlie and his team had faced similar challenges. They were professionals, but that did not mean it became easier each time. It just meant that they knew what questions to ask, what were the range of outcomes, and how to talk to frightened clients. They all knew that before anything they had to meet together and agree on a common viewpoint. The worst course of action would be for each portfolio manager to take individual positions that could result in the firm voicing conflicting messages to the client base. As always Charlie was determined to avoid disparate communications. Everyone would be encouraged in the meeting to express his opinion on what to do and say. Ultimately, however, Charlie's task would be to reduce their judgments to a consensus that everyone could endorse.

As Charlie thought through this process of coming to the firm's position and communicating it to the hundreds of clients personally, he knew his resolution to focus on the murder investigation was doomed. His top priority had to be the business crisis. Solving a crime was important—but not today or tomorrow—even though he felt competent and motivated to pursue his investigation. Indeed, because of the attack in New York, he had more incentive than ever. He was, however, beginning to understand the weakness in being an amateur sleuth—he could not focus full time. His family and job took precedence. Damn the Israelis, the Palestinians, and the Iranians. The investigation was on the back burner for now.

The meeting with his staff went surprisingly fast, considering the magnitude of the decision. Charlie put forward his analysis of what happened and what they should do. There were few dissents. The consensus view was that the new conflict would last several weeks, that the superpowers in the world would successfully pressure Israel and Iran to cease hostilities, and that the stock markets would initially sell off but recover partially as a cease-fire became more likely. However, longer term investors would be more cautious than before, because the situation in the Middle East and the world in general was now more unstable and uncertain. Charlie's investment team would adjust client portfolios to increase cash, defense and oil stock holdings and sell down stocks with high valuations. Simultaneously, they would call each client, explain their planned actions, and urge calm.

As Charlie left the conference room to return to his office, he saw Rocky sitting in the lobby with his head hung down. Charlie knew from the conversation at the hotel this morning that Rocky was dispirited by the news of the attack on the Baileys. The one chance he would have had to prove himself had occurred without him.

"Rocky, come into my office," said Charlie, determined to make his bodyguard feel better. Rocky said nothing but stood up and followed Charlie—never changing his hangdog expression.

"It wasn't your fault. I told you to leave us alone for the night. Clearly, if you had been there, you would have nailed the guy."

"No, boss. I should've been there. I could've waited until you and Mrs. Bailey went to bed. Bad job by me."

"Forget it. Water under the bridge. What's important is to look ahead." Charlie smiled at the sour-looking security guard.

"I'll get the bastard," Rocky vowed with emotion.

"I wouldn't want to be him when you find him. Now, if you excuse me, I have several phone calls to make. The world fell apart this afternoon. We'll talk later."

Charlie liked Rocky. The man was diligent and made no excuses. He had no doubt that when Rocky learned who attacked Kate and himself, he would show no mercy. That prospect amused Charlie.

The current chaotic situation—Kate injured, the markets in turmoil, and his investigation on hiatus temporarily, energized Charlie. He thrived in tumult. He hated routine. He enjoyed being the captain of the ship when the winds were blowing all out and the seas were tossing the hull up and down, right and left. In such times Charlie would recite the lines from his favorite poem, Henley's *Invictus*: "I am the master of my fate. I am the captain of my soul." Today's challenge was tomorrow's history lesson.

In such a state, the afternoon and client calls flew by for him. Only when he entered his apartment building after work did his confidence falter. He was unsure if Kate was feeling better and how she would receive him. He should have called her. Granted, he had been distracted by the client calls, but that was not a good enough excuse.

Charlie found Kate in the big, brown leather armchair with a pile of magazines strewn on the rug.

"Welcome home, my handsome husband. I missed you. How was your day?"

Charlie leaned down, kissed her lips, and then stepped back to look at her. Oddly enough, she never looked so attractive to him. The bandages on her head and hands aroused a tenderness in him and her ponytail, blue jeans, man's shirt with the sleeves rolled up, and bare feet excited him in another way. She was wearing an outfit that he found extremely sexy. He doubted that she intended to look sexy, but the effect on him was the same.

"All hell broke loose at the office, but how are you?"

"I saw the news. I sympathize for what you had to do. Me? I'm feeling much better. I even felt up to calling my office and doing some work that they pay me so poorly for."

"You do sound better. Can you forgive me?"

"Forgive you? You probably saved my life by falling on top of me. Usually when you are in that position, we aren't in the street."

"You must be feeling better. Let me know when you are really in a good mood. I can be ready."

"Thanks, Romeo. Maybe in a day or two. On a more serious matter. I know I have had mixed emotions about your investigation. I thought the whole thing was too dangerous. Obviously it has become dangerous. Still, now I want you to get that guy. How dare he try to kill us? I just think that we should have all the help we can get. Promise you'll tell that Jackie Farrell what happened."

Kate said this while looking Charlie straight in the eyes. She was serious and persuasive. Charlie understood that she was buying into the investigation completely but that the price was that he stop ignoring the FBI. He knew she was right.

* * *

Keeping his promise, Charlie tried to reach Jackie Farrell from the office the first thing in the morning. She did not answer, so he left his cell phone number on her machine.

He spent the next day and a half executing trades and talking to clients on the phone. Their response was uniformly supportive of the program he outlined. They had lots of questions and concerns, but they trusted Charlie and appreciated his contacting them.

Midday on Thursday Kathy, his secretary, announced that Charlie's mother was on the phone and sounded upset.

"Mother, what's the matter?"

"Dear, I received a letter today. Only it was just an envelope. It was filled with a white powder. No note. Very strange. Do you think it has anything to do with the other nasty note?"

"Did you touch the powder?"

"Yes. I tried tasting it—sort of bland."

Charlie's mind raced through the multiple meanings of an envelope full of powder. Alarms were sounding. Anthrax? Ricin? He had read about terrorist attempts to poison populations with powdery forms of toxins.

"Mother, go immediately to the emergency room of Lake Forest Hospital. I'm leaving now to meet you there. Have Stan put on gloves and put the envelope in a plastic bag. No one is to touch the powder directly. The hospital will have to do tests to determine what the powder is. This is serious but try to keep your calm. Okay? Also, write down the postmark."

"Charlie, you scare me."

Chapter Twenty-One

When Charlie entered the Lake Forest Hospital emergency room, he looked out of place in his business suit next to the doctors, nurses, and patients with their casually attired relatives. As he followed directions to his mother's location, he noticed Stan and James seated out in the waiting room and nodded to them. He found his mother dressed in a hospital gown and lying on a bed behind a curtain. She looked fine, but an IV line was attached to her arm.

"Mother, how are you?" He bent down and kissed her cheek. "Have you seen a doctor?"

"I feel fine. The doctors don't know what to do with me. My vitals are good, but they need tests to determine what the powder is. It looked like talcum to me. But what do I know? I'm just an old lady."

"A very important lady to Kate and me. What happened with the envelope?"

"It was in the mail I received this morning. I opened the envelope and the powder spilled out on my hands. As I went to the hall bathroom to clean my hands, I tasted some to see what it was. I guess I shouldn't have done that."

Charlie waited with his mother for most of the next hour. They talked about Kate's injuries and the fire drill going on at his office since Tuesday. He left her for a few minutes to talk to Stan and James to see if either of them had had skin contact with the powder or had breathed the powder in the air. They both replied negatively. Shortly after he returned to his mother's bedside, a youngish doctor wearing glasses came in with a smile on his face.

"Good news. Someone was playing a practical joke, and a not very funny one. The chemist says the powder is a combination of cornstarch and zinc oxide. In other words, baby powder. Harmless. Mrs. Bailey, you may go home. It's fortunate that the powder wasn't a toxin like ricin. We would have had to send you to Northwestern Hospital in downtown Chicago. So all's well that ends well."

"Doctor, do you suppose my mother could take home that envelope?"

"Of course. It's in the plastic bag she brought at the nurse's station. We don't need it."

Charlie thanked the doctor and the nurses on the way out and drove his mother home in his car. While they were driving, Claire Bailey was reflective, "Son, I don't know if I can take all this excitement: threats, theft, murder, assaults. I feel old. I saw Dr. Jensen, my cardiologist, earlier this week. He said that I have a leaky valve. I'll need more than duct tape to fix it. I'm taking medication but I may need surgery. I'm supposed to avoid stress. Fat chance now. This envelope was another threat, wasn't it?"

"Yes, another scare tactic. He wants us to know how serious he is. He certainly has my attention."

"Nasty person. Why did you ask for the envelope? The mere sight of it gives me the shakes."

"I'm sorry, Mother. I'm going to give it to the FBI. I also wanted to look at the postmark. Based on where it was mailed, we might have a connection to a suspect. Unfortunately, it is not very helpful. Stamford, Connecticut—about halfway between New York and New Haven."

Charlie pulled into the driveway and parked in front of the imposing house. He helped his mother inside as Stan and James arrived.

"I suggest you take a nap," Charlie said tenderly.

"I will. I will. What are you going to do now? You mentioned the FBI. We need their help."

"I called just yesterday. They owe me a return call, but I'll call again after I talk to Kate. I talked to her on the way up. She'll want to know how you are."

"She's a dear girl at heart. Now I will go to bed," Claire announced. She kissed Charlie and headed for the stairs.

Charlie sat down in the library and called Kate. She picked up immediately—as if she was waiting by the phone. Charlie assured her that his mother was exhausted but fine. The powder was a hoax, undoubtedly intended to scare them.

Kate said, "I'm so relieved. I have wonderful news. Hugh Vance called for you a few minutes ago and said that the Childe Hassam painting is coming back to Yale."

Charlie was incredulous at the news. An hour before his mother might be dying and now the lost painting was being recovered. What a change in his emotions—fear to joy! He had run the gamut of feelings. He needed details.

"What did he say? How did it happen?"

"A middleman approached the gallery and said that they had a client who was offering to sell the Hassam painting back to Yale." Hugh explained that he was eager to do the transaction but that he had to get approval from the insurance company first. Apparently that was no problem. The company agreed to the price contingent on the good condition of the painting. He said this all happened yesterday. They should have the painting in a week or ten days."

"Did he mention a price? And what about the Degas sketch?"

"I forgot to ask about the price. Does it matter? Oh, I did ask about the sketch. He said that it was not offered. Vance says he guesses that the thieves didn't think it was worth much. Maybe he is right. I don't know. I really liked it."

"Maybe the thieves will offer it after the Hassam is back. Did Vance talk to any of the thieves directly—or just to the middleman?"

"He didn't say. You need to call him. He wants to talk to you. I will say he was quite full of himself. After all the criticism he endured, I imagine he is a happy man."

"I have his number and will call him immediately. All is well with you?"

"The prospect that this nightmare may be over perks me up. I am a little confused of course. Why scare Claire if the thief is returning the painting? Why shove us into traffic? This guy strikes me as basically cruel. Who knows? Tell your mother the news and call Mr. Vance."

Charlie decided to let his mother sleep. She needed the rest. This turn of events was unexpected. Everyone from Seth Price to Jackie Farrell to Ron Gelb had warned him that the probability of seeing the paintings back soon was near zero. He had no explanation. Maybe the thief was concerned that the investigation was coming too close to him and that the return of the painting would end the probe. Maybe the thief just wanted to cash in and surmised that he could pull off the ransom with impunity, or maybe the transaction was all a deception—like the baby powder. I wonder.

High Vance picked up Charlie's call after the first ring and enthusiastically repeated what he had told Kate. Charlie detected a boastfulness in his account, which likely overstated Vance's role. Nevertheless, Charlie was willing to forgive him if the *Flags* painting physically changed hands.

"This middleman, do you know him?" asked Charlie.

"It was Ronald Boothby of Art Anonymous in New York. That company maintains a database of stolen art to rival those of the FBI, Interpol, and the Art Loss Registry in London. They also help negotiate the return of stolen art—for a commission, of course. Knowledgeable thieves know where to go. Boothby was acquainted with our missing painting and thought the price was fair. When I told him Chubb was our insurer, he said that was a positive. In his opinion, Chubb was reasonable and sophisticated. So after our insurance man talked to the claims adjuster at Chubb, I called back Boothby, and the deal was done. The whole transaction took only an hour and a half yesterday afternoon. Boothby stayed at his office quite late to accommodate us."

"I assume Boothby did not reveal the identity of the other side."

"Of course not. No one talks. That way those returns are possible. Art Anonymous provides a useful service."

"Of course. But what about the Cassatt sketch?"

"It was not offered. I asked Boothby, and he said he would ask about it to the other side, but it is not available at this point."

"Do you have a theory as to why it is not available?"

"No. It is only worth a fraction of the *Flags* painting, but it is worth something. I'll ask when we talk again next time. The public will be excited by the two paintings we do have. Your father's memory will be honored very appropriately."

"I may be a pest, but I would like to see the original gift intact."

"We'll try. Now I must be off to a meeting. If you want to talk further, I'll be in the office tomorrow. Goodbye, Mr. Bailey."

Charlie reflected on this conversation and was impressed by the speed of this transaction. Nothing had happened for weeks and then suddenly the painting was coming back to Yale. He wondered if the police or FBI had anything to do with this arrangement. He wondered what they thought of the Ronald Boothbys of the world?

Charlie did not have time to wait for his mother to wake up. He left her a detailed note instead and promised to call her that night. He had to return to the office to ascertain how the calls were going, and he wanted to be with Kate to see how she was feeling.

The anticipated recovery of the *Flags* painting was a marvelous event. Why didn't he feel fulfilled? To the art world Yale now had the two important works of art. The sketch was only a footnote to Mary Cassatt's work. Cynthia Newgate was dead, but then it seems she had been a collaborator in a theft. If she were alive and arrested, she would be ostensibly going to jail. Charlie could understand if some people felt that the incident was over. Time to give Peaches his exclusive.

But, Charlie was not satisfied. He was not done. Certainly the Newgates wouldn't be satisfied. Justice demanded that the thief and killer be caught, return the sketch, and pay for the seduction and murder of his ingenuous cousin.

Late in the afternoon, Jackie Farrell finally called Charlie back at his office.

"Mr. Bailey, do you have something for me?"

"I was going to ask you the same question. Failing that, I should tell you that the Hassam painting is being ransomed by Yale."

"I heard that an hour ago from the New Haven Police. Good news. It's rare that a stolen work of art is offered back so quickly. Yale's lucky, although the recovery was very costly. You and your mother must be happy. Now you can get on with your lives."

Charlie looked at his phone in disbelief. Jackie Farrell couldn't be serious.

"Is that it? Are you finished? Do you care about Cynthia's murder or the sketch?"

"Of course. We'll talk to our contact at Art Anonymous. We may be able to find out something about the seller. I believe if the transfer of the painting goes well, the sketch will be offered next. Why would the thief leave something valuable on the table? I just meant that whatever your efforts, we can handle everything from here in the future."

Charlie rolled his eyes in disbelief. What had the FBI accomplished? They were just lucky that the thief decided to cash in now. In a fit of pique because he felt as if Jackie was dismissing him, Charlie began to detail what he and Kate had done since he last talked to her. He mentioned visits with Jacob Stern, Larry Kendall, John Hamilton, Susan Parker, Ron Gelb, and Sandy Rasmussen. He also describing the threats and attacks on his mother, Kate, and himself.

"My, you have been busy," Jackie responded sounding sarcastic. "I told you to stop playing detective. If you had listened, no one would have attacked you. You obviously struck a nerve. I was trying to look out for your safety. However, since you did these interviews and may have had contact, however unauthorized, with someone who wanted you to back off, let me ask you what you learned?"

Charlie seethed. He was angry with her attitude but was also mad at himself for telling her so much. His emotions had gotten the best of him. Still, if he were to solve the case out of harm's way, he needed the FBI. Reluctantly, he mentioned Larry Kendall's statements on Cynthia's drug usage and Sandy Rasmussen's confirmation of the same. He added Sandy's comments about a possible amorous relationship with someone at work. He also highlighted Gelb's minimizing his contacts with Cynthia. Charlie concluded his review by stating that he was convinced that Gelb knew more about Cynthia's life than the man was saying.

"You have been busier than I thought. Of course we have interviewed most of the same people. Have you concluded anything from all this work?"

"Concluded? No. Nevertheless, I do have some theories."

"First, the drug angle," he continued. "I know that Cynthia was a workaholic and a straight arrow. I could see how she might have started taking drugs to keep up her work pace. I doubt she was using them for any weight problem. Then, if she began to rely on the pills, someone might have manipulated her—especially if she was reluctant to go to a doctor for more pills. Her conservative parents wouldn't have approved. She was smart and may have hidden her condition at work. Her colleagues were accustomed to see her grind it out. But addicts need their fixes. If she developed her interest in drugs in New York, perhaps someone who had ulterior motives may have been her source and continued to supply her when she returned to Yale."

"Okay, but what would the ulterior motives be? Sex, money, something else?"

"Sex, maybe last summer. Money—no, while her parents are relatively affluent, she had nothing to pay for a drug habit. Our donation—maybe she became more interesting to someone in the art world when she started talking about our gift: new paintings worth a lot."

"I see. That would imply that someone in the art world—maybe from Ludyard Gallery or elsewhere in New York, became her source and co-conspirator. Maybe Mr. Gelb, whom you don't like. But why him? My research card says he is doing well at his uncle's art gallery. Owns an apartment on Park Avenue. Great education. Most art thieves we see are shady characters—low lifes."

"Maybe he is living beyond his means. Maybe his uncle doesn't pay well. Greed has no limits."

"So, a Svengali theory. Any others?"

"From your tone, I doubt you are interested. Despite your plodding approach to this case, you probably already have enough evidence to bring to trial the killer and return the sketch. I'll read about it in the papers. Congratulations," Charlie said slamming down the phone.

* * *

Bailey messed up my plan. It would have been safer and I would have been able to get a higher price if I could have waited for the interest in the theft to die down and for prices in the market to increase. But he was getting too close with his questions. The police and the FBI were going nowhere from what I could see. If Bailey was talking to them, things could get hot.

I tried to scare him off—the letters and the body block. Most people would have stopped. Bailey is pig-headed. Maybe it runs in the family. Cynthia was a problem from time to time. The amphetamines did the trick though. First, the Adderall I had from a prescription. She took to it. She had a tendency to be depressed and tired. The Adderall picked her up and helped her concentrate. No danger there. A legal drug. Probably a third of the students in New Haven took it or Ritalin. Once she told me about the paintings that her boss was negotiating to come to Yale, I knew I needed something more powerful. There had to be a balance. I needed her dependent but she couldn't look like a drugee. A little speed every so often worked and made her a borderline addict. I would have fed her more powerful stuff if she had not gone along with my scheme. No need. She got me in the door.

The Art Anonymous deal worked well. They did all the work. I feel safe because this is a big business for them. They can't afford to rat on anyone. My check will go to the Cayman Island Corporation and then to Switzerland. They will pick up the painting wrapped in brown paper in the Grand Central Station storage bin after I mail them the key. The painting is in mint condition—thanks to Mrs. Bailey.

The other little treasure I'll hang on to. I don't want them looking at it too closely. After all, the Hassam was essentially a red herring.

Chapter Twenty-Two

After hanging up on Jackie Farrell, Charlie dialed Marty O'Connell's cell phone. Marty was the only police source he felt comfortable with. Farrell only irritated him. While Marty was restricted in what he could reveal, he had been open to confirming points that Charlie raised.

"Marty, the Yale Police must be thrilled that the Hassam painting is coming back. Kudos."

"How did you hear, Charlie?"

"High Vance called me with the good news. The thieves must have been nervous holding a hot item like that painting. You and the FBI must have been too close to them for comfort."

"I wouldn't say that. The offer came out of the blue. We are happy to recover the art, but the University is out the deductible, and the insurance company is out a lot more money. We still need to catch the thieves. More important, there's the girl. No celebrations with an unsolved murder."

Charlie was glad to hear that last statement. The theft of the painting was an expensive loss and a temporary blot on the university's reputation, but a dead student was much more serious.

"That's correct. Have you made any further progress on Cynthia's death?"

"Nothing I can talk about."

"One thing I heard is she was taking drugs. That might explain her behavior. Have you found that to be the case?"

"It's in the medical examiner's report. He found evidence of Benzedrine in her system. The arsenic killed her—not the amphetamine. It's hard to say how the drug affected her before her death. Lots of graduate students take bennies and speed. Helps them cope with pressure. You need a prescription normally, but it is also easy to get on the street."

"I'm sorry to hear that she used drugs. Would you have told her parents?"

"No, unless they asked. I'm not sure it's relevant to her death."

"So where do you go from here?"

"We continue to work with the New Haven PD and the FBI. We need a break—like a credible witness or forensic evidence."

Charlie thanked Marty for his unit's continued work and wished them success in finding that breakthrough. After he hung up, Charlie reflected that he was lucky to be able to talk to Marty. It would have been easy for Jackie Farrell to confirm Cynthia's drug use, but she clearly did not want to reveal anything to me. She was content to have him talk about things he had learned, but it was a very one-way street. He had not convinced her that there was value in a partnership between himself and the FBI. He would just have to try to stay one step ahead of them. Maybe later they would want to want to work with him.

Considering Kate's condition Charlie decided to order in dinner from the Racquet Club, which was just a handful of blocks away from their apartment. He picked up the food on his way home. When he arrived, he checked on Kate and learned that, while she looked terrible with her bruises, she was feeling much better—so well, in fact, that she said that she would go to work the next day.

"Don't push it," Charlie advised her as he set the table and opened a bottle of ten-year-old Château Pavie.

For the first time in three days her appetite was good and she even took a sip of wine. They talked at length about Claire and her second scare in a week and focused on the lamentable effect this strain might be having on her health.

"If we could only get her to take a vacation with one of her friends, she might put the current unpleasantness out of her mind," Charlie said. "Unfortunately she's a stubborn old bird. She won't be happy until all the art is recovered and Cynthia's killer is in jail."

"Did she brighten up when you called her about the one painting coming back?"

"She did perk up a bit. Nevertheless, she also asked about the sketch and the prospects for catching the thief. Still, for someone who has lived such a charmed life, these topics depress her. She insists that you and I are at risk. She wants it all to end."

"We have to encourage her to talk to her cardiologist regularly," Kate insisted.

"Agreed."

Charlie then summarized his conversations with Jackie Farrell and Marty. He did not hide his irritation with the former and his fondness for the latter.

"Farrell's attitude was 'take your painting and go home'. She criticized me for interviewing everyone we did. She said that if you were assaulted, it was your own fault. Friendly lady."

"She doesn't like us. Did you get any credit for what you unearthed?"

"She did show a little interest in a drug motive for Cynthia," Charlie admitted. "She also asked about Gelb. I wouldn't be surprised if she follows up on him."

"Did she say anything about the sketch?"

"She thinks that after the Hassam arrives, the thieves will call about the sketch. She implied that the return of the sketch was a given in time—an anticlimactic event."

"Since you told me this afternoon that only the Hassam painting was offered to Yale, I have been thinking about the sketch and that writing on the back. It's curious that the thief split them up. As you always tell me, I'm the suspicious type. I pulled out that enlargement you had made, which was sitting in a pile on your desk. Let me get it."

She returned with a manila file and sat down at the dinner table in the kitchen. She took out the photograph of the backside of the sketch of the dying Degas and a sheet of paper with the top half in French and a translation underneath.

"As you can see, the writing on the back of the photograph is a bit hard to read," said Kate. "Mary Cassatt's handwriting is not clear. It's as if she was jotting down a list in a hurry. I typed out on my computer my best guess of what was written. My English translation is below. When I saw *washing*, *breakfast, fruit, dancers,* and *the Louvre,* I assumed it was a list of things to do or places to visit. However, this afternoon I remembered that there was a better translation. To make sure, I found that large coffee table book you have on Degas and leafed through the illustrations. I saw the same words in the titles of several paintings and sculptures. Clearly this is a list of artworks by Degas and one by Cézanne. Just look. Each painting is described as a pastel, charcoal, or oil. It's obvious. We didn't pay much attention to this before, but in light of the sketch being withheld, this list may be important."

While Kate was talking, Charlie was studying the two papers. Everything Kate said made sense to him.

"You're right about the lists. Actually, it looks like two separate lists—one *JF* and one *ZC.* Any idea what the initials or abbreviations mean?"

"I have a guess," said Kate, becoming more excited. "Your Degas book mentioned that he had a niece, Jeanne Fèvre, who came to Paris to take care of him toward the end: *JF.* He also had a housekeeper, Zoë Closier: *ZC.* A coincidence? More than that."

The Photograph – French

JF
Petite Danseuse de Quatorze Ans - sculpture (cire)

ZC
Danseuse à la Barre - pastel
Les Blanchisseuses (Le Repassage) - pastel
La Toilette (Le Bain) - pastel
Portrait de l'Artiste - fusain
La Chanteuse - pastel
Le Petit Déjeuner Après le Bain - pastel
Au Louvre - pastel
Nature Morte aux Fruits - peinture à l'huile (Cézanne)

Translation

<u>JF</u>
Small 14-year-old Female dancer – sculpture (wax)

<u>ZC</u>
Female Dancer at the Barre/Handrail – pastel
The Female Laundress (Ironing) – pastel
The Washing and Dressing (Bath) – pastel
Portrait of the Artist – charcoal sketch
The Female Singer – pastel
Breakfast After the Bath – pastel
At the Louvre Museum – pastel
Still Like of Fruits – oil painting (Cézanne)

"I like your guess, Kate," said Charlie. "You're clever. Why not? Maybe Cassatt was indicating some things that the two women liked or that they were to do something to the pictures—clean them or store them. Or maybe Degas gave them to them."

"At today's prices—pretty fancy gifts."

"Right. But I don't know what they were worth then. It is only a guess. Did you see that one of the paintings seems to be by Cézanne? I wonder what that means."

"I suppose an art historian might be able to make something out of these lists," said Kate.

Charlie smiled. "You mean like Cynthia Newgate?"

"Of course, Cynthia would have been able to explain what the lists meant. Art historians probably spend days and weeks discussing this sort of minutiae. Original research and intellectual trivia."

"Do you suppose these lists have anything to do with the theft?" Kate asked.

"I can't imagine how. So what if his sister and housekeeper received some paintings? Let's send the file to Seth Price. He knows people who are experts on Degas. Let's see what they say."

"Great. You know I am curious. The lists do seem to add a colorful side story to this piece. When Yale gets it back, maybe they will add the list to its description of the sketch."

Kate picked up the translation sheet and continued to look at it.

"Not satisfied?" asked Charlie, seeing a puzzled look on Kate's face.

"There still has to be a reason the sketch was separated from the painting."

* * *

The next morning Charlie called Seth Price at his Northwestern University office and asked him for his help in explaining what the lists meant. He had messengered the file up that morning to Evanston. Seth said he would pass it along to someone in the department who was intimate with the Impressionists.

"Seth, while I have you on the line, I want your opinion of a gallery in New York. I visited it last week and need to know its reputation. It is the Ludyard Gallery; the principals I talked to were Jacob Stern and his nephew, Ron Gelb. The gallery specializes in European and American paintings, 1850 to 1930."

"I've heard the name, but I'll have to ask around. I'm sure I can get a handle on both the gallery and its people. I'll call you back in a day or two."

An hour later, Hugh Vance called to tell Charlie that the Childe Hassam painting would be in New Haven at the end of next week. He reassured Charlie that Yale would employ special security measures in receiving it and storing it. He went on to report that there was still no offer to return the sketch. The lack of an offer puzzled him, but he was hopeful it would come soon. He said that he had already talked to the insurance company about it, and Chubb was being very accommodating.

Sensing a conclusion of this sorry affair, Charlie wondered if he should mention the handwritten list on the back of the sketch and then impulsively decided to go ahead.

"Did you know that Mary Cassatt wrote a list of Degas paintings on the back of the sketch?"

"No, I don't remember that. I only recall viewing the actual sketch."

"Is it unusual that an artist would write on the back of a sketch?"

"With a sketch, an artist might do anything. By nature a sketch is informal. Cassatt probably drew it in a few minutes—perhaps to pass the time of day when Degas was sleeping or incoherent. He was quite sick, you know."

"Would the handwriting make it more valuable or less?"

"It would depend on what the artist wrote. If it is just a list of some of Degas's paintings, it probably neither adds nor subtracts from the value. Of course, I shall take a look at the backside when we recover it."

During the next couple of hours, Charlie was on the phone constantly with clients. The stock market had continued to go down during the week, and the clients were understandably nervous. The calls took time, but the conversations were substantive and congenial. It was fulfilling to be helpful.

Still, when he received the call slip that Professor Price had phoned, Charlie made that the next call.

"Seth, I am talking to you twice in one day. I would have thought you would be off on an early start to the weekend," Charlie joked.

He took out a legal pad to take a note.

"The search for truth by us academicians takes no holiday. Charlie, to change the subject, I see that the markets are down. Is it time to sell? Should I move my paltry academic retirement fund over to you before I lose everything? I know nothing about finance and I panic easily."

"I'd be happy to look at your retirement fund, but didn't your mother tell you? We already have your family's trusts here. I know you are doing fine on those. Next time I talk to your mother, I'll suggest she bring you up-to-date."

"Don't worry. I know you people are doing well by my family. My mother likes to talk. She couldn't keep a secret on a bet. I was just joking. Now let me get to your questions. First, the lists. I gave the file you sent to Irene, our expert on the Impressionists. You know I am capable of commenting only on the Italian Renaissance. She came back to me immediately—amazing considering the work she did. I guess she was fascinated by the sketch: Cassatt drawing Degas in the deathbed. Not a bad drawing either—considering that Cassatt had cataracts at the time. Irene told me that Cassatt had two surgeries on her eyes, but both times the surgeries failed.'

"Irene looked at the photograph on the backside and opined that, although the handwriting is difficult to decipher, those are titles of paintings and sculptures that Degas might have done. Curious, she went to her reference books to see if she could find the same works of art. Apparently Degas did several sculptures and paintings with the same names. Some of the titles on the list matched with known works. She conjectured that the lists might be a partial inventory of what was in Degas's apartment. She said Degas was famous for not wanting to sell his own work and for collecting the work of his friends and contemporaries. For instance, that Cézanne still life on the list was typical of what Degas bought and saved.'

"Am I going too fast, Charlie? We do this kind of research all the time."

"No, I'm okay. I'm taking notes."

"If indeed the list was an inventory of what existed when he died, Irene reasoned that the artworks would have been sold in the couple of big sales of his paintings by dealers after his death. So she tried matching the list to the sales results. Some matched, but to her surprise, others on the list do not appear on any of the dealers' reports of what was sold. In fact, because of the similarity of names, it could be that none of the paintings on this list was actually sold.'

'Remember, his estate said all his paintings and other artworks were sold. I wonder if his relatives kept some and hid that fact to help keep prices up. I don't know, and neither does Irene. That's one mystery."

This last commentary struck a chord in Charlie's brain. Maybe there were important works of art that had stayed in the families of *JF* and *ZC* or that were simply missing to the art world. If so, Cassatt's lists might be valuable for scholarship or for identifying long lost works of art. Of course this idea was pure speculation.

"There is another mystery," Seth continued. "Irene noted that there were letters signifying each list. She thinks they might be locations where the art could be found or descriptions of categories. The C, for instance, might stand for *clôture*, an enclosure. Z could mean *zone*, a zone or area. On the other hand, *JF* could mean *jeune fille*, a young girl, because the sculpture is of a young girl."

If Irene's interpretation is correct, thought Charlie, Kate's theory about the niece and housekeeper is wrong. So much for guessing.

"What these initials mean, we'll never know. At any rate, Irene had fun researching the list. But the document is almost one hundred years old and, pardon my pun, a bit sketchy. I hope we have been helpful."

"Certainly. Thanks a lot, Seth. These lists just add a bit of intrigue to the sketch. Good. Any luck with Ludyard Gallery?"

"Yes. I called a friend at Columbia. He knew the gallery, as did Irene. Ludyard has a good reputation and deals mainly in the high end. They have been around for fifteen to twenty years on the East Side of Manhattan. The owner, Jacob Stern, is thought to be cranky and a hard negotiator. Being a dealer is a tough business. My friend thought he is honest and knowledgeable.'

"You asked about his nephew, also. He is learning the business from his uncle. He is thought to be less discreet—dates a lot and goes to parties. My friend met him and did not like him. He said he was a bit full of himself. That's it. That's all I know. Is that helpful?"

"I think so, Seth. I guess it would be safe to buy a painting from them."

Chapter Twenty-Three

Jackie Farrell had a busy week with several cases. With the upcoming return of the Childe Hassam painting she reasoned that her job in the Yale case was mostly done. Then she could free up time to focus on the other work piled high on her desk. When the Yale people received their painting, they would be pleased. The insurance company was out a good deal of money, but that was part of their business. They certainly factored in a certain amount for losses when they priced their policies. Of course the Baileys would need some time to get over the trauma of the episode, but eventually they would move on.

Presumably the sketch would be offered up soon—unless the thieves foolishly threw it out as being worth little. Unfortunately the failure to apprehend the thieves would overhang the good news of the recovery of the artwork, but Farrell thought that she had little hope of finding the thieves. When a ransom had been paid in most other cases, it did not result in an arrest. Without a good tip or confession, the chances of catching thieves without their holding the artwork were very low. Of course the case would remain open, but little work would be done. All trails would go cold quickly. With the picture returned, who would be pushing the investigation anyways?

The murder was another thing. The murderer had to be found. The parents of the girl deserved justice. Obviously the theft was linked to the murder, but Jackie's job wasn't homicide. That was the work of the local police authorities and other people in the FBI.

When she had first learned of the theft and the murder, Farrell had asked Penn Olson which other department of the bureau she should call in. She was told that her job was to focus on the theft. The murder was probably related, but, until it was definitely tied, the murder was a local matter. Other than coordinating with support services like forensics and the lab in the initial investigation, she should work solely on the theft. He had said that at some point it might be that they needed someone from Violent Crimes—but not at this point. Now with the return of the painting, she assumed that the focus of the FBI involvement would change.

Unfortunately her boss was on vacation that week, so she had to wait for direction until Penn returned. If the lead on the case was reassigned—as she assumed, Jackie would work more as a background consultant on the art world. In other words, she would be available for analysis but not responsible for pursuing leads.

The news of the prospective return of the Hassam painting was a surprise to her. Experience had taught her that art thieves waited until interest in the event abated and the investigative agencies had moved on to the next significant case. When the thieves felt comfortable, they approached the victim directly or, more likely, through an intermediary. That this transaction was happening so soon was unusual but lucky. Catching the thieves was important to the FBI, but the return of the artwork is what made the victim and the press happy. So this case was a success in the eyes of the Bureau and the public. She wondered however, if Charlie Bailey's unconventional efforts had pressured the thieves to act sooner than they had planned. If true, perhaps she shouldn't have been so hard on him. No, she insisted, Bailey shouldn't have interfered.

The bottom line was that in a short time Art Anonymous would effect a transfer of the painting. Despite the unlikely event that she would learn something specific about the thieves, she felt duty-bound to meet with her contact at the New York firm. She had talked to Ronald Boothby several times. He had told her that his firm could not bring the FBI into ransom transactions because their presence—overt or suggested—would spook the other side. He had said, however, that he was happy to meet with Jackie at any time to discuss the structure of the arrangements they typically made for the return of stolen works of art.

She was able to meet with him the next day at an architecturally significant office tower in mid-town Manhattan.

"I expected your call, Jackie," Boothby began as they sat down in his ornate office decorated with copies of famous works of art. "The Yale painting was extremely high profile. We were pleased to assist in its recovery. In fact, we expect to deliver the Hassam oil by the end of next week. We should pick it up next Monday."

"Do you mind if we tag along?"

"Ho, ho. You are funny. I don't think the other side would be amused. I can't detail how we'll gain physical possession of the painting, but in this case we don't know the identity of the seller. We are just instructed to have Chubb wire the money to a Panamanian bank to the account of a shell company. Upon receipt and acknowledgment by the bank we'll receive the art."

"What is the name of the company?" Jackie asked.

"Ask Chubb next week. My experience is that any attempt to trace such an account to the owners will run into a brick wall. Try if you will."

"Do you seriously expect me to believe that you don't know the name of the thieves—oops, I mean seller?"

"Our role is to facilitate the transfer of art on a no-names basis. Sometimes the less we know the better."

"You're being compensated, aren't you?"

"Of course. Our standard fee is based on a third party estimate of the auction value. Christie's supplied the appraisal—assuming the painting is authentic and in good condition."

"What about the missing sketch?"

"The seller did not mention it, but we are prepared to arrange its return as well."

Jackie left shortly thereafter. She had not expected that Boothby would break any confidences or supplement the usual information of these transfers. Still, she had had to meet with him—just in case.

Back at her desk, Jackie called over her colleague, Alice Cho, to review the case file and discuss suspects. Alice was not assigned to the Yale case, but she and Jackie had discussed it several times and Jackie often sought her opinion since she had many years of experience in similar cases.

"I expect that Penn will appoint a new lead next week," Jackie said, just in case Alice did not expect a change. "Whoever that is, he will want to know who we suspect and why. Based on the New Haven PD, the forensic evidence, and our investigation, I still think our top two suspects are Larry Kendall and Christopher van Buch. Neither one had a confirmed alibi the night of the theft and both knew the victim well."

"Yes, but neither is a slam dunk," countered Alice.

"Granted. Let's begin with Kendall, the boyfriend. In his interview he acknowledged that they had dated for more than a year. In fact, he thought that he and Cynthia would marry. He was unhappy that they broke up. He said that she had changed after last summer. He attributed her change to drug usage. He knew she took Adderall. In fact, he conceded that he did the same from time to time. Apparently he suspected she was into heavier drugs but she wouldn't admit it. That pissed him off. I also had the impression that he believed that she had engaged in another romantic relationship in New York. That pissed him off even more."

"Enough to kill?" asked Alice.

"That is hard to believe. I think he was in love. He felt angry and hurt. Disappointed in her. Not the usual motives for murder. Still we can't ignore him. He was her intimate companion. If she was going to steal the paintings, wouldn't she have talked to Kendall and asked for his advice and help. How could he not know? He didn't strike me as an angel. Moreover, he is a chemist. He knows poisons and drugs. He even knows the fucking molecular structures. Right?"

"Right," agreed Alice. "He's got to be a suspect, even thought it's hard to see him killing the girl he wanted to marry."

Jackie sat back in her chair and twirled a pencil with her right hand. She brushed back her mid-length brown hair over her shoulder with her other hand. From experience Jackie knew Alice would wait until Jackie was ready with a theory of the case.

"Okay," Jackie began leaning forward. "Maybe Cynthia's new moods and personality cooled his attraction to her. Maybe he even discovered a real boyfriend from New York. He had agreed to help her steal the painting, but now did not trust her. Greed took over. After the theft she was not needed. In fact, she would be a threat to him if the police got too close. He couldn't rely on her. So he poisoned her."

"Jealousy and greed. That's a story, but is there evidence?"

"We have his fingerprints all over her apartment."

"So what? They were sleeping together for months. Also, Jackie, how would Kendall know how to fence the paintings? He's a chemist, not an art dealer?"

"Maybe Cynthia had told him what to do?" Jackie suggested without much conviction.

"If this storyline is true, Kendall should get an academy award. The interview notes say he was all broken up by Cynthia's death. You were at the interrogation. What did you think?"

"He seemed to be in pain," admitted Jackie. "Maybe he is a good actor."

Alice shook her head but said nothing. Jackie assumed she had not bought the Kendall story yet.

"Let's move on to Mr. von Buch," said Jackie. "He's the assistant professor in the Art History Department."

Jackie pictured von Buch in her mind from their interview. He was short, stocky, and balding. He dressed immaculately with his tie complementing the colors of his suit and dress shirt. He wore round, wire-rimmed glasses and spoke with a slight accent—possibly European.

Alice was leafing through the file and found the Christopher von Buch interview. She scanned the paper and then placed it on Jackie's desk.

"Von Buch admitted he had seen Cynthia last summer in New York?"

"Yes, it's not in the interview, but subsequently he told us that after she was in his class, they frequently shared lunch at a panini café in New Haven and did the same in New York when she was an intern at the Ludyard Gallery. He admitted that he had her over for dinner at his apartment on the East Side."

"Romance?"

"Not that I know. At a minimum they were friends. He is only five years older than she was."

"What about the expensive lifestyle?"

"I checked into his background. He grew up in the moneyed environment in Zurich. Cultured family. Father was a banker. The parents sent Christopher to boarding school in England and then to Columbia to study art history. He earned a Ph.D. at Yale and was offered his present position after his degree. Along the way—almost five years ago—the father was arrested and convicted in Switzerland for money laundering. I assume that the parental financial support has dried up. Unless von Buch has secret bank accounts, he must need money to pay his bills and operate his Porsche."

"Not to mention his place in New Haven," Alice added. "I can see why you have your eye on this one. Any others?"

"I'm thinking about one. Remember Charlie Bailey I told you about?"
"Bailey's a suspect?"

"No, no," Jackie laughed. "I talked with him yesterday. When I first heard that the Hassam painting was coming back, one of the thoughts I had was 'Hallelujah, that nuisance, Charlie Bailey, will be gone.' He had complained about the pace of the investigation and was potentially undermining our efforts by meddling.'

'Then I talked to him and learned that his mother had received threatening letters and he and his wife had been body-blocked into traffic near the Carlyle Hotel a few days ago. That was an 'I told you so' moment. Play with fire and you can be burnt. Of course, I know that thought was childish. I don't wish hurt on anyone. It got me thinking, though. Someone—probably the thief and murderer—is watching Bailey. No one knew he was doing his own investigation except people he visited or their close friends."

"I see," said Alice, her face brightening. "Find out whom he talked to, and you may find a thief."

"Exactly. He told me that he talked to a few people at Yale and two men at Ludyard Galleries. At Yale, Kendall directly and Susan Parker of the Yale Art Gallery. Also, John Hamilton, Cynthia's academic advisor. He or Parker could have mentioned something to von Buch. In addition the attacker on the street was a man. Either of my suspects qualifies."

"Or there could be more than one thief or a hired thug."

"You're a pain, Alice. Always shooting holes in my theories. You are almost as much a pain as Bailey. He's no dummy, though. He brought up the drug angle. Drug addiction could be behind Cynthia's perceived personality change that a few of our interviews noted and her involvement in the theft. At least Bailey would like to think that—partially excusing the conduct of his distant cousin. It might explain for him how the shy, conservative girl, dedicated scholar, and well brought up relative could have been involved in a disgraceful theft."

Alice glanced down at her watch and moved her chair back from Jackie's desk, signaling a desire to end the conversation.

"What's next?" Alice asked.

"One more thing—again from my talk with Bailey. He had a bad feeling about Ron Gelb. He's the man who supervised Cynthia at the Ludyard Gallery last summer. I didn't interview him because he had nothing to do with Yale and the gallery has a good reputation. From the little background check we did, Gelb is a successful—thirtyish, unmarried and living in an expensive Park Avenue apartment. I hate to think that Bailey might be on to something, but Gelb knew Cynthia and knows art. It's only a hunch but still worth a chat. Let's have him in."

* * *

The next morning Ron Gelb followed the FBI receptionist to a small windowless room with a table and three chairs. On the table was a glass of water. Jackie welcomed him.

"Thank you, Mr. Gelb, for coming in. You are appearing voluntarily, and we are going to ask you some questions to help us understand certain matters regarding the death of Cynthia Newgate and the theft of some works of art belonging to Yale University. Are you familiar with the theft I just mentioned?"

Jackie thought Ron Gelb looked exactly like the person she brought up on the Ludyard Gallery website. Maybe he was wearing the same clothes: tweed sport coat, solid blue dress shirt, dark blue trousers, and a red silk tie. She was happy that he came alone. That he did not bring an attorney meant Gelb was comfortable in the situation. Usually those who had much to conceal lawyered up right away.

Jackie followed FBI policy and had another agent present in the room. She had briefed Harry Engel on the case, but Harry was there only to listen and to serve as a witness if there was a later disagreement about what was said.

Gelb hesitated before answering Jackie's question. He appeared to be surprised at the blunt nature of what was asked. Jackie guessed he expected to begin with a series of easy queries about his job and background.

"Familiar? I did hear about it—if it is the right incident. An American Impressionist painting was stolen, I believe. Our gallery specializes in European and American Impressionists, so we pay attention to events like that."

"What about Cynthia?"

"Of course, we were shocked to hear of her death. She interned with us last summer. She worked very hard and was liked by everyone. Why do you ask about her and that theft? Certainly those two events aren't linked. If they happened at about the same time, they must be entirely a coincidence. She was totally devoted to art and completely honest."

"Whom did she work for at the gallery?"

"In a small company like ours, interns do work for anyone who asks. Technically I was her mentor. If she had a question, she could start with me. She mainly did research and cataloguing for us. We have to confirm authenticity and provenance before we sell or take on consignment of any work of art. It can be tedious work. Cynthia had a knack for it."

"Did she return to Yale in good graces?"

"Oh, yes. In fact, my uncle Jacob Stern wrote to her supervisor at Yale and praised her work and comportment. As I said, we all liked her."

"Did you have any contact with her after she returned to Yale?"

"Yes, I talked to her once. She had an academic question and considered me a source—an expert, if you will. She may have called others at the gallery. We did not discourage her."

"Did she mention any paintings by Mary Cassatt or Childe Hassam?"

"Not that I recall. I remember that she called me for some background on Berthe Morisot. She was one of the French Impressionists and was married to Manet's brother Eugène. I was happy to oblige."

"Did Miss Newgate ever come back to the gallery after she returned to New Haven?"

"I don't think so. I assume someone would have mentioned it. But she would have been welcome."

"Do you know of the Art Anonymous company?"

"Of course. It maintains a large database of stolen art. It competes with the Art Loss Registry in London. We subscribe to its publication. We can't be too careful about what we buy and take in. In the end, an art dealer has only his reputation."

"Doesn't it also facilitate the return or ransom of stolen artworks?"

"I've heard that, but we wouldn't have a reason to use that service."

"So you have never been offered any stolen artworks by anyone?"

"Thank goodness, no. But it could happen, so we have to take a close look at everything."

"If a painting by a famous artist was stolen—as in the Yale case—what would happen to it?"

"One never knows. For instance, if a collector is behind the theft, he will keep it under lock and key. Otherwise, the thief tries to sell it to a dealer, at auction, to a museum, or back to the original owner. Reputable dealers, auction houses, and museums would not touch stolen goods, especially with high visibility artworks like those from Yale. Most likely the thief would try to sell it back to the owner."

"For insurance money?"

"Perhaps. Or maybe the owner would buy it back with his own money. I don't really know. I have never been involved in such a transaction. I'm just saying what I have heard or read. You probably know much more than I."

"In your opinion was Miss Newgate a happy person?"

"I suppose so. She mainly struck me as young and serious. Very pleasant once you got to know her."

"Did you notice another side to her? A party person? Someone who might have become involved in the wrong crowd? Drug users, perhaps?"

"That would be totally out of character. But you never know what happens with people after hours."

"Did you ever take her out—after hours as you say?"

"No. She's not my type. Besides, it is not good form for a supervisor to spend time socially with an intern. I suppose some of the staff at the gallery may have gone out with her after the gallery was closed, but no one ever told me that Cynthia was anything but a quiet, serious person. Obviously from your questions, you think her death was connected with the art theft. That seems unlikely to me. I assumed she committed suicide. She told me that she had a boyfriend at Yale. Maybe he broke her heart."

"I doubt that, Mr. Gelb. People commit suicide over a lost love only in romantic poetry. No, her death is related to the theft. Are you surprised?"

"Completely. I would have never thought so. I hope you catch whoever hurt Cynthia."

"Oh, we will," said Jackie confidently, looking straight at Gelb. He appeared unnerved. A couple times during this conversation he had tried to appear relaxed, but his composure was slipping. Now he was tense, bit his fingernails, and shifted in his chair.

Jackie went on the offense. "I think you are not completely candid with us. I think you knew Cynthia better than you say. Why hide that part? She was an intelligent, attractive woman. You are single. There's no harm in socializing."

"Well, it didn't happen," he said loudly and reached for the water. "This whole interview is preposterous. I only had a professional relationship with Cynthia and you do a disservice to a lovely person to state that her death was related to this notorious theft. I think it is time to leave."

Ron Gelb looked for the door and stood up. He avoided shaking their hands, and slammed the door as he left. Jackie Farrell sat down at the conference room table and Harry Engel followed suit.

"Harry, what do you think? You were watching him. Did he seem credible?"

"No. He was trying to be smooth at the beginning. He was downplaying everything. For instance, he started by saying he wasn't sure he knew about the Yale theft. Then he said those paintings had high visibility. When you turned up the heat, he almost fell apart. A red flag went up for me."

"Me too. Of course, I was fishing where I didn't know if there were fish. An honest man would have answered differently. He became indignant—not sincere. I think I hit his hot button. There must have been more of a relationship than he wants to admit."

Harry spoke up and offered an alternative, "On the other hand, that kind of lie doesn't mean he had anything to do with her death, her drug problems, or the theft. He may just have wanted to avoid being involved in a murder investigation. He may be angry with himself for knowing a woman who was killed. He may fear the embarrassment and the innuendo attached to our questions."

"Sure, Harry. Or he did it."

Chapter Twenty-Four

When Jackie Farrell's supervisor, Penn Olson, returned from vacation on Monday morning, Jackie stopped by his office as soon as his secretary would let her. She wanted to bring Penn up to speed on her investigation of the Yale theft and obtain some guidance. Olson's office was large by Bureau standards, but the furniture, bookcase, fluorescent lights, carpet squares, and drab draperies were like everyone else's at his level. They were classic government issue. The only things that personalized the space were six citations and awards that hung on the walls and seven or eight family pictures on his desk and the windowsills.

Jackie sat on one of the three steel-and-cushion chairs in front of the desk and began her report. She recapped the news of the Hassam painting, summarized her conversation with Art Anonymous, expressed her continuing suspicions of Kendall and von Buch, and suggested that there were other persons of interest she was looking at, and gave vent to her conversation with Charlie Bailey.

"Bailey is a pain in the butt," Jackie said. "Somehow though he caught the attention of the thief—witness the letter threats and the physical attack. A normal person would stop fooling around in the middle of our case, but Bailey persists. He even expects us to work with him. I discouraged him, but it occurs to me that maybe we should pay more attention to what he is doing—in case the thief makes another run at him. What do you think?"

"Don't you think now that the thief is returning the painting and getting paid he might not feel as threatened—by Bailey or us? The money is what he wanted."

"True, but he still has the sketch to sell. Remember, Bailey won't quit. He told me that he won't be satisfied until Yale has the sketch and the killer is arrested. Of course, the thief should be more concerned with our investigation, but maybe he thinks that one less person nosing around is better. Maybe Bailey got too close."

"Okay, but no security and only for a week or so. A rich guy like Bailey should pay for his own security. I'll call our Chicago office and have him tailed. Bottom line—has Bailey found anything new and useful?"

"Sort of. He accepts that Cynthia Newgate was an accomplice. He explains her participation as the result of drug addiction—possibly linked to her partner or partners. Most interesting though is his hunch that her partner or Svengali is Ron Gelb."

"Gelb? Who's he?" asked Penn looking askance.

"Gelb was her supervisor where Cynthia interned last summer. He was always on our radar—but not high on our list of suspects. Frankly, he should have been higher. I brought him in for questioning last Friday."

"What did you learn?"

"That he doesn't want us to know much about his relationship with the deceased. He minimized everything. He said he knew almost nothing about the biggest art theft of the last six months. He expressed surprise that Cynthia hadn't committed suicide. He didn't know anything about Cynthia outside the gallery. To get a second opinion, I had Harry sit in on the interview and he agreed that Gelb was hiding a lot. According to Bailey he talked to Gelb about the art theft and about Cynthia's murder. Gelb was pretending he didn't know things he already knew. I say he's worth investigating."

"As a suspect?" asked Penn.

"Yes"

"Surveillance?"

"Definitely."

"Alibi?"

"Nothing much."

"You know that the Bureau is cutting back. Budget issues. I'm losing resources as we speak."

"How about just a week or two? If Gelb is hiding something, our conversation may put him off enough in the short term so that he makes a mistake."

"A long shot." He paused. "It is against my better judgment. Okay—two weeks."

"Thanks, Penn."

"I guess Bailey has been helpful. Is he telling you everything he knows?"

"I doubt it. He doesn't like me telling him to cease and desist."

"Not surprising," said Penn. "The surveillance is the good news. Now the bad news. Since the major work of art is coming back, the emphasis on the case will shift significantly to the murder. Sam Petrino from Violent Crimes called me this morning and said he will be assigning a lead from his department. As only he would say: 'we're moving from art to blood.' Despite Sam's unfortunate way with words, I agree with the shift. If we run into some heavies later in the investigation, I'll feel better if you have your back covered."

"I'm so relieved," added Jackie sarcastically.

She left Penn's office feeling upbeat. She had feared that she would get no help, and if she wanted to know was Gelb was doing, she would have to do the stakeout herself—not the kind of work an art cop did. Having won support from Penn, her focus turned to Gillian Heitz, the researcher she had been using on the case. She wondered if Gillian had come up with anything on Gelb from school records, the Internet, police reports, and other public information since they talked Friday.

When she reached her cubicle, she was pleased to find a folder put together by Gillian. Fortunately, there was quite a lot of data. Ron Gelb was born on Long Island to Jewish parents. His father was a part owner in a small heating-equipment company and his mother was a housewife. Gelb had one sibling, a sister who was married and lived in Oakland. Gelb had gone to the local high school, where he participated in art and music programs. He was on the junior varsity tennis team.

His excellent grades and test scores earned him admission to Brown University. There he majored in art history and enhanced his studies by working summers in his uncle's art gallery. He graduated cum laude and immediately went to work full-time at the gallery. He had never had another employer. At first he rented an apartment in a middle-class neighborhood in Queens but eventually moved to the West Side of Manhattan. When his parents died in a car accident, he must have inherited some money, because six months later he bought a small apartment in a Park Avenue cooperative building. He was still living there.

Gillian did have a chance to talk to two individuals friendly to the Bureau who worked in the industry and to a doorman at Gelb's apartment building. The industry contacts said that Gelb had a good reputation as a dealer in a successful gallery. They agreed that his social life was active. They saw him at parties and industry social events, often with an attractive woman in tow. They added that at some of the events, drugs were widely available, and they would not be surprised if Gelb was a recreational user. Both of these sources and the doorman remembered the young woman in the photograph of Cynthia Newgate. The doorman thought she visited Gelb in his apartment, and the others thought they had seen her at a party several months before. No one suggested she and Ron Gelb were romantically involved—just friends. One source remembered seeing her at a party, seemingly on drugs.

The report concluded that there was nothing particularly unusual about Gelb. He could have been one of hundreds of well-educated, well-dressed, thirty-something singles on the make with a good job. However, these interviews did make one thing clear: Gelb had known Cynthia Newgate better than he admitted. In addition, the sources suggested that she probably used drugs.

Jackie closed the file and thought that nothing in it pointed to Gelb's involvement in the theft, but then again, nothing said he could not have been involved. Gelb seemed to be ambitious and to like the things money could buy. He did not come from money nor was he likely to be earning investment banker type paychecks from his job. Arguably he would have been happy to come into a large sum of money. Whether such a desire translated into theft and murder remained to be seen.

Still, he had been Cynthia's boss, could have known she took drugs, and might have heard from her that the Bailey pictures were going to Yale where she would work closely with them. His potential involvement was plausible. In fact, compared to the circumstantial evidence Jackie had on her other suspects, the case for Gelb's involvement appeared stronger. Nevertheless, she had no hard evidence. Her best bet was that the surveillance effort would lead her to some new connection—a drug dealer, the missing sketch, some suspicious activity on Gelb's part.

Jackie had to admit that it was Charlie Bailey who had convinced her to look closer at Gelb. Bailey's involvement had been irritating, but she acknowledged that he had good instincts. Still she wondered if Bailey had let her know of Gelb only when Bailey had hit a dead end and thought that the Bureau's resources could prove useful. Based on their interaction so far, Bailey seemed as distrusting of the Bureau as Jackie was of Bailey. Maybe, as Penn had suggested, Bailey knew more that he had told her. Just in case, she would have to talk to Bailey again.

Jackie had had Gillian look into Bailey's history as well. Her report said that Bailey had Yale and Harvard credentials, grew up in a moneyed lifestyle, lost his first wife in an accident, married a high-profile woman in a much publicized social wedding, and owned a money management firm catering to the very wealthy—all very proper. About a year ago Charles Bailey was questioned about a murder in Lake Forest, but it appeared that he was cooperative with the investigation and the case was successfully resolved.

Jackie lingered over that item and wondered if that incident had whetted Charlie's appetite for police work. Maybe that experience had been exciting and helped explain his eagerness to be involved now. If so, it was bad luck for her.

She struggled with the idea of crediting a rank amateur like Bailey with developing any clues or evidence. After all, she had worked hard to achieve her position. She was proud of overcoming an institutional bias against women and being accepted in an esoteric field like art without an elite school education. Nevertheless, she had to call Bailey again.

Jackie knew she had to be careful in her conversation with him, but she had to find out if Bailey knew more about Gelb than he had said without encouraging the man to continue his investigation. To cover her real purpose, she decided to use the pretext of the painting's return in the call.

"Mr. Bailey, I'm sorry to interrupt you during business hours again, but I'm certain you will be happy to know that I can confirm that the Childe Hassam painting will be back at Yale on Thursday. Yale said that Art Anonymous notified them today. I'm sure it will be displayed prominently with the

Mary Cassatt painting. No doubt, the sketch will turn up soon as well. We are still on the lookout."

"That's good news. Finally!" Charlie said sounding combative and sarcastic to Jackie. "I must say that, if I were you, I would be more eager to find the sketch. It may contain more information than you think."

Jackie smiled to herself. He is leading me to something he thinks is important. That was her purpose for placing this call.

"What do you mean? Have you learned something special about it?"

"Do you remember the photograph we sent you depicting the back of the sketch? Did you look at it?"

Jackie heard a change in Charlie's tone. He sounded hostile at the end of their last conversation and at the beginning today. Suddenly, he sounded helpful. He is acting the teacher and I am the student.

"Yes, we examined the back several days ago. There was a list. Does it have significance?"

"I think so. We think it is a list of paintings and a sculpture owned by Degas which would be distributed possibly to his niece and his housekeeper. Mary Cassatt made the list. Perhaps Degas asked her to do it. He was too ill to write anything himself."

"That's an interesting interpretation. Why is this list so important?"

"I am not sure, but if the sketch continues to be withheld, the thief must attribute some extraordinary value to the list. Remember, the thief passed up taking the Cassatt oil when he had the chance. I'm guessing the list is worth more to him than the fabulous Cassatt painting."

"Fascinating. I'll put our researcher onto this mystery. In the meantime, we did take your suggestion and talked to Ron Gelb. We're not done with him yet."

"Great," said Charlie eagerly. "Did he tell you much about his relationship with Cynthia? I think he is key to knowing how she became involved."

"Why do you think that?"

"Look," said Charlie. "Isn't it obvious. How does a conservative, intelligent, graduate art student go to New York for three months, become a druggie, and drive away her decent, infatuated boyfriend of some time? Someone corrupted her. My guess is that it was her boss, Ron Gelb. Sex may have been involved—but that wouldn't matter as much as the drugs."

"Okay, Mr. Bailey. Slow down. Couldn't she have been corrupted—as you say—elsewhere? By someone at Yale, for instance. A Yale Svengali instead of a New York Svengali?"

"Cynthia had spent her whole adult life in academia. Her experiences were there. Yale was 'normal' for her. The one new experience was working at the New York gallery. If you were looking at change in a person, look at change to her 'normal' life."

"So did Svengali kill her?"

"Of course. After the theft he did not need her. Her existence was a threat to him and greed would demand that fewer splits meant more for Svengali."

"Arsenic?"

"Easy to get and to administer. An efficient killer."

"Wow, that's quite a theory! Do you have any evidence tying Gelb to drugs or the paintings?"

"That's your job. I invest people's money in the markets. I am simply telling you what I think happened. I can't do police work. But I do believe I am right."

"I can hear that. Still we need evidence to prove a theory. The courts demand it. Nevertheless, you make some interesting points. In the meantime, we'll keep a close eye on Mr. Gelb. Is there anything else we should know about this case?"

"Not at this time. What do you think?"

Jackie hesitated in answering his question. Despite her exploration, his theory of the case matched hers closely: manipulated insider allows thief access to the paintings and is killed to ensure her silence. She didn't want Charlie to know she agreed with much of what he said. She thought she might appear weak not to have a distinct view. Where Jackie differed from Charlie was in the identity of the thief/murderer. He seemed certain; Jackie was open to a few possibilities. Her training demanded hard evidence. Everything so far was circumstantial.

"You have me thinking," Jackie responded trying to be conciliatory. "We still have a lot of work to do."

Chapter Twenty-Five

"What a day!" Charlie sighed as he walked into the library, bent over, and kissed Kate, who was sitting in her favorite chair reading a client marketing plan.

"How's my girl? You look so much better. Ten days can make a huge difference."

"Yah. I look like I won the fight now instead of lost it."

"You always look like a winner to me."

"Flattery will get you everywhere," she said grinning. "Well, what happened?"

"First, now that the Middle East is quieting down, so too are the client phone calls. The portfolio changes were made and seem to be working out. However, maybe the good Lord doesn't want me to slow down, because I had some phone calls today that got my attention."

"Like what?" Kate asked, putting down her report.

"Marty called from Yale around noon. He told me that the Yale PD just talked to a woman who lived in an apartment across from Cynthia's place. She said she and her husband left for their summer vacation the weekend Cynthia was killed. They have a cottage in the backwoods of Maine, which explains why she did not hear of Cynthia's murder until she returned yesterday. She called us the first thing today to report that she saw a man leaving Cynthia's apartment late that Saturday night with two objects wrapped in brown paper. She added that one of the packages was the size of a framed painting. The other appeared to be a cylinder. Apparently she was taking some garbage out to the apartment building chute on her floor. The man seemed surprised when she opened the door and turned his back to her. He was tall with curly brown hair and was wearing a tan raincoat. He hurried down the stairs and did not look back.'

"I asked Marty if she recognized the visitor and he said that they showed her photos of some suspects and non-suspects. She recognized Kendall's picture, saying she had seen him at Cynthia's many times, but the visitor definitely wasn't Kendall."

"Charlie, did they show her Gelb's picture?" Kate asked excitedly.

"I asked, but Marty was not familiar with Gelb. Remember, he is not the lead on the murder. I think he continues to talk with me because I bring up something new to him, like Gelb. I explained Gelb's relationship with Cynthia and then a light bulb must have switched on in his brain. He said, 'That must be the guy the FBI alerted us to a couple of days ago. So I'm sure we showed her his picture. At any rate, she had not seen enough of the man to make an ID. Still, what she did see did not eliminate Gelb. He's tall with curly brown hair. I think this is the best clue we heard so far."

Kate looked at Charlie with a puzzled look. "There are a lot of tall men with curly brown hair."

"True, but how many knew Cynthia and wrap paintings in brown paper wrappers? The universe of men has really narrowed."

"Charlie, your mind certainly jumps to conclusions," she laughed. "Clear across the abyss of ignorance to the happy home of fact. Wow! You know, you're probably right."

"I know I'm right. He lied to us about Cynthia and he poisoned her."

"Okay, cowboy, was that all?"

"No. This one is funny. Rocky called me. I'm being followed."

"I know about Rocky."

"The follower is someone else—from the FBI. Remember, we gave Rocky our daily schedules so he could watch out for both of us. After you go into your office he leaves you until you have an appointment outside. Since I go out more often, he picks me up when you are inside. The plan is working, I guess. Anyway, he noticed someone following me the last two days. He said, 'They tailing you, boss.' I asked him who was tailing me. He said that from previous assignments he recognized the 'tail' as an FBI agent. Rocky took it very seriously."

"I guess Charlie Bailey is a suspect," Kate surmised lightheartedly.

"I guess the FBI thinks I stole my mother's paintings. It's remarkable how smart they are. I can't get away with anything."

"Fess up, Charlie, and save the government some money."

"Lock me up and throw away the key."

"Seriously, I think you should take their action as a compliment. They think you will lead them to the thief."

"I never thought of that. You are a sweetheart—a clever sweetheart. There are times, though, when I think they will never get their act together."

"From your description of your conversation a couple of days ago with Jackie Farrell, you and the FBI are now in love. N'est pas?"

"Maybe a truce. At least she didn't tell me to stop talking with anyone this time."

"Charlie, give yourself some credit. Marty confirmed that they are focusing on Gelb. That was your doing."

"Maybe. Enough of this good news," said Charlie changing the subject. "There is some bad news. Peaches called. Our erstwhile friend whose job it apparently is to chronicle the foibles and misfortunes of Chicago's moneyed class called this afternoon to warn me about an article on the Baileys this weekend in the *Trib*. He found a PR release from Yale yesterday announcing the recovery of the Hassam painting. He reminded me of our agreement that he would wait to publicize the loss of the Bailey gift until its recovery in return for an 'exclusive' with me or mother. He was calling in his marker."

"Can you say no?" Kate asked.

Charlie got out of his chair and walked around the room stopping at the window to look out at Lake Michigan. He had hoped that Peaches would have moved on to other news or forgot. After all, Peaches was flaky with a short attention span. But Charlie had not expected that the painting would come back so soon. Even Peaches could remember something from two weeks ago.

"I don't want to talk to him, Kate. Even though the theft wasn't our fault, it makes us look silly. Give to Yale on day one; pictures gone on day two. Also the gift draws attention to Mother's wealth. We don't need the attention. I suppose we could take an ad out in case some thief out there missed Peaches's column. I told him that the story was old news and that no one was interested in it, but he didn't buy my argument. He will say I made a commitment to him, adding that if I didn't talk to him, he would ask Mother. If she declined, he would run the story anyways. I think I am dead. I'll have to see him tomorrow."

"I'm sorry," Kate commiserated. "Don't be upset. I know you'll do a good job to soften the article."

Charlie sat down again and leaned over towards Kate. "You know what I really want to do? I want to go to New York and confront Gelb. After what Marty told me about the neighbor, I want to get the bastard."

"No, no, no," Kate said at once. "I want to get him, too, but it's too dangerous. You must call your new friend, Jackie. This is the FBI's job. I want my husband around for the next fifty years. You're too hyper now. The prospective *Trib* story has unsettled you. Maybe the best thing for us to do is get away. Let's take a break—that vacation we've talked about."

Charlie looked at her as if she had gone insane.

* * *

"Jackie, the hottest agent in the FBI," Danny Flood shouted as he came up to her desk. "It seems that we are going to be working together again. I guess you artsy people got the painting back but can't figure out who stole it. Probably my killer. I'm glad to help you out."

Danny Flood was well-known to Jackie. They had partnered on the two other art-related crimes during the past five years; that had included a homicide. His arrogant bonhomie would have turned off most people in the bureau, except that he was uncommonly successful. He was a big man in everything: large physique, big drinker, huge ego, and ebullient personality. Quick with the jibe. First in line to accept praise and reward. Last in line if there was a glitch. A hundred guys in the bureau would have fought to be the first to throw him off a cliff if he failed—except that he did not. He was smart and driven.

"Danny. Why am I so lucky? Penn gave me the bad news this morning. Fortunately for you, we don't do murders on this floor. You can be a hero again. I'll give you my files so you can get started right away."

"Just send them to my office. I'll get to them eventually. Penn gave me a summary and a status quo. Schoolmarmish Cynthia Newgate gets poisoned the night of a big time art theft at one of our elitist universities. Terribly embarrassing to the Ivy League. Newgate, a Marian the Librarian if there ever was one, learns about the other side of evil in New York, comes home a druggie, and helps out some bad guy or guys steal some *chèr* artworks. Poor lamb is extra after the pictures are out the door and she is sacrificed. Bad guys ransom the paintings and disappear. You art guys can't find them, so you call me to do your dirty work. Clever guys, you all. Do I have the story right?"

"A little more respect for the dead would be nice, but in general you have the story right."

"So who do we have in the lineup? Manipulative lover, drug dealer into art, sneaky colleague? Tell me I don't have to go to dirty old New Haven."

"You might. But first, you have to get up to speed on four individuals: Larry Kendall, Yale student and ex-boyfriend; Christopher von Buch, academic and sometime mentor; Ron Gelb, art expert at a New York gallery and her summer supervisor; and Charlie Bailey, son of art donor and amateur sleuth. Our best leads involve these four."

"A veritable rogue's gallery. I'll leave Bailey to last, if at all. Like I need to talk to an amateur sleuth," he added sarcastically. "The other three, at least, fit the usual profile. Gelb is in New York. Being naturally lazy, I'll start here."

"Hold on, Red Rider. We have Gelb under surveillance. We interviewed him and the notes are in the files. We should follow him for at least a few more days."

"That was good until now. Least you forget: I am now in charge. Who's doing the watch on Gelb?"

Frowning, Jackie answered, "Stu Gretz, Solly, and a third guy who is a part-timer."

"Okay. Let's call Stu now so I can give him the good news that I'm on the case."

Jackie grimaced but knew she could not do anything to stop Flood. She dialed Gretz on location and gave him the handset.

"Stu, this is Danny Flood. Crimes is now in the picture. Tell me what is going on with this Gelb guy, suspect, or whatever he is."

Jackie reread her file while they were talking. After five minutes Danny told Jackie to punch this extension at the desk nearby so Stu wouldn't have to repeat what he was saying.

"Jackie, if you are on?" Stu began. "Last night my partner, Solly, followed Gelb to a club in the East Village. Typical club. It gets going around one o'clock. Loud. Hip-hop and rock. Chicks in short dresses from the East Side who should know better. Guys with day jobs on the prowl. Booze and powder and pills in a back room and the men's room. Dancing, kissing, feeling, snorting, and popping. Anyways, Gelb shows up by himself. Took a taxi from his apartment. Solly follows him inside. Gelb says hello to three or four guys—one an owner and the others customers. Talks mainly to one guy who looks gay. About two o'clock Gelb goes to the back room and scores some coke. Solly could see him from the door. Then he pays cash for some pills from a dealer we have seen before. Half an hour later Gelb has an argument with the gay guy and leaves in a huff. Takes a cab home."

Jackie watched Flood during this recitation. He seemed bored and impatient, while Jackie was absorbed. Finally there was evidence that Gelb was into the drug scene. She needed that connection to tie Cynthia more firmly into him.

"Solly goes back to the club and calls the local PD. He arranges for our good guys to detain the dealer as he is leaving. They strongly suggest he sings about our boy Ron. The dealer caves and says Ron is a regular customer—small stuff. He says that last year Ron bought more—enough to resell maybe, but cut back this year. Always pays cash, no markers. Our coppers say okay. They warn the dealer, tell him not to talk to Gelb, and let him go.

"So, Danny, Gelb's a user and sometimes carries more than he needs personally—or at least used to. Did we miss anything?"

Danny shrugged his shoulders while looking at Jackie. She spoke up, "No, great work. Of course, we have to assume the dealer will talk to Gelb about us. Maybe that's not a bad thing. It'll make Gelb nervous. Jumpy guys make mistakes. We'll keep the surveillance on to see what else we can learn. Thanks for doing such a good job."

Jackie smiles and stood up excited. Good evidence.

"Danny. The surveillance is paying off. Gelb could have been Ms. Newgate's source and the person who manipulated her in the robbery.

"Big fricking deal," scoffed Flood. "We'll need a lot more than this. You notice that I didn't ask Stu how our boys got the dealer to talk. His testimony is probably inadmissible. I live with this all the time in my world."

As he wandered off with her file, Jackie got a call from the New Haven PD. Her contact told her about the eyewitness the Yale PD found and her description of Cynthia's visitor.

"If the neighbor is right," Jackie commented, "then two of our suspects may be in the clear. Fax me the text of the interview."

Her contact agreed and then asked about the new suspect, Ron Gelb, that she had alerted them to earlier in the week.

"He's still in the picture. Thanks for the info."

Earlier in the week Jackie had asked for Gelb's telephone records and credit card charges. Nothing substantiated a Gelb presence in New Haven the weekend Cynthia died. What she wanted to see were his computer and cellphone. Gelb possibly kept a record of his whereabouts in these devices. She wondered if she had enough for a judge to issue a search warrant for Gelb's apartment.

As Jackie contemplated the steps she had to complete to get a warrant, Gillian Hertz appeared at her desk and sat in the steelcase chair next to it. Gillian was a multi-talented researcher. She did background checking and, because of a degree in art history and four years at Sotheby's in its American Paintings Department, she researched artists, provenances, dealers, and other art related topics. Jackie had asked her to look into Charlie Bailey's claims about the writing on the back of the sketch.

As Gillian sat down Jackie wondered how she could get Danny Flood to act respectfully toward this highly intelligent researcher who also had the good fortune to be young, auburn-haired, well-endowed, trim, and beautiful. He was enough to drive her out of the bureau with sexist comments. Jackie could not afford to lose her.

"Jackie, I've had a chance to look at those photographs you showed me."

"What did you learn?"

"First, the sketch is not listed in any compilation of Mary Cassatt's work. Miss Cassatt was prolific and knew Degas well. So I suspect the purchaser bought it directly from the artist or from a dealer who did not show it in a public exhibition. From the sketch's style and subject matter, I concur it is authentic."

"I don't doubt that. But what of the writing on the back?"

"I was getting to that," she responded, obviously irritated to be pressured. "The writing is a list of paintings and sculptures, presumably by Degas. One is by Cézanne, but the others correspond broadly to known works by Degas. I checked the record of his artworks sold at auction after his death, and a couple seem to match items that were sold. But I cannot be certain, because many of his paintings and sculptures had similar titles. He did a lot of ballet dancers, washerwomen, and singers.

"The handwriting? Isn't it Mary Cassatt's?"

"It looks that way. I can only speculate why she made the list. Maybe these were items she really liked or maybe they were on the walls of Degas's apartment. Do you think the list is important?"

"I don't know. The donor—or at least her son—seems to think so. He guessed that the lists are paintings to be given to one of Degas's relatives and his housekeeper. I say so what? What does a list of a hundred-year-old group of paintings have to do with a murder and an art theft a few weeks ago? Bailey thinks that because the sketch wasn't sold back to Yale by the thief with the Hassam painting, the list has some specific significance. What do you think?"

"He makes an intriguing point. I'll go back and consult a few more books on Mary Cassatt and Degas. I will say that any one of those paintings on the list is worth millions today."

Chapter Twenty-Six

"He's gone," Stu Gertz roared, his voice further amplified by the speakerphone in Danny Flood's office. Jackie sat across the room, wondering how Danny would react.

"Gone? How gone? Where gone?" Danny shouted back. "You're supposed to know where Gelb is all the time. That's what surveillance is."

"Penn had us on partial surveillance. The guy goes to bed; we go to bed. He gets up; we get up."

"Christ, that's surveillance?" Danny bellowed. "He disappeared; you're gonna disappear—fired. Find him."

"His doorman said he left in a cab last night about eight with two suitcases. He didn't say where he was going. We're checking the airline and car rental records now. He can't vanish forever. If he is using his name, we'll find him."

"You hope. Don't let me hold you up with this chit-chat, you clowns," Danny said sarcastically. Then he hit the End button on the speaker.

"Can you believe that?" Danny said rhetorically. "I should have picked up Gelb two days ago when we heard of the eyewitness ID. Admittedly there are lots of tall, curly brown-haired men, but... I shouldn't have let you talk me into just doing surveillance."

Jackie rolled her eyes in disbelief and disgust at Danny's attitude. She would have pushed back with someone else, but it would be a waste of time with him. He was a big shot and knew it. His office proved it. A star in the FBI gets you an office with glass walls like Danny Flood's instead of a metal desk in an open area like Jackie Farrell's. Danny was brash and flamboyant, but his record supported his status. Only in his early thirties, his arrests of high-profile suspects were numerous; and they almost always led to convictions. Certainly his reputation was aided by the general understanding in the FBI that agents who deal with terrorists and drug-related crimes ranked higher than those dealing with white-collar crimes—art theft or securities fraud. The public, more interested in straightforward crimes of passion and violence than complex or technical breaches of the law, reinforced this situation.

She would have to roll with the punches. Danny was the lead. Penn had told her yesterday that he had to call in a favor from Sam Petrino to get Danny Flood. According to Penn, Danny objected to working an art crime again—not up to his macho standards. Penn supposedly assured Danny that he would get all the support he needed and would be done in no time. When she heard that, Jackie laughed inwardly, knowing that her cases always took longer than expected.

"Danny, I'll tell Solly to meet me at the Ludyard Gallery. Maybe Gelb told someone there where he was going. An innocent man would tell his uncle how to reach him."

"And a guilty man takes off at night not telling anyone," Danny said, amending her comment. "Go ahead, but I'm going to ask my favorite judge for a search warrant. Gelb may have left behind something juicy in his apartment."

Jackie met Solly outside the Ludyard Gallery. When they showed their FBI badges to Christina, they were escorted back to Jacob Stern's office.

"Ron? He's on vacation," said Stern. "He didn't say where he was going—just that he would be gone for more than a week. He wasn't working on any deals; so this is a good time to take off. The summer is slow. What this about? Is Ron in some sort of trouble?"

"Is there a place he usually goes—on vacation?" Jackie asked calmly.

"No. Is this about Cynthia Newgate? Ron said he talked to the FBI a few days ago. I trust he was helpful."

"We just want to talk to him again."

"When he calls in, I'll tell him to call you"

Out on the sidewalk afterwards Jackie admitted that she could not tell if Stern was being truthful. Solly simply said that Gelb would never call.

"I agree," Jackie said, feeling frustrated. "No way can we wait for that. If he has the sketch, he's not coming back."

Rather than go back downtown to the office, Jackie called Danny's office to see if he had secured a search warrant for Gelb's nearby apartment. Danny answered and said he was just leaving and would meet her there. He added that they had learned from KLM's manifests that Ron Gelb had flown from JFK to Amsterdam-Schiphol overnight and passed through passport control already. The FBI there officially requested Dutch police assistance in detaining Gelb; but Danny had little hope the Dutch would find him now that the EEC's borders were entirely open.

He had better luck with the warrant and brought along his computer whiz kid in case Gelb had left behind his computer. The superintendent of the building had a key to Gelb's apartment and let them in with no hassle. The apartment looked like a typical bachelor's pad belonging to a man in a hurry—unmade bed, rumpled towel, clothes on a bedroom chair, sparsely provisioned refrigerator. On the other hand, there was ample evidence of his profession—art books, catalogues, exhibition tickets, and several American Impressionists paintings on the walls.

After searching for forty minutes Jackie concluded "He left in a rush, but there's no Cassatt sketch or any other stolen goods that I can tell. Any luck with the computer, Henry?"

Gelb had left behind a computer notebook on his desk in his bedroom. Henry Kim, the FBI's technical expert in New York, had immediately started to work while the search of the apartment was taking place. He needed less than five minutes to get past the password and firewalls.

"He did post a calendar," Henry reported. "And he didn't trash his emails. What are we looking for?"

"Try 'Cynthia Newgate', 'Art Anonymous', 'Cassatt', 'Hassam', 'Degas', and 'Bailey art collection'." Jackie proposed immediately.

Henry took some time locating all these suggestions but he had finished by the time the physical search ended.

"Okay, I'll print out all the hits. I found a lot."

"Danny, look at this," Jackie aid with wonder ten minutes later looking over Henry's shoulder. "He didn't delete all these meetings with Cynthia.

There must be twelve meeting from last summer through last month. The notations indicated that the meetings were in New Haven, New York, and Stamford. For some reason he didn't email her after she started her internship. There are only two emails from before welcoming her and telling her what she needed to know to start work. As time went on, he must have been nervous about creating a record of their correspondence. But he had to have contacted her to set up the meetings on his calendar. We'll check his phone bills. I suspect we'll see a lot."

Danny was also leafing through the printouts Henry was producing as Jackie was talking. He showed no emotion and handed each page to Solly when he was finished. After a while, he did not need to see anything more.

"Jackie, analyze all this evidence," Danny ordered. "Obviously, this guy lied to us and is running as fast as he can. Too bad we didn't see this stuff before the insurance company paid up. He's got a lot of dough to hide with. Meet me in my office in an hour."

Jackie watched him leave the apartment but could not read his body language. From his comments Danny had no doubt that Gelb was the culprit. The question was how do you capture Gelb when he is in Europe—or maybe Asia by now? He had access to a ton of money and presumably had travelled abroad frequently as part of his work. He knew how to get around. Could they count on foreign authorities locating Gelb—or even wanting to help? Based on her impressions of Danny Flood, she wouldn't expect him to be comfortable sitting and waiting.

Danny clarified Jackie's questions an hour later.

"As much as I hate to leave muggy, rainy New York in August, I think this calls for a trip to Paris. Maybe this case isn't so dreary, after all. You want to come? I don't speak French. Do you?"

"Enough to read the signs and get by."

"Okay. You doing anything tonight? We'll fly out tonight if we can. Right now, I'm going to call Interpol to alert them we're coming and why. Do you know anyone in their works of art area? My only contacts are in their drugs and organized crime departments."

"Yes. I've worked with Aldo Laval a couple of time. Interpol must have the Yale paintings on their database, since we notified them weeks ago. Aldo is in Lyon, but I'm sure I can get him to meet us in Paris."

"Good. You call. Tell him to meet us at the DeGaulle Airport. Travel will get us the flight number. I'm going home to pack. Off to see the frogs."

Jackie winced at his Gallic insult. She fretted that Danny would be a handful in France. She just hoped that he wouldn't offend Aldo on day one—or day two. She didn't like Danny's style but she had to admit she liked decisiveness. Before he could leave the room, she asked, "Why Paris? Gelb flew to Amsterdam."

"Amsterdam is a left fake. Gelb didn't just leave to lose us. That sketch means something to him. He kept it for a reason. Your dead artists—Degas and Cassatt—lived in Paris. I'll bet that's where he is going, Darling."

PART TWO
FOUND

Chapter Twenty-Seven

Sitting in the first class cabin of his United flight to Paris, Charlie relaxed for the first time in weeks. Kate had convinced him to take a break. The financial scare had diminished. His clients had stopped calling with their concerns. And closer to his healthy mental state, the awful events surrounding his mother's gift and Cynthia's murder were past.

"You solved the case for the FBI," Kate congratulated him after takeoff. There is no more danger from Gelb to you or your mom. I assume they have arrested him by now."

"I hope so. Jackie Farrell took a long time to come around to agreeing that Gelb was the thief and murderer. The eyewitness of his exit from Cynthia's apartment finally convinced her. All she has to do is to pick him up and charge him."

"Hasn't she done that?"

"Jackie doesn't keep me informed as she should. I told her everything I had learned and led her to Gelb. And this case is about mom's artwork and my blood relative's murder. I'm frustrated at times."

"Well, the FBI will take care of everything."

Charlie nodded but thought if they don't finish off the case, I may have to cut short this trip."

"What are you thinking, handsome?" Kate asked.

"Paris in the summer," Charlie lied.

"This vacation is so exciting. The only other time I was in Paris was when my parents took me when I was a freshman in college—'April in Paris'. Or rather, it was March in Paris."

"It's different at this time of year. A lot more flowers and a lot more tourists. The weather should be warm and pleasant. Fortunately, we are staying at a hotel with air conditioning."

"Do you mean that some hotels don't have it?"

Charlie chuckled, "Some hotels that cater to the French. Many Europeans don't like processed air. They are not conditioned to air conditioning."

Kate rolled her eyes at the lousy pun and took a sip of her mimosa. "Tell me more."

"You'll love it at this time of year. Most of the stores and restaurants will be open. Because you speak a little French, everyone will be happy with you. To tell you the truth, my favorite month is August—but then I'm old."

Charlie proceeded to tell Kate what occurred in August. He said that most Parisians leave for the country, the seashore, or foreign countries. Factories coordinate the annual vacation closings, and the rest of the populace follows suit. The timing makes sense, since it is between school terms and the weather can be hot and sultry in the cities. This practice is common in France, Italy, Spain, and some parts of the rest of Europe. Tourists are aware of this phenomenon; so many avoid Paris during that time, knowing that some restaurants and small businesses are closed. Still, a few hearty souls like himself prefer that time to visit the city because most of the big-name stores, hotels, and museums are still open and uncrowded. Traffic is light, and seats on the Mêtro are abundant. He enjoyed the leisurely pace, the empty hotels and museums, and the idea that one could go on the spur of the moment and still stay at his favorite hotel.

"Aren't we staying at your favorite hotel?" Kate asked.

"Yes, the Georges V."

"I'm going to do a lot of shopping. At home I am always working and never seem to have time to shop. What are you going to do? I hate to leave you alone. You could come with me."

"Shopping. No, you'll do fine without me. I have some plans. There is a new Impressionist exhibition at the Musée d'Orsay. I also want to visit some old 'paintings friends' at the l'Orangerie in the Tuileries Gardens—Monet, Cézanne, Renoir, Rousseau, and Matisse. Then there is the gallery of Henri Archambault on Quai Voltaire, which I visited with Mother over the years. I haven't been there in ages. I have lots of things to do."

"Good. I worry about you," Kate said. "The one thing that I won't miss is Rocky following me everywhere."

"The FBI agent, also. I'm sure Rocky would have liked to come, but I don't see why we would need him. We're safe in Paris. In fact, hardly anyone knows we're here."

"Gulp. I bragged to some people at work. Don't be angry."

Charlie laughed, "Okay, this one time."

Kate opened the novel she had brought and let Charlie have his thoughts. He admitted to himself that one of the reasons he had suggested they visit Paris was a secret nostalgia brought on by all the time he spent remembering and discovering anew the era and places of Degas and Cassatt. The Belle Epoque, the time of the Impressionists, Bohemians, Montmartre, and the Moulin Rouge. Walking the streets and visiting some of the places these great artists frequented appealed to him. He hoped that Kate might share his enthusiasm.

The plane landed at Charles de Gaulle in the morning. Charlie disliked flying east because the time change meant he and Kate were only able to get a few hours of sleep on the plane. At least the hotel driver was prompt and met them at the luggage carousel. They were at the hotel an hour later.

"Charlie, you didn't exaggerate," Kate gushed, taking in the inlaid marble floors, flower arrangements, rococo-style furniture, and decorative paintings of the lobby. "This is as beautiful or better than the Four Seasons in Chicago."

"*Bien sûr*, my pet, let me show you more. Open courtyard and a three-star restaurant in the back."

"I'm feeling romantic, Charlie."

The assistant manager showed them to the suite that Charlie remembered from a previous trip. When they were alone, Charlie kissed his wife and promised "Tonight".

"I know you are tired," Kate said sympathetically. "Shower, take a long nap, and be ready for dinner tonight. I'm too excited to sleep. I'm going to plot my attack tomorrow on the Avenue Montaigne and the Rue du Faubourg St. Honoré."

"You have good taste—and are understanding."

When Charlie woke up, Kate had returned from a walk in the neighborhood. They dressed and wandered around outside until they found a little bistro on Rue Marbeuf for dinner.

"Kate, I know that you will be off shopping tomorrow. Don't hate me if I don't join you. As you know, I'm not a great shopper. You'll make much better time without me. I can entertain myself and meet you back at the hotel at five."

"I don't know, Charlie. I thought you would love following me around, watching me put on shoes and try on dresses. Oh, well, you are going to miss out, poor baby. I'll worry about you all day long."

"Fat chance. At least we agree. Of course, if you see a tie at Hermes, I could use a new one. But don't go out of your way."

"You're in luck. Hermès is on my list. But what are you going to do?"

"If the weather is good, I'll stroll through the Tuileries, then go across the river to the St. Germain-des-Prés area. Maybe have lunch there.

"Très bohemian."

"Of course, that's me. After a while, I'll wander back toward the hotel. I want to walk across the Alexander Bridge—my favorite in the whole world."

"Sounds good. I'll be back late afternoon. I'm so happy we have this time together to relax and do our things."

"No argument here," Charlie said sipping a glass of burgundy. "I am pleased the markets finally calmed down and we are out of town for the fallout from that Peaches article."

"You tried your best to kill it."

"You're kind, but I failed. You and I saw the headline, 'Social Local Benefactors Victims of Crime'. My father always advised me to stay out of the society columns and never talk of your wealth. Up to now mother and I have done pretty well. That article is a disaster."

"You can't control the press. As you say, let's be glad we're here. Salut."

As they walked slowly through the streets back to the hotel, Charlie's mood softened. He felt that the stresses experienced in Chicago were far away. There was a magic in the night: the stars, the mild temperature, the beautiful buildings adorned with flowers everywhere, the memory of a satisfying dinner, and his beautiful wife. The spell lingered as they walked through the marble lobby to the elevator, which brought them to their floor in seconds.

His sense of time continued to blur as they entered their room, undressed each other, and met in bed. At this moment making love was more natural than sleep, and they joined in the act of physical giving that expressed their need for each other. Their movements revealed a familiarity gained over time. Later he held her gently and close until he sensed she was sleeping. Then he fell asleep.

* * *

As they planned, after a late breakfast the next morning Charlie and Kate went their separate ways—she in a taxi heading to the shops and he walking leisurely down to the Champs-Élysées, then around the Place de la Concorde, to the Tuileries Gardens. Part way there Charlie stopped to buy an *International Herald Tribune* and a *Wall Street Journal*. His plan was to read them this warm, sunny morning on a park bench near the first large, round fountain and water basin in the gardens.

Ten minutes later he had positioned himself on a bench with the sun behind him and his sunglasses perched on his nose. He read and occasionally looked up to enjoy seeing the young mothers strolling with their babies and toddlers over the crushed stone pathways. The world seemed pleasantly aligned at that moment, and as the newspapers reported, even the financial markets were behaving.

During one of these moments of looking up, Charlie noticed a man in a navy-blue sport coat and khaki trousers walking swiftly by the other side of the water basin. Although he could see only the man's profile, he thought he recognized Ron Gelb. In a minute the man was past, walking up the stairs toward the l'Orangerie Museum. Charlie hesitated, then stood up to follow him. He couldn't be Gelb. I have Ron Gelb on my mind. I'll follow him to prove that I am being silly. Suddenly the man disappeared among groups of tourists. Charlie thought it had been Gelb, but in truth he had only met him once and could not be sure. Of course, it was possible that Gelb had come to Paris just as he had, on vacation. Charlie instantly regretted that he had not acted quicker and followed the man. As he sat back on the bench, he dismissed the idea that it was Gelb as too improbably a coincidence. Plus, the FBI should have arrested him by now.

A few minutes later his curiosity got the best of him and on the chance that the man had entered the l'Orangerie, Charlie folded up his papers, stuck them in his coat pocket, and headed toward l'Orangerie. But after an hour and a half of not seeing the man, Charlie gave up hope that he would ever see him again. He proceeded with his original plan and had lunch on the Left Bank, walked by the holiday-shuttered gallery of the art dealer Archambault, and crossed the Alexander Bridge with its remarkable gilted, art-nouveau sculptures and lamps.

About a block from his hotel, Charlie looked up and was surprised to see the same man he had seen in the Tuileries earlier crossing the Avenue Georges V. Once again the man seemed to focus on his task. As the fellow crossed the street he did not bother to look at the traffic entering the avenue. At the corner where the hotel stood, he glanced at the doorman and preceded down the street, Avenue Peter the First of Serbia.

This time Charlie did not hesitate. He rushed up to the corner and watched the man, who looked more and more like Gelb, stop at several townhouses, looking up and consulting a piece of paper.

Charlie followed him at a distance, wondering what the man found so interesting. Suddenly he turned around and seemed to recognize Charlie. He hesitated a moment, then headed directly towards Charlie. As he came closer, Charlie became convinced it was Gelb. His face was flushed with anger.

"Why are you following me?" Gelb demanded. "I told you what I know in New York. I have no time for you. Stay away!"

"Wait!" Charlie said. "I wasn't sure it was you. I had no idea you would be in Paris."

Gelb pointed over Charlie's right shoulder, and Charlie turned instinctively in that direction. He then felt a sharp, heavy blow to his left temple and he fell to the sidewalk. Temporarily he lost awareness of where he was. Alert again he saw that two men had rushed over to help him. Others on the street gathered around. Charlie was in pain as he got up, but searched the men surrounding him for Gelb.

"Qu'est l'homme qu'est me frappe?" Charlie asked in his high school French. One of the bystanders pointed in the direction of the Place d'Irène Mêtro station but Charlie could see nothing through the crowd. Gelb had disappeared.

By that time the doorman from the Georges V had arrived and recognized Charlie.

"Monsieur Bailey. What has happened? Come with me into the hotel. We'll get a doctor *immédiatement*."

* * *

How unlikely can it be? What are the odds of Bailey being in Paris now? Is it a coincidence or am I paranoid? I guess I overreacted by sucker-punching him but I was pissed off that he seemed to be following me. I thought that I noticed him in the Tuileries, but there he was again near the Georges V. The FBI spooked me in New York—calling me in after Bailey asked me questions. It was good that my drug dealer called me after the FBI asked him about me. I knew I had to push up my trip to France at once. Thank god the insurance money came quickly.

Everything was going smoothly until Bailey showed up. Cynthia started the whole deal by telling me of the prospective Bailey donation. She was very excited. I saw immediately that her intimate knowledge of the timetable for the donation and the inner workings of the gallery's security measures made her key to a theft. Of course the theft and resale of just the Bailey gift was not attractive enough for me to risk my whole career. It was when she told me about the list of unsold paintings on the back of the sketch that I became interested. Her viewpoint was that of the art history scholar: she had found some priceless Degas works of art never notated in the publications. She thought this discovery could be the basis of a thesis. I thought they could be the basis of a fortune. I did my own research and concurred that most of the paintings had never been sold. Mary Cassatt may have stored them somewhere after Degas's death. Or she distributed them to the two individuals intended. If so, I'll find them.

Cynthia would never have agreed to steal the Bailey paintings unless she was compromised. She took the Adderall at first but only became addicted later with the street speed. Even then I wasn't certain she would go ahead with my plan until she came out the back of the museum with the two paintings. I think that I convinced her that we needed to steal the sketch so that no one would be able to see the list on the back and damage her chances of proving a scholarly "find". I also made the case that the Hassam would be returned to Yale through an insurance buy-back. In the end Yale would have the Cassatt and Hassam paintings. She persuaded herself—with my help that Yale wouldn't miss the sketch, since it had little artistic merit, and she would have the only source document for her thesis. The money was also nice. I don't know whether it was her need for a fix or my arguments that had the greatest effect on her, but the combination worked. She came around—after many meetings.

Of course, Cynthia was erratic and unreliable—changing her mind regularly. There was no way to trust her afterwards. So my drug dealer helped me out. He told me how arsenic worked. If arsenic were mixed into red wine a drugee would never taste it. He said that the poison was unnoticeable for several hours but ultimately effective. He was right.

I thought my plan was clever. I particularly liked my decision not to take the Cassatt painting. Since it was worth several millions, the police would assume the thieves were not experts in art valuations. Only someone outside the art world would take the sketch and leave the Cassatt. I wanted the theft to appear like an amateur production.

The only thing that went wrong was the unexpected appearance of Cynthia's neighbor taking out the trash. I turned away before she could see my face. But, the incident gave me a scare.

I hope I am discouraging Bailey. If he persists, I'll have to take care of him. My goal now is to find that trove of paintings. Works of art of that quality and provenance cannot go unnoticed for one hundred years. They have to be misplaced in storage somewhere, and whoever has them has no idea of their worth. The trail starts with Mary Cassatt, the person who made the list. The search should be straightforward, but I need to be careful—don't stay in anyplace too long, never charge anything in my name, trust no one, and let nobody see the sketch.

Chapter Twenty-Eight

"I think you'll have a black eye," Kate pronounced after examining the bruise that ran from Charlie's left eye to his temple. "Does it hurt?"

"Yes, but my pride more than the scrape," said Charlie. "I fell for the oldest schoolyard trick—a distraction—followed by a sucker-punch. If my old marine buddies heard about this, I'd be laughed out of the corps."

"Charlie, you don't have to worry about that. You left the marines at least fifteen years ago. Still, I get your point."

As Kate dabbed his abrasion with a wet hand towel, Charlie eyed Kate's purchases spread on the bed. "That looks like a good haul. You have been busy."

"Yes, I have," Kate said excitedly. "It's so long since I have really shopped all day looking at gorgeous things. If you're up to it, let me show you."

"If you model them, I'm all eyes," Charlie said as he moved over to sit in the fauteuil. To his amazement Kate proceeded to exhibit coquettishly a pair of shoes, a dress, a scarf, a skirt, two blouses, and two pieces of luggage. At the end of this fashion show, she picked up a tie box and presented it to Charlie.

"See, I didn't forget you. I looked in Hermès but didn't see anything I liked. This afternoon I found this at Celine, and I love it for you. You can wear it to work and at parties."

Charlie went along with the mood Kate had created and opened his gift with a flourish. He found a light blue tie sprinkled with tiny red dots. He held it up to his chest and grinned.

"Gee, thanks. Now I have a real French tie to go with my Brooks Brothers and Ferragamo ones. I'll be the envy of all my friends."

"Enough of the humor. I like it."

After Kate put everything away Charlie proposed a celebration, opened a bottle of champagne in the suite, and poured two glasses.

"Kate, I'm going to nail Gelb. He has gone too far. I assumed he FBI had arrested him in New York. They must have hesitated, or he slipped away from them."

"Hold on, Charlie. I know I have flip-flopped on the issue of your involvement. I was as gung ho as you after the Carlyle incident, but after today I'm scared again. Scared that this murderer could hurt you. Be sensible. Let's bring in the French police, the FBI, even the marines. Let them take care of Gelb."

"I hear you and I'll call Jackie Farrell in a minute. I'm just not confident in the FBI at this moment. They had an eyewitness ID but obviously did not arrest Gelb. They need help. Something is screwy. If Gelb is running from the FBI, why is he in broad daylight on the streets of Paris? If he were fearful, he would be hiding in some small town in the Black Forest. No, he's motivated. He's looking for something. I think it has something to do with the sketch. If we solve the riddle of the sketch, I'll bet we'll find Gelb nearby."

"Charlie, you amaze me and frighten me. You don't listen to my concerns for you. You are obsessed by Gelb. He has a grip on you. Until he's in prison, you won't let go of the personal wrong he did to your mother and the tragedy he inflicted on Cynthia and her family."

"Yes, he did." Charlie said.

"You have always been successful through your charm and intelligence. Now the situation is different. This is the real world of bad guys. Gelb doesn't care about charm and intelligence. I ask you again—no, I beg you— walk away. Tell Jackie your theories, and let's return to Chicago."

Charlie conceded Kate's passion. He saw it in her face and her body language. He understood that she meant well. He even appreciated that most people would agree with her. However, unless this issue was so important to her that his stubbornness would damage their marriage, he was going ahead.

"Kate, I respect your viewpoint. But you know it goes against my very nature to be less than fully committed to stop this lowlife. Call me obsessive if you will. I have faults. I can't change. I must go ahead, and I hope you will work with me as you have. I need you. I love you."

Kate started to cry softly. Charlie walked over to her sitting on the couch and hugged her. After a few minutes she said, "Okay. You call Jackie Farrell now. I need to be alone." She stood up and went into the bedroom shutting the door.

Charlie slumped on the couch. He did not like to upset Kate. The last time they argued on this same topic it took several days and a physical assault on her to get her to come around. Hopefully now she would need less time.

While Kate was still in the bathroom, he asked the hotel operator to call Jackie Farrell's number. After a few rings, Alice Cho picked up and told him Jackie was out of the office.

"What I have to tell her is important to her investigation of the Yale thefts."

"If you are patient, I'll try to patch you through, Mr. Bailey. I'm putting you on 'hold'."

Five minutes later, Charlie had Jackie on the phone. He told her where he was in Paris on vacation with Kate.

"But the damnest thing happened today," he said. "I saw Ron Gelb on the street."

"Where did this happen?" Jackie asked in a flat voice.

"Once in the Tuileries Garden and the other time near my hotel, the Georges V."

"Was he following you?"

"No, but he recognized me and accused me of following him. Then he punched me in the face and fled the scene."

"Are you hurt?"

"A little bit."

"Were you following him?"

"Of course not. I had no idea Gelb was in Paris. I thought you had him on your radar screen and possibly had arrested him in New York."

"Gelb is still a person of interest to us. My colleagues and I would like to talk to you about this encounter and what you intend to do in France. Can you meet us tomorrow morning at nine in your hotel?"

"Are you in Paris?" Charlie asked, puzzled by Jackie's offer.

"Yes. Is that time convenient?"

What a surprise! The FBI—and Gelb—were here. What a coincident! Yet this situation was not pure chance. Rocky had said that the FBI was watching us in Chicago. After we left it would have been easy for them to check the airlines to locate us. They were likely also following Gelb. He probably led them to Paris.

Charlie wondered if the FBI thought that his vacation was a ruse to mask his investigation of Gelb. Jackie had seemed suspicious of his explanation. If he took the FBI's point of view, he concluded that it was odd that both Gelb and he had come to Paris at the same time.

Kate emerged from the bathroom with swollen eyes. She came over to Charlie and hugged him for a moment saying nothing. Charlie interpreted her behavior positively. She might have wished that he took her advice, but she was still his partner.

He told her of his phone call and the planned meeting tomorrow.

"Join us. I would welcome your support. Besides, you should meet these agents who are currently part of our lives."

"What are you planning to do after the meeting?"

"I need to do some research to understand where Gelb is going. I want to know more about Mary Cassatt and Edgar Degas."

"Here we go again," Kate muttered.

Chapter Twenty-Nine

"Danny, your instincts are good. It's confirmed. Gelb is still here in Paris," Jackie reported when Flood returned to their conference room after her phone call with Charlie. They had been camped out in the headquarters of the Central Directorate of Judicial Police on the Rue des Saussaies in the middle of Paris since they arrived at the Charles de Gaulle airport in the morning.

"What did I miss?" Danny asked.

"Bailey called me, out of the blue. New York patched him through. He saw Gelb today—on the street. They even had a scuffle. Gelb ran off. I set up a meeting with Bailey first thing tomorrow morning."

"Weird. Why not tonight?"

Jackie felt deflated suddenly. She was pleased that she had this remarkable news for Danny but now she worried that she made a mistake. "I thought we could use the time to plan our interview with Bailey," Jackie stammered unconvincingly. "Besides, we have jet lag."

"No wonder you're doing artsy stuff. Come on. That lead could be hot."

"Should I call him back?"

"No, you need your sleep," Danny said sarcastically.

Jackie was tired of Danny Flood after only one day together in France. He had been in a foul mood ever since they landed. First, he had received an email from his office that said that Ron Gelb had checked into the Hotel de la Trémoille in Paris the day before but had checked out already. No other hotel had reported him yet. That fact made him curse out loud. Then after an expedited passage through Passport Control, they found Aldo Laval waiting for them at the luggage carousel. Jackie recognized Aldo immediately. They had met two years before at a symposium. Jackie could see that Danny was unimpressed.

Laval was a short, trim, brown-haired man wearing a gray suit and tie. He appeared permanently sleepy because his eyes drooped with heavy bags. He managed a brief smile when Jackie approached and greeted her. "*Jacqueline, bonjour et bienvenue à Paris.*"

"Aldo, thanks for coming on short notice. Let me introduce my colleague, Danny Flood, who is lead on this case."

"Welcome to Paris, Agent Flood. I trust we can be of service to you both."

"Right," said Danny crankily.

They retrieved their bags and crammed into a black, staff Citroën with a driver. During the long drive into the city, Jackie reviewed the case for Aldo, with particular emphasis on Ron Gelb and Charlie Bailey.

"How certain are you that Monsieur Gelb is *coupable*—guilty?" Laval asked.

"Very. He had motive and opportunity. He lied to us during interrogation. We have a partial ID from an eyewitness. And he fled the country when we got near him. We know he has been in France. As a consequence, we are here to facilitate his arrest and deportation."

"*Bon.* If you wish, I'll contact the Police Nationale to pick him up. In the meantime, we can drive to their offices and wait."

"Where is that?" asked Jackie.

"It's part of the Ministry of the Interior. The building is practically across the street from the Élysée Palace, right in the middle of Paris."

"Why are you so confident that you'll find Gelb?" Flood asked with genuine curiosity.

"People leave traces—hotels, airplanes, credit cards, phone calls. Our police are good."

During the drive, Jackie gave Aldo a photograph of Gelb and various personal information like cell, credit card, bank account, and passport numbers.

When they arrived, Aldo led them to an empty conference room and then left to make arrangements for an all points bulletin for a detention of

Ronald Gelb. While he was gone, Danny made fun of his accent and questioned whether an Interpol detective specializing in art thefts had the right credentials for what they needed.

"We'll find out," Jackie said, annoyed at his second-guessing.

Aldo returned after fifteen minutes.

"I hope we'll find Mister Gelb quickly. In the meantime, you can enjoy the sights of Paris. This is a good time to be here. Exhibitions, shopping, great restaurants—all *ouvert*."

"Great, but we're not here to play," said Danny matter-of-factly. "By the way, is this room secure?"

"Yes, no two-way walls or hidden microphones," Aldo laughed.

"Look, I am confident that your local police are good," Danny continued. "But we need to approach this case as if Gelb is hard to find."

"*D'accord*," Aldo agreed. "I admire your serious approach. I must leave you now for a few hours. I have another case I need to tend to. *Au revoir*."

Sitting in that small room with only limited air circulation for several hours calling and emailing back to the States, eating fast food sent in to them, and hearing no news from the French only worsened Danny's disposition by the time of Charlie Bailey's call. So Jackie delighted when Danny agreed to go to bed. They walked together to their hotel, checked in, and went to their rooms.

Jackie was relieved the next morning over breakfast at the hotel that Danny had stopped criticizing her. Aldo joined them halfway through the meal. He had called Danny earlier to ask to join them with Charlie Bailey.

"Here's the procedure this morning," Danny began when Aldo sat down. "I ask all the questions. You two watch Bailey to see if he is holding back on us. I have no idea why he and his wife are in Paris. There are hundreds of places to go on vacation. He picks the one place where Gelb is. Then he sees Gelb, supposedly by chance. What are the probabilities? He must think I believe in Santa Claus and the tooth fairy as well."

"The tooth fairy?" Aldo asked, not comprehending.

Danny ignored him.

"How far do we have to go?" Danny asked no one in particular.

"With traffic now, our driver will take fifteen minutes," Aldo answered.

"Let's go."

The trio of agents arrived before the Baileys and positioned themselves in chairs in the middle of the massive lounge to the right of the reception area. Jackie was surprised when she saw that Charlie was accompanied by his wife. Nonplussed for a second she nevertheless made all the introductions. They all sat down facing each other.

"Jackie, I guess you brought the A-team with you," Charlie said, apparently trying to keep the tone light. "I always wondered what someone from Interpol looked like. Mr. Laval, are you an art-theft expert like Miss Farrell?"

"*Oui*. We have a lot in common."

"But we don't have a lot of time, Mr. Bailey," Danny barged in. "Let's get down to business. We have a few questions for you in light of your reported sighting of Mr. Gelb."

"Certainly. It's our pleasure to meet you all. As I am sure Jackie has mentioned to you, my mother and I are anxious to recover both artworks stolen from Yale and to bring to justice Cynthia Newgate's murderer. So far, only one painting has been recovered. So there's more to be done. I am encouraged that you flew here from the States. My surmise is that you are taking this sad episode more seriously."

"Yes, obviously," said Danny impatiently. "What I don't understand is why you keep popping up in this investigation. After all, your mother gave the pictures to Yale. It's Yale that should be worried. And they are from what I hear. They are happy with you. Your mother gave a very generous gift. They are grateful. But they don't expect you to recover the stolen sketch for them. Yet you seem determined to be involved—despite Jackie telling you to keep out. What's the deal?"

"The deal is that my mother feels violated," Charlie said with emotion. "The works of art had great personal significance and emotion attached to them. She is an elderly woman and cannot rest until her whole gift is intact and in the hands of Yale. She is also understandably concerned about the death of her grandniece. My wife and I worry about her. She has a history of heart issues. These events don't help. With all due respect, the local police and your organization have not succeeded with your investigation. The Childe Hassam painting was returned—for a price and without your assistance. The sketch is still missing and the killer is still at large. And there have been times when I felt that the FBI was doing nothing to solve the case. Frankly, I have been disappointed."

"What do you know about police work?" Danny countered. "Any fool would know it is dangerous—especially murder cases. Amateurs fooling around can only get hurt. And you, Bailey, are an amateur."

"Touché. That is the most passion from the FBI I have witnessed all summer. Perhaps you are committed to this case, after all. By the way, you can't hurt my feelings. I am used to criticism. Let me add, though, I don't think you would be over here looking for Ron Gelb without the help I provided to your investigation. So if the histrionics are over, I am prepared to answer your questions."

"Finally," Danny sighed.

Jackie looked at Aldo, who appeared alarmed at Danny's approach. She was used to him; Aldo was not. Jackie was more amused than dismayed. Charlie seemed to be a match for Danny.

"Okay. Why are you here? Have you been following Gelb?"

"Not at all," Charlie laughed. "Kate and I had hoped to escape all the pressures of the past few months by taking a spur-of-the-moment vacation. We agreed that Paris at this time of year would be beautiful and romantic. The last person I expected to see was Ron Gelb."

"When and where did you see Ron Gelb?"

Charlie recounted in detail his sightings of Gelb and the assault he endured outside the hotel. He added that Gelb warned him to quit following him.

"It seems like both you and Gelb want me to disappear," Charlie joked.

"You seem to find this situation amusing, Mr. Bailey. I do not. Was Gelb alone both times you saw him?"

"Yes."

"Could you tell what he was looking for before he saw you?"

"No. He seemed to be interested in a building on the street to the right of the hotel as you go out. Why? I don't know."

"How long do you intend to stay in Paris?"

"A few more days. I want to visit some museums, and Kate still has shopping to do. Since Jackie had us followed in Chicago, I'm certain you'll know where we are."

Jackie nearly fell out of her chair. She had no idea that Bailey knew about the surveillance. That was one more thing that Danny would criticize her for. This trip was a nightmare so far.

"Now that you have been spotted, you may be in danger," Danny continued. "I think it would be best if you left sooner than later. In the meantime, I am going to give you a local telephone number to call if you happen to see Gelb again or remember anything you forgot to tell us."

"It's been a pleasure, gentlemen," Charlie said as he stood up and took the card. "Happy hunting."

Kate stood up following Charlie's lead. She shook the agents' hands and thanked them for their efforts.

Jackie judged that Kate had better manners than her husband. Charlie's intensity sometimes made him seem rude.

When the Baileys had left, Danny turned to Jackie and said, "Your description of him was right on. I can usually tell if a person is lying or hiding something. I have a sense developed over the years watching and listening to scumbags, addicts, inveterate liars, and innocent people. Bailey is straight. He might hold back on some things, but he'll tell us all he knows when he is ready. On the most important point, based on his past behavior, he is not going to walk away from Gelb. He thinks we are the Keystone Kops—inept bozos. So he needs to do something on his own. Aldo, we must have him followed. I have an odd feeling that if the locals don't find Gelb, our friend Bailey will."

Chapter Thirty

Back in their hotel room after the FBI interview, Charlie asked Kate, "How do you think it went?"

"You were honest. You told them what they wanted to know. On the other hand, Agent Flood was unpleasant. He left his manners in New York—if he had any. I applaud you for keeping your cool. I wouldn't have faulted you if you had let him have it."

"He was just doing his job," Charlie said excusing him. "He probably thought intimidation and bullying would make us go home. Fat chance."

"Yes, I know only too well: 'fat chance'," Kate sighed. "What's next? Are we going to pretend that nothing has happened and enjoy a vacation here, or do you have another plan?"

"Yes, I do. We are going to find a missing trove of Degas paintings, if they still exist."

"You mean the list on the sketch?"

"Precisely. Gelb must think the paintings are somewhere in France or he would have sold the sketch back to Yale. Why else did he come here?"

"Do you think Cynthia thought there was a missing trove?"

"Absolutely. She probably discussed the list with Gelb—most likely from a scholarly point of view. Discover the trove and publish an article. She may have seen the subject as a way to burnish her credentials for a Ph.D. and a curatorship. Remember that Seth Price's colleague suggested that some of the titles never appeared in the auction data after Degas's death? If we could uncover that fact, then it's likely that experts like Cynthia and Gelb concluded the same thing. The paintings may have been stored somewhere for decades. They may have thought that if they could locate and obtain the paintings somehow, they would have works of art worth tens of millions of dollars and earn invaluable academic recognition to boot. A scholarship payoff."

"Wait a second, Charlie. I am starting to catch up to you. Cynthia must have told Gelb that the list was facing a blank wall in your mom's house for decades. No one knew the list existed because no one would have had a reason to look behind the sketch. That's why Gelb is keeping the sketch to himself. He thinks no one knows about the list."

"A good assumption—except for one thing. Unknown to him my father had the front and back photographed for insurance purposes. So we know about the list also, and he doesn't know we know."

"I get it. We are both looking for the same priceless group of paintings. Gelb may not be concerned about us in his search because he thinks we are interested only in the return of the sketch and the identity of Cynthia's killer—nothing else. If he can evade the FBI, he can search unimpeded at his own pace."

Charlie nodded agreement and added, "He's likely unaware that we are looking for the same thing as he is. It's an advantage to be aware of what he is doing while he is ignorant of what we are doing."

"I suppose we could say that, if we find the trove, we'll also find Gelb."

"Unless we get there first. Nevertheless, you're right either way. Even if we find the art first, I expect that Gelb won't be far behind."

"Okay, so your objective is to find the treasure before Gelb?"

Charlie did not answer her. He couldn't predict how their efforts would work out. Looking for the same thing as Gelb, he imagined that they would meet Gelb along the way. It would be exciting to find the trove. However, it was essential to apprehend Gelb.

"Either way the attempt is dangerous, considering that we think Gelb is a murderer," Kate warned.

"True. Remember though, Jackie Farrell and Danny Flood should be following us. At any rate, when we find the trove, we'll call them immediately."

"Why not just let the FBI and Interpol do the work?"

"Because I think they are better at finding and tracking human beings than works of art."

Kate sat back in the well-cushioned sofa and sipped a glass of water. Her look suggested to Charlie that this conversation was kindling her enthusiasm. She was smiling and looking down at her drink.

"So it's a chase—just like in the movies," she said. "You and me against Gelb. Who finds the missing trove first? We'll try to avoid him because he can be trouble. At the end, we find the paintings and Gelb walks into a trap. Who plays me in the movie?"

Charlie laughed and was delighted Kate was warming to the mission.

"The Katherine Hepburn *du jour*. Tall, beautiful, intelligent and sexy."

"A brunette, I hope. Maybe Angelina Jolie. You can be a blond, Brad Pitt."

"That's a deal."

"Charlie, I hate to be a spoil-sport, but what if Mary Cassatt or Degas had given or sold the paintings to a private collector ninety years ago? The collector and his family may have just kept the treasure to themselves. Why do we think we can find something that art scholars have missed for decades?"

"They haven't been looking. My initial guess is that the trove is sitting in a closet or old garage or warehouse forgotten or not recognized for what it is. But you are right. There is certainly a risk that we'll never find the trove. At a minimum, in looking we'll probably come across Gelb who we can turn over to the FBI. That would be reward enough, I suppose."

"Knowing you, I doubt it. You want to find both the paintings and Gelb. In my mind I have been trying to distance the chase for the trove from confronting Mr. Gelb as two different events. I was naïve. You won't be avoiding Gelb. You'll take him down whenever you have the chance. Gelb is the cake, and the trove is the icing. That's the real assignment."

"Yes. The trove is the bait in the trap."

"Back to 'dangerous'." Kate declared.

Having confirmed his mission, Charlie told Kate that first he needed to do some research to learn more about Degas and Mary Cassatt. He wanted to see where they lived who were their friends and business associates, who were their relatives, where their art was exhibited during their lives, and where they traveled outside Paris. The more he knew, the greater the likelihood that he could interpret the meaning and purpose of the list. He admitted that they were lucky to be in Paris, since a great amount of information would be in the art libraries of the city. In addition, they would be able to visit the apartments and studios where the artists worked and walk the streets they had walked.

To begin the research he mentioned to Kate that he needed to call Seth to find out how he could get in the academic libraries. Seth was certain to know. At this hour in Chicago Seth would not be in his office yet, so he suggested to Kate that she might go shopping or join him for a lengthy lunch in an hour at a café on the Champs Élysée. Kate chose the lunch, saying she was in no mood to shop and anyway she wanted to participate in the research. She went so far as to say that she was eager to get started.

After killing an hour in their room, they went out and found an outdoor café on the famous boulevard where they enjoyed the food and people watching. They amused themselves guessing who might be the policeman assigned to follow them. At two o'clock Charlie paid the bill and they walked back to their hotel to call Seth.

"Seth, I need another favor."

"I am happy to help you, Charlie, if I can. What do you need?"

"Of course, you remember the art theft. You were extremely helpful to us. Currently Kate and I are in Paris on vacation. While we're here, I thought it would be useful in understanding the motive behind the theft to learn more about Degas and Cassatt. Where would you go if you wanted to do some historical research?"

"Well, I agree that you are in the right city. As you know, French Impressionism is not my field, but you might start with the pictures in the museum. After that, go to two libraries, both of which should be superb for your purposes. First, the Sorbonne. That's what people call the school—but actually the Sorbonne is part of the University of Paris. They have an esteemed Department of Art History as part of the school. You would need me to call an acquaintance of mine to get you access to their library. I can certainly do that."

"That would be wonderful," Charlie said with sincerity.

"The other library to visit is part of the Louvre. It is a true research center. I've been there. By appointment only. On a little street just off the

Tuilleries Gardens. But wait...Impressionists. I would bet that more would be over at the Research Center at the Musée d'Orsay. I'll go through our computer contacts files and find my colleague there. I'm sure it will be okay for you to visit. When do you want to go to both places?"

"Today, if it is possible."

"Then I'll call now. If you have any trouble, let me know immediately. I must admit that I find it flattering that my brilliant schoolmate is interested in art history scholarship. I would be very interested to hear about your experience when you are back in town."

"I am indebted to you. I'm obviously just a dilettante compared to you, but I think this project will be great fun. Could you add Kate also? She wants to join me."

"Of course. I'll email you the arrangements. Good luck."

Within an hour Seth confirmed his conversation with contacts at the two research centers and gave Charlie instructions how to find the libraries. Their first stop was the art-history library in the Musée d'Orsay.

When they found the library and read the brochures describing its contents, Charlie was relieved that Seth had guessed correctly. Indeed, a multitude of books relating to Impressionists were in this library—many more than at the main Research Center for the Louvre on the Rue St. Rock off the Tuilleries. Seth had done his job calling, because the front desk had their names. The library staff assigned them to a cubicle with a computer from which he quickly ordered up biographical books and articles about Mary Cassatt and Edgar Degas. A huge amount of material was available, and the staff produced it efficiently in twenty minutes. Not surprisingly, much of it was repetitive. What interested Charlie mostly were descriptions of where the artists lived and who were their friends, foes, and acquaintances; when paintings were completed; and how and to whom the artworks were sold during their lifetimes and after death. All these facts were easily accessible—even to someone like Charlie with three years of college French.

By closing time, they had accumulated a vast amount of pertinent information transferred to notes on his iPad. Charlie certainly felt that now he knew these two artists and their milieu well. A thought that occurred to him after digesting the material was whether any of the places referenced still existed after more than one hundred years. He welcomed the idea of walking the streets of Paris and visiting the referenced places. These places, if still standing, just might give him an appreciation and a feel for these individuals and their lifestyles. Perhaps—just perhaps—this immersion in the surroundings of Cassatt and Degas might also give him additional insights to the list on the back of the sketch. So in the taxi ride back to the hotel he discussed with Kate his desire to take a walking tour the next day.

"That sounds like a terrific idea," she said excitedly. "I learned a lot today, but a book is just a book. Visiting the places described puts color on the picture. Did you discover anything especially significant in your reading?"

"I did. Did you know that Mary Cassatt lived for a time in an apartment just around the corner from the hotel—on the street where I saw Gelb yesterday? Remember, I said that he was looking up at some buildings. He may have been trying to locate the precise building where she lived. Why? I don't know, but it may be significant. Perhaps he thinks the trove is there."

"Should we call Jackie about that?"

"No. Let's wait. I'm just guessing. Instead let's plan our walk tomorrow. While we are at it, let's visit the Sorbonne in the morning on the way. Its library may have something in addition to what we saw today. After that we can visit the neighborhoods where Degas and Mary Cassatt had their studios."

"A lot must have changed over the past hundred years."

"Of course, but some of the buildings will be the same and the distances between places haven't changed. We won't know unless we go."

"What about the place near the hotel?"

"We can drop by there on the way back tomorrow."

Over dinner at a bistro within walking distance of the hotel, they compared notes about the biographical information they had studied. Charlie emphasized the student-mentor relationship that Mary Cassatt had with Degas early in her career. They had their disagreements over the years—principally attributed to Degas's dyspeptic personality. Nevertheless, Cassatt recognized Degas's immense artistic talent and worked hard to maintain their friendship. Even in his later years when he was almost blind and very ill, she visited him often to keep him current on the latest news and gossip and to offer her assistance to his niece, Jeanne Fèvre, and his housekeeper, Zoë Closier, who took care of him.

Charlie's fascination with this latter part of Degas's life was related to the missing sketch. Quite likely Cassatt would have spent at least one of her visits at Degas's bedside sketching him to pass the time and serve as a remembrance of her mentor and friend. Perhaps she did other sketches as well, although none was mentioned in the material he had read earlier in the day.

Kate said she was taken by the feminist issues in the Mary Cassatt history. She admired the artist as a pioneer for women in a male-dominant profession. Mary left her affluent Philadelphia family to pursue a painting career in a foreign country. It hurt her that many people in her social class frowned on her choices. Ladies in her day were permitted to appreciate art but not to pursue it personally. Mary broke the rules. She was a single woman sketching models in exotic places like Italy and France. Such behavior was not proper or respectable. If such biases were not enough, the French establishment ignored or demeaned female artists in general—particularly the few American artists. Just as significant in labeling Mary as a rebel, she had chosen to paint in an Impressionist style. Surprising to Kate, she read that art dealers and collectors found Impressionism scandalous and unworthy of a serious consideration for decades. In fact most of the famous Impressionists, whom Kate felt were among the greatest artists of all time, lived impoverished during most of their careers. The all-powerful Académie des Beaux-Art steadfastly refused to exhibit their style of painting.

"Charlie, Mary Cassatt could easily have given up. Her brother was one of the most successful businessmen in America. She could have gone home, married, and lived a comfortable life in the upper reaches of society. Instead she persevered, developed her talent, introduced wealthy American tourists to the next generation of great artists, and created a collection of works of art admired and coveted by museums and art lovers worldwide. She's a great American story."

Charlie smiled, delighting in Kate's enthusiasm. He had hoped that she would feel that way. Their tastes in art were not identical, but he was happy that she had developed a passionate regard for an artist he also admired. It was another interest they could share.

Of course, when it came to the creation of art, Kate was way ahead of him. After all, after school she had hoped to make a career in art-painting and sculpture. But her tiny gallery had failed commercially. So she changed jobs, joining her current advertising company in the art department. Quickly she became so well thought of in the firm that they promoted her upstairs to her present executive position. But she understood artists. She was one herself.

Walking back to the hotel, Charlie took Katie's arm and felt her snuggle close to him. This shared enthusiasm and the lively and romantic city made the moment warm and magical. He could not wait until tomorrow—working with Kate.

Chapter Thirty-One

"According to the map, we are only a block from Mary Cassatt's apartment," Charlie said, looking at his travel guide and pointing his finger at an area on his map. "But if you are as hungry as I am, we can stop at one of these restaurants on the boulevard here. What do you say?"

"I'm game. Besides, if we spend some time walking around Montmartre, I'll need some nourishment because of the hills."

Kate was relieved they were stopping. She was mentally tired. They had spent the morning in the Sorbonne library, thanks to Seth Price's contacts. Sharing a cubicle with two computers, they selected books and articles they had not seen during their research the day before. Over a nearly three-hour period Kate found the work both educational and exhausting. They rarely spoke to each other. She was absorbed but found reading so much in a foreign language under what she perceived as time pressure stressed her. Every so often she would glance over at Charlie, who was rapidly skimming pages and taking notes. He didn't seem to tire which she attributed to his high energy and intense personality.

At twelve-thirty he stopped as promised and asked her if she was finished. Kate answered that she had learned enough for today and would appreciate seeing the sun again. Once outside, Charlie released some pent up energy by pointing out the nearby sites.

"This is the Latin Quarter, and the Sorbonne is the seat of the University of Paris. Its one of the oldest sections of the city and known for its artists, bohemian students, and history of political unrest."

"It looks peaceful enough this glorious summer day," Kate observed.

"That building over there is the National Museum of the Middle Ages, known as Cluny," Charlie continued as they crossed the Rue des Écoles holding hands.

"I wish I knew French history in more detail," Kate lamented. "Then I would appreciate better what you are describing."

"You know plenty, dear wife. I hope you don't think I'm condescending with my tour-guide *patois*. I'll stop if you wish."

"No, continue. I'll speak up when I have something to add or when I've had enough."

Sometimes Kate humored Charlie by letting him go on. To her mind he was a frustrated teacher who needed a chance to show off. No harm done.

"Where to now?" she asked.

"To the St. Michel Mêtro Station and then on to Anvers."

When they emerged up the Mêtro stairs at Anvers into the strong sunlight near the former studios of Degas and several other impressionists, it was a natural time to stop. They settled on the first restaurant with outdoor seating and were directed to a table where an awning was shielding the sun. The menu was typical of hundreds of Parisian restaurants, so they spent little time studying it. Steak, frites, and a salade with a glass of house red wine suited them both. The busy street where they were sitting, Boulevard de Rochechouart, was wide but not particularly memorable, with stores on the sidewalk level and apartments and offices above. There was a grassy island populated with trees in the middle of the street, separating the traffic and the noise of the cars and buses. Despite this mundane urban setting, they were content sitting, watching the people hurry by, trying to imagine what Paris had been like over a hundred years before, and eating a passable lunch common to the daily French diet.

Feeling the relaxing effect of the wine, they discussed the research they had done in the morning. Charlie had focused on biographical information, places where the artists had lived and worked, and the art they produced. Kate was more interested in relationships between the artists. She was pleasantly surprised how well acquainted were such famous artists as Manet, Cézanne, Renoir, Monet, Pissaro, and Degas. She imagined an animated conversation over dinner in a café between Monet, Cézanne, and Degas about the use of color, the importance of drawing, and subject matter. If she could have only been a fly on the wall. She wondered how the two women in the group, Berthe Morisot and Mary Cassatt, were treated and judged. Degas had encouraged them, but others in the art community only accepted their work begrudgingly.

As Kate contemplated this issue, Charlie paid the bill with cash. Charlie said, "Let's explore the neighborhood."

"*On y va*," Kate responded standing up.

Walking slowly, they stopped briefly to study the façades of two historic buildings, the Élysée-Montmartre, the renowned *can-can* dance hall, and the Grand Trianon, one of the first movie theaters in the city. Then they headed south through Place d'Anvers to the wide tree-lined Avenue Trudaine. Kate located number 13 across from a school. She had read that Mary Cassatt lived there with her family for several years. Her studio had been nearby. The street was essentially residential with the school occupying half of its length. Charlie explained that while this street was technically a part of the Montmartre district, it was decidedly on the edge. He mentioned that most of the artists who lived in this district settled on the Boulevard de Clichy or north nearer to the Sacré-Coeur Basilica, which dominated the skyline. Kate guessed that Mary had found this street quieter and slightly more upscale but still near the center for the artistic and creative world of Paris. Charlie pointed out that the principal meeting places in Montmartre in Mary's day were the Boulevard de Clichy or the Place du Tertre, about a fifteen-minute walk up the steep hills of the district. There, artists would meet to eat and discuss their latest project.

"Today I am told," Charlie said, "the Place du Tertre is mobbed by tourists serviced by quick portrait artists and souvenir sellers."

"How disappointing," Kate said. "Your description shatters my romantic picture of the square."

Charlie said that he had hoped to be inspired to some new insight by finding Number 13. But Kate saw that from the outside there was nothing to learn from it, other than it existed and was near where other Impressionists had lived.

"Should we ask someone about her apartment in the building?" Kate asked.

"Okay. I'll ring the bell. Maybe we'll be lucky about the trove."

There were several bells to choose from, as each floor must have had one or two apartments. As he was about to ring the first one, a woman came out the main door. She asked them if she could help, and Kate immediately explained that they were looking for the apartment of Mary Cassatt. The woman said she was of course familiar with it. She added that tourists and art experts come by every month or so, but that there was nothing to see. All the apartments were occupied and none of the residents were artists. At any rate, the apartment was the only one on the top floor—up five flights. Kate apologized for her question but explained that Mary Cassatt was her favorite artist, and she had wanted to see where she lived.

"Could we go up?" Kate asked.

The woman appeared annoyed by the request and said that the apartment was a private residence, which had nothing there from Mary Cassatt. She added tersely that her neighbor had mentioned that another American had been there the day before with the same request. He was told no also. With that the woman said she was late and hurried away.

"Charlie, could that American have been Gelb?" Kate asked.

"Possibly," Charlie said, catching Kate's smile. "If so, he's looking for the trove like we are. We may be on the right track."

"That's exciting. Do we go on or try to find a way to visit the apartment here anyways?"

"No. I assume for now that anyone living there would have found the paintings—if they were there. That news would have been in the material we read yesterday and today. I think we are looking for an empty or abandoned large apartment, warehouse, or garage.

"That makes sense," Kate agreed.

"At least we found the building. I think it must have been a nice place to live. From the top floors she and her family could see that park we passed and Montmartre above and Paris and the Seine below. Great view. Now do you want to look for the other addresses we found? Let me find my notes.

Here, 19 Rue de Laval. Another studio she worked in, I think, before this one. Or we could try 2 Rue Deperré."

"Both would be good, but I can't find either street on my map," Charlie said, disappointed. "I know from our research that these were off the Boulevard de Clichy, but they don't seem to exist now. Maybe the streets' names were changed at some point."

"This search may be more difficult than I thought. So what's next on your list?"

"Rue Victor-Massé, Degas's studio for many years before he became sick."

Kate noted that Rue Victor-Massé was only a short walk from Avenue Trudaine. As they strolled Charlie mentioned to Kate that Number 12 was the home of the *Chat Noir*, a very popular artistic cabaret during Degas's time. What they saw in general was a street lined with apartment buildings, some quite ornate, dating from the nineteenth century. Degas's home and studio was at Number 37. Charlie said that Degas leased the whole building and lived there from 1890 to 1917—not far from where he had lived elsewhere in the district.

"I can understand now how Mary Cassatt visited Degas so frequently," Charlie observed. "The proximity explains it. In fact from the 1870s for fifty years at least, this area must have been teeming with artists. No wonder that so many of the Impressionists knew each other well. Degas was different from other artists because he had family money—except for Mary of course. She also came from affluence. Maybe because Degas had access to funds, he bought many of his friends' paintings. Remember, a Cézanne was on the list. The books all said he was an avid collector."

"And hoarder," Kate added. "I read that he never sold anything. An exaggeration, perhaps, but since he had money, he didn't need to sell anything."

"True."

"You said 'friends'," Kate said, seeking clarification. "I read that Degas was a very difficult person to be around. He alienated just about everyone at one time or another."

"Okay. Not 'friends', but 'acquaintances'."

Kate spotted Number 37 and recognized the signs of extensive reconstruction. There would be no secrets left in that building.

Charlie said, "Clearly we aren't going to be able to visit the original studio in this building. Let's go up to the Boulevard de Clichy apartment where he died."

They walked to the Place Pigalle on the Boulevard de Clichy in less than five minutes. The change in atmosphere was immediate and depressing. Kate saw a large circular intersection dominated by strip clubs, porno shops, cheap cafés, and bars and peopled by street hustlers and a multitude of tourists of every nationality. It lacked charm and struck her as probably dangerous at night. Fortunately, they did not have far to go.

"Here it is, Kate. 6 Boulevard de Clichy. I wonder which floor he rented. According to one book I skimmed, his studio/apartment was huge. He needed the space to store his vast art collection. One book said that Degas moved eight times in his life in Paris—all within a ten-block radius. He obviously liked the neighborhood."

"If that was the case, this area must have been quite different over a hundred years ago. This street looks like the sin capital of Paris. I assume that years ago this was a bohemian village on the fringe of Paris, full of students and artists—lively but poor. *La Bohème*."

"I'm sure you're right, but I think the streets and nightclubs had their quota of prostitutes and drug dealers even then. The artwork of the period tells the story. Rich men had their dance-hall mistresses. Remember the movie *Moulin Rouge* and the Toulouse-Lautrec posters. Sex and art."

"So you think that this is the building where Mary Cassatt drew the sketch of the dying Degas?" asked Kate looking up at Number 6.

"Yes, I'm quite sure of it."

Charlie said that they would try to stop someone exiting the building to ask them which floor Degas occupied. But after ten minutes no one came out, and Kate felt restless. "Charlie, I don't think we'll learn anything more. We have to feel for the neighborhood. I am struck how close everything is. Just think, Renoir, Pissaro, Cézanne, Van Gogh, Seurat, Picasso, all lived within blocks of each other around the same time. Remarkable. I would have loved to have been sitting at the next table in one of the coffeehouses at the time. But standing here now, this street gives me the creeps. Can we move on? And don't ever bring me here at night."

"Of course, let's go. Our last stop will be the cemetery up the street—just past the *Moulin Rouge*. That's where Degas is buried."

They walked up the Boulevard de Clichy, avoiding the street artists, hustlers, daytime prostitutes, and mass of tourists until they saw the *Moulin Rouge* just past Place Blanche. The garish marquee and red windmill were still there.

"I thought the windmill would be taller," Kate said, disappointed.

"Yes, it's an icon. But famous places are often smaller or less impressive in reality than one imagines. The Statue of Liberty is beautiful, but it shrinks in comparison near some of the immense office buildings in lower Manhattan. It looks like the nightclub is open tonight. I bet you they still do the *can-can* and the women are half naked. Sort of a Las Vegas show for the impressionable. Plus they probably charge an arm and a leg for the spectacle. I'm glad you want to skip it."

"I do?" she questioned, then laughed. "But I'm happy to have seen it. I can tell my friends back home when they mention the movie or the Broadway musical. Besides, I can do my own *can-can* for you. Now you are actually going to take me to a cemetery?"

"Yes, to the right."

Kate had read that the Cemetière de Montmartre was the resting place of many famous painters, composers, poets, dancers, writers, and celebrities. A map found at the entrance directed them to the gravestones of interest. To her surprise Kate became engrossed by the cemetery immediately. She walked slowly, reading practically every gravestone. The markers were extremely close to each other, walkways were narrow, and trees lined the few wider paths. While she found the tombstones of the famous noteworthy, she was even more fascinated by the many graves of children and young adults. These tombstones gave her a sense of a community that had survived for centuries. These people had been born, grown up, worked, married, had children, and died nearby. They were not famous but were integral and important to the Montmartre district. They gave it vitality, joys, and tragedies as much as Degas, Nijinsky, and Truffaut, who were buried next to them. Ironically, the dead made Montmartre come alive to her.

"Kate, here is where Degas was buried. The undertakers did not have to take the body far. I read that Mary Cassatt went to his funeral and saw him buried. She wasn't in the best of health herself by then. She was probably quite sad to lose her old if irascible friend."

"Do you wonder if Gelb came here? I have the feeling that we are on parallel paths."

"My guess is that he is only interested in finding the trove. It's not buried here. I brought you here to help us understand who these people were."

"Thank you for that," said Kate sincerely. "Even if we couldn't visit inside the buildings, I appreciate better now how close Degas may have been to Mary and why he may have given her the trove when he was dying."

Kate and Charlie meandered through the cemetery until they reached the street. He said that he still wanted to go by the apartment building where Mary lived and housed her visiting family for several years. Her residence had been on the street near the hotel where he saw Gelb. Admitting they felt tired, they agreed to pass up another Mêtro trip and instead hailed a taxi.

They found the building, but like the others they had visited, it had been modernized. It was improbable that the trove had been secreted there for all those years.

"I give up," Kate said. "We did our best today. Finding the paintings is no clinch."

Charlie agreed and suggested that they return to their room, order room service, and plan for the next day. He mentioned for the first time that he had in mind a more likely place outside the city.

"Tell me more upstairs," Kate said, trying to be positive. "However, first I want to call your mother. We need to find out what the cardiologist said. I'm worried, and we are so far away."

Chapter Thirty-Two

"*Enfin*". We have a good lead," Aldo Laval announced enthusiastically to Danny Flood and Jackie Farrell as he entered their conference room in the Central Directorate of Judicial Police. The FBI agent had sat there with no new information for a day and a half since their talk with the Baileys at the Georges V. Aldo had arranged for an undercover policeman to follow the Baileys and had reiterated his request through police channels to locate the American visitor Ronald Gelb. Until now they had heard nothing but a few apologies from Laval for their lack of success.

Aldo's promising statement brightened Jackie's disposition. Spending a day with Danny tapping his fingers on the table and complaining about the ineptitude of the French had completely tested her patience. She was prepared to leave him there alone, until Laval had some news.

"I hope it's good," Danny said sarcastically. "I'm starting to think Bailey is correct in challenging our competence."

"This is good," Laval argued. "An American living in Paris in the Sixteenth Arrondisement near Avenue Foch put Gelb up in his apartment last night. This man, William Hecht, knows Gelb from New York, where he used to live. Gelb showed up at his apartment unannounced, saying he lost his travelers checks and credit card that day—probably to a pickpocket. He needed a place to stay for two days while he had money wired to him. Hecht agreed. He said that they had a nice dinner last night. Today Gelb said he was off to visit art galleries. Meanwhile Hecht went to his job at a global bank. When he came home at lunchtime he found several things missing: a suitcase, valise, passport, ATM card, VISA card, and a handgun. He went immediately to the local police to report the theft. Even though he found it hard to believe that his friend, a reputable art dealer, would rob him, he assumed that Gelb took everything."

"A good assumption," Danny laughed and rolled his eyes. "When can we meet Mr. Hecht?"

"I'll have him here in an hour."

Aldo left the room to make the request of the Parisian police to bring Hecht in.

"Progress, I guess," Danny remarked lacking confidence. "Hecht was the dup Gelb needed to help him get more cover. He must know that Hecht would go to the police. So the VISA and ATM cards have limited value after today. The French would be notified the minute they are swiped."

"Why wouldn't Hecht cancel them?"

"Because we want Gelb to use them, so we know where he is."

"But he will be gone by the time the police arrive."

"We'll have a trail—if he uses them. As I said, unless he makes a mistake, the cards have limited value to him—and us."

"What about the passport, Danny?"

"Hotels ask for them. Again, limited value. He would have to look somewhat like Hecht and after today all the hotels in France will have the names Gelb and Hecht. What I don't like is the handgun. That's a problem."

Twenty minutes later Aldo returned to report on the activities of the Baileys. The tail had called in.

"If I didn't know better, I would say that the Baileys are typical tourists sightseeing the Musée d'Orsay, the Sorbonne, and Montmartre. Alain Rosen, our man following them, is bored. They are doing conventional things."

"But you do know better," Danny reminded Aldo. "They are on a mission to find Gelb."

"*D'accord*," said Aldo. "They are following the art. The art may bring them to Gelb. Bailey did not just go to the Musée d'Orsay. He went into the art library. He ordered up books and pamphlets about the Impressionists including Degas and Cassatt. They did the same thing this morning at the Sorbonne art library. The average tourist does not spend his vacation researching artists."

"Bailey must be looking for a clue to lead him to Gelb," Jackie suggested. "He's not telling us something."

"Both Baileys left the Sorbonne and rode the Mêtro to the Anvers station in Montmartre. As Jackie knows, that is where the Impressionists lived and had their studios. Our man said that they stopped in front of a handful of buildings. They never went in any of them. Finally they visited the famous *Cimetière*. Degas's grave is there."

Danny looked at both of them impatiently.

"Of course he was looking for Gelb. They didn't come here on vacation and Bailey didn't come to Paris to study art. He thinks we are a bunch of bozos. He wants revenge on Gelb for violating—in his mind, his mother and his father's memory. I don't think he even cares if he gets back the missing work of art. He thinks Gelb stole the painting and he wants to get Gelb. Bailey is a smart guy. As I said before, if we don't find Gelb first, I think Bailey will lead us to him. So we'll keep trailing him."

"You don't mean that we should stop looking for Gelb ourselves, do you?" Jackie asked.

"No, of course not. But I have this feeling about Bailey. As much as I normally hate amateur detectives, this guy may help us. Now, Aldo, maybe you can turn up the heat on the locals and your buddies at Interpol to find Gelb—just in case Bailey falls flat on his face."

Aldo nodded.

"We know two things about Bailey," Danny continued. "He is insanely persistent and he doesn't trust us. So we watch him from a distance. We can always shut him down if we need to."

A short time later a detective opened the door to announce the arrival of Hecht.

"Bring him in," Aldo said.

William Hecht was wearing a light blue cotton suit, white shirt, and red tie. Jackie noticed perspiration on his cheeks, which she attributed to the summer heat and his anxiety over his missing possessions. He was a heavyset man in his thirties with dark hair sporting horn-rimmed glasses. She thought he must have never had time today to change out of these business clothes. He resembled Gelb only vaguely.

The agents introduced themselves and offered him coffee and water.

"Thanks, but I am interested in getting back my stolen passport and credit cards. I am impressed that the FBI and Interpol are interested in my loss, but you must be here for another reason. Did I do something wrong?"

"Did you?" Danny asked.

Hecht did not answer but looked askance at Danny.

"Let's begin with Ron Gelb," Danny said after a pause. "How well do you know him?"

"Not too well. I met him socially in New York. He knew a good friend of mine. I found him an impressive person and had an interest in his work. I know a few people in the art world, and clearly Ron Gelb is an important and knowledgeable dealer. I regret that invitation now."

"I bet you do," Danny said sardonically. "So you think Gelb stole your things. Not very friendly. What was your 'interest' in his work?"

"Oh, I like art—especially Impressionists. We had an enjoyable conversation over dinner last night. We talked about Monet and Cézanne. It was fascinating to me."

"Sure. Fascinating. Did Gelb mention why he was here?"

"He said he comes often on business. He usually stops at the Tremoille. This time someone stole his travelers checks and credit card." Hecht shook his head. "I still can't picture him as a thief."

Danny looked up at the ceiling and smiled. Jackie also held back a laugh.

"Appearances deceive," Danny pronounced at last.

Changing direction Danny asked, "Why do you own a gun? Are you in a dangerous business?"

"I'm a banker. My father gave me the gun—for security purposes. I've never shot it."

"Did you have ammunition?"

"A box. It's missing, too."

"Do you have it registered?"

"No. I never thought about it. It was in the bottom drawer of my desk. I'm surprised Gelb found it."

Danny turned to Aldo and asked him if an unregistered gun was a problem. Aldo said it was, but if Hecht was helpful, the authorities might give him some leeway.

"You may be lucky, Mr. Hecht," Danny concluded. "In New York, you would be in a world of hurt. Back to Gelb, did he mention specifically anything about Degas, Mary Cassatt, or Childe Hassam?"

"He mentioned Degas a bit but not the other two."

"Did he mention a theft of some artwork from Yale University?"

"No, but he did say that he would be a good source for the FBI in the event of a theft of Impressionist paintings. He said he might volunteer to help when he was back in the US."

Danny looked at Jackie and shook his head at such a provocative suggestion. Jackie thought that Gelb had a lot of chutzpah to make such a comment.

"Did Gelb leave anything behind in your apartment?"

"No. He cleaned me out and took his things as well. Should I replace everything or wait until you catch him?"

Jackie thought that was a naïve question and wondered what Danny would say.

"I suggest you deactivate what you can—in a few days. In the meantime we may be able to find Gelb if he charges anything. You won't be responsible for his activity and you will be helping the police."

Danny continued to ask questions, but Hecht had nothing substantive to add.

After he left Danny offered his instant opinion. "I don't think he is involved. He's a fool who trusted a bad guy. Happens all the time."

* * *

Thank you, Billy Hecht. You were so trusting. I brought along a lot of cash, but I maxed out your ATM card today anyways. In the future, Billy, don't write your passwords on a piece of paper in your desk. I put the Renault rental on the VISA card because it may confuse the people looking for me. I assume that Billy will cancel these cards in a day or two, so I'll toss them then. The passport may come in handy although I don't look much like him. We'll see. The sooner I find the missing trove, the sooner I'll not be bothered by these logistics.

Gelb walked back to his rental car and rearranged his luggage. He took out Billy's gun, loaded it, and put it in the glove compartment. Then he studied his roadmap for the best route north of Paris.

Mary Cassatt's place on Avenue Trudaine was a disappointment yesterday. I knew it was a long shot after all these years, but I had to try. The woman who lives in her apartment said that she and her husband remodeled it and nothing from the Cassatt era survived. When she wouldn't let me up to see, I asked her if she had found any artwork left there. She laughed and asked if I were crazy. If there was anything to be had, I think she would have bragged. Anyways I am on to the next place now — out in the country.

Sooner or later the FBI will learn of Billy's loss. They must be in France by now and have local help. I'll have to ditch the car tomorrow. The wild card is Bailey. I would like to know if he is following me or just here by chance. If he shows up at any of the places on my list of likely locations for the stash, then I'll be thankful I took Billy's gun. I wonder if he knows the significance of the sketch's list. The sketch was in his mother's house for decades. They did nothing during that time. So if he knows about the trove, he learned recently. Unlikely. I am just being paranoid. Stick to the plan. Find out where Mary Cassatt left the paintings.

Chapter Thirty-Three

"Picardie? Where is that again?" Kate asked while Charlie adjusted the rear view mirror of his car.

"It's a region about fifty miles north of Paris. Look in the glove compartment. There must be a map." Charlie pointed his right hand as he tried to adjust the seat of the rented Citroën, which the concierge had arranged for them.

"There, success," he added as the seat clicked into his preferred setting. "You are sweet to join me. I know you have to talk to your office."

"I can reach them on this global phone while we drive. Let's go, Monsieur Chauffeur. This sounds like fun. I've never been outside Paris. I'd love to see the real France. Tell me about Mary Cassatt's country house. The material I skimmed at the library mentioned it but I paid no attention. I was concentrated on the apartments she rented here in the city."

Charlie pulled the car out into the traffic in front of the hotel. When he felt comfortable driving, he answered Kate,

"The house, or rather the château, is called Beaufresne. She owned it for thirty years and is buried there with her parents, and her brother and sister. I hope it is still there."

"It must be. It's probably landmarked. She is likely the most famous person to have lived in that little town. I wonder if she painted scenes from the area, like Monet?"

"I don't remember any landscapes, but maybe. Well, at least the weather is nice. This should be a pleasant adventure. Oh, I forgot to mention I tried reaching Mother twice this morning while you were with the concierge. I left a message on the answering service. I'm worried that she didn't pick up or return my call."

"Let's try again later. She gets distracted sometimes. I'm concerned as well. I'll try texting her? Maybe that will get through."

After their tour of Montmartre the day before, Charlie had proposed this trip. If Mary Cassatt had taken the paintings on the list and the art world had not accounted for them, they must have been secreted somewhere—a closet, a basement, an attic, a garage, or something of the like. Anything stored in the apartments he and Kate had walked by would have been found years before. A big country house in a remote village might be different. Charlie had decided that it was worth a try.

Armed with directions from Google, they drove off toward the Arc de Triomphe and then to the Porte Maillot. They turned down the ramp on to the Ring Road, and headed in the direction of St. Denis. At the A15 exit, they turned north in the general direction of Beauvais. Soon they were out of the Paris environs and driving through farmland and past small towns. Five turns and about fifty miles later, they passed through the town of Bachivillers and veered right toward the village of Le Mesnil-Théribus.

The Picardie region of France was not picturesque by most standards. It consisted of rolling hills of farmland speckled by groves of trees. The populace congregated in villages and small towns more functional than charming. Overall the landscape was monotonous. Charlie guessed that the character of the area had not changed in decades.

He said little as Kate spent most of the drive on the phone with a colleague from her office. He was able to understand from her comments that no emergencies had arisen and her absence was being tolerated—at least for now.

Mary Cassatt's former country house was in the village of Le Mesnil-Théribus, which consisted of only eight or nine streets. Everything was within walking distance. In looking for the village center, Charlie drove by the Château de Beaufresne without noticing it. He was intent on finding someone on the street who could give them directions.

When they found a collection of small shops with apartments above, they parked on the side of the street and climbed out of the car. For a minute they saw no one but then Kate spotted a middle-aged woman walking toward them carrying a string bag filled with vegetables. Kate politely stopped her and in her best French asked directions to Beaufresne. The woman looked at Kate quizzically and defensively and asked why. Kate told her that they were Americans with a keen interest in Mary Cassatt paintings and had read that the artist once lived there. The woman paused a few seconds as if she seemed to weigh the pros and cons of offering information. Finally she said that Mary Cassatt had indeed lived at the château, but that was a hundred years ago. The building was now a school. The students and teachers were on holiday. She paused, thinking, then added that the new term is to begin soon. Perhaps someone would be there now. With some hesitation, she told Kate how to walk there.

Charlie had seen a picture of the château in one of the books he had scanned and was struck, when he saw it, by how little the structure had changed over the years. It was a large three-story, brick-and-stone house with rows of high, shuttered windows lining the first two floors. The ends of the house had turret-like structures topped by cupolas. There was a garden in front and a garage and outbuilding to the side. The property, which extended back into a large meadow, was lined by thick stands of trees. Charlie seemed to remember a picture of a pond in back of the house, but none was there. He did note the small stone building to the side. He remembered that the artist operated her printmaking press there.

While Charlie was wandering around the property, he noticed Kate entering the school through the open front door. He hurried after her and found her in the hallway with a woman dressed in a smock. Kate was explaining their mission, and the woman seemed relieved. She responded in English that she was the headmistress and that she was preparing the classrooms for the term, which was about to begin. She explained that the school took care of disturbed and abandoned children—some of whom lived in the château year round. No children were in residence today, as a benefactor had taken them on holiday.

Kate introduced Charlie to the headmistress, Claudette Pidot, and they shook hands. She said they were welcome to look around the school and the property but explained that she knew little about the American artist, Mary

Cassatt. She knew that Cassatt had purchased the house from a wealthy, local family and had passed it on to a relative when she died. Later the relative had donated the mansion to the organization that ran the school. She added that the former headmaster had been enthusiastic about the building's history and had started a local Association for Mary Stevenson Cassatt. He had also established a small exhibition of historical photographs about her and the château in one of the buildings in the village. Since Cassatt was undeniably been one of the most famous residents of the village, there were occasional visitors, such as Kate and Charlie. Some came to see the school; others went to the local cemetery where the family was buried in a vault. Most just stopped in the village for only an hour or two. As an example, she said that by coincidence, there had been an American art historian who dropped by the school the day before—their first visitor in a month. He had looked around the property and then left. She implied that he had not been very friendly. "Perhaps he was disappointed," she said.

Charlie was alert to this last piece of news.

"Do you remember his name?" he asked.

"I do not remember what he said. I suppose I did not pay attention. He said he was a scholar affiliated with a university in the United States."

"Was he tall or short, dark or light, how old?" Charlie continued to ask. "You see, I have been looking for someone who is in France now. He is an art historian with an interest in Impressionists. This might have been him."

She went on to describe generally someone who could have been Gelb—but who could have also been anyone with brown curly hair in his late thirties over six feet tall. Then, as if just remembering something, she added that the man had asked her if she had had visitors recently whom he described as a couple who looked like Charlie and Kate.

The woman brightened, "Maybe then, it was your friend."

"I hope so. I would like to meet up with him."

Then Kate asked her if there were any paintings by Mary Cassatt or her friends on the walls or in storage.

"No," Madame Pidot said. "The school is not rich. If something as valuable as that had been here, it would have been sold long ago to provide funds for our operations. Look around. If you find something, let me know. I would be very happy."

On that joking note the Baileys thanked her and said they would wander about the grounds for a while, to soak in a feeling of how Mary Cassatt lived. Charlie led Kate over to the garage and the outbuilding. He expected to find nothing, but he wanted to go through the motions nevertheless. Kate humored him by trailing along. They entered each building and saw school supplies, a rusty bed frame, dusty student desks, easels, and a bicycle, but no paintings.

Giving up, Charlie turned to her and said, "What's important is that she told us that Gelb was here."

"Wait a minute. You are jumping to conclusions. The man yesterday could have been anybody."

"Not so. The description matches. He asked about me. And I saw him three days ago. It had to be Gelb. Too many coincidences. He must be looking for something important, or he would have vanished after he saw me near the hotel. His coming here can't be idle curiosity. Mary Cassatt means a lot to him. That's why the sketch wasn't put up for repurchase. He's after the same thing we are—first in Montmartre and now here."

"If it was Gelb, he didn't find the trove here," Kate added.

"I agree, but he is thinking like us. First, go to the source. Mary Cassatt made the list. If she didn't hide the paintings, maybe she gave them to someone. So go there. Let's think this through."

Chapter Thirty-Four

"I've got it," Charlie exclaimed to a stirring Kate in bed. "We have to go to the Riviera—or wherever the niece lived. Her family may still be around, and they may have stories to tell."

"What are you talking about?" a drowsy Kate asked.

"I think I know where Gelb is headed. He is running around France a step ahead of us. But to be sure we must talk to Jeanne Fèvre's descendants. They may know what happened to the paintings."

Charlie had barely spoken on their drive back to Paris from Beaufresne. He had also been quiet at dinner. He had hoped Kate understood. He did not intend to be rude. He was convinced that there was a missing trove and that Gelb was also trying to track it down. Mary Cassatt's residences were the obvious places. Apparently Gelb had thought so, too. Since the paintings had never surfaced in a public sale and did not appear to be at her residences, Mary Cassatt may have given them away according to Degas's wishes.

Degas's niece, Jeanne Fèvre, presumably the *JF* of the list, made sense because she had nursed him for years. He was probably grateful to her. Identifying the *ZC* was more problematical. His housekeeper was Zoë Closier. She served Degas for many years. On the other hand, there could be other people or institutions with *ZC* initials. Moreover, what would a housekeeper do with all those paintings? If Degas wanted to reward her, wouldn't she want cash? If she did receive the art, wouldn't she have asked Mary or someone else to sell them for her? The Zoë explanation did not make sense to Charlie.

As he thought, half awake in bed, he concluded that they should pursue the Jeanne Fèvre connection. That meant traveling to her hometown, Nice, before she came to Paris to help Degas.

When Kate sat up, Charlie climbed out of bed, put on the hotel robe, and standing in front of the bed went through his analysis. He was confident that his interpretation of the list was sound but welcomed Kate's opinion.

"All this happened almost one hundred years ago," Kate began. "If we can locate Jeanne Fèvre's descendants, would they remember what happened? Also, if I recall what I read at the library, Degas's family organized the three or four auctions of his work—with his dealer, of course. The family seemed to have wanted the proceeds rather than the artwork."

"Granted, but they were getting a lot of money," Charlie said. "They may have held back some personal favorites, including those on the list. Maybe a painting or two are hanging on a wall in a descendant's house. Let's go to Nice and ask."

"If they are hanging on a wall, Gelb won't be pleased. He didn't kill Cynthia to find that out."

As soon as they were dressed, Charlie called the concierge to book a morning flight to Nice. He requested open tickets. Fortunately, there were several flights each weekday from Orly. They did not bother to check out of the Georges V and brought along only small hand luggage.

On arriving in Nice, they immediately took a taxi to the city library. Charlie guessed it would have a section devoted to local residents, particularly those with any fame.

After they entered the impressive building, Kate volunteered to converse with the librarian behind the information desk. She learned that the section they were seeking was in a corner on the second floor. The Baileys found the area easily and began to peruse the shelves. There were many books about the city's history and local celebrities as well as books written by local authors.

On a wall next to a window was a card catalog organized alphabetically. Kate dived in to the listing with enthusiasm.

"Charlie, there a handful of listings under 'Fèvre', 'Degas', and 'de Gas'. There are dozens of cards. Not surprisingly, this is a well-known family. Where do we start?"

"I'll skim the references for any contemporary descendants."

"While you are doing that, I'll ask the woman at the information desk if she knows of any descendants of the family of the famous artist Degas still living in Nice."

Charlie soon exhausted the card catalog because all the references were old. Disappointed he joined Kate at the information desk.

"Charlie, I'm glad you're here. This lovely lady, Sofie, has been very helpful. She remembered an article in the newspaper several years ago about Degas's descendants. She then called her friend Marie, a curator for the city's art museum. While Sofie chatted with her friend, I interrupted to say that the descendants name might be Fèvre. Apparently that name produced some recognition at the other end of the phone. After a short give-and-take she handed me the phone and asked me to discuss the matter directly with Marie."

"Marie was not at all curious why I was asking this question. She went on at a frantic pace about Degas and his famous family—several of whom had notable successes in their own right in business in France and the United States. She said that the museum possessed several paintings and sculptures donated by the family and regularly invited prominent members of the family to attend whenever the museum had an exhibition featuring Degas's artwork. She recalled that one of the branches of the family was named Fèvre. Marie believed at least one of the Fèvres lived in the small suburb southwest of the city named Saint-Hèléne. She added that that person was probably listed in the Nice phonebook. She even suggested that the family liked to talk about their famous ancestor."

"Nice going," Charlie said. "Let's find a phonebook."

Sofie must have heard Charlie, because she reached under her desk and produced it. Charlie thanked her and quickly found two listings for Fèvre in Sainte-Hèléne. He wrote them down and saw Sofie pointing to a public phone across the lobby.

Kate had luck on the first call. She talked to a woman who confirmed that she was a descendant of the de Gas family and would be happy to talk to an American art collector about her famous relative and her great-grandaunt, Jeanne Fèvre. They agreed to meet after lunch at a café overlooking the beach on the main street that ran through Saint-Hèléne.

Pressed for time, Charlie and Kate stopped for lunch at a nearby McDonalds. Kate was amused that American "French fries" were simply *frites* in Nice.

"I wonder what the French call 'Italian sausage', 'German potato salad', 'Irish coffee', and 'Belgian waffles'," she joked.

"How about 'Swiss cheese'?" Charlie joined in.

"Is there anything I should know about the Fèvre family?" Kate asked, getting serious.

"The de Gas family was affluent when Degas was growing up in this area. From the material at the library, I inferred that they were prominent in business also, well after he died. Jeanne Fèvre was his young niece, and in the books at the Sorbonne, there is no mention if she ever married. Degas himself never married or had children."

"In short, we know little about *JF*," Kate concluded.

The trip to Sainte-Hélène was not far, and the taxi driver knew the café. The Baileys entered the café, and the owner directed them to a table outside on the sidewalk. The table was occupied by a modestly dressed woman with graying hair, wearing clear glasses. She had already ordered a demi of white wine. When Charlie and Kate sat down, the woman eyed the couple and, by her mood, decided apparently that the Baileys were trustworthy people.

Kate introduced Charlie and herself and expressed her gratitude that Madame Fèvre was willing to talk to them. Kate explained that Charlie's family collected art and had a particular interest in Degas's relationship to the American artist Mary Cassatt. They knew that for several years before his death Degas relied on Jeanne Fèvre to take care of him. And Jeanne knew Mary because Mary visited Degas frequently during the period about one hundred years ago.

The woman, Suzanne Fèvre, said that she knew of Mary Cassatt very well and the history of Edgar Degas.

"The de Gas family was important in Nice during that time. Instead of going into business or medicine, Edgar scandalized his family by running off to be an artist in Paris, living a bohemian lifestyle. Instead his sister married a Fèvre, from another prominent family, and settled in a beautiful villa not far from here. I think the family was quite surprised that Edgar amounted to anything. The Fèvres had a daughter, Jeanne, who went to Paris to nurse Edgar when he fell ill. In fact, her sacrifice resulted in the Fèvres being named Degas's primary heirs. Those famous auctions after his death generated a large amount of money. You know Edgar was a collector as well as an artist. He had a big apartment and practically filled it up."

"So we understand."

"Edgar was a major benefactor to my family. But that was a long time ago. Since then we have had wars and depressions. We live modestly today."

"My husband has read up on the auctions. Because of those sales, the world enjoys access to many wonderful paintings and drawings from his collections. Who were some of the artists, Charlie?"

"Ingres, Daumier, Delacroix, Monet, Cézanne, Van Gogh, Gauguin, and Morisot, to name a few."

"It was wonderful that your family decided to sell," Kate said to Suzanne.

"Of course we did not sell everything. Some pieces of art were kept and later donated to museums."

"That was very kind of your family. We did wonder about one thing, though. Recently we had the opportunity to compare a list of paintings with the listings from those famous auctions. But they did not match up completely. Did the family hold back many works of art?"

"I don't know. That was long ago—before I was born. But I do remember a story my mother told me. She did not like your Mary Cassatt very much. She said that Madame Cassatt meddled with Edgar's collection when he was ill. You know he was very weak toward the end. I think Mother said Madame Cassatt took some paintings that should have been ours. Something like that."

"You mean that Mary Cassatt stole some of Edgar Degas's artwork?"

"No, no, that was not it exactly. Wait. Now I remember. There was a housekeeper, Zoë something. Old, fat woman, a servant. Mary Cassatt told Jeanne that this Zoë deserved something for working for Edgar for many years. Apparently Mary was a pushy, domineering person. She insisted that Zoë get a patrimony. Jeanne was younger and impressionable. She went along, but my mother said that Jeanne was unhappy with the arrangement. She felt that we were cheated out of some paintings worth a great amount.

Anyway, that story has come down to my generation. Somehow Mary Cassatt and Zöe stole from us."

"But certainly Edgar must have agreed to give some artworks to Zöe?"

"I doubt it. He was dying and a difficult person. Mary Cassatt and Zöe ganged up on a sick man and a young woman, Jeanne."

"Has the family ever filed a claim?" asked Kate.

"Not that I know of. Again it was long ago. But my mother was bitter until she died."

"So if Zöe received some artworks, where are they now? Did she sell them?"

"Heaven knows. Zöe was just a servant. Who knows what she did."

"Do you know where she lived after Edgar's death?"

"Of course not. I don't think my family wanted anything to do with her after Edgar's death. Why should we have?"

"Have you talked to anyone else recently about this Mary Cassatt episode?"

"No. It's an unpleasant story."

"Do any more relatives live around here who know about your family's past?"

"Frankly, not many of us are left. I have a cousin here in Sainte-Hélène and another in Nice. There are some distant relatives in Venice, but I never see them. I doubt any of them know anything more that I have told you."

"You are knowledgeable about your family's history," said Kate, praising her. "It's a fascinating tale. I can't imagine what it is like to have a famous ancestor."

"It's a blessing and a burden. But it would be worse if my name were Degas."

"True. I'm curious if you have ever been contacted by an American art dealer, Ronald Gelb," Charlie asked.

"No. I've never heard that name."

"One last thing. We read that Degas gave to Jeanne a sculpture he did of a fourteen-year-old dancer. Does the family still have it?"

"In a month when I have heavy bills, I wish I did. My grandfather donated it to the art museum in Nice. It's on a pedestal off the main lobby. I'm told Edgar did a few of these. It is delicate and beautiful."

"I can imagine."

The Baileys thanked Suzanne Fèvre warmly for the informative conversation and then found a taxi back to the Nice airport. Charlie felt energized and wanted to talk.

"We learned three important things: Zöe received the paintings on the list; Gelb has not been here; and the sculpture went to Jeanne Fèvre, as the list indicated."

"Does this mean we are now ahead of Gelb in this search for the trove?" Kate asked with a smile.

"Maybe. The sketch listed only the sculpture under *JF*. Under *ZC* there were several paintings. Gelb may be pursuing the larger trove first. Suzanne Fèvre confirmed that Zöe was given the paintings. Despite the Fèvre's misgivings, I am touched that Degas gave Zöe those remarkable works of art as a sort of pension for long service. He may have been an ill-tempered man generally, but in this case he was kind and generous."

"Zöe may have even picked out which paintings she liked and told Degas or Mary," Kate suggested.

"That would make a nice story. Now we have to find them. They are probably in the possession of Zöe's descendants—although it's difficult to believe they wouldn't have sold them by now."

"Maybe they don't know what they are," Kate speculated.

"We'll see. First we have to find them."

"What if the trove doesn't exist any more?"

"That doesn't matter as long as Gelb thinks it exists. We'll find him where he thinks it is. Finding him is our goal."

Chapter Thirty-Five

"As I look through the notes I took at the Sorbonne, I see that I wrote down 'Zöe Closier' only once," Kate admitted having reviewed the file she brought along while flying back to Paris. "It says that Zöe was Degas's housekeeper. Not much to go on to find her descendant."

"I don't remember that she was mentioned much either," said Charlie. "I must confess I wasn't focusing on her anyways. I do recall a photograph of Degas in one of the books with her in the background. The picture must have been shot in his apartment. I suggest we go back to that library and search more thoroughly. It will be too late today when we get in to Paris, but we can go the first thing tomorrow morning."

"Okay. At least we can assume for now that she had those eight pictures on the list at some point. Do you think Gelb knows?"

"I'm counting on it," Charlie said.

"Let's call your mother again tonight. I'm worried about her. She sounded weak last time we talked."

"I agree. She didn't sound like herself at all. We have to finish here and get home."

* * *

Charlie made the call from the hotel as soon as they arrived. "Mother, how are you? How was your doctor's appointment?"

"I saw the cardiologist today. He doesn't like the fluid in my lungs or that I'm coughing so much. He said I shouldn't drink or have relations."

"What? He said that?"

"I think he was trying to make me laugh. Don't worry, son. I don't have any boyfriends. I would like a drink, though. He said one of my valves wasn't working the way it should. I guess stress is the cause. It's been an eventful summer. When are you coming home?"

"Soon."

"Have you and Kate enjoyed Paris? I imagine it's lovely."

"We have, but we are worried about you. Did the doctor give you some medicine?"

"Of course, they always do. But I'm still coughing. He said he needs to fix that valve soon. I'll feel better when you two are back here with me."

"I have a little project to complete. Then we'll leave immediately afterwards."

After saying goodbye Charlie and Kate discussed the conversation with Claire. Kate suggested that they should fly to Chicago the next day.

"Let Jackie Farrell and that Flood character do their job. For all we know, they may have arrested Gelb today. Your mother's health comes first."

"This is tough" Charlie said, feeling uncertain. "For all the reasons you know I want to grab and smash Gelb, I'm sure my mother will feel better once he is apprehended. If we can find Zöe's family, I think we'll be this close to nailing him." Charlie held his thumb and forefinger up an inch apart.

He paused and gathered himself. "Please bear with me one more day. Then we'll go back."

Kate looked at him sternly. "I think your priorities are screwed up. I went along with you for the past few days. Now circumstances have changed. I'm unhappy with you. Am I more concerned about your mother than you are?"

"One more day, please."

Kate stood up and went into the other room in the suite, shutting the door behind her.

Her action was familiar to Charlie and he cursed himself silently. He was ambivalent—guilty about his mother and spiteful towards Gelb. His plea for an additional day was a faulty compromise. It didn't serve his mother's situation nor likely provided adequate time to find Gelb. He wished he had Kate's clarity of mind. He also wished she was not so upset. But he stuck to his decision.

* * *

Charlie and a reluctant Kate were at the door of the Sorbonne library when it opened at ten o'clock the next morning. The security guard recognized them and waved them through the door. They selected a large reading table and marked it off with paper pads, attaché case, and personal computers. Kate stayed there while Charlie went over to a computer with the book catalogue. His query for Zöe Closier brought up nothing, so he came back to the "Degas" listings he had consulted previously. He ordered all the books and pamphlets that seemed remotely promising.

Thirty minutes later they had a pile of material from the stacks to peruse. Quickly they found several citations of Zöe Closier, but they were brief and repetitive. They learned that Zöe was the last of a series of housekeepers Degas employed during his life. She was hired in 1890 when Degas was fifty-six and moving into his apartment/studio on Rue Victor-Massé. She was a former schoolteacher and a bit younger than Degas. Apparently she was able to put up with Degas's famous impatient and demanding personality, as she stayed with him twenty-seven years until he died. Kate found the photograph of her in the background behind Degas. It was taken by Degas's brother, René de Gas, in the late 1890s. Zöe was overweight, modestly dressed, wearing large, round eyeglasses. One source mentioned that she never married and lived in a single room in the back of the large apartment.

"Charlie, from the books I have skimmed, there is not much to go on. Zöe doesn't appear to have had any children, and there is no mention of brothers and sisters. Whatever secret she may have been part of may have died with her. This could be a waste of time."

"Perhaps, but I am not ready to give up. One reference here reveals more about her background. It says she had taught school in Sceaux before taking the job with Degas in Paris. It could be that she originally came from the area around Sceaux."

"Where is Sceaux?"

"I just looked it up on my search application. Sceaux is a town south of Paris about halfway between Versailles and the Orly Airport. I guess you could call it a suburb. A train runs by it. Now it is mainly residential, but a hundred years ago it may have been farmland."

"If that is where she grew up, I suppose she might have returned there after Degas died. At her age, I doubt she would have sought a new job."

"It's worth a try. Let me finish the rest of this stack of books to see if I find anything else. Failing that, we can try Sceaux. We might be lucky."

An hour later they gave up. Zöe was not particularly interesting to the legion of Degas biographers. She had been a loyal employee for almost three decades and had assisted Jeanne Fèvre in taking care of the dying Degas. After he died, she disappeared in all the texts. If she took possession of the artwork listed on the back of Mary Cassatt's sketch, there was no mention of her doing so in any of the biographies or art histories. Certainly such an event would have been noteworthy, so the lack of any mention in so many texts suggested strongly that it did not happen. Not one historian cited evidence of a collection of paintings passing to Zöe.

"The absence of any reference of a gift or pension to Zöe is discouraging," Charlie admitted. "Still the list of artworks compiled by Mary Cassatt remains. That trove went somewhere. Based on our conversation in Nice, I continue to think Zöe is the most likely candidate. Unfortunately, our only lead at this point is that she came from Sceaux before she signed on with Degas. It may be a dead end but it's all we have. Maybe the concierge at the hotel can help us."

When they entered the marbled lobby of the Georges V, Charlie headed right to the concierge desk. He told the concierge on duty that he was looking for someone who lived in or around Sceaux. The family name was Closier. He asked if there was a telephone listing for anyone of that name. The concierge went into a room behind the station where the local directories were kept. He returned with a book and pointed to a listing.

"There is this only one. 'H. Closier'. The town is Bièvres. It must be a village near Sceaux. Is this the right person?"

"I'm not sure, but would you write down the telephone number and the address?"

"Yes, of course. Right away."

Charlie and Kate hurried back to their room. Charlie was suddenly feeling energized again. It seemed possible that a Closier family had lived in the area around Sceaux for many years. The current residents could be descendants from Zöe's original family.

"Kate, let's rent a car and drive there now. I feel good about this information. Maybe the H. Closier is the link to Zöe. We can call ahead when we get near Bièvres. I'll have the concierge get a car and a map."

"Okay. But if H. Closier is no relation, you know we are finished with this. He is our only chance to find Zöe. If he looks at us strangely and asks, 'Who is Zöe?', we'll have to pack our bags and return to Chicago. I know how much you want this man to lead us to the solution to the mystery, but if he cannot, I hope you won't be too disappointed. This trip has been a great adventure, but our search would be over."

"Granted. I can handle disappointment. We have to get back to Mother. But we have been a great team on this search. That alone makes the trip worthwhile. Let's see what Monsieur Closier can tell us."

* * *

The Citroën that Charlie rented had a good GPS to guide them. They drove through Sceaux in half an hour and reached Bièvres ten minutes later. As they had driven south from Paris, the villages had grown smaller, and they had seen forests and farmland interspersed with residential housing.

Bièvres was a village with a modest commercial center. Charlie reached the central roundabout and followed the GPS instructions west to the third farm, which was identified by a small sign 'Closier'. They turned onto a crushed stone driveway about a quarter of a mile long that ended at a two-story white house with an orange-tile roof.

There was nothing grand about the farm. The main crops seemed to be hay and corn, and Charlie noticed some livestock off to the right. A dusty red Renault was parked by the front door. The Baileys climbed out of their Citroën and, seeing no one outside, knocked on the door.

An older woman answered the door and looked at them quizzically. She appeared confused that two well-dressed strangers had stopped at her house.

Kate explained that they might be lost but were hopeful that this was the home of Monsieur Closier, a descendant of Zöe Closier, who was an acquaintance of Degas, the famous artist. They were art collectors who were trying to learn more about Degas and his acquaintances.

The woman looked at them skeptically but warmed a bit after a second, and they made introductions. She said her name was Brigitte.

"Yes, Hèrcule is related to the Zöe you mentioned. She lived here many years ago."

"What can you tell us about her?" Charlie asked as the woman ushered them inside.

"From what Hèrcule told me, Zöe never married. She worked for Degas in Paris for years, then came here to the farm to live with her brother and sister-in-law. By then she was relatively old. No one has asked about her in years—except for another American this morning. He came here without calling, just like you, and talked to Hèrcule. Funny, all those years, and now three people are asking about Zöe. We don't even mention her in town. People think we made up the story about Degas, so we avoid the subject. You should talk to Hèrcule. He is probably in the tool shed out back. I'll tell him you are here. Come in and sit in the parlor."

Charlie and Kate followed her and sat down. Charlie could not believe their luck in finding a descendant of Zöe's. His mind was also rapidly speculating about the previous visitor; it had to have been Gelb. The coincidence was overwhelming. But how, he wondered, had Gelb found Hèrcule Closier? Before he could think that through, Hèrcule Closier entered the room in his work clothes and mud boots.

"*Bon jour. Bienvenue.* My wife tells me you are here to learn about my great-aunt, Zöe. It appears that she is suddenly famous."

"Yes, we heard that someone else came asking about her today," Charlie said. "*Oui.* He said he is writing a book. He wanted to look around. Get an inspiration, I assume. I don't know why you and he are interested in Zöe. She was just a housekeeper. Degas did not pay her much. For some reason she liked that job better than teaching school, which she had done. After Degas died, she was in her seventies, and came back here to live. This farm had belonged to her father, my great-grandfather. If you look in the back, way back, there is a small cottage—a sitting room, kitchen, and bedroom. She lived there to be out of the way of her brother and his family. I vaguely remember her. She was quite old, and I was just a small boy. She was fat and had bad eyes. She's buried in the family plot on the west end of the property. That's all I know."

"That's a lot," Charlie offered. "Did she ever talk about Degas? Did he like her? Did he ever give her anything for her service, such as a painting or money?"

"Not that anyone told me. Our family has lived on this farm for decades. The land has taken care of us. We are not rich, but we get by."

Then Kate asked, "This man who was here this morning, what did he look like? What did he want? Do you remember his name?"

"Mr. Verdi. He was an American, taller than me, stocky, curly brown hair, and eyeglasses. Maybe forty years old. He asked me about Zöe—just like you. He also wanted to see where she lived. I showed him. My younger brother's daughter lives there now. Lisètte. She is a student in Nanterre, but currently she is on *vacances* in Burgundy. If you would like, you can also see the cottage. The only thing there that reminds us of Zöe is an old photograph taken when she was quite old."

The three of them stood up and walked out the front door and halfway around the house. They could see then the small cottage in the distance down a path through the fields. It took almost five minutes to walk there. Hèrcule Closier used a large key to unlock the door. The simple whitewashed home was as promised: small, basic, furnished in a utilitarian fashion. But immediately Kate noticed three striking paintings on the walls. She nodded to Charlie, but he had already walked closer to one. It depicted a young ballet student at a barre. It was unmistakably a Degas pastel. Front left he noticed a watering can beneath the barre. That detail made the painting distinctive. He pivoted left and saw the other two pictures: one of a laundress at work and another of a singer at a nightclub. They were also pastels in the Degas style.

"Oh, I notice you are looking at the pictures," said Hèrcule, teasing Charlie. "Don't get too excited. They are copies that Zöe brought with her. She says a student copied Degas's originals. She said they were poorly done, but they brought back good memories for her. My father told me that they were worthless. There's one in the kitchen that looks like a bowl of fruit, and a couple in the bedroom. Lisètte likes them, although I think she prefers her poster of a rock star."

Charlie moved into the bedroom and recognized two more pastels, which had been listed on the back of the sketch. They were exquisite and well preserved. The colors were faded a bit, but the impact on him was electric. The themes and the execution were those of the mature artist on top of his game. He examined each closely and, despite not being an expert, he felt certain that these were originals. Zöe had brought these home to be near her as she grew old.

Kate whispered, "Let me think about the list. How many pictures were there? Of course, now the *ZC* makes sense. There were eight pictures and one sculpture. The sculpture had gone to *JF*—Jeanne Fèvre, obviously." With this identification in mind, they walked into the kitchen and saw the painting of the bowl of fruit Hèrcule had mentioned. Charlie knew that the still life was not a Degas. It was an oil painting in the style of Cézanne, as stated on the list. "Remember that Degas collected works of art that he liked by his contemporaries. This picture, too, has to be authentic."

They returned to the main room and Charlie said, "Monsieur Closier, your great-aunt had excellent taste. These pictures are beautiful. Did she save any others?"

"Yes, there are two in our main house. My wife is fond of them. I could do without them, but you know women. One is a picture of a man—perhaps an artist. The other looks like a room in an art museum. I haven't been in a museum in years. I say that I already have a museum in my house—those pictures. I know that is a weak joke, but it is my excuse not to have to go all the way into Paris to visit a museum."

"Of course," Charlie mumbled, still carefully studying the dancer pastel. "I'm interested in what your visitor this morning thought of these pictures. Did he say anything?"

"Oh, yes. He liked the frames. He said that they don't make frames like this anymore. He said that they would look even better if they contained really good paintings. In fact, he said he would be willing to buy all the pictures Zöe had put in this cottage and up at the house. He looked at them again and said the frames were antiques; so he was willing to pay two thousand euros for the lot of them. I thought that sounded like a lot of money for some old picture frames, but I said I would think it over. What I really wanted to do was talk to Brigitte and Lisètte to see if they would miss them. I know women attach sentimental value to these sorts of things."

"What did they say?" Kate asked.

"Well, Lisètte is not here. And Brigitte is reluctant, although she would like the money. I think she suspects the frames are worth more. She thinks three thousand might be better. Anyways, I need to make up my mind. The man said he would be back after dinner. He said he needed an answer today. He had to go somewhere tomorrow. Can you imaging two thousand euro in cash? That would buy a lot of seed."

"Yes, indeed. Might we be able to see the pictures you have in the main house? I'm interested in what Zöe liked so much."

"Of course. Are you finished here? I'm going to lock up."

Charlie and Kate started off together to return to the home when Closier stayed behind to lock up.

"Charlie, I don't believe it! After all these years, this trove exists! The list is real. And if the ones in the house are similar, these are all the ones listed on the sketch. I am happy for Zöe. She was rewarded for all her work. I think it is wonderful she kept everything and did not sell them."

"I agree, but she may not have had a choice. People may not have believed then that she obtained the collection legally. The de Gas family might have come after her. After all, as Madame Fèvre complained, they continue to think Mary and Zöe cheated Jeanne and Degas himself. Mary would have stuck up for Zöe, but remember Mary was starting to fail physically. Who knows? Of course, after she retired, Zöe would have insisted that the pictures were fakes or copies. She had to for security sake. They were just too valuable."

"Gelb is a bastard. He's a murderer and a thief, and he is trying to cheat these people. Two thousand euros! He knows that the trove is worth at least thirty to forty million euros. Scoundrel! Scumbag! We need to protect the Closiers. Gelb is dangerous, but so are a lot of other people if the word gets out that thirty million euros of Impressionist works of art are hanging, unprotected, on the walls of this farmhouse."

By that time Closier had caught up to them and led them back to the main house. Once there, he found his wife and told her that the Americans just wanted to look at the two of Zöe's pictures in the house. She motioned to Charlie and Kate to follow her up the stairs and took them into a bedroom in the back of the second floor, where two similar-sized pictures hung next to each other on the far wall.

Charlie shook his head in amazement and recognition. "What do you think?" Charlie asked Kate quietly.

"It's them, all right. The portrait of the artist is a charcoal, a *fusain*, just as the list describes, and this museum is of the Louvre, a pastel. I remember both of them from the list. That makes eight pictures—all the ones cited under the ZC heading. Unmistakable."

"And they all appear to be in good condition," Charlie added.

"So what do we do now? Call Jackie Farrell?"

"We have to talk to Mr. Closier first."

Charlie smiled at Brigitte, who was in the hall, and thanked her. Then they followed her downstairs where Hèrcule was waiting in the sitting room.

"Mr. Closier despite what Zöe told your family many years ago, we believe that these paintings are Degas originals except one, which is by Cézanne. Zöe must have had her reasons for saying they were copies. We know Degas gave them to her. Mr. Verdi, whom we think we know, is trying to steal them from you."

Hèrcule and Brigitte looked shocked. They were speechless for a minute.

"Originals? How is that possible?" he stammered. "Someone would have said something."

"*Mais*, Hèrcule," Brigitte aid, "Only our neighbors and relatives have seen them all these years. We told them they were fakes. How would they know?"

"Are they worth a lot?" Hèrcule asked innocently.

"A great deal," Charlie said.

"You were going to sell them for two thousand euros," Brigitte carped at Hèrcule. "What a fool! You never liked the pictures. It's a good thing Lisètte and I wanted to keep them."

"Hush, witch," Hèrcule warned. "You would have sold them for three thousand euros."

"Please, don't fight," said Kate. "You should be happy the paintings are valuable and you still have them. Before anything, though, we need the police to arrest Mr. Verdi."

"What has he done?" Hèrcule asked. "We aren't going to sell to him."

"We know who he is. He is a fraud and very dangerous," Charlie warned them. "We'll help. May we stay until he and the police arrive?"

"Of course. He said 'after dinner'."

"We'll just wait."

"Join us for dinner," Brigitte offered.

They all looked at the front door then, as they heard barking outside. Hèrcule and Charlie went outside and after a minute the barking stopped.

"*Mes chiens* were barking at a van which was turning around up the driveway. He must have made the wrong turn.

"Could it have been Mr. Verdi?" Charlie asked.

"*Mais non*, Verdi had a black Renault. This was a white van."

"Excuse me," Charlie said. "I need to make a phone call."

Chapter Thirty-Six

When the phone rang in the conference room Aldo Laval was the first to reach it.

"*Allô*. Laval *ici*."

Aldo turned and gestured to Jackie and Danny that the call was significant. "Monsieur Bailey. What can I do for you?"

He nodded and said "*oui*" and "*merveilleux*" several times, wrote down a name and address, and promised that they would be there as soon as possible.

When he hung up, Danny was the first to ask, "Bailey? Where are we going?"

"Bièvres. South of the city. He says that Gelb is coming to meet a farmer there sometime this evening. He said that he would explain everything once we arrive. He cautioned that we arrive discreetly so that we don't scare off Gelb."

"Okay. What does he think we would do? Set off fireworks. Let's go," Danny said without hesitation. "Anything to get out of this room."

"On the way out I'll have the duty officer notify the local gendarmerie near Bièvres to position themselves near the farm and to use no sirens. Depending on traffic, we'll be there in forty to sixty minutes. We can call Rosier from the car to find out what he has seen. *Allons-y*."

Jackie was eager to hear Pierre Rosier's report. He was the officer following the Baileys across France for the past five days. He would call in around dinnertime and give a detailed account of what he witnessed. Aldo would put the call on the conference phone so all three agents could hear. Pierre spoke excellent English.

Jackie thought back about Pierre's reports as the driver sped through Parisian traffic to the main road towards Sceaux. She knew the Baileys had spent a half day in Montmartre walking near the studios and haunts of the Impressionist artists. Considering the art history content of her job, she would have liked to join their ramble through the art district.

Then they drove out to that little town in Picardie where they visited a school. Only by calling back to the local police after tailing the Baileys to their hotel did Pierre learn that the school was formerly the summer home of Mary Cassatt. That information provided at least a rationale for the Baileys' trip. What they were looking for Jackie didn't know. Up to that point the Baileys were acting like academics or art researchers collecting background for a book. She knew that explanation was wrong; so she hoped that the Baileys were aware of something that their actions were designed to bring them to Gelb.

At first the trip to Nice meant nothing to Jackie. Again they had gone to a library and then had coffee with a woman at a seaside café. Luckily Pierre decided to let them go off after that conversation and instead caught up with the woman. Her name, Suzanne Fèvre, rang a bell with Jackie—the same last name as Degas's niece. She remembered the speculation that the *JF* initials on the back of the sketch had been those of the niece. Maybe the Baileys thought the same. The niece was clearly a factor in their movements.

The concierge at the Georges V had been helpful—first by alerting Pierre to the Baileys booking a flight to Nice and now looking for Hèrcule Closier. When Pierre called in to report that he was following the Baileys to the Closier address, he was eager to add that the Closier name had come up in his conversation with Suzanne Fèvre. He recalled that Madame Fèvre had said that the Baileys seemed to be interested in Degas's housekeeper—also named Closier. She complained that the housekeeper had stolen some art from the dying Degas.

The puzzle suddenly fell into place for Jackie. ZC was the housekeeper. The paintings had gone to her. The Baileys knew that and maybe Gelb did, too.

"We're going to the right place," she said confidently.

Of course, Jackie recognized that the investigation would have gone much easier had the French been able to locate Gelb. He had simply eluded them. She and Danny had felt helpful and clueless. They weren't used to sitting around completely dependent on police organizations outside their control and influence to conduct an effective investigation. Each day they read the *International Herald Tribune*, called the office in New York, did crossword puzzles, leafed through magazines, wrote emails, reviewed reports on other cases sent confidentially via the American consulate office, and waited for Aldo to show up with an update on the search for Gelb.

Jackie could tell Danny's ego had been taking a beating. He was a star detective in the FBI. He usually worked several cases at a time and people came to him constantly for advice. Here in France he had a single case and was isolated. He had said to her that something had to break soon on the Gelb case or else he vowed to fly home and leave Jackie alone to wait for the French to come up with leads.

Jackie had also been bored, but she understood the pecking order. Danny was in charge; she had to soldier on silently, no matter what she felt. Still, she was as furious as Danny that Aldo and his compatriots had not come up with anything except for the Hecht episode.

Now that they were in the car headed to a possible confrontation with Gelb, Jackie noticed that Danny's mood had improved dramatically. He was talking civilly to Aldo about politics, handguns, and the lack of air-conditioning in the hotel they had been staying at.

"Jackie, didn't I tell you," Danny bragged. "Follow Bailey and he will lead us to Gelb. I don't understand the art connection, but we know Gelb is greedy. He and Bailey think there's other paintings to be had. Otherwise Gelb would have disappeared entirely. Now he and Bailey end up at a farmhouse in the middle of France at a descendant—I presume—of Degas's housekeeper. It's not a coincidence. I don't trust Bailey, but at least he called us. I don't think it's a set-up. Bailey wants to nail the bastard, but he needs our muscle. Only too happy to oblige.

"So, Aldo," Danny continued. "Remind me where we are going."

"We are going in the direction of Sceaux. It's an ancient town not far to the south of Paris and not far from Orly. According to our information this Hèrcule Closier is a farmer living near the village Bièvres. The area is mainly farmland."

"Let's go directly to the farmhouse," Danny said. "Tell the locals to hold back but block the driveway if Gelb goes in there. Is Rosier there?"

"I'm trying to reach him," Aldo said. "He's not answering."

"We can't wait for him," Danny said. "We'll be the only ones going in at first. Remember Gelb has a handgun."

* * *

The sun had set while the Closiers and Baileys ate dinner in the small kitchen. Charlie was too hyper to spend much time on his food. He got up and went to a window looking for Gelb's arrival. While standing there, he explained to the Closiers why he was certain the paintings were originals. He described Mary Cassatt's relationship to Degas and the list she had made on the back of the sketch. The combination of Zöe's initials and Suzanne Fèvre's embittered comments convinced him that these original paintings would have come to Zöe. That they were still here completely and in good condition was a tribute to Zöe's cleverness in convincing her family that they were copies which she wanted to keep as mementos of her service to Degas. The family had no reason to doubt her since who would believe that a gift of such magnitude would befall to a mere housekeeper? In fact, even after hearing Charlie's explanation Hèrcule was still skeptical.

"How is it possible?" he wondered aloud.

Brigitte asked, "How much are they worth?"

"I can't say," Charlie answered. "Certainly millions. If you would like I could arrange for an art appraiser to come to give you an idea."

"That kind of money might change our lives," Hèrcule worried. "We need to go slowly."

They stopped talking the moment they heard barking again.

"Someone is coming, but I don't hear a car on the driveway. Maybe our dogs saw another dog on the property."

The barking became louder. Then they heard two loud noises like 'pop' or 'bang'. The barking stopped.

"Gunfire!" Charlie shouted.

They all jumped up and went out the front door. It was very dark out with the only light coming from the house.

"I think the noise came from the direction of the cottage," Hèrcule said, pointing toward the path through the fields.

Charlie started to run, immediately leaving the others behind.

"Stop, Charlie," he heard Kate scream. "For God's sake, don't go that way! Wait for the police. Please stop!"

In a matter of seconds Charlie had plunged into the darkness. Gelb had to be there at the cottage. He was stealing the paintings there. Maybe he had seen Charlie at the farmhouse or had never intended to scam the Closiers by buying the frames. Charlie had to stop him. He might never have another chance.

He made a left turn down the path and saw the cottage with a light on inside. By the door he saw the two dogs lying lifeless on the ground. The dogs. Dead. Then he heard another loud noise and felt a heavy blow to his left shoulder. Then heat and pain. He was falling. Then blackness and silence.

Chapter Thirty-Seven

Ron Gelb drove his van flat out on the dark roads, turning often with no plan except for going in the general direction of Paris. His heart beat rapidly as he endeavored to get as far away from the farm as possible in a short time. He saw a few cars on the roads, but none followed him.

After twenty minutes he slowed and relaxed. He smiled and felt ecstatic. As he drove, he considered what he did. *How did Bailey find the Closier farm? That question bothers me. I was certain that Bailey had not been following me since that sighting in Paris. I had been careful doubling back and forth on the Métro, staying in no-name pensions that don't ask for anything other than cash, and buying a used Renault off a suburban lot—again for cash. No credit cards. I had used the Hecht ID for the car registration, which wouldn't have reached the government motor-vehicle database before I ditched the car. No, Bailey had not followed me.*

Yet, there he was in front of the farmhouse which the Closiers when I pulled the van into the long driveway earlier. I had no option but to turn around immediately and drive off. Since the Closiers had seen me in the morning in a black sedan, it was unlikely that they connected the white van with me. Just a delivery van finding a place to reverse direction. No, they expected me to return to their house after dinner driving a black Renault. Considering that the presence of the Baileys changed the situation, now I feel smart—and lucky, that I had abandoned the sedan in a carpark this afternoon and bought the white van in Sceaux. My reason had been that I needed a van to transport all the paintings—or frames—I was going to buy. Now I had another reason.

The Baileys being there changed my plan from buying framed Degas "copies" to stealing originals. I had to forgo the two paintings in the main farmhouse, but the rest were conveniently hung in the remote and unsecured cottage. Faced with a last minute change in plan, I am proud of myself for having bought the necessary packing materials to protect the paintings from damage, for having purchased a flashlight and tire iron, for having noticed a dirt path running next to the wire fence marking the boundary of the property, and for having taken Hecht's handgun. I had everything I needed.

When I returned to the farm after dark, I drove past the driveway about a quarter mile and found the little road. It was just wide enough for the van to pass. I remember feeling my heart beat faster and my palms sweat as I turned onto the utility road. I was particularly nervous because I thought I had seen a police car waiting of the road near the driveway. I knew I had reached the point of no return. Still the prize was worth it.

A quarter moon had provided enough light to drive without headlights. I drove slowly down the narrow pathway and after what seemed an eternity, I saw the white cottage to my right. I stopped the car, grabbed the flashlight, the handgun, and the tire iron and walked down a short path to the cottage. All was dark inside. In the distance I could see the lights from the farmhouse, but the only sounds I heard were crickets.

I broke the large window on the side of the structure and cleared the shards from the frame. I had no trouble climbing up and through the window. I turned on a single table lamp. Then I quickly gathered the six paintings and placed them by the door. When I unlocked the door, I peered out carefully but saw no one. Relieved and feeling bold, I walked to the car and took out the packing materials. I brought the boxes back to the cottage and used the dining table to pack each painting. It took me no more than ten minutes to do a cursory job. After I was done I took two at a time back to the car. As I was leaving with the last two, I heard a noise that sounded like someone running through the fields. I dropped the boxes and pulled the gun from my pocket. Then I heard growling and loud barking. I pointed the flashlight at the noise and saw two large, panting dogs staring at me from four feet away. Both barked angrily again and I must admit I panicked. I aimed at one dog's chest and shot. The dog was blown back by the force. The other dog looked at his dead companion and then lunged at me. I shot him in the head. The dog squealed and dropped down. Both were dead. I tossed the gun aside and picked up the boxes. I ran as fast as I could back to the car. I climbed in and locked the doors, but no dogs and followed me. Then I remembered the gun. I might need it, so I opened the door and ran to it. As I was picking it up I saw a figure making the turn from the path leading back up to the farmhouse. As the person emerged from the darkness into the light from the cottage, I fired twice. The man dropped immediately to the ground. I waited to see if I needed to fire again. Then I heard people's voices shouting and thought I heard a woman say "Charlie".

I ran to the van, maneuvered it around, sped down the utility road, turned right and drove rapidly in the direction away from the village. I looked in my rear view mirror repeatedly for five minutes, but no vehicle followed me.

Now an hour later I am feeling almost calm recollecting the events that had just transpired. Most of all I am puzzled by the question of Bailey's presence. I admit that Bailey certainly had a motive for wanting to find me and turn me over to the police. I stole the Bailey paintings and poisoned Cynthia. A motive, yes, but what is the probability of Bailey showing up today in a little farm town in France where eight paintings have been hidden for over a hundred years? It defies chance.

Unless he knew about the secret of the sketch. The sketch had been in his mother's house for decades and they had done nothing about the list of art on the back. Cynthia and I had discussed the possibility of the Baileys knowing what they had and we dismissed that as unlikely. Then we had specifically taken the sketch so that no one would notice the list and decipher its meaning. Our plan was foolproof. Yet there was Bailey at the Closiers.

Cynthia and I talked several times about where the trove might be now. We had agreed that it made most sense that Mary Cassatt kept the paintings. I knew that the sculpture associated with JF had been donated by the Fèvre family to the Musée Massena in Nice. I had seen it there.

The paintings were another thing. We doubted that Mary would turn over these remarkable works of art to the housekeeper. She might have told Degas that she did to make her old friend feel better, but we assumed she stored them in her studio or country house until she decided what to do with his legacy. It's possible that she forgot about them, because her health kept declining for years afterwards.

Cynthia was planning to join me this summer in our search. I didn't need her or want her. I confess I was disappointed that none of Mary Cassatt's different residences and studios were promising. I thought Beaufresne would be the place—in some upstairs room, garage, or barn. Nothing had been there.

I then went back to the beginning and wondered what if Mary had given the paintings to Zöe. If so, I would have thought she or her relatives would have sold them. But then, we would know that through all the research done on Degas.

Not having high hopes, I traced her relatives to Bièvres. Remarkably, she had hung on to the paintings. Maybe they represented good memories to her. She may not have cared about the money. Obviously the current Closiers believed the paintings were copies or fakes. Whatever Zöe's motivations, I feel lucky. My plan worked. I have the trove in the back of my van.

I'll probably never figure out how Bailey found the trove also. He may have stumbled on the sketch's list and solved its code. Maybe he is working closely with the police. That would explain why I saw that police car near the Closier driveway. Maybe there were police in the farmhouse tonight waiting for me. But I was too slick for them. I hope it was Bailey I shot. I'll find out if the papers pick up the events of tonight. Serves him right if he's dead.

My present concern is to get to the Left Bank and switch the paintings to Philippe de Beauvais's blue van. He leaves it on the street with the key under the driver's seat. He only has one key and his backroom boy has to drive it from time to time. His van is equipped with wooden slot frames to transport paintings from his gallery to exhibitions—perfect for my purpose. What a friend I am! The police will return it to Phillipe after I have no more use for it. No harm done.

I need to make the switch because the police may be looking for a white van. Bailey and the Closiers will have put the lead police on to me. Even though I'm in France, the FBI may be involved as well. But if all goes well, I'll be out of the country by morning.

PART THREE
LOST and FOUND

Chapter Thirty-Eight

The drop in temperature made his shoulder ache. Charlie looked up at the leaden sky and thought it might snow, as the local New York weatherman had predicted. He was walking up Madison Avenue in early December wearing a business suit, topcoat, and hat. He had just finished a lunch with a client reviewing his portfolio. The meeting had gone well and Charlie felt energized enough to skip the car ride and walk to the Carlyle Hotel to wait for Kate to return from her meetings.

Charlie liked to take Kate to New York City about two weeks before Christmas. They had made the trip then a couple of times before they were married. It was an ideal time to combine business with shopping—and to take in a Broadway play. The cityscape was magical before Christmas. Holiday lights lined the midtown streets; the stores put up special displays; museums had memorable exhibitions; snow festooned Central Park's trees and paths; hansom cabs crowded the streets; and skaters were abundant at Rockefeller Center and the Wollman Rink.

His shoulder and the proximity of the Ludyard Gallery brought back recollections of the day last summer when he had been shot. Everything was a blur after he felt the impact and heat of the bullet. Kate told him afterwards, "Hèrcule and I reached you at about the same time. You were on the ground bleeding and moaning. You appeared to come in and out of consciousness. We had arrived too late to see the shooter. We only heard him drive away. The local police appeared in a matter of minutes. Brigitte had called them and the car parked just outside the driveway drove up to the house. I was frantic as the police ran down the paths near the cottage while I yelled at them that you needed to be taken to a hospital. After ten minutes another squad car arrived and I persuaded them to load you in the back and drive us the twenty minutes to the hospital. I was so frustrated. At least they had a towel that I could use to stanch the blood from your wound. It was a scene from hell."

When Charlie woke up in his emergency room bed, Kate was there by his side. He felt confused, medicated, and tired, but he was alert enough to understand Kate's account of what happened. She praised the doctors and nurses for their care and competence. Although the bullet had exited the back of his shoulder, it had done considerable damage to bones, muscles and tendons. He had also lost a substantial amount of blood. As Charlie listened, his eyes focused better and he noticed that some of the blood was still on Kate's blouse and skirt.

"You're going to be all right," Kate said, tears welling up in her eyes. "I need to get you back home where you can recover. The doctors say that we can leave in four or five days."

Growing more lucid, Charlie joked, "What a vacation!"

"You were lucky, my love. Six inches to the right and there would be no joking."

"Did the police catch him?"

"No. He got away."

"Was it Gelb?"

"Undoubtedly."

"He took the paintings?"

"Everything in the cottage," Kate confirmed.

"Part of the trove."

"Yes, you were right about that. Jackie Farrell and the other two agents are outside. They arrived at the farm just as we had you positioned in the squad car. They were exercised that they missed Gelb. I saw them at the hospital about an hour later. Apparently they mobilized all available police cars in the area to search for Gelb. From their comments they were not successful. I told them everything I knew. Just as you thought, they had someone following us. Someone named Rosier. Jackie, the FBI agent and the Interpol agent were livid at Rosier. He had lost us in Sceaux and failed to call his boss to let him know. In general, they knew where we went the past few days, but they weren't certain why. They guessed that we would lead them to Gelb although they did not know about the trove—until today. When I explained to them what the list meant, Jackie admitted that they had not appreciated the lead you had given them. They had looked at the list and failed to interpret it. She finally figured out when she heard that we and Gelb were at the Closiers. I think you impressed her."

"That's progress," Charlie replied.

"Danny Flood, on the other hand, is hopeless," Kate continued. "He didn't even ask how you were. He just complained that we withheld important information from the FBI. He demanded to question you as soon as you woke up. I'll try to keep them outside as long as I can."

"Thanks," Charlie said and he went back to sleep.

Charlie remembered talking to Danny and Aldo Laval. The only fact they seemed to think was important was the white van Charlie recalled vaguely. After an hour they left him alone.

As he was feeling better in the hospital the next day, he asked Kate to see if the media was reporting anything about the Closier theft and shooting. She found nothing. Charlie concluded that the police still had failed to capture Gelb and had suppressed the Closier news. Kate decided that they were embarrassed by the episode and felt publicity would be harmful.

"After all, a valuable piece of their patrimony has slipped through their hands," Kate said sardonically.

* * *

The trip back to Chicago had gone uneventfully—except for a phone call to Claire Bailey. Kate had insisted to Charlie that his mother should know. Charlie had wanted to wait until they reached home, but he acquiesced ultimately. They should have known that the news of Charlie being shot would be a harsh shock to his mother. Unfortunately, the news was one blow too many for a frail heart. Charlie learned later that Claire felt a pain while she was still on the phone. She sat down and called James. James drove her to

Lake Forest Hospital and called her cardiologist. By the time Charlie and Kate reached Lake Forest, Claire had had mitral valve surgery. The doctor told them that excessive stress over the past few weeks had triggered a malfunctioning in her heart. She had nearly died.

* * *

As Charlie recalled these incidents in France and Lake Forest, he felt guilty. His single-minded pursuit of Gelb had put Kate in danger and led to his mother's heart problems. The stress had been overwhelming for her. He had been impetuous and foolhardy. Kate had tried to temper his passion, but he had not listened. And for what? Gelb had escaped with most of the trove—plus the insurance money. Moreover, he still had the sketch. Yale had the two paintings. The Closiers now knew about the two valuable Degas paintings still in their house. But Cynthia Newgate was dead and her murderer faced no retribution. To be blunt but honest, he felt he had failed.

It started to snow and Charlie considered going into a store to pass some time to see if the snow would stop. Recognizing that he was only a block from the Ludyard Gallery, he grasped what he really wanted to do. He wanted to confront Jacob Stern. Considering all the mistakes he had made, Charlie could not just walk away. Finding Gelb would repair some of the damage Charlie had done. Stern had to know something.

When Charlie entered from the sidewalk, a receptionist he did not recognize offered to take his coat and hat and to get him a cup of coffee. Charlie gave her his coat but declined the coffee. A cursory glance at the paintings hung in the first, large room reminded him that this gallery dealt only in the high end of the Impressionists. Most paintings looked as if they belonged in major museums around the world.

Before long, Christina Hildalgo, the saleswoman from the summer, appeared.

"Good afternoon, sir. May I assist you? I recognize you. You have been here before."

"Yes. I was here a few months ago seeing Mr. Stern. Is he in?"

"I expect him back shortly."

"How about Ron Gelb?"

"Ron is no longer with us. I think he went off on his own."

"Where?"

"I have no idea. Perhaps Mr. Stern knows. He is Ron's uncle. In the meantime, is there an artist or period in which you are interested?"

"No one in particular," Charlie responded. "I'll look around and find you if I need help."

Charlie wandered off to examine the paintings more closely. He would look until Stern returned. In a smaller room off the main gallery he instantly recognized a painting that he may have seen only a few months before. It was a Degas ballet dancer. Naturally he was skeptical that it was part of the Zöe Closier trove of Degas's from the little farm cottage south of Paris. He knew that Degas had painted many young ballerinas practicing their positions; so this one must have come from an entirely different provenance. Still, something distinctive about it triggered an image in Charlie's brain. And there it was: the watering can front left. He recalled that the painting in Zöe's cottage had struck him because of the watering can sitting on the floor beneath the barre in the dancers' studio. He had thought at the time that that detail had been odd—and here it was again.

He stepped back to examine the complete picture. It was a pastel. The dancer wore a white bodice and tutu with a blue waistband. In her hair she had tied a red, white, and blue ribbon, which reminded Charlie of the French flag. Pink slippers and a black choker completed her outfit. The background wall was yellow. The painting was entitled *Grand Battement à la Seconde*. It was a beautiful study of a young woman practicing. The complete painting was remarkable, but Charlie remembered most the watering can. There could not be two paintings exactly alike. If he had been in a different gallery, he would have been more skeptical, but this find could not be coincidental.

Charlie motioned to Christina to join him. Even though he felt confused and excited, Charlie fought hard to appear calm.

"I rather like this Degas. It's magnificent. Why do you have it in a back room?"

"Mr. Stern wanted it here. He wanted it for serious collectors. Street traffic rarely wanders back here."

"What is its provenance? It looks familiar."

"Indeed, it may seem familiar because there is a similar painting in the Havemeyer collection at the Met. The difference is that there are two dancers in the Met's painting. You probably have seen that picture. This is one from a private overseas collection. This is the first time it has been seen in New York. But if you are interested, we could talk to the collector's agent. Are you serious?"

"No, I am sure it is too dear for me, but I may know someone who might be interested. Could you take a photograph of the painting? I'll show my friend, and he might come in."

"Of course, but a photograph won't do it justice. Perhaps I could talk to your friend."

"No, he is shy of salesmen. But he is quite fond of Degas. I'll talk to him. In fact, I'll call him now. Maybe he is free."

Christina led him to a small room used for private showing. There was an easel and two Chippendale chairs. When she stepped out, Charlie used his cell phone to call Jackie Farrell. They had not talked since France, but Charlie was certain she would take his call. Jackie picked up on the second ring.

"Hello, Mr. Bailey. How's your shoulder?"

"It'll be fine. I'm doing rehab now. Thanks for asking. I have something for you that you should want to take action on. I have just seen one of the stolen Closier paintings."

"Where?" Jackie asked sounding interested.

"The Ludyard Gallery. They are displaying a Degas painting which I am sure I saw in Zöe Closier's cottage. A ballerina in the second position."

"Are you certain? You told me that you only saw the painting briefly. Degas painted many ballerinas. What makes you sure?"

"The watering can. At the time I thought it was unusual to have a watering can in the picture. I had rarely seen that item before in all the Degas paintings I've seen. The saleswoman at the gallery said the painting had never been to New York and came from a private overseas collector. It must be on consignment."

"Did this salesperson say who the collector is or how the gallery obtained the painting?"

"No. And I didn't want to send the wrong signal—make her suspicious of my interest. I don't know if she realizes it's from Gelb."

"I understand."

"Look, I came to the gallery looking for Stern. He's not here right now but will be back soon. You should get up here with a couple of agents and nail him."

"That we will. You stay there. I need you to ID the painting. Remember I've never seen it."

Charlie felt pleased with Jackie's response. She seemed to credit his judgment more than before. He then tried Kate on his cell phone but had no answer. So he texted her to recommend she join him at the gallery for a colorful event.

She was there with him for forty minutes before Jacob Stern arrived. Stern looked surprised when he saw Charlie in the back gallery, hesitated, and turned back to the street entrance. Charlie hurried after him and grabbed his arm. At that point Jackie Farrell and four agents raided the gallery. They detained Stern and asked Charlie to show them the painting. Immediately two agents confiscated *Grand Battement à la Seconde*.

"Jacob Stern, you are under arrest as an accessory to a theft and a potential fraudulent sale," Jackie announced loudly and read him his Miranda rights.

Two agents led him out of the gallery while Christina Hildalgo stood speechless and astonished.

"Good going, Jackie," said Kate sincerely.

"We got a great tip," Jackie said winking at Charlie. "We'll interview the staff now. Could you come downtown later to give us a statement?"

"Of course," Charlie answered.

"Thanks. You know, it's reckless of Gelb to try to sell a painting through his former gallery. He must think we are really stupid and wouldn't check the gallery from time to time. After Paris, we questioned all of Gelb's relatives—including Stern—and the staff here. No one gave us a decent lead."

"Will the painting go back to the Closiers?" Kate asked.

"Of course. It's evidence, but it's also theirs."

Chapter Thirty-Nine

"Your timing is good," Jackie said to Charlie and Kate when they arrived at her office floor. "I want you to listen in on my interrogation of Stern to see if he lies about what you know about Gelb and the Closier paintings. You have a special perspective."

She led them to a room with several chairs and a one-way window looking into another room where Stern and a man in a dark blue business suit sat on one side of a clean table.

"That's Stern's attorney—Sam Rosenberg, high profile and very competent. Stern lawyered up the moment we brought him here. We had to wait until Mr. Rosenberg could get here. Actually we are lucky because now you can hear the questioning. I'll be in there with my boss, Penn Olson."

"What about Danny Flood?" Charlie asked.

"He's off the case."

"What? I thought he was the star of the FBI. Has the case lost importance to you?"

"No. Penn said to me, 'Stars must perform'. Gelb escaped our watch twice. Back to the bench, star."

Charlie and Kate nodded, grinned, and sat down while Jackie left the room.

"This will be a novel experience," Kate said, and smiled. "Will this adventure never end?"

Jackie began the interview with the usual recitals about rights, honesty, decorum, and the seriousness of this meeting.

"You have no right to arrest Mr. Stern," Sam Rosenberg stated. "He is an honest businessman and has done nothing wrong. Make this fast. He has to get back to work."

"The pending charges against your client are weighty," Jackie said. "You have a chance to mitigate if you help us. I advise you to do so."

Charlie saw Stern whisper to his lawyer and then sit up attentively.

"Because my client has not broken any laws, he'll cooperate fully."

"Where did you get the Degas painting we removed from your gallery?" Jackie asked.

"It's on consignment from a dealer in Europe whom I've known for years."

"What's the dealer name and address?"

"Franz Überle. His gallery in Frankfort is named for him. He rarely handles Impressionists, so he called me for help."

"What kind of help?"

"To sell it, of course. He said it was a pristine Degas from a secretive collector who wanted to be anonymous. Franz is very well thought of in my world. I took his word."

"Is the painting authentic?"

"No doubt. It's a magnificent Degas. We found no citation of it in any book. It must have been in private hands for a century—probably bought directly from the artist."

"How did it come into your hands?" Jackie wanted to know.

"Franz shipped us the painting over two weeks ago, and it has been very well received by potential purchasers. I had expected to sell it by Christmas. But now you have changed the prospect."

"So you never suspected anything?" said Jackie in disbelief. "An important Degas shows up out of the blue after a hundred years, and you aren't incredulous? Degas is the most researched artist of his time. The idea that a painting such as this has never been seen defies credibility. Get real."

"That's what happened. If it was stolen you should talk to Franz. I don't deal in stolen goods. All I have is my reputation."

"Where is your nephew, Ron Gelb?" Jackie asked changing the focus.

"I don't know. He vanished during the summer. I haven't heard from him. I thought he might be ill. When you people came and talked to me and my staff last summer, I assumed you needed him as a witness or that he did something wrong. I figured he would come back here at some point."

Kate leaned over to Charlie and noted, "Stern appears nervous and defensive. See him glance around and the perspiration on his cheek."

"Yes. It's time for Jackie to nail him."

Jackie leaned forward looking squarely at Stern—eye to eye. She said bluntly, "Cut the crap. I advised you to tell us the truth. But you give us this half-baked story. We know Gelb stole a Hassam painting and a Cassatt sketch from Yale earlier last summer. We also know that he stole some Degas paintings in France. Franz Überle will tell us he received that painting from Gelb. Franz certainly would have told you that your nephew brought it to you. Gelb probably told him you would be accommodating, and you have been. Okay, your last chance, or things are going to go bad for you."

Rosenberg stopped Stern from replying and asked for a minute with his client. They talked quietly and then seemed to agree. Charlie could not make out what they were saying.

"He's going to take the Fifth," Kate guessed.

"Then he'll get no deal," Charlie countered.

At last Stern looked at Jackie and appeared defeated.

"I didn't know he stole them," he asserted weakly.

"The painting comes to you under unusual circumstances," Jackie scoffed. "From your missing nephew. It's a highly expensive work of art which you know he could never afford. He went through your German friend, but what Gelb wants is for you to fence it for him. You are not naïve. You know what the deal is. Plus you're greedy. That Degas would bring a tidy commission."

"No, believe me!" Stern pleaded. "I didn't know Ron stole the painting. I thought he was acting as agent for someone—dealing on his own out from under my shadow. I assumed he went through Franz because he thought I might be angry with him since he left his job without telling me. This could ruin me. Ron would never try to ruin me."

"Sure," Jackie said sarcastically. "Where is your nephew?"

"I don't know," Stern appealed for understanding. "But Franz should know. After all, if the painting sold, Franz has to talk to Ron. I'll call him right now."

"No you won't," said Jackie, stopping the questioning.

She and Penn turned off the tape recorders, and she said to Rosenberg that an agent would join them to assist in the preparation of a statement. Depending on what he admitted, she would talk to the prosecutor on Stern's behalf.

"Don't make me have to come back," Jackie threatened.

Then Jackie joined the Baileys in the observation room.

"What do you think?" she asked.

Charlie said, "I hope you don't believe that he didn't know Gelb stole the painting. First, there was Cynthia's murder and the Yale theft. Now Gelb is using a middleman to cover the trail of stolen art. It smells to high heaven. I presume that Stern thought that this arrangement protects him if the fraud comes out later."

"Don't worry. I know Stern is trying to save his rear end. It won't work. Still, unless we get Gelb to confirm Stern's involvement and knowledge, Stern may be hard to convict on what we have now. He will use the 'unwitting dupe' defense."

"Nonsense," Charlie protested. "He and Gelb were close. Nevertheless, I don't understand why he and Gelb thought it would work to offer a stolen painting through Ludyard Gallery? It seems far too risky."

"Obviously, it was too risky," Jackie agreed. "Bad guys make mistakes, too. Gelb may have felt our case was cold and we wouldn't notice the painting being offered. Ludyard Gallery with it reputation for selling high-end Impressionist paintings was a natural. And Uncle Jacob wouldn't say no. He didn't expect that you would walk in the door. Thank you, Mr. Bailey."

"Charlie, that makes sense," said Kate, affirming Jackie's hypothetical scenario.

"What was most significant about Stern's statement is that we now have the best lead regarding Gelb's location since France," Jackie said confidently. "Überle will take us to Gelb. That means I am going to Frankfort. I want you to come with me, Mr. Bailey."

"No," Kate said emphatically.

"Why, Jackie?" Charlie asked.

"You have seen all the stolen paintings," Jackie explained. "I have not. After the shooting we talked to the Closiers and they showed us the two paintings in the farmhouse. To be sure of their authenticity, Aldo Laval had a museum expert come down the next day. He certified both Degases—the portrait of the artist and the scene in the Louvre. He also appraised their market value which we passed along to the Closiers. They were overwhelmed by the estimates. We also advised them to put the works of art in a bank vault for now."

"That was good of you," Kate said. "Are you sure that there aren't photographs of the paintings? The Closiers must have taken pictures at some time."

"No. Remember they were told they were copies—fakes. They believed that the frames were worth more than the paintings. Understand, I would not ask you to come with me if we had a way to ID the pictures as those from the Closiers when we find them through Gelb. Today you proved you can ID them."

"My husband has been shot—nearly killed." Kate interjected. "Isn't there another way? Hèrcule Closier himself."

"I should have said that Mr. Closier is overwhelmed in all ways. He isn't composed yet. Don't worry. Your husband will be safe. We won't let him near Gelb. Will you come, Mr. Bailey?"

"When?"

"Tomorrow. We don't want Gelb hearing of Stern's arrest."

"Katie, don't you see? I have to go. I'll call the office and see if I can rearrange my schedule. I want to help. Cynthia's parents need closure. The Closiers need justice. My mother may feel better with Gelb behind bars. And my shoulder hurts. The bastard shot me."

Chapter Forty

Charlie, Jackie and Aldo met Agent Kart-Heinz Rüderger at three in the afternoon in a Schnell-Imbiss café in Frankfurt across the street from Franz Überle's gallery. Charlie had learned from Jackie that Aldo had asked his German Interpol counterpart to meet them there.

"Our investigation went cold two months ago," Aldo confessed, bringing the others up to date. "We found the blue van Gelb stole in Paris—three days after the robbery in Strasbourg. It was empty of the paintings but full of Gelb's fingerprints. Since then everything has been quiet. No sign of Gelb nor any news of the paintings put up for sale."

"How can someone disappear like that?" Charlie asked. "There must be records—deeds, telephone bills, credit card charges and the like. The world is electronic today."

"True," Karl-Heinz said. "Obviously. He must have planned this part of his scheme quite well. Plus, 'Gelb' is a relatively common name in Germany. After Aldo called, I looked in the Frankfurt telephone directory and found forty-seven 'Gelbs'—six with the first initial 'R'. That's assuming he is using his name. Obviously none would be him, but the number of listings prove how common it is."

"However difficult the investigation has been, we now have a breakthrough," Jackie reminded the Interpol agents. "We are here thanks to Mr. Bailey's recognition of the ballet dancer painting. Karl-Heinz, do we have local *polizei* support?"

"Yes, I asked for a squad car and two officers on foot. When we enter the gallery, they'll stand at the door."

Charlie looked out the window and saw two policemen on the sidewalk across the street.

Impressed he asked, "Do you expect that Überle will try to run?"

"No, we just need to scare him," explained Karl-Heinz. "Franz Überle is a short, frail man in his sixties. The locals tell me his usual day consists of a few conversations with clients and other dealers, some random walk-ins to the gallery, lunch with his banker, and some scholarly research. We are hoping that our unannounced appearance will unnerve him. Aldo suggested to me that Jackie ask the questions in English. That may make him uncomfortable. I can nudge him if he lapses into German."

Accepting this approach, they stood up and walked across to the gallery. Jackie asked to speak with Überle, and he appeared two minutes later. When he saw the group and learned their purpose, he requested that everyone leave the sales floor and follow him to his large conference room.

Jackie wasted no time in asking about Jacob Stern, Ron Gelb, and the Degas painting. Charlie heard Überle answer nervously—hesitating after each question, repeating himself, shifting his eyes around the room.

"*Ja*. I know Jacob a long time. Ronald brought me the painting. I rarely deal in French Impressionists. *Und* a Degas is too big for me. I told Ron to call Jacob. He said he and his uncle have troubles between each other. He has angst to call Jacob. He promised instead that, if I call and the painting sells, I would earn a commission. I said okay."

"Didn't that arrangement seem odd to you?" Jackie asked.

"*Ja*, but I trust Jacob."

"Did you ask Gelb how he had the painting?"

"*Natürlich*. He said he was acting as agent for an important collector. He could not say the name of the collector now but would later. I was a little nervous, but Jacob told me not to worry—his nephew was honest. With these expensive works of art, sellers often have tax, estate, or even divorce issues. They demand confidentiality."

"So you see this arrangement often?" Jackie followed up.

"*Nein*. My business is more simple. My sellers do not have these problems. Understand?"

"Did you know that the painting was stolen?"

Charlie thought Überle's complexion turned white and he started to sweat.

"No. No. *Unmöglich*. I do not deal in stolen property. Jacob would warn me, I'm sure. *Nein*."

"You are in trouble," Karl-Heinz said. "You should have asked."

Charlie thought Überle might cry; he seemed so shaken.

"What is Ron Gelb's address?" Jackie asked. "You have to know."

"Heidelberg. I drove down there to examine the painting before taking it on consignment. He rents a house in the forest on the hill near where the old castle is. It has a good view down to the Neckar River. I wrote down the address. I'll get it for you right away."

Charlie was overjoyed. They were near. Heidelberg was only an hour or so south.

"Did Gelb show you any other paintings?" Jackie asked.

"No. But he said the collector might be persuaded to sell other comparable quality paintings if this sale went well."

Jackie continued asking questions to learn of subsequent conversations, financial arrangements if the painting sold, and any physical alterations in Gelb's appearance. Überle handed her the address and promised not to talk to anyone about this conversation.

"Don't leave Frankfurt," Karl-Heinz ordered. "We are not done with you."

"How did we do?" Jackie asked her colleagues after they left.

"Excellent," Karl-Heinz declared. "I'll call the Heidelberg police and have them check if Gelb is still there. We'll arrest him tomorrow morning at seven-thirty a.m. at the house. I need the time to get the warrant and to arrange everything. At seven-thirty it will be just becoming light. I don't like to work in the dark. Things can go wrong."

* * *

Charlie stood among a stand of trees about fifty yards left of Gelb's rented house above the Old Town section of Heidelberg. As the dawn light brightened the sky he could see two police cars parked on the road blocking the driveway and Karl-Heinz and two officers standing by one of them drinking containers of coffee. Charlie felt the cold penetrating his body despite his ski jacket, gloves, and hat. His shoulder throbbed. A new, thin layer of snow had fallen during the night giving the house, which was set amidst a forest, the look of a Christmas card. Beyond the house Charlie could see through an opening in the trees down to the Neckar River bisecting the city. Under different circumstances he would have enjoyed the view and even snapped a picture.

Instead he concentrated on the plan. In a few minutes Karl-Heinz would signal Jackie and Aldo standing a few feet from Charlie to come toward the house. The German agent would lead a group of armed police to the front door and arrest Gelb when he opened it. If Gelb resisted or showed a firearm, more police would rush the house and lay siege. Jackie's role was to stay in back and give a positive identification as soon as she could. Charlie was to remain in the woods until Gelb was captured. Then he was to enter the house and identify the stolen works of art if they were there.

"There's the sign," Aldo said. "*Allons-y*."

Charlie's breath quickened.

"Stay put, Mr. Bailey, "Jackie reminded him. "I'll come get you."

Charlie watched the groups walk toward the front of the house. He noticed a light through a second story window and assumed Gelb was up. The plan should play out in a couple of minutes. Unexpectedly his eye caught some movement behind the house. At first he thought the object was a deer. Then he saw more clearly it was a man in a brown overcoat—creeping across the open space towards the trees and shrubs.

All Charlie could think of was that Gelb was going to escape a third time. Instinctively Charlie began to run toward the dark figure.

"Jackie, he's in the back!" Charlie yelled and did not stop.

The ground was slippery and Charlie struggled to keep his balance. He stumbled a few times but did not fall. He saw the man disappear momentarily down a path cut in the woods. When he reached the path he could see distinct footprints in the snow. Ignoring the icy footing, he ran as fast as he could and saw the figure twenty yards in front of him. The path zigzagged down the slope of the hill overlooking the city. Because the bushes were bare he could always see the man ahead.

He was gaining and then suddenly he saw the man spin around and pull a handgun from his coat pocket. Charlie jumped to his right, grabbed the nearest tree, and positioned himself behind it. In an instant he heard the 'pop' of a gunshot but felt nothing. He looked around the tree and recognized unmistakably Gelb. A second later the man turned and continued running. Charlie followed.

Fifty yards farther Charlie could see where Gelb was headed. The path ended at a set of concrete stairs with a metal handrail leading down ten or twelve feet to a city street below. Charlie's superior speed had narrowed the gap considerably, and as the path zigged for the last time down the hill, Charlie leapt across the slope onto Gelb's back and shoulders. They tumbled down to the head of the stairs. They were entangled on the wet ground, and Charlie reached for the hand with the gun. Not succeeding, Charlie hit Gelb in the shoulder and neck causing him to lose his grip on the gun. It bounced down the stairs. Charlie's punch also sent an intense pain down through his own left shoulder. They continued to wrestle on the ground butting heads and trying to gain leverage with their legs and feet. Charlie's heavy coat and position on top of Gelb's back restricted his ability to hit Gelb cleanly. But he was able to hold him down effectively. Slipping repeatedly on the snow, ice, and mud they rolled to the edge of the wall cut into the hill. Then they toppled over. Charlie sensed he was flying through the air. He felt his body slam into Gelb and he briefly lost consciousness.

* * *

"Mr. Bailey, are you all right? Can you hear me?" Jackie asked. "Say something if you can," Charlie heard Jackie pleading. He was leaning against her on the bench of the back section of what appeared to Charlie to be an ambulance. It was parked on the street with the backdoor open. He saw the lights and heard the sirens of two police cars positioned twenty yards away on the same street.

"Where is he?" Charlie asked—confused but remembering fighting with Gelb.

"Thank God you're all right," Jackie said, sounding like she meant it. "How are you?"

Charlie recognized that, as he became more aware of where he was he also began to feel pain in his body. He saw that he had deep scrapes on the backs of both hands and his head ached from a laceration in his scalp. He hurt but was very much alive.

"Where's Gelb?" Charlie repeated.

Jackie pointed around her body to a shape in a brown jacket lying on the pavement. Blood circled the head. There was no movement and two officers and a medic stood nearby talking.

"Gelb's dead," she answered. "His head hit the street full force. You two must have fallen off that high wall. We found you next to him—on your back. His body must have cushioned your fall. You were lucky—but also brave. Did you know he had a gun?"

"Yes, I remembered he fired it at me. Again, missed this time."

"I heard you call to me at the house. It took us a minute to figure out what you meant. Then we chased you both down the hill, but your fight was over by the time we arrived. You are fearless. Courageous but a bit insane. Civilians don't run after armed murderers. Still, you saved the day. I'll never forget you."

Chapter Forty-One

"Then Charlie did a belly-flop onto Mr. Gelb. He squooshed him," Claire Bailey said with a twinkle in her eye. She was regaling her dinner guests with her version of Charlie's triumph a month after he returned. Joining her in her Georgian antique-furnished dining room were Yale's President Chauncey Adams, curator Susan Parker, Kate and Charlie.

"Charlie, you really should lose a few pounds," She laughed. "You killed the poor dear. But you are a hero."

"Mother, please, Charlie responded. "I fell, and I don't remember much else. It was an accident. Still, we are all better off that Ron Gelb is dead."

Charlie was amused by his mother's colorful and flawed rendition of this episode. Her quips evidenced to him that she was getting back to her former outlandish self. The stress of the summer events and her operation had made her depressed. Her mood tonight signaled that that dark period was over.

"Charlie, you are much too modest," Chauncey offered.

"The real hero here is Kate," Charlie countered. "She put up with my obsessive behavior, and she first recognized the significance of the list on the back of the sketch. She was the brains on our team. I was merely the brawn."

"Forever the charmer," Kate reacted. "Back to the story. Charlie, tell Chauncey and Susan what happened after you saw that Gelb was dead. All the works of art are back where they should be. Correct?"

"True. After Gelb's body was sent off to the morgue, FBI agent Jackie Farrell and the Interpol agents Aldo Laval and Karl-Heinz Rüderger drove me back to the house. The police officers had already found the paintings.

They were in a closet covered by a blanket leaning against the wall. The sketch was also there rolled up in a cylinder container. I recognized all the paintings from the Closier cottage. Surprising to me, there were only four, instead of five. The 'ballet dancer' was obviously in New York but the one titled *La Chanteuse* was missing. We searched further throughout the house but could not locate it. Incidentally, we did find passports for Ron Gelb and William Hecht, $83,000 in cash, and a receipt from Überle Gallery for the 'ballet dancer'.

After about an hour of fruitless search, a police technician shouted out that he had found the answer. He had hacked into Gelb's laptop and opened up a file listing the paintings. A note in the file documented a consignment two days earlier to the Hirsch Gallery in Munich."

"Eureka," Claire said with enthusiasm.

Charlie saw that her guests smiled at her in agreement.

"We had accounted for everything at that point," Charlie continued. "Gelb, the paintings, passports, money. The agents still had lots of administrative details to take care of, but I had a simple priority: return the works of art to their owners. So we split up the task. Karl-Heinz went to Munich to retrieve the one painting for the Closiers. Jackie brought the sketch back to you, Susan, and then had the 'ballet dancer' at the Ludyard Gallery shipped to France. Aldo returned the four paintings in Heidelberg to the Closiers. As to me, the two agents suggested that I fly directly home, but I insisted that I accompany Aldo to the farm. I wanted to make sure that the Closiers were aware of what happened and that Zöe's legacy was recognized for its significance."

"I imagine the Closiers were delighted," Chauncey submitted.

"They were thankful, of course," Charlie said. "They were also overwhelmed by the change in their 'situation'. They were happy with their life before. Now suddenly they were immensely wealthy. Hèrcule told me he hoped the news could be kept secret so that their relationship with their friends and relatives would not change and so that salesmen and others would not be hounding them. I reacted sympathetically but was inwardly not optimistic."

"You were correct to fear the worst," Chauncey sighed. "We have seen several articles from both here and abroad about the thefts and the return of the paintings. The works of art were too high profile to keep this story buried. Regrettably Yale was mentioned in part of the stories. We would have preferred no mention."

"I understand," Charlie agreed nodding.

"I was irritated that the FBI, Interpol, and the German police all played up their roles," Chauncey confided. "Boasted in fact."

"I guess they publicize their successes as a deterrent to future thieves," Kate suggested. "The headlines might make evil-doers think twice."

"I hope so," said Chauncey. "I also noticed that in none of the articles was there mention of the efforts of you two. I guess the FBI didn't want you to share the spotlight."

"Thank God!" both Charlie and Kate said in unison.

Everyone laughed at their response.

Chauncey looked directly at Charlie and asked apparently amused, "Does your answer mean that your crime-fighting career is over?"

"Both Kate and my mother have demanded that I never again get involved in a criminal investigation."

"Your response?" Chauncey continued.

"I agreed, of course. I'm not stupid."

Everyone laughed at that response. Claire signaled subtly to James that it was time to clear the dishes and offer coffee.

"What will happen to Jacob Stern and the dealers in Frankfurt and Munich?" Susan Parker asked Charlie.

"Jackie Farrell called me from her office in New York two days ago. I had the same question. She said that Gelb's death eliminated the only testimony that could confirm the extent of their involvement and show their intent. They are all saying they were duped by Gelb. Off the record she thinks Überle and Hirsch are probably telling the truth and Stern is lying. But even Stern is unlikely to be prosecuted."

"Too bad," Susan declared. "I think he should have protected Cynthia from his nephew. She was an innocent who was taken advantage of."

"If you mean in over her head, I agree," said Charlie.

"On her own, she wouldn't have been involved," Claire stated with finality. "Let's move into the living room for coffee and stronger spirits."

They sat down on a couch and chairs forming a rough circle. Chauncey Adams was the first to speak.

"Susan and I came here to deliver several messages from Yale. Hugh Vance would have been here also but for an unbreakable conflict."

"I won't miss him," mumbled Claire, revealing her continuing displeasure with the director of Yale's art gallery.

Chauncey ignored her comment and said, "First, I want to thank you again, Mrs. Bailey, for your most generous gift. It's very special. Second, Charlie and Kate, thank you for making it possible for us to recover the stolen works of art but also for seeing justice done for Cynthia. Finally, I learned today about the Closier gift. You all are clearly responsible for it as well. You will always have a place of honor at Yale. All I can promise you in addition is that our security procedures are greatly enhanced."

"Thank you," said Charlie and Kate.

"What Closier gift?" asked Claire.

"Let me explain, Mother. About two weeks ago I received a call from Hèrcule Closier. He said that he was trying to come to grips with the unexpected treasure trove he inherited. He did not trust anyone who had contacted him to offer to help. Instead, he asked me to recommend an art and financial advisor to sort things out for him. I confessed I did not know anyone in France, but I could ask someone who did. So I called Seth Price. Chauncey, he is an art-history professor at Northwestern and a friend. He immediately thought of Jacques Beaupré—formerly of the Musée d'Orsay and Christie's. I gave Hèrcule his number but heard nothing from him until two days ago.'

"Hèrcule has decided to sell all but one of the paintings at auction—Christie's in London. He was not comfortable with the security measures required by such valuable art. What good would millions of euros of art sitting in a vault do him? After the paintings are sold, the proceeds will be invested based on the Closiers' needs and estate planning. Hèrcule and Brigitte agreed that they wanted to continue to farm, live in their little village and enjoy the blessing of having the resources to help other people in the area when a need might arise.'

"As a sentimental touch Hèrcule told me that he was having copies of the originals made and would hang them in the same places where the originals had been. Then at the end as a surprise to me, he also asked if our firm would manage the lion's share of his wealth. He said simply that he trusted me."

"A good idea," said Chauncey.

"Enough," Claire said impatiently. "What's the gift?"

"Degas's *Au Louvre*," Charlie said, smiling slyly. "They're selling seven paintings and gifting one to the Yale Art Gallery. In honor of Zöe Closier. They wanted Zöe's name to be held in esteem in perpetuity. Hèrcule told me that the Louvre Museum curator argued with him that the subject matter and patriotism demanded that it go to them. Hèrcule said no. He wouldn't be donating this painting if it wasn't for the Baileys and their association with Yale."

"Hèrcule, Brigitte, and Lisètte will be in New Haven in February to make the presentation," Susan announced. "I hope you can come."

Claire leaned forward and waved her hand with a flourish, "This calls for champagne—Krug Grande Cuvée.

* * *

The following article appeared in the *Chicago Tribune* in the weekend edition Society section:

Yale President visits Claire Curtis Bailey

Yale's President, Chauncey Adams, dined recently with Claire Bailey and family at her Lake Forest mansion. He came to thank her for her gift to the school of two Impressionist paintings. Also present were Susan Parker, Yale Art Gallery curator, and Mr. and Mrs. Charles Bailey, prominent socialites. They celebrated the return of part of the donation that had disappeared last summer in mysterious circumstances. Sources reveal that Charles and Katherine Bailey played an important role in the recovery. Perhaps there is a new career in the offing for this popular Chicago couple.

George Kenney

THE END

Acknowledgments

Several individuals assisted me significantly in writing this book with technical knowledge, coaching, advice, deadline setting, inspiration, and encouragement. I would still be writing but for them. Marlene Adelstein worked on several drafts emphasizing plot and character development. Laurie Rosin dug deeper in every aspect from line and copy editing, pacing, coaching, and narrative. Kenzie Saunders from Dorrance Publishing supported me through each step of the publishing process, keeping me on a schedule without sacrificing quality and integrity. Elaine, my beloved wife and head cheerleader, encouraged me and added administrative backing from start to finish.

Four persons inspired me with their expertise and example in artistic creation. Vincent Scully, my teacher and an icon in the art and architecture world, opened my eyes and heart to the history of art. Jock Reynolds brought the Yale Art Gallery into the modern world, educating millions in the appreciation of our artistic heritage. Dr. Nancy Mowell Mathews is the scholar and first source of Mary Cassatt. Finally, my friend, Jane Davis Doggett, innovator and artist, taught me what is possible, practical, and excellent. Her insights and model have influenced a generation.

"The novel is the one bright book of life." — D. H. Lawrence